RICHES
AT HIS BIDDING

Rags to
RICHES
COLLECTION

April 2017

May 2017

June 2017

July 2017

August 2017

September 2017

Rags to
RICHES
AT HIS BIDDING

Leanne
BANKS

Rebecca
WINTERS

Brenda
HARLEN

MILLS & BOON

HarperCollins
PUBLISHERS
— Since 1817 —

Published in Great Britain 2017
By Mills & Boon, an imprint of HarperCollins*Publishers*
1 London Bridge Street, London, SE1 9GF

RAGS TO RICHES: AT HIS BIDDING
© 2017 Harlequin Books S.A.

A Home for Nobody's Princess © 2012 Leanne Banks
The Rancher's Housekeeper © 2012 Rebecca Winters
Prince Daddy & the Nanny © 2011 Brenda Harlen

ISBN: 978-0-263-93091-7

09-0717

Our policy is to use papers that are natural, renewable and recyclable products and made from wood grown in sustainable forests.
The logging and manufacturing processes conform to the legal environmental regulations of the country of origin.

Printed and bound in Spain
by CPI, Barcelona

A HOME FOR
NOBODY'S
PRINCESS

LEANNE BANKS

This book is dedicated to the babes:
Coco, Ann, Terri, Mina, Rose, Peggy, Sharon,
Jane, Kathy, Kathy, Kim, Sandy, Catherine, Terry.
You are a constant source of inspiration to me.

Leanne Banks is a *New York Times* bestselling author with over sixty books to her credit. A book lover and romance fan from even before she learned to read, Leanne has always treasured the way that books allow us to go to new places and experience the lives of wonderful characters. Always ready for a trip to the beach, Leanne lives in Virginia with her family and her Pomeranian muse.

Chapter One

His daughter hated him.

Benjamin Garner carefully opened the front door to his sprawling two-story house and paused. Even though he was six foot four and had been described as two hundred pounds of muscle due to the hard work he put in on his cattle ranch of over ten thousand acres, he'd become a stranger in his own home.

Why? Because his five-month-old daughter couldn't stand him.

Every time he came toward her, she gave a shriek that would wake the entire country of New Zealand, and New Zealand was a good fifteen-hour flight away from the town of Silver City, Texas.

He stepped as lightly as he could in his boots. Coco

Jordan, the young nanny who had seemed to work magic with baby Emma from the first time the two had met, had assured him that Emma could sleep through regular environmental noises, but he didn't quite believe her.

Sometimes Benjamin wondered if his daughter had special powers and could smell him or hear him breathe even from the front door when she was upstairs in the nursery. Benjamin scowled at himself. This just showed what a nutcase he was becoming.

His dog, Boomer, limped out to greet him. Boomer had been one of his best herding dogs, but after he'd gotten his leg twisted in some barbed wire, he couldn't run fast enough. Benjamin figured the dog had earned his retirement, so Boomer spent his days trying to catch scraps from his housekeeper's cooking and dozing on the sofa. Benjamin reached down to give the mixed-breed dog a rub on his head, but was quiet about it. At least his dog liked him.

Heading for his office at the back of the house, he strode past the kitchen.

"Ah!"

His stomach knotted. He knew that sound. He knew that voice. He kept on moving.

"Benjamin." The low, sweet voice of the nanny called to him. "You can't avoid her forever."

"Ah!" Emma said.

Taking a deep breath, he turned and faced the two of them, standing in the kitchen doorway. His daughter stared at him with big blue suspicious eyes, while

Coco was all soft, pretty encouragement. Emma wasn't screaming—yet. Maybe she was just gearing up for it.

"She just finished eating, so she should be in a good mood. Don't you want to hold her?"

Hell, no, he thought. A rattlesnake was easier to handle. He shifted his hat back and shrugged. "I haven't washed up."

"That's okay. A little dirt won't kill her."

"Okay," he said, opening his arms, preparing himself for his daughter's rejection of him. "I'll hold her."

Coco moved closer and Benjamin noticed that Emma's eyes seemed to grow larger with each step she took. "Here you go," she murmured to Emma. "This is your big strong daddy and he will always take care of you. There's no need to be afraid of him. He's on your side."

Coco gently placed Emma in his arms and he drew her close to his chest, holding his breath. Emma stared up at him, her eyes wide. He counted silently. One. Two. Three. Four. Five.

She pressed her lips together and glanced toward Coco. As soon as her lower lip jutted out in a perfectly defined pout, he knew what was coming. His daughter let out a high-pitched sound of distress that quickly grew in volume. He met Coco's discouraged gaze and shook his head.

"Here," he said, handing Emma back to the nanny. "There's no need to torture the poor thing. That's why I hired you."

Coco patted Emma on the back in a soothing motion. "But we have to get her used to you. We have to find a way—"

"Maybe by the time she hits her first birthday, she'll like me better," he said and turned away, tamping down his own sense of discouragement.

"Wait," Coco said, and he felt her hand on his arm.

He glanced over his shoulder.

"Maybe she doesn't like your hat," she said. "Maybe if you take it off, she'll—"

"I'll give it a try next time," he said. "Right now, I need to enter some stock updates on the computer. Later," he said and strode the rest of the way to his office.

His muscles twitched. He could manage this ranch with one hand tied behind his back, but he couldn't hold his daughter for even one minute without scaring her so much she shrieked in fear. Somehow, someday, he needed to change that, but he didn't know how to do it.

He scrubbed his forehead with his hand. What had Brooke done? He wondered if his ex-lover had told Emma he was a horrid man. He wondered if, before Brooke had died riding on the back of her most recent lover's motorcycle, she had corrupted Emma's brain. Was that even possible?

He and Brooke had shared a sexual affair that had lasted a weekend. He'd come to his senses, as had she. Until weeks later, when Brooke had learned she was pregnant. Benjamin had immediately proposed, even though he and Brooke had both known they didn't belong together. She'd refused his proposal but accepted his support. He'd reluctantly realized that he would be a twice-a-month father. He only saw Emma three times before her mother's death.

Suddenly he'd become a full-time single father. Who made his daughter cry at the very sight of him.

His gut clenched again. Sometimes he wondered if he would ever hold her without her screaming in fear.

Sucking in a mind-clearing breath, he focused on the computer screen. He wasn't going to fix his problem with Emma today. Thank goodness he had Coco. Emma felt safe with her. That was why he had hired Coco. She was magic for Emma. She had been the first time she'd held her. Somehow, Coco was an ordinary woman with superpowers when it came to babies, which was exactly what Benjamin needed. Lately, he'd wondered if she could be…more…

Benjamin shook his head. Crazy thoughts. His computer cursor was blinking at him. He should enter the appropriate numbers in his Excel spreadsheet.

There was plenty of trouble in his day before he even thought of Coco.

Coco stared after her tall, broad-shouldered boss as he disappeared into his office. She jiggled Emma to help her settle down. The baby clung to her like a tick, bless her heart. Coco was certain Emma still missed her mama even though her mama had been the type to come and go as she pleased.

Coco was pretty certain Benjamin had tried to hire Emma's previous nanny, but not everyone wanted to live on a ranch in the middle of nowhere, Texas. Nowhere, Texas, suited Coco just fine after all the days she'd spent with her mother in hospice care. It was nice not to have to live by herself in a tiny apartment, always aware that she wasn't just alone for the night. Now that her mother had passed away, Coco was truly alone in this world.

Caring for a baby was therapeutic for Coco. Even though Emma was terribly insecure and frightened, she represented light and hope to Coco. After the strange visit Coco had received yesterday from the even stranger two men who had shown up on the front porch of Benjamin's home, though she'd shooed them away, she was afraid. What did they want from her? Was there some other debt her mother had owed that Coco would need to pay?

She panicked at that prospect. By the time her mother had passed, there'd been nearly nothing left. Coco had taken out a loan so that her mother could have a proper burial and she would be paying college loans for a long time. Coco had quit just shy of getting her degree and was determined to finish it. But that was for later. Now, she just needed to get some of her equilibrium back. From the first moment she'd stepped onto this ranch, something had clicked and she'd known this was the place for her. It didn't hurt that Emma needed her.

Benjamin's long-time housekeeper, Sarah Stevens, made a clucking sound as she entered the hallway. "How long is it going to take that man to just sweat it out and hold that baby until she stops crying?"

"I can't totally blame him," Coco said. "Emma hasn't been at all cooperative."

Sarah's generously lined face softened. "Well, it's true the baby has been through a lot of changes. Who knows what kind of environment she was living in with that Brooke Hastings." Sarah gave a snort. "Party girl. Don't know how he ever got involved with her."

Coco had kept her curiosity to herself about the odd pairing of one of Dallas's most notorious party girls and solid rancher Benjamin Garner. "They must have seen something in each other."

Sarah snorted again. "Enough for a fling. Of course, as soon as Benjamin found out little Miss Brooke was pregnant, he tried to do the right thing and offered to marry her, but the woman refused. She didn't want to be tied down. Too much life to be lived."

"Did she keep partying throughout her pregnancy? That could have been terrible for Emma."

"I think Brooke dialed it down during the pregnancy, but as soon as Emma was delivered, she was hitting the circuit again. Thank goodness you showed up when you did. The little peanut was usually okay with me as long as I held her every minute, but I couldn't get anything done around the house. I'm still catching up," she grumbled.

"It was good timing for me, too," Coco said. "But I may need to take a couple hours off soon for personal business."

Sarah sighed. "It's only fair. You've been working two weeks straight with her. I just know that I'll be the fill-in." The older woman lifted her finger to Emma's cheek and cracked a smile. "She's adorable when she's not screaming."

"I'll try to schedule my break when she's taking a nap," Coco said.

"You're overdue," Sarah said. "We'll just have to adjust. Maybe I'll finagle a way to get Benjamin together with her. Never would have believed a little baby could scare the devil out of a man like him," she said and laughed. "You let me know when you need your break. I'll be here for the little one."

"Thank you, Sarah," Coco said and wondered if perhaps she should just take Emma with her. She was reluctant to cause any more trauma for Emma or Benjamin.

Later that night, Coco slept in the room next to the nursery. The baby could still be a bit unpredictable. Coco was still bothered by the men who had come to visit her and wondered what she should do. Were they bill collectors? Should she consult a lawyer? It took her hours to go to sleep

A shriek jerked her awake. Coco sat upright, adrenaline pumping through her as she tried to pull herself together.

Another shriek pierced the air and she realized it was Emma. Another bad dream, she thought. Who would have guessed that a baby could have bad dreams? Coco jumped out of bed and darted out of her room toward the nursery next door. She didn't bother with a light because she knew the way by heart.

Except this time she plowed into a human wall.

She felt her breath leave her body in a rush. Automatically bracing herself, she put her hands on his shoulders. Hot flesh over sinewy muscles. Her heart slammed against her ribs. She felt his arms slide around her to stabilize her.

Coco's eyes finally began to adjust to the darkness. "Sorry," she managed, a strange sensual panic racing through her.

"I heard Emma and she wasn't stopping," Benjamin said in a rough voice that made goose bumps rise on her arms.

Coco took a step back. "Sorry," she said again. "I was fast asleep."

"You need a break," he said, raking his hand through his hair.

"We'll figure it out," she said and pushed through Emma's partially opened door. The volume of Emma's screams increased exponentially without a pause. Coco rushed to the crib and picked up the baby, cooing at her.

"There you are," she said. "You're fine. You're okay, sweetie. You don't need to be upset. You're safe."

Emma alternately whined and made hiccupping sounds.

Coco hated that the baby was so upset. She bobbed up and down. "There you go. See. You're okay."

Emma gave a heavy sigh. Then another. She felt the tot fasten her mouth against her shoulder and make buzzing noises and couldn't help laughing under her breath.

"I take it she's okay," Benjamin said from a few feet behind her.

Emma continued her happy buzzing noise and Coco turned around to face Benjamin. He was dressed in a pair of pajama pants and nothing else. "Sure sounds like it to me."

Emma paused a half beat then continued.

"Why does she keep waking up screaming?" he asked, resting his hands on his hips, clearly perplexed.

Jiggling Emma, she stroked the baby's back. "It's not every night. She's just still adjusting. I think she'll calm down soon."

"She has an appointment with the pediatrician soon. Maybe he can tell us something. I'll want you to go to that appointment," he said. "If I take her, she'll just scream the whole time."

"That's fine. I'd like a few hours off tomorrow or the next day, though. I have some personal business to take care of."

"No problem. Sarah will cover for you. I may need

to hire someone part-time so you'll have backup," he said with a sigh.

"We can give her a little more time. With little ones, they can turn a corner before you know it." Coco could feel Emma's rigid frame start to relax against her. "Maybe she wouldn't be so afraid of you in the dark. Come closer and see."

"I did that earlier," he said in a dry tone.

"But this is different. It's dark and you're not wearing your hat. Maybe—"

"Maybe not tonight," he said firmly. "I don't want to get her riled up again tonight. See you tomorrow," he said and left the room.

Coco slid into the rocking chair with a sigh. She hated that Emma and Benjamin were so tense around each other. When she'd first accepted the position to take care of Emma, she'd thought Emma's screaming when her daddy came close was just a phase. True, it had only been a few weeks, but it seemed as if the two of them were growing more tense with each other, instead of less. Benjamin wanted to avoid upsetting Emma, which gave them fewer opportunities to interact.

Coco wondered if she should just set Emma in his arms and leave so the two of them could work it out, but she knew that was probably her lack of sleep talking. She felt Emma's sweet little body go limp with relaxation. The baby's trust in her never failed to grab her heart. Rising, she returned Emma to her crib and went back to bed. This time, she fell asleep before her head hit the pillow.

Late the next morning, after Coco put Emma down for her morning nap, she dressed to go into town. Just as she descended the steps from the front porch, she saw a black Mercedes pulling toward the front of the house. Her stomach dipped. This was the same car that had brought the strange men who'd visited her two days ago.

Sweating, she glanced over her shoulder, praying that no one would see the visitors. Her heart pounding in her chest, she walked toward the vehicle as it stopped.

The man in the passenger seat opened the door and rose from the car. He was short with gray hair and squinty eyes. "Miss Jordan, my name is Paul Forno. I represent the House of Devereaux. My associate and I need to discuss an important matter with you."

The *House of Devereaux?* Coco wasn't sure if it was a fashion label or a collection agency. When the driver opened his car door, panic raced through her. "Listen, this is private property. This is also where I work."

"Yes, ma'am. Please accept our apologies, but this is news that must be delivered in person. If you could give us a few moments of your time—"

"Not right now," she said. "I'm on my way out."

The man sighed. "As you wish, miss, but we don't have a lot of time. Please accept my business card and call me at your earliest convenience," he said and offered her the card.

Confused, but not wanting to show it, she gave a brisk

nod, stuffed the card into her small purse and strode to her car. *We don't have a lot of time.* What could that possibly mean? And who was *we?* Her hands shook as she stuck the key into the ignition of her five-year-old economy car. Looking in her rearview mirror, she felt a microbit of relief when she saw the black Mercedes pull away from the ranch.

Coco opened her car window and took several breaths. The men looked like the same kind who had frequented her mother's home the last two months before she died. Her mother had fallen deeply in debt, and lenders had become impatient with her inability to pay her bills. Coco had helped as much as she could, but near the end she was only working part-time. Her mother's care had required the rest of her time and energy.

She wondered if somehow she was responsible for some of her mother's bills. She'd never cosigned loans, but she had used a credit card when they'd had an electrical problem and her car had needed an emergency repair. She'd thought she'd paid it off, but now she thought she needed to review her check register.

Her mind reeling, Coco drove off the property onto the highway into town. All the time, she wondered what she should do. She remembered a friend who had been a legal assistant. Maybe she could call her.

Reaching the small town of Silver City, she pulled alongside the town diner and got out of her car. She wanted a good cup of coffee or hot chocolate or hot apple cider and maybe a little sympathy from her friend Kim, a waitress at the diner. She'd known Kim back in high school, and Kim had since married and moved to Silver City. Coco and Kim had shared a meal when Coco had first come to town last month. Since then, Coco had dropped into the diner with Emma a couple times.

Coco walked inside the homey diner and the hostess immediately greeted her. "How are you doing, miss? Can I seat you?"

"Fine, thank you. Yes," Coco said. "Please do. Just one."

"We've got plenty of room. I'll put you in a booth."

As soon as Coco slid into the red booth, Kim Washburn winked and waved at her. Coco shot her a weak smile in return.

A couple moments later, Kim trotted to Coco's table. "Where's the little one today?" Kim asked.

"I finally got a couple hours off so I left her sleeping with Sarah at the ready to take over. I need to run some errands."

"I would say so. You haven't taken a break since you signed on for this gig, have you? What can I get you?"

"Hot chocolate," she said. "Or apple cider."

Kim laughed. "You want both?"

"No. I'll take hot chocolate with extra marshmallows."

Kim studied her thoughtfully. "Something wrong? Now that I think about it, you don't look too happy."

"Just distracted," Coco said.

Kim shrugged her shoulders, but clearly didn't believe her. "If you say so. But if you need some help, I'll give it my best try," she said, then headed for the kitchen area.

Coco bit her lip. She was so used to fending for herself that she almost didn't know how to accept help when it was offered. Kim returned with a mug of hot chocolate overflowing with marshmallows.

Coco smiled. "Thanks. Can you keep something confidential?" she asked in a low voice.

"Sure, what is it?"

"I may need some legal advice," Coco said reluctantly.

Kim's eyes widened and she slid into the booth across from Coco. "Well, you're not married, so you don't need a divorce. I can't believe you've committed any crimes."

"It's not that," Coco said. "I just need to check on what happens to a person's debts when they die. I need to know if I'm responsible for my mother's debts."

"Well, I can tell you that. As long as you didn't co-sign anything, you're not responsible. How do I know? When my husband Hank's parents died, they had a boat-load of debt and none of the kids had to pay. Now the repo company took everything his parents owned and that meant no inheritance for the kids, but the kids did not have to pay." She frowned. "Why are you worried?"

"These strange men have come to Benjamin Garner's house. They remind me of the bill collectors who kept coming around when my mother was sick," Coco said.

"Well, if they're angling to get some money out of

you, they're just crooked. You should tell Benjamin. He'll take care of them in no time."

"But he's my employer. It would be embarrassing to have to tell him about this," she said.

"If they keep coming around the house, he's going to find out anyway. Better to nip it in the bud. And trust me, there's no one better-suited to take care of someone trying to pull some sort of money scheme on you than Benjamin." Kim thumped the table with her knuckles. "I gotta get back to work. Enjoy those marshmallows and talk to Benjamin."

Coco stared at the marshmallows, her stomach churning at the prospect of discussing her mother's debt issues with Benjamin.

"She's okay as long as I bob up and down. I just hope it doesn't make my fillings fall out. You'll have a high dental bill if that happens," Sarah warned Benjamin as she jiggled Emma.

Emma had spotted him and was throwing a hard glance at him. It amazed him that a kid under six months old could kill a man with her eyes. Maybe she was a chip off the old block after all. He turned to go to his office.

"Not so fast," Sarah called. "The least you can do is come here and say hello to your daughter."

"I'll just make her cry," he said.

"I'll take that risk. You can't run from your own child forever," she said.

"I'm not running," he said. "I just don't see any need in upsetting her."

Benjamin slowly walked toward Sarah and Emma. The baby glared at him like a gunfighter ready for action.

"Boo," he said in a low voice.

Both Sarah and Emma gasped. "Why'd you do that? You're just gonna scare her even more."

Benjamin shrugged and walked closer. He lifted his hand to the sweet skin of the baby's chubby arm. "Hey, Princess, sooner or later, you'll realize that I'm gonna be around a long time. I can just tell you're gonna give me hell till you figure that out."

Emma frowned, but she didn't cry. She shot him another hard look and stared at his hat.

"Does this bother you?" he asked, removing the hat from his head and extending the Stetson toward her. He thought about the sweet nanny he'd hired. At first sight of the woman, Benjamin had sensed a tender heart. "Coco said it might."

Emma stared at the hat then at him and for one sliver of a second, he saw a softening in those intense blue eyes of his daughter.

The front door opened and Coco's footsteps sounded in the foyer. He knew her step already. Benjamin automatically turned and Boomer limped to greet her. "Hey, boy," he heard her say to the dog. Seconds later, she appeared, breathless, clearly a little concerned. "How was she?"

"Ah!" Emma said.

"She's fine as long as I jump up and down," Sarah said in a grumpy voice as Emma stretched her hands toward Coco. "Did you take care of your business?"

Coco's gaze darkened, taking Emma into her arms. "Mostly, but I—uh—I'd appreciate it if I could maybe talk to you sometime soon," she said to Benjamin.

Surprised, he shrugged. "No problem. Just let me know when. I'm in the office this afternoon and I have a cattlemen's meeting tonight."

Coco stared at him for a moment. "So when is a good time?"

He got an odd feeling in his gut at the expression on her face. He hoped this didn't mean trouble. Benjamin didn't need one more iota of trouble in his life. And he sure as hell didn't need trouble from his daughter's nanny. He'd hired the woman to alleviate his problems, not exacerbate them.

"I can see you up until six today or after nine tonight," he told her.

She took a deep breath. "After nine. Emma will be in bed by then."

He nodded and placed his hat back on his head. "Nine o'clock. Come to my office."

"Can we, uh, meet in the den?" she asked, surprising him with the request.

He shrugged. "Okay. See you at nine. I've got work to do," he said and walked away.

That night, just before 9:00 p.m., Emma fell asleep with no struggle. Coco set the baby on her back in her crib. Emma was totally relaxed and Coco had a feeling the baby might sleep through the whole night. She quietly walked from the room and left the door open just a sliver. She had a monitor, but Coco liked the idea of having more than one modality to hear Emma if she cried.

Now she was second-guessing her decision to talk with Benjamin. She'd almost hoped Emma would take a long time to get to sleep, so she wouldn't be able to meet with him. Her stomach knotted with nerves. Benjamin was a tough man. She just hoped he would be on her side.

Chapter Two

Coco hesitated at the entry to the den. Now she wondered why she'd chosen it with its brown leather furniture and masculine tan, rust and brown palette. Maybe the office would have been better.

Suddenly, Benjamin stood in front of her. Her heart stopped.

"You look like you need a drink," he said.

She shook her head. "No. I'm fine."

"Hmm," he said doubtfully. "Come on in."

She followed him into the den and gingerly sat across from him on the sofa. He'd sat in the well-worn leather chair. He looked at her expectantly and her throat went dry.

She opened her mouth and a croaking sound came out.

He set his shot glass next to her on the couch. "You need a swallow of something. May as well be some good whiskey."

She took a sip of the alcohol. It burned all the way down.

"Another," he said.

She hesitated, but his nod encouraged her and she took a second sip. "Enough," she said and gave the glass back to him. "I need your help."

He took a swallow from the squat glass he'd shared with her. "I figured that. What's the problem?"

"I'm not sure. These men have been trying to see me."

"Men?" he repeated, a shot of displeasure rising through him.

"They've already come to the house twice and—"

"Which house?" he asked, sitting up in his chair.

"This house," she said. "Your house."

"Why in hell are they coming here?" he asked. "And why haven't any of my staff seen them?"

"They're here to see me." She pulled a card from her purse and handed it to them. "I have no idea who the House of Devereaux is." She took a quick, desperate breath and pushed her brown hair nervously behind her ear. "As you know, my mother died a few months ago. She didn't have much money at the end." Coco bit her lip. "Bill collectors started coming around. These men reminded me of them."

Benjamin frowned and set down his drink. He studied the card. "Did you cosign any of her loans?"

She shook her head.

"I'll call my brother—he's an attorney—and see if he knows anything about this House of Devereaux. In the meantime, if those guys show up, I want you to call my cell right away."

She looked hesitant.

"Is there anything else I need to know?" he asked.

She shook her head. "No. I'm just not sure I should have dragged you into this."

"These men came onto my property without an invitation. You are an important employee. That makes it my business."

The vulnerability she showed grabbed at him, although he sure as hell wouldn't admit it. Coco had a fresh-scrubbed face and slim body, making her look younger than her years. Sweet and innocent, probably hoping for a Prince Charming to sweep her off her feet. Not his type at all. Benjamin had usually gone for low-maintenance women who knew their way around a man and wouldn't expect too much of him. Except for Brooke. He'd made a big mistake with Brooke.

"I need your word that you'll call me if they come around again," he insisted.

She sighed and nodded reluctantly. "I will, but I'm hoping I'll fall off their radar."

Benjamin had a feeling that her wish wouldn't come true. "Just so we understand each other," he said and stood. "I'll see you tomorrow."

* * *

The next day as Coco dressed Emma, she pointed to the photograph of Benjamin she had placed on a dresser in the baby's room. "Daddy," Coco said. "That's your daddy."

The baby was cheerful and a little less clingy than usual. Coco was pleased with Emma's progress and hoped there might be an opportunity for Emma and Benjamin to make a little peace.

The doorbell rang as she was feeding Coco her lunch.

Sarah entered the kitchen. "Two men are here to see you. Dever-something?" she said.

Coco's stomach clenched. She wondered if she should send them away, but remembered her promise to Benjamin. She swallowed over the lump in her throat. "Tell them to wait in the front room, please," she said and pulled out her cell phone. As soon as Sarah left, she punched Benjamin's number on her cell phone.

"Benjamin," he said in a curt voice.

"It's me, Coco," she said. "The men are here. They're in the den."

"Do you know what they want?" he asked.

"Not yet. I've been feeding Emma. I only called because you made me promise," she said.

"I'll be there as soon as I can," he said and hung up the phone.

Coco handed the feeding of Emma over to Sarah and made her way to the front room. The two men immediately stood. "Miss Jordan, thank you for seeing us.

Again, I'm Paul Forno, and this is my colleague Gerald Shaw."

Tense, Coco laced her fingers together in front of her. "If this is regarding my mother's debt, I'm afraid I can't help you."

Mr. Forno's face crinkled in confusion. "Your mother's debt?" he echoed. "I wasn't aware that Miss London had any debt issues. According to our information, she's been well cared for, per her agreement with your father."

"Miss London," she echoed, not certain who was more confused—she or Mr. Forno. "That's not my mother's name. You must have the wrong person."

Mr. Forno studied her. "You do know that you were adopted, don't you?"

"Of course, but—" She broke off, struggling to keep her emotions under control as she tried to make sense of the men's visit. "Is this about my birth mother? I tried to find her years ago, but I was told she didn't want to meet me. Has she changed her mind?"

Mr. Forno exchanged a look with his associate. "Unfortunately—"

The front door opened and Benjamin stepped inside, his gaze sweeping the front room. "Problem?"

Coco immediately felt a sense of relief. "I think there's a lot of confusion right now."

Benjamin addressed the two men. "It shouldn't take long to clear up any confusion given the fact that you've been bothering Miss Jordan. If you have a legitimate reason to see her, then spill it or leave."

Mr. Forno cleared his throat. "This is a matter of a delicate nature. We, uh, prefer to speak to Miss Jordan privately."

"That's up to Miss Jordan," Benjamin said.

"I'd like Mr. Garner to remain," she said. "Whatever you say to me, you can say in front of him."

Mr. Shaw sighed. "Then, sir, we must request that you sign a confidentiality agreement."

"I'm not signing anything," Benjamin said. "You're in my house and you're wasting my employee's time and mine, too."

Mr. Shaw looked nervous and perplexed. "Then I must beg of you to keep what we are about to tell you in the strictest confidence."

Benjamin lifted one shoulder in halfhearted agreement. "Still waiting."

Mr. Forno waved his hand. "Allow me to introduce ourselves, Mr. Garner. I am Paul Forno and this is my associate, Gerald Shaw, with the House of Devereaux. Perhaps we should sit down."

Impatience simmering from Benjamin, he sat down. The others followed.

"As I said, we are representatives of the House of Devereaux," the man began.

"What is that?" Benjamin asked.

Mr. Shaw blinked. "The royal House of Devereaux. The ruling family of the country of Chantaine."

"Never heard of it," Benjamin said.

Mr. Forno looked at Coco and she shrugged. "Sorry. Neither have I."

"Oh, my," Mr. Forno said. "Chantaine is a small, but beautiful island country off the coast of Italy. The Devereau family has ruled the country for centuries."

"And what does this have to do with Coco?"

Mr. Forno sighed. "Your birth mother was Ava London. She had a long-term relationship with Prince Edward of Chantaine and you are—" He cleared his throat. "A product of that relationship."

Coco frowned, blinking at the man's announcement. Her birth mother? Her birth father? After all these years, she would learn who they were? She shook her head in amazement. "Are you saying that Ava London and Prince Edward are my biological parents?"

"Yes, they are," he said.

She was so stunned she couldn't comprehend it all. "My father is a prince?"

"Yes, he was," Mr. Forno said.

"Was?" she echoed, her heart racing. "Oh, my goodness! Is he alive? Is my birth mother alive?"

"Unfortunately, no. His Royal Highness passed away several years ago, and his son, Stefan, has since ascended the throne. Your birth mother passed away just over a week ago," he said.

"Oh," she said, feeling a surge of sadness. Since her mother had died, she had felt so terribly alone. She'd had no close relatives, no siblings.

"What does this mean for Miss Jordan?" Benjamin asked.

"Well, the House of Devereaux wishes to extend an invitation for you to visit the country of Chantaine and also to meet the Devereau family," he said brightly.

"Visit Chantaine? But how?" Coco asked.

"The usual way these days," Mr. Forno said, continuing to smile. "A transatlantic flight."

Her mind whirling, she looked at Benjamin and she immediately knew she couldn't go. He was counting on her. Emma was counting on her. She shook her head. "Oh, I couldn't. I've just started working here and Emma needs me. Thank you for the invitation, though," she said.

The men looked surprised. "You're turning down the invitation to meet the Devereaux."

"It's not a good time for me or my employer," she said, glancing at Benjamin, who was wearing an expression of shock.

"Are you sure about this?" he asked.

"Of course I'm sure. I've made a commitment. I have every intention of keeping it," she said and stood. All three men were gaping at her as if she'd grown an extra head. Her mind was racing. She finally knew who her biological parents were. She also knew they hadn't wanted her. She had a brother, a prince, who probably wasn't thrilled with her existence. "Are there other Devereaux? Do I—" She stopped at the insane thought. They weren't her full brothers and sisters, yet she couldn't tamp down her curiosity. "Did Prince Edward have other children?"

"Yes, he did," Mr. Shaw said. "There's Prince Stefan, Princesses Valentina, Fredericka, Bridget, Phillipa and Prince Jacques."

Mr. Forno and Mr. Shaw exchanged a look. "Prince Edward also fathered another child with your birth mother. A son."

"Another," she said, disbelief racing through her. "My, he was quite the busy one, wasn't he?"

Mr. Shaw cleared his throat, but didn't respond.

Benjamin gave a low laugh. "I have to agree."

His chuckle distracted her from her own state of shock for just a few seconds. "Now, let me get this right. You're telling me that my birth father has six—no, wait, seven—other children. And one of these is my full biological brother. I have a real brother? Where is he?" she wanted to know. "Who is he?"

"He's currently in Australia. An engineer. He's been quite difficult to reach," Mr. Shaw said. "We aren't at liberty to give any more information about him. However, the news could break at any moment."

"News?" Benjamin repeated. "I thought you said this was a confidential matter."

"It is, but we fear the news of Prince Edward's newly discovered children could be leaked to the press any day," Mr. Shaw said.

"That's why you've been so determined to get to

Coco," Benjamin said. "Why you've invited her to Chantaine. Control Coco and you can control the spin."

"It's quite understandable that the Devereaux would like to have an opportunity to meet with Miss Jordan," Mr. Shaw said in a snippy voice.

"Hmm. Well, this is a lot for Miss Jordan to take in, so I'm sure you don't mind giving her some time to process it."

"Of course," Mr. Shaw said. "If she would just sign a release stating she won't discuss the matter with the press—"

"She's not signing anything without an attorney looking at it," Benjamin said.

"Sir, it's in her best interest not to discuss this publicly. Once the story breaks, she'll be flooded with requests from the paparazzi. Signing this document will provide her with an easy excuse to avoid interviews."

"She won't need an excuse," Benjamin said and rose to his feet. "Now, as long as she has your contact information, I think we're done for the day."

Both men appeared disappointed. "Call us if you change your mind about the release or visiting Chantaine," Mr. Forno said to Coco.

Her mind was reeling with all the information, and Benjamin was right. It was going to take some time for her to digest it. "I don't think I'll be changing my mind, but I have your phone number," she said and watched as the two men walked out the front door.

She felt Benjamin's gaze on her. "You okay?"

Not wanting to appear as rattled as she felt, she lifted her chin. "Of course I'm okay. The news is a bit bizarre, but I've always known I was adopted. I also knew that neither of my birth parents wanted to meet me. Now I know why."

Sarah walked into the room. "Are they gone? Good. I was in the middle of placing my grocery order. Do you mind taking the baby?" she asked.

"Of course not," Coco said, automatically holding out her hands for Emma.

Sarah quickly walked away and Coco caught a whiff of why the housekeeper was eager to have Coco take Emma. "Someone needs a change," she said and tapped Emma on her nose. "Excuse me. Duty calls."

"Just a minute," Benjamin said.

"Trust me. Waiting will just make this worse," she said and headed down the hallway toward the stairs. She heard his footsteps behind her as she made her way to the nursery.

Feeling Benjamin's presence behind her, she quickly changed the messy diaper and picked up the baby. Coco turned to face him. "Thank you for being with me during the announcement."

"I'm not sure you realize what an impact this could have on you," he said. "Your father was a prince. It's possible you have an inheritance. Hell, in a way, you're a princess," he said, with a hint of horror in his eyes.

Coco scoffed and jiggled Emma as she fussed at the sight of Benjamin. "Oh, that's ridiculous. I'm no princess, that's for sure. I'm sure there's no inheritance for me. They would have mentioned that right off the bat," she said and took in his doubtful expression. "Wouldn't they? After all, I'm illegitimate. They've probably got all that sort of thing covered. I can't believe Edward was the first man in the Devereau family to spread his seed. I mean, some men just can't keep it zipped and—"

She stopped when she realized Benjamin might construe her words as criticism of him. "I mean, he fathered, or *sired,* eight children. That's different than one or two or—"

"It's okay. Let me know when you want to get in touch with the Devereaux," he said.

"When?" she said. "That will never happen. They don't really want me. Their father never wanted me, either." She suddenly felt vulnerable because she'd been so sure before that she was alone in the world. She'd coached herself to believe that she would be okay. Now she could hardly believe what she'd just been told—at the same time, she sensed that her newfound family wouldn't welcome her. "I have enough going on in my life. I don't need to—"

"You'll change your mind," he said.

She scowled at him. "You can't know that."

He hooked his thumbs in his pockets. "I know you will. At some point, at some time, you're going to want to meet those brothers and sisters. Anyone would want to know their relatives, especially if they thought they had none. I would," he said.

"Would you?" she asked.

"Yeah," he said. "I've got three brothers. Two in town and one up in Claytor Junction, Colorado. They've always been important to me. More so after my dad died and my mom took off for Costa Rica."

"Costa Rica?" she echoed.

Benjamin shrugged. "Mom always wanted to travel. Except for a few vacations, she just waited until after my dad died to do most of it. It's her way, she's running. One day, she'll stop."

Coco gnawed the inside of her lip. "You don't resent her? Don't you wish she was here?"

Benjamin laughed. "Hell, no. She needed to go. My dad's death was hard on her. I'm glad she had the guts to get out of town. Everyone has to mourn their loss in their own way."

"Is that why you got involved with Brooke?"

He paused a long time then sighed. "Maybe. I had to be strong for a while there. None of my brothers wanted to take over the ranch and it was going to be a big job."

"Why didn't they want to help?" she asked.

"They don't have ranching blood in them. One is a lawyer in town. One is an investment specialist. The other's a computer specialist. That left me," he said.

"I don't know much about ranching, but it looks like you're doing a pretty good job."

He cracked a half grin. "Thanks. I am doing a pretty good job."

Emma made an unhappy sound. "And if I can get

my daughter to stop crying every time she sees me, I'll be in good shape."

"You can start by taking off that hat," she said.

"I don't know if that makes a difference," he said.

"Give it a try," she said.

Sighing, he removed his hat.

Emma stared at him in silence.

"I can't believe it's the damn hat," he said.

The baby extended her hand out to his face.

"Lean closer," Coco said.

He slid her a doubtful glance, but bowed his head toward the baby. Emma gave a disapproving growl. Yet, the baby extended her hand to Benjamin's chin.

"Ah!" Emma said.

"Improvement," Coco said, unable to withhold a trace of victory in her voice.

Enduring the baby's probing strokes across his mouth and chin, he grimaced. "That's a matter of opinion."

"She's not screaming," Coco said.

"True," he said, gumming at Emma's tiny finger.

The baby's eyes widened and she pulled back her hand.

"Don't scare her," Coco scolded.

"How ya' doin', darlin'?" he asked Emma.

Her rapt gaze held his and she waved her hand at his face. "Ah!"

"Ah!" he echoed and caught her hand within his. "You're my girl. Don't ever forget that," he said and kissed her hand. "Ever," he said.

Emma kicked her feet and stared into his eyes, but
for the first time in forever, she didn't scream. Maybe
Coco was right. Maybe the hat had frightened her. More
important, maybe Coco was right and he needed to chill
and just love his child. That assignment could be a bit
more difficult than he planned.

Over the next few days, Coco tried to ignore the new
information she'd received about her birth family. Her
birth parents had never wanted her. Her half brothers
and sisters weren't truly interested in her. If so, wouldn't
one of them have come to meet her? And what about
her full brother? He apparently couldn't give a flying
fig about her existence.

The knowledge stung, but after her father had died,
a part of Coco had always been fearful. One day, her
mother would die. She knew that one day she would be
all alone in the world. For a while she'd believed that
was a long way off, but then her mother had gotten cancer and everything had gone downhill.

Staying with her mom during her last days had been
the most important, yet the hardest thing she'd ever
done. Coco had hoped it would give her peace, but since
her mother had passed, she'd felt restless. She'd wake
up in the middle of the night in a panic.

Taking the job with Benjamin and Emma had given
her a strange sort of relief. Emma had immediately
responded to her as if there were already a bond between the two of them. Even though Emma was jittery,

there was a sense of calm to the daily routine. Although Emma screamed and cried, she also smiled and cuddled. Something about the baby soothed Coco's sadness. She wanted to help heal Emma's fear. In the short time she'd spent at the Garner ranch, she'd grown extremely protective of Emma and was determined to bring peace between the baby and her daddy.

At this point in her life, nothing else was more important.

Each hour, however, she felt herself grow a little more curious about the royal family. In her few spare moments, she checked out the Devereau family and Chantaine online. Most of the siblings looked snooty to her—except for the one with curly hair named Phillipa. Coco was surprised to discover that one of the princesses—Valentina—actually lived in Texas with her husband and daughter.

Her half sister was in the same state. She could actually drive to meet her, she thought. That said, Princess Valentina might have no interest in meeting her. In spite of the fact that she insisted she had no expectations of her new semisiblings, Coco felt restless day and night. When she went to bed, her mind whirled with possibilities. In the deepest, darkest part of her, Coco wanted family—sisters, a mother, a father, cousins, aunts, uncles. Her adoptive mother and father were dead. Her birth mother and father were dead. She'd thought she was all alone. Was she? Was she crazy to think she *wasn't* alone?

* * *

The next day, Coco strapped Emma to her chest and took a fishing pole and tackle box out to one of the streams on the Garner ranch. In Texas, people took their infants out to do things that celebrated everything great about the state. That meant the general population wouldn't be surprised to see an infant at a professional ball game, fishing or even horseback riding, with their mama or daddy, of course. Thinking back to all the fishing trips she'd taken with her daddy before she'd turned ten, she cast her line into the stream, sat on the shore and waited. And waited. And waited. Then she got a bite and reeled in a medium-sized trout. She threw him back and cast her line again.

Early on, she'd learned that waiting was a big part of the game. Her father had made that easier with stories he'd told her—stories he'd clearly conjured. She reconstructed one of those stories and repeated it to Emma, who promptly fell asleep.

Hey, it was a cool story even if it made Emma snooze. Coco caught another three fish that she tossed back into the stream. One of Benjamin's workers stopped by to chat with her for a few minutes, and by late afternoon, she felt great. All her worries had disappeared. She gave Emma a bottle. The sun was shining on her head, she was sweating just a little bit and she began tramping back to the house.

Back at the house, Benjamin paced his office. Coco and Emma were gone. Coco had told Sarah she was going fishing, but Benjamin hadn't gotten around to showing her the real fishing spots on the ranch. So how the hell had she gone fishing?

He thought about Tweedledee and Tweedledum, the two guys representing the Devereau clan who'd visited Coco. He wondered if, despite their dweebiness, they had darker motives. What if they had gone after Coco and his daughter?

Benjamin headed for the front door, intent on tracking down Coco and Emma when he saw Coco stomping up the steps with a fishing pole, a tackle kit and a beaming smile.

Her smile was contagious. "You look happy."

"I am," she said. "I caught four fish and threw them back in the stream."

"You could be lying," he couldn't resist teasing. "What proof do you have?"

Her eyes darkened. "Your daughter is a witness."

Benjamin looked at his sleeping daughter and laughed. "She's a bad witness."

"You don't believe I caught those fish?" she asked, lifting her chin.

"Why should I?"

"Because I told you and because I'm an honorable woman. The only tales I tell are the kind that keep you occupied when you're waiting to score a fish. My daddy told me a lot of those kinds of stories when we went fishing," she said.

He met her gaze and felt a strange sensation in his

chest. She'd surprised him. He wouldn't have expected her to be a fisherman even though he'd known she'd grown up in a small town.

"And you're trying to teach my daughter how to fish at five months?" he said, nodding toward the baby pack on Coco's chest.

"Do you mind?" she asked.

"No. I don't mind. It's good for her to get outside."

"Do you want to take her?" she challenged.

Whoa, he thought. "She'd scream bloody murder if I tried to take her fishing."

Her eyes softened just a little. "I'm not talking about fishing. I'm talking about you and your daughter doing something enjoyable together. Both of you need that."

Chapter Three

The next night, Benjamin met his brother Jackson at a bar in town. They sat down over couple of cold beers. "So, what's up?" Jackson asked. "You don't look too good."

Benjamin slid a sideways glance at his younger brother. Jackson, an up-and-coming lawyer, had always been fast on the draw. He'd finished high school in two years, college in three, then gone on to collect his law degree at a prestigious university.

"Wanna trade places for a month or two?" Benjamin joked.

"Sorry." Jackson lifted his mug to his lips. "Even I know you would get the easier deal. Ranch and a new baby. Me? I'm a single guy with no plans for a wife or kids anytime in the next century."

"I hadn't planned on children yet, either," Benjamin said wryly but couldn't keep from cracking a smile. "How's the practice going?"

"Good," he said. "It would be easier if I were in Dallas, and there was that offer in New York."

"So why don't you go?" Benjamin challenged, already knowing the answer. His brother was committed to Silver City.

Jackson shrugged. "I don't know. This just feels right."

"Then quit bellyachin' about it," Benjamin said.

Jackson shot him a mock-hard glance. "You're the one who wanted to trade places," he said and took a swallow of his beer. "What's going on?"

Benjamin sighed. "Besides the fact that my daughter hates my guts?" he asked.

Jackson appeared to swallow a laugh and took another sip of beer to cover it. "That could be tough."

"Yeah," Benjamin said.

"But there's something else," Jackson prodded.

Benjamin sighed again. "The new nanny."

Jackson frowned. "I thought she was magical. She calmed your screaming daughter. She was perfect."

"Close to perfect," Benjamin muttered. "But we've hit a bump."

"She's illegal?" Jackson asked.

Benjamin shook his head. "No. It's worse that that."

"What could be worse?"

Benjamin looked from side to side and leaned toward his brother with a low voice. "She's a princess."

"What?" Jackson asked loudly.

"Keep it down," Benjamin said with a scowl.

"What are you talking about?" Jackson whispered.

"She was given up for adoption and she just found out her father was a prince."

"Holy crap," Jackson said. "You know how to pick them."

Benjamin frowned. "Thank you for your support."

"What do you need from me?"

"Some representatives of the royal family tried to get her to sign some forms," Benjamin said.

"Absolutely not," Jackson said. "Let me take a look at them first."

"I already said no. They've invited her to visit their island country, but again, they want her to sign papers. She says she doesn't care about meeting them, but I think she does."

Jackson scrubbed his face. "And you're wondering what this means legally? Do you want to fire her?"

"Hell, no. Emma loves her," Benjamin said.

"Okay. Well, there's a remote possibility that she's due an inheritance, but since she's out-of-wedlock and an adult, it's unlikely. Royals have ways of tying up their funds."

"I'm sure Coco would appreciate the infusion to her

bank account, but there are other concerns," Benjamin said.

"Such as?" Jackson asked.

"Such as the royal reps said she would be contacted by the media when the news breaks," Benjamin said.

Jackson winced. "That's true. There's a huge infatuation with anything royal. She could get pestered...."

"My men and I can handle a little pestering," he said.

"This might be more than a little," Jackson warned.

"I think she wants family," Benjamin said. "She didn't have any brothers or sisters growing up. Her father died when she was young and her mother died within the last few months."

Benjamin felt his brother studying him.

"This is starting to sound personal. Do you have something going on with your baby's nanny?"

"No," Benjamin said immediately. "I'm just telling you what I've observed."

"So, no hanky-panky. No kisses. No middle of the night sleepwalking into each other's beds."

"No."

"Hmm," Jackson said, drumming his fingers on the bar as he studied Benjamin. "I don't know. What does she look like?"

His brother's intent expression irritated Benjamin. "There's nothing going on between Coco and me. Between Brooke and the baby, trust me, I've had enough trouble with women lately. Emma feels safe with Coco. The last thing I want to do is mess up that situation."

"Well, if you have any more legal questions or if I can give you a hand with anything, let me know. Since you're more likely to saw off a leg than ask for help, you must consider this more important."

"Yeah," Benjamin said and decided to change the subject. "Who's in your fantasy football lineup?"

He and his brother talked football for a while, then Benjamin headed home. He noticed the porch light and floodlights were on and wondered if Sarah had left them lit. After a blazing-hot summer, Benjamin welcomed the cooler temperatures. He could almost see a hint of vapor when he exhaled.

Pulling open the front door, he stepped inside and cut the lights.

"Wait!"

He immediately identified Coco's breathless voice and turned the lights back on. "What are you doing?" he asked as he saw her trotting toward the steps.

"I just needed some fresh air, so I walked around the house a few times. I've got a remote intercom in case Emma wakes up," she said, pushing her hands into the pockets of her hoodie sweatshirt as she walked up the steps. Her nose was pink and her cheeks were flushed from the cold.

"How long have you been out there?" he asked.

"Not that long," she said. "I'm okay. I just didn't want to get locked out."

He sensed a restlessness vibrating from her. She

pushed back the hood of her sweatshirt and pulled her hair free. "You sure there's nothing wrong?" he asked.

"No," she said, but she didn't meet his gaze. "I used to walk around my mom's house that last month she was alive. Sometimes I just feel better after walking a little bit."

"I can understand that. I get itchy if I stay still too long," he said.

She finally looked at him. "Really?"

"Yeah, really. You want a cup of something to warm you up? It smells like Sarah may have left something warming in a crock."

"Apple cider," Coco said. "And it's delicious."

They went to the kitchen, and Coco pulled down the mugs and poured the cider. Benjamin took a sip too soon and it burned his tongue. "Ouch," he muttered and waved a hand for her to join him at the small table in the kitchen nook.

Coco smiled and sat across from him. "It smells so good. It's hard to wait."

She looked so young and sweet she could have been a teenager.

She met his gaze. "You're looking at me strangely. What are you thinking?"

"I'm remembering how I had to look at your driver's license twice before I believed you were twenty-four," he said.

Coco laughed. "I've always looked young for my age. My mother always told me there would come a time that I would appreciate that quality. Hated it in high school, though."

Benjamin took another sip; this one didn't scald his tongue, thankfully. "So, what made you want to do your little 5K around the house tonight? Have you been thinking about your new-to-you family?"

Coco's smile fell and she sighed. "I don't know what to do. I have a hard time believing they really want to meet me. It's not as if they've been beating down the door or calling me."

"There may some legal reasons that they're waiting for you to contact them," he suggested.

"Really?" she said, more than asked, in disbelief. "Well, all I know is if I had found out that I had a sister or brother, I would try to meet them."

"Then why aren't you?"

She shot him a dark look. "Because I don't like to go where I'm not wanted."

"You don't really know that you're not wanted," he said and leaned toward her. "Listen, if you want to go to Chantaine and meet them, we can work something out."

"I don't know how," she said, staring into her mug and cradling it with both hands. "Emma isn't settled in yet. She needs more time to feel at home and to get into a routine."

"That's true, but she'll get there," he said, even though he sometimes wondered if his daughter would ever feel at ease in his house. He was damn determined to do what was necessary to make it happen, though. "I don't want you to feel that you can't go," he said.

She bit her lip. "It's not like I would have anything in common with them."

He stared at her for a minute. She looked young, but he knew she'd carried a lot on her shoulders while her mother was sick. She'd taken charge with Emma and dealt with the baby's nightmares with no complaint.

"What are you scared of?"

She took immediate offense. "I'm not scared."

"Sure looks like it to me," he said.

"Well, I'm not. But you have to admit that these people are definitely in a different league."

He shrugged. "Still gotta put one sock on at a time."

She shot him a sideways glance and her lips twitched. "Unless they have a servant who puts on their socks for them."

Benjamin laughed. "That would be pretty pathetic." He put his hand over hers. "You don't have to make any rash decisions. You can take your time. Give yourself a break."

She met his gaze and took a deep breath. "I guess you're right. I don't need to work myself into a frenzy over this."

"Exactly," he said, and the moment stretched between them. The warmth in her eyes gave him a strange feeling in his gut. Realizing that his hand was still covering hers, he quickly pulled it away. It was one thing to try to comfort his daughter's nanny, but he didn't want Coco to misconstrue his sympathy as something else.

He cleared his throat. "Well, I should hit the sack," he said and rose to his feet.

"Me, too," she said, following him to her feet. "I'll take care of the mugs."

"Thanks," he said, wondering why his voice sounded so rough. He headed toward the doorway.

"And, Benjamin, thank you for talking me down from that cliff I was climbing," she said to his back.

He smiled at her description of her emotional state. "No need to scale a cliff unless it's absolutely necessary. G'night."

"G'night," she said as he entered the hallway. He felt another twitch at the sound of her soft voice, and he rubbed his stomach. He'd better take some antacid.

Two days later, as she was about to feed Emma, Coco saw Benjamin enter the house. Midlift of the spoon, Coco thought about the fact that Benjamin had been avoiding his daughter once again. She couldn't allow this to continue.

She pulled the spoon back from Emma. "Benjamin," Coco called as the baby frowned at her in confusion. Emma's soft, plump lips puckered in disapproval.

Benjamin poked his head in the doorway. "Yeah?"

Coco immediately stood. "Emma's ready to be fed and I…uh…I need to powder my nose."

Benjamin wrinkled his brow. "Powder your nose?"

"Use the ladies' room," she said.

Realization crossed his face. "Oh, okay. You want me to watch her?"

"I actually want you to feed her," she countered.

He frowned. "*Feed* her?"

"It's not that hard," she said and reached for his Stetson, but he was faster. "She hates your hat."

"I *like* my hat," he said.

"You don't need to wear it in the house while you're feeding a baby," she said and held out her hand for him to give her his hat.

"I'll put it on the table in the foyer," he said, lifting his hat from his head.

"Ah!" Emma called.

"Oops, better hurry. She's getting impatient," Coco said.

"Well, she can wait one minute," he said.

"Not unless you want her to start screaming so much she can't stop," she said. "Gotta go," she said, covering her ears as she ran to the upstairs bathroom. She wasn't sure she could hear Emma's screams at full blast and not respond.

She went into the bathroom closed the door behind her and turned on the fan. "La-la-la-la-la," she said as she covered her ears, determined to prevent herself from hearing Emma's screams. She continued for several moments then stopped her la-las. No baby shrieks pierced the sound of the fan. Giving in to her curiosity, she cut it off.

Still no sounds of alarm. Gingerly, she opened the bathroom door and listened. Silence greeted her. Coco felt a spurt of hope and tiptoed down the stairs.

"There ya go," Benjamin said. "Another bite. You're getting stronger. You're a Garner. You've got to be ready for everything."

Coco couldn't help smiling at Benjamin's words. When Emma gurgled, she had to cover her mouth to keep from giggling. She knew that sound signaled they were nearing the end of mealtime.

Peeking around the corner, she watched Emma give a huge raspberry, sending her latest bite of food and drool all over Benjamin's shirt.

"Whoa," he said and glanced down at his shirt. "What's up with that?"

Emma shot him another raspberry. This time, he had the sense to back away. "You got some power with that," he said, laughing as he wiped off his shirt with a napkin. "Do you do this every time you eat? It's a wonder Coco hasn't quit. I guess this means you're done."

He dabbed at her face with a napkin and she scowled and screeched at him. "Ah, you don't like the cleanup. Well, that's what happens when you're messy. You gotta get clean."

He wiped at her face and she screeched again.

Coco decided it was time to intervene. "I usually sing a song right now."

He glanced at her. "Nice of you to show up."

She bit her lip, but couldn't conceal a smile. "Well,

it looks like my timing is perfect. Seems that you two worked it out," she said.

"Temporarily," he said. "She sure can spit."

"I try to cut it off before that point. Once she starts gurgling, it's the beginning of the end."

"What's the magic song?" he asked.

"Wash your cheeks," she sang in a soft voice. "Wash your mouth. Shine like a sparkly star. That's what you are," she said and tapped Emma on her nose. "A sparkly star." Feeling sheepish, she shrugged. "I'm a triple threat with my deep lyrics, incredible vocal range and the ability to clean a baby's face at the same time."

"But can you dance and lasso cattle?"

"I don't know. If I tried to lasso cattle, then it might look like I was dancing," she said. "You want to pull her up from her high chair?"

He shot her a blank look. "Why would I want to do that?"

"Because she's finished eating and needs to get out of her chair, and the two of you need to get used to each other," she said.

Benjamin sighed and she noticed that his eye twitched slightly, but he unfastened Emma from the high chair and picked her up in his arms. The baby stared at him for a moment, then looked away and started making babbling noises.

Benjamin glanced at Coco. "What does that mean?"

"She's allowing you to carry her," Coco said and couldn't withhold a chuckle. Benjamin appeared as if he were carrying a live grenade and it would go off at any moment.

"What do I do now?"

"She's probably due for a diaper change," Coco said, goading him just a bit.

He shot her a dark glance. "I think the smashed pea shooting is enough for one day."

"In that case, carry her upstairs and I'll join you in a minute or two," she said.

"What am I supposed to do for that minute or two?" he demanded.

"Bond with her."

Benjamin groaned and walked into the hallway.

Coco cleaned up Emma's messy high chair and counted to three hundred. Carefully, she crept up the stairs to stand outside the nursery. She heard Benjamin talking. Peeking inside, she saw Benjamin pick up one of Emma's bunnies and move it from side to side in front of the baby.

Emma reached for the stuffed animal and squeezed it for a few seconds then dropped it.

"Oops," Benjamin said, reaching down to scoop up the bunny. Emma reached for the bunny again and dropped it again. "Fickle little thing, aren't you?" He caught sight of Coco and gave a nod.

"I see you've reached a peace agreement," she said.

"For now," he said and handed the baby to Emma.

"You just need to keep spending a little time with her. Soon enough you'll be giving her horseback-riding lessons," she said as she put Emma on the changing table and changed her diaper. "Helping her learn to ride a bike, then teaching her how to drive." She looked up to meet his horrified gaze.

"Driving," he echoed and shook his head. "Maybe she won't want to drive."

Coco laughed. "Now you're just dreaming."

"Let's take this one step at a time. The next step for me is to change out of this shirt that's covered with strained green peas." He glanced from Coco to Emma to Coco again. "See ya later," he said.

As soon as he left, Coco turned to Emma. "Good job!" she said. "You'll make a daddy out of Benjamin Garner before you know it."

The next day, Benjamin rode on horseback to check fences with one of his assistant foremen, Jace. Jace was young, but a hard worker, and both Benjamin and his foreman Hal valued good work ethics in their employees.

"Looks like there could be the beginning of a problem in the northeast corner," Jace said from his horse.

Benjamin lifted his binoculars and nodded. "Good catch."

"I should be able to get to it this afternoon," Jace said.

"That'll work," Benjamin said. "Let's check the other pasture, then we'll be done."

"Hal mentioned that we should be on the lookout for strangers coming on the property," Jace said.

"Have you seen anyone?"

"No. Hal also said it was something to do with the new nanny. She's not in danger, is she?"

"No," Benjamin said. "Coco's fine."

"Well, speaking of the nanny, she sure is nice," Jace said.

Benjamin glanced at Jace. "How would you know?"

"I met her when she was going fishing one day. Looked like she was pretty good at it," he said and laughed. "For a woman. I was wondering if it would be okay if I asked her out sometime."

"Coco?" Benjamin said.

"Yeah. She's pretty and nice. She seems like she would be fun."

"No," Benjamin said instinctively and without hesitation. He didn't have to think it through.

"No?" Jace echoed, clearly surprised.

"No," Benjamin repeated, bemused by the odd gnashing feeling inside him. "We're trying to get the baby used to living here. Coco is the most important ingredient in that equation. I don't want her distracted or bothered."

"I wouldn't bother her," Jace muttered.

"That's right. She's off-limits. Feel free to spread the word to the rest of the men," Benjamin said. With no female employees besides his housekeeper, Sarah, dating hadn't been an issue, until now. Even though Coco was attractive and appeared *fun,* he didn't want any additional complications in the picture with her. There were enough with the whole royalty thing. He hoped she would be able to put that on the back burner, but if she couldn't they would have to work something out. He had to think about what was best for Emma, and what was best for Emma was Coco.

Coco dressed Emma in a light jacket, tucked her into the stroller and took her for a walk. There was a slight nip in the air, but it was sunny and the time outside would do them both good. Coco headed for the back of the house, where a trail divided two fields. Chatting about the cattle and the trees, Coco alternately walked and ran. Emma let out a giggle when Coco ran.

"So you like a little speed in your stroller, do you?" Coco asked, glancing at the baby. "Your daddy's not gonna be happy if you feel the same way when you get your first car." Coco ran and Emma giggled again.

She turned around to return home, alternately walking and running. As she approached the back of the house, though, she noticed that Emma had fallen asleep, her head drooping to the side and her baby lips gently parted. Her heart twisted at the sight of her, so relaxed and at peace. As she rounded the corner to the front of the house, she wondered if she should take her up to her crib for a quick little snooze before dinner.

Three men and a woman immediately lunged toward her. She heard the click of cameras in between their questions.

"Miss Jordan, is it true that you are the illegitimate daughter of the former Prince of Chantaine?"

"Who are you?" Coco asked, shocked by their approach. She instinctively stepped in front of the stroller to protect Emma. "How did you find—"

"Your Highness," the woman began, "how does it feel to become a princess? You must be so excited."

Coco shook her head in confusion, distracted by the man shooting photographs of her. "I'm not a princess."

"Is it true that the Devereau family wishes to deny your place in the royal family?" a man asked.

Emma began to fuss.

"What place?" Coco asked and turned to pull Emma from the stroller. What a ridiculous question, she thought.

"Your rightful place in the royal family," the man said. "Surely you know you're due certain rights and privileges."

"Not really," Coco said as Emma began to wail.

"But you're a princess now," the female reporter said.

"I'm not a princess," Coco said flatly. "And you're making the baby cry. Are you proud of that?" she said more than asked and walked up the steps to the front door.

Chapter Four

"What I want to know is how in hell four reporters got past my men," Benjamin said to his foreman.

"We haven't been policing it 24/7, Ben," Hal Dunn said. The two had known each other since Benjamin was eight years old and Hal had been a young new worker on the ranch that Benjamin's father had then owned. Now Hal was Benjamin's right-hand man. "They could have sneaked through the wooded area in the front of the property."

"Well, I don't want to hear about anyone sneaking in anywhere," Benjamin said. "And 24/7 starts now."

"Got it," Hal said. "But I can tell you that whoever pulls that midnight shift is gonna want extra pay."

"Done," Benjamin said. "Just don't make it too much

or you'll get squabbling over who gets to take the night shift."

"That's for darn sure," Hal said with a rough laugh then turned sober. "Hope they didn't upset the little one or the nanny too much."

"Coco said Emma started crying but stopped as soon as they stepped inside the house. Coco seemed pissed off, but I think she may have been more rattled than she wanted to admit. I don't think she really expected any extra attention from the press, even though we were warned."

"Well, hell, she's royalty. That's big news around here," Hal said. "Maybe big news everywhere."

"Because it's going to change the world if Coco is a princess," Benjamin said with more than a touch of sarcasm.

Hal gave a combination of a wince and shrug. "Guess that's true. What else do you want us to do?"

"Just guard the perimeter," Benjamin said.

"Will do," Hal said.

A few moments later, Coco bounced down the stairs with Emma bundled in a fleece outfit "We're ready to go to the doctor," Coco said.

"What?" Benjamin said. "Why does she need to go to the doctor?"

"It's a regular appointment," she said. "Remember, you told me you wanted me to go with you?"

"Yeah, I remember," he said, thinking he should have added the appointment to his cell calendar schedule.

He must have put it on a different calendar. Having trespassers on his property had gotten him sidetracked. "Maybe I should have someone drive you to the pediatrician," he mused.

"Absolutely not. If we start behaving differently, then we'll have to do it for the next year. There's no need for such insanity."

"I could have one of the men follow her," Hal said.

"No," Coco said. "If we take the casual route, then the press will back off."

Benjamin gave it a second, and even third, thought. "I think it would be a good idea to have one of our men backing you up."

"Overkill," she said.

"Better safe than sorry," he said, enduring her scowl. "We have to think about both your safety and Emma's safety."

Her complexion paled. "I would guard Emma with my life."

"I know you would," he said. "But I don't want it to get to that point."

She took a deep breath and nodded. "Okay."

Benjamin scrubbed his jaw with his hand. "I'll reschedule my other appointments for this afternoon. I need to stay on top of Emma's health."

Coco blinked and took a quick breath. "Uh, okay. That's a great idea. You just need to remember to take off your hat."

Benjamin felt Hal's confused gaze. "Emma doesn't like my hat."

"Damn," Hal said. "That's a shame."

"Tell me about it," Benjamin said and sighed. He took off his hat and clutched it in his right hand. "Let's go," he said to Coco and led the way to his SUV.

"Her car seat is in my car," she said.

"No problem," Benjamin said and transferred the seat from Coco's car to his. He watched as Coco wedged Emma into the car seat and shook his head. "Bet she hates that."

"If you give her enough toys, she forgets about it," she said. "But I'm glad we don't have to go on any long trips."

"You and me both," he said as soon as everyone was buckled in place.

He pulled away from the house and drove down the long drive to the public road. He noted a few cars parked alongside the public road and frowned but hoped they weren't newspeople.

Driving toward town, he checked his rearview mirror, relieved when it didn't appear that he was being followed. "So what's the purpose of this appointment? Any shots?"

"It's a regular checkup. Yes to the shots," she said.

"Damn," he muttered. "One more opportunity for her to associate me with pain."

"They really do forget quickly," she said.

"I'll let you hold her during the shots," he said.

Knowing the bond between Emma and Benjamin was still a bit tenuous, she acquiesced. "This time," she said.

He slid her a sideways glance. "This time?"

"Yes," she said. "There may be times when Emma will need support. She may break a leg—"

"Not on my watch," he insisted.

She smiled. "She may fall and need stitches."

"You'll teach her to be careful," he said.

"Accidents happen. How many broken bones and stitches did you get when you were growing up?"

"That's different," he said. "I'm male."

"Ooh," she said, drawing out the one syllable in a way that clearly indicated she disagreed. "Big mistake to think that because she's female, she won't have accidents. Plus there are illnesses that could take her to the hospital."

Benjamin's stomach turned. "I don't like the sound of any of this."

"Too late," she said. "You're already her father. The good news is that you can take this all one step at a time. Plus you're already the type to man up, so you've got that on your side."

Benjamin turned the corner to the road where the pediatrician's office was located. "What makes you so sure about that?"

"You wouldn't have gone after Emma right after Brooke died if you weren't a responsible man. You wouldn't have hired me ASAP. You wouldn't have taken off your hat for Emma and allowed her to spit peas at you."

"Well, I guess there's that," he said dryly and brought the car to a stop in front of the pediatrician's office.

"Do they give you a beer after this?" he asked.

She laughed. "No. Not until you get home. Let's go. It won't be as bad as you expect."

Automatically returning his hat to his head, he ushered Coco out of the car and freed Emma from her car seat. She was staring hard at him.

"Hat," Coco prompted.

"Oh. Okay," he said and removed it again, setting it in the front seat.

He handed off Emma to Coco and escorted them inside. They sat in the waiting room for fifteen minutes. Afterward, Emma was weighed and measured while they waited for Dr. Apple.

The jovial man walked into the examination room with a friendly, booming voice. "Hello to Emma and mom and dad."

"You didn't read the report. Emma's mother died last month. Coco is her nanny."

Dr. Apple frowned. "Oh, please accept my condolences. This must be a difficult time for you."

"Yes, but not in the way you're thinking," Benjamin said. "Emma's mother and I weren't married."

Dr. Apple's mouth formed a perfect O.

"Yeah, and Emma hates me. She screams bloody murder every time I come around," Benjamin said.

"She's not screaming now," Dr. Apple said.

"This is the exception," he said.

"Not true," Coco said. "All you have to do is take off your hat."

Benjamin couldn't deny her statement.

"Hmm," Dr. Apple said. "Let's check out your baby."

The doctor conducted the examination and ordered the vaccinations. Emma was above average in her weight and height. She had gained in both since her last appointment. According to Dr. Apple, Emma was thriving. Benjamin was certain the primary reason for that was Coco.

The nurse entered and administered the punishment. Emma screamed in fury and agony. His heart wrenched. He watched Coco wince then immediately turn into comfort mode. "There you go," she said rubbing the baby's arm. "What a brave girl. All over in no time. You're such a good girl."

Emma quickly became distracted by Coco's words of praise. Her cries subsided and she gave a few extra sobs then sighed.

"You can give her a low dose of baby acetaminophen if she appears uncomfortable," the nurse said. "She's a beautiful baby."

Coco smiled. "Thank you. We think so, too."

They walked out of the office and Benjamin helped Emma into her car seat and escorted Coco into her seat. Emma sucked on her pacifier.

"Poor thing," Coco said. "They go through so much they don't understand."

"Yeah, but it's necessary to keep them alive," Benjamin said. "I would be a rotten father if I didn't protect her against the diseases she could get."

"That's right," Coco agreed. "And you're nowhere near a rotten father." She glanced behind her. "Besides, she's sleeping now."

Benjamin felt something inside him ease. "Good. Just tell me we have that baby Tylenol ready."

"We do," she assured him. "Along with your beer."

The next day, the story hit the Dallas and Houston papers. The weekly Silver City paper wouldn't be far behind. The house phone started ringing. Everyone from newspaper reporters to radio DJs to television reporters wanted to interview Coco about her association with the Devereau family.

Sarah fielded the calls when Coco was busy with Emma, but she was getting antsy by late afternoon. "I don't think I can do another day of this. These phone calls have totally interrupted my cooking and cleaning schedule."

"I'm sorry," Coco said as the phone rang again. "Maybe we should let the calls go to voice mail."

Sarah scoffed and shook her head. "It'll fill up in an hour. I swear, it must be a slow news day for everyone to get worked up over this." She picked up the phone. "Garner Ranch." She paused a few seconds. "Miss Jordan has nothing to say to the press. Pass that along to all your colleagues so they'll stop calling. Goodbye," she said and hung up the phone.

"They'll stop when they figure out I don't know anything about the Devereaux. As long as I continue to be boring, they'll get bored, too," Coco said.

Sarah snorted. "I don't know what you've been drinking, but this is a great story. Pretty girl, orphaned by her adoptive parents, finds out she's a princess—"

"I'm not a princess," Coco said. "I'm a nanny."

"Hmmph," Sarah said. "Try telling that to the reporters."

"I have," Coco said.

The phone rang again and Coco reached for it. She didn't want Sarah getting any more cranky than she already was. "Garner Ranch," she said.

"This is Annie Howell. I'd like to speak with Coco Jordan," the woman said.

Coco sighed. "Speaking."

"Oh, Your Highness. I'm so happy to talk to you," the woman gushed. "I'm the president of the Silver City Ladies Society. We would love for you to come and speak to our group next month."

"Thank you for the kind invitation," Coco said. "But I must tell you that I'm not any kind of highness and I'm very busy working for the Garner household right now."

"But you *are* from royalty," the woman said. "We're so excited to have royalty right here among us."

"But I'm really not royalty. A true royal person is raised to be royal from birth and, trust me, I was not.

I'm sorry I can't help you. Have a good day. Goodbye," she said before the woman could respond.

"These people really don't get it," she murmured.

Emma's cry vibrated through the baby monitor, interrupting her thoughts.

Coco ran upstairs, scooped up Emma, changed her diaper and returned downstairs just as the doorbell rang.

"I'll get it," Sarah said. "Might as well be Grand Central Station in here today with all these interruptions."

Carrying Emma, Coco wandered toward the front room.

Sarah opened the door and looked surprised. "Eunice and Timmy, what brings you here?" she asked, drying her hands on the dish towel she carried.

"May we come in?" the woman outside asked.

"Of course," Sarah said and stepped aside. "What can I do for you, Eunice?"

An older woman with bright red lipstick and unrealistically black hair and a middle-aged man stood inside the door. The woman carried a fruit basket and the man cleared his throat and pressed down his hair.

"We hear you have a princess living in your house and we wanted to welcome her to the neighborhood," Eunice said.

Coco took a silent step backward so she wouldn't be seen.

Sarah paused a half beat then sighed and reached for the basket. "That's nice of you. I'll be sure and tell Coco you dropped by."

"Oh, we were hoping to meet the princess," Eunice said.

"Well, she's busy with the baby right now," Sarah said.

Emma looked down at the dog and made a loud gurgling sound.

"Oh, is that them?"

Emma let out another loud gurgle.

"Coco," Sarah called as if she realized it was no use trying to hide Coco any longer. "You have guests."

Coco entered the room and smiled. "Hello," she said.

"Coco, this is Eunice Chittum and her son, Timmy."

"Tim," the man corrected and cleared his throat.

"Tim," Sarah repeated. "Well, the Chittums have brought you a fruit basket. I'll take it into the kitchen for you."

"Thank you very much," Coco said. "What a nice gift. It's nice to meet you."

"Oh, our pleasure," Eunice gushed and dipped in a curtsey. "Your royalness."

Frustration rippled through Coco. "Oh, no, please don't do that. I'm just Coco Jordan. Really."

"There's no need to be so humble with us. We're very honored to meet you. I especially wanted you to meet Timmy."

"Tim," the man corrected.

"He would be a perfect escort and you should know that he *is* eligible."

"Mother," Timmy said, rubbing at his hair self-consciously.

Coco covered her dismay by shifting Emma to her left hip and extending her hand. "It's nice to meet both of you and so friendly of you to stop by. I wish I could invite you to stay longer, but I need to bathe the baby."

"Oh, of course. We wouldn't dream of imposing, but I do want to leave you with my phone number and Timmy's," the woman said with a bob of her head and handed Coco a floral card with several phone numbers on it. "That last one is Timmy's cell and he always answers. Please call us for anything you might need. Anything at all."

Coco nodded and murmured her thanks again as she closed the door behind them. As soon as they left, she walked to the kitchen where Sarah was cooking. "Just tell me this won't last long," she said over Emma's babbling. Emma was turning into quite the chatty baby. Coco just wished she understood the baby's language.

Sarah shot her a look of sympathy. "Oh, sweetheart, it's just getting started, but maybe if we ask Benjamin to keep it to no visitors for a while, it'll die down faster."

"I hate to be unfriendly," Coco said.

"It's about survival," Sarah said. "We have to survive the incoming."

The phone rang.

"I'll get it," Coco said as Emma continued to babble.

"I'll let you," Sarah said and turned back to stirring her pot.

Coco scooted around the corner to grab the phone

in the den and almost collided with Benjamin. "Oh, I didn't know you were here," she said.

Emma stared at Benjamin's hat and immediately stopped babbling. "She really doesn't like that hat," Sarah muttered.

Rolling his eyes, Benjamin removed it. "I'll get the phone," he said, picking up the receiver.

Coco went after him. "You might not want to do—"

"Garner Ranch," he said and listened. He wrinkled his brow and his face became more and more perturbed. "Wait a minute. Wait, wait a minute. You say you're a DJ at a radio station, and you want to interview Princess Coco Jordan?"

Benjamin glanced at her. She cringed and shook her head.

"She doesn't want to be interviewed," he said and opened his mouth as if he were going to say goodbye. He listened a moment longer and his eyes grew wide with disbelief. "You want to have a reality competition for men who want to marry a princess? That's the most ridiculous thing I've heard in my life—" He broke off and shook his head. "You say you've already got fifty men signed up? I don't care if you've got a million. It's not gonna happen. Ever. Got it? Goodbye."

He hung up the phone and turned to her. "We're gonna need a different strategy."

That night after she put Emma to bed, Coco returned to her bedroom, pulled on a sweatshirt and crept downstairs and out the back door. Her mind whirling a mile a minute, she circled the house. She started out at a fast jog. *What was her blood brother like? Were any of those royals worth knowing? Would any of them consider* her *worth knowing?*

Coco had always dreamed of having brothers and sisters, but her parents had told her she was their everything. In retrospect, she'd felt more than a little pressure from that. She'd always wanted to be the best student, the best artist, the best singer, the best fisher, the best athlete, but in truth, she'd been mostly average.

Oh, she'd been a good speller and her grades had spiked into Dean's List territory every now and then, but along the way, she'd learned that she couldn't be Miss Perfect. And she'd felt a little guilty about it, especially when she'd overheard her parents arguing about money and learned that her parents had spent their life savings to adopt her.

After a time, she'd seen that her requests for a sibling had pained her mother and father, so she'd stopped voicing them. But she'd never stopped wanting a brother or sister or both. And now, she technically had brothers and sisters, all for the taking. Yet she felt as if it were all a bad joke, because she sensed they would regard her as a complication, perhaps a threat.

Which was so ridiculous, because she wasn't a nasty person.

Why couldn't she put this craziness out of her mind? The onslaught of the press didn't help, but she just

wished she could turn it all off at night when she went
to bed. So far, no luck.

Suddenly, Benjamin appeared by her side, walking
with her. "Something bothering you?" he asked in his
low drawl.

"It's been a strange day," she said a little breathlessly.
She inhaled quickly, superaware of his height and muscular frame.

"I'll say," he said. "Which bothered you most?" he
asked. "Eunice and Timmy? Or the reality competition
for your hand in marriage?"

She shot him a dirty look. Ordinarily, she would have
been more careful with her reaction to her boss.

He chuckled and gave her a quick elbow. "Looks like
you've got some extra energy. You need to run," he said
and started to jog.

She couldn't *not* accept his dare, so she quickened
her stride. Coco noticed that Benjamin wasn't breathing hard. "Were you a football player when you were
in high school?"

"And college," he said. "Why do you ask?"

She shrugged and upped her speed a bit. "Just curious. You're big, but fit," she said.

"Big?" he echoed. "I was one of the little guys on the
team. But thanks for the compliment. It helps to move
around a lot during the day. You should know with all
the moving you do for Emma."

She nodded, concentrating on her pace and breathing.

"You still didn't answer my question about why we're running," he said.

"I don't know why *you* are running," she said.

"Okay, I can settle that. I'm running to keep up with you. Why are you running?"

She ran several more steps. "I don't want to have to deal with all this right now. I just started taking care of Emma. Sarah has been a good sport, but it's not fair to her to have to answer all these crazy phone calls."

"Yeah," he said. "What else?"

She continued jogging then slowed. Then walked. "I don't want to want to meet them," she said, her heart pounding in her chest. "I don't want to care if I ever see one of them face-to-face."

"But you do want to meet them. I would want to," he said, walking beside her.

"You said that before," she said, looking at him.

"Sure. I've got brothers, but I've always known them," he said.

She nodded, taking a deep breath. "The trouble is I don't want to go by myself, and I can't think of anyone to go with me."

"Hmm," he said.

Her heart twisted. "And it's such bad timing."

He rubbed his chin. "It could be worse."

"How?" she asked.

"It's not calving season," he said and met her gaze. "How would you feel about having Emma and me tag along for your trip to Chantaine?"

She gaped at him in amazement. "Are you joking?"

"Don't get the wrong idea. I'm not doing this out of the goodness of my heart," he said. "You're the best one for Emma, and I'll do whatever I have to do to keep you."

Coco blinked while his words sank in. *Allrighty.* She was totally confused for an entire moment, until she realized that Benjamin was still desperate to keep Emma happy, even though his daughter had stopped screaming at the very sight of him.

Chapter Five

The next day, numerous bouquets of flowers, invitations and fruit baskets arrived. The arrivals kept Boomer busy as he tried to greet each deliveryman. Benjamin made a new message for the voice mail and no one was required to pick up the house phone. His men kept all visitors at bay.

Coco breathed a sigh of relief several times throughout the day. Sarah was more relaxed. Even the baby seemed more at ease. The conversation she'd had with Benjamin made her feel alternately uneasy and anxious. Was she really going to Chantaine to meet her half siblings? Had Benjamin really agreed to go with her? And take Emma?

Coco wondered if she'd dreamed it.

"There's no way we can use all this fruit," Sarah said. "Even if we give it to the men."

"Is there someone in the community who could use it?" Coco asked as she slid Emma into her high chair for dinner.

"I could call the church. They might know someone who could take it," Sarah said as she stirred stew on the stove. She gave a slight smile. "It sure has been nice ignoring the phone today, hasn't it?"

"Yes, it has," Coco said as she began to feed Emma. The baby kicked her feet in anticipation of her green beans.

Coco smiled at the baby's puckered lips. "Compared to yesterday, it's been heaven."

"I'm thinking after word of Benjamin's message gets around, the phone won't be ringing near as much tomorrow," Sarah said.

"Why is that?" Coco asked, giving Emma another spoonful of beans.

Sarah chuckled. "It's not exactly a welcoming message."

"I haven't listened to it," Coco said and decided to do that as soon as she finished feeding Emma. "I can't imagine what he said."

"Something along the lines of how you wouldn't be back in touch until after the turn of the next century and trespassers would be prosecuted to the full extent of Texas law," Sarah said, then chuckled. "It's fun when Benjamin gets a little huffy. He's usually not the pushy type. Like his father, he doesn't get riled unless the occasion calls for it."

Sarah made Coco curious. "What was his father like?" Coco asked.

"He was a good, solid man. The ranch was his life. Except for Benjamin, his boys went in different directions. I think Benjamin fought it for a while, but once his father died, he knew his destiny. Except for that crazy affair with Brooke Hastings." Sarah rolled her eyes. "But we all have our foolish moments. This one turned out pretty good when you look at that baby."

Coco smiled at Emma, and Emma gave her a toothless smile in return. Sheer delight rushed through her. "She is adorable, isn't she?"

"When she isn't screaming bloody murder," Sarah said.

"She's still adjusting," Coco said, feeding Emma another spoonful. "What about Benjamin's mother? I haven't heard much about her."

"Well, that's another story," Sarah said as she adjusted the temperature on the burner. "Georgia is her name and you've probably heard she lives in Costa Rica. At the moment, anyway," Sarah said. "Georgia wanted to travel. Benjamin's father, Howard, couldn't and wouldn't. I'm not sure which of those were first."

"It does seem that ranch life is very absorbing."

"It is," Sarah said. "A rancher is married to his ranch and his wife needs to understand that. Georgia went along with it for a long time, but as she and Howard grew older, she wanted them to take vacations. He was resistant. Sometimes, she went on her own. Don't dare repeat this, but their marriage was turbulent because of it."

Coco frowned. "It must have been difficult for both of them if she wanted to travel and he didn't."

Sarah nodded. "Yep. It was. Some people thought she was flighty, but she hung around until her boys were grown."

"What do you think?" Coco asked, knowing Sarah had been employed by the Garners for a long time.

"It's not my place to comment one way or another, but when I saw her, she was a good mother and a good wife. She just got a little wanderlust and some empty-nest syndrome. I know she's grieving now. Traveling won't fill the loss, but it might provide a distraction. Sometimes we all need a distraction."

Coco absorbed Sarah's words. "Very true. You're a wise woman, Sarah."

Sarah smiled, her face creasing in a thousand wrinkles. "Well, thank you very much, your royalness."

Coco laughed. "You know I'll be changing a dirty diaper within thirty minutes."

Sarah nodded. "You're a good girl. You're better than any princess—I'll tell you that much. And you work magic with that baby. It's no wonder Benjamin is willing to do almost anything to protect you. If you ever meet those royal people, you remember they're not better than you. Hear me?"

Coco's heart twisted and her throat swelled with emotion. "I hear you."

"Good, and don't forget what I said," Sarah said.

Later that evening, Benjamin found Coco wading through the flowers and messages she'd received during the day. She pushed a strand of her hair behind her ear and shook her head in frustration. "This is ridiculous," she muttered.

He took a drink of water from his glass. "Long day? You didn't have any visitors, did you?"

She shook her head and looked up at him. "No visitors. Just deliveries and the phone ringing off the hook. It's these crazy requests. These men don't even know me, but they're asking for dates, offering to take me on trips. I feel like I need to put out a press release saying, *I'm broke. You can stop calling now.*"

Benjamin chuckled at her, but at the same time, he felt sorry for her. She hadn't asked for any of this. He admired her for keeping her feet on the ground. Many women would have been demanding a tiara and breakfast in bed if they'd learned they had royal blood in them. But not Coco.

"You don't have to answer them," he said. "These offers you're getting are completely unsolicited."

"I know," she said. "I just wish I wasn't getting them at all." She shrugged. "If I were engaged or married, these men wouldn't be making all these offers."

"True," he said and his mind wandered to his assistant foreman, Jace. Jace would be more than happy to act as Coco's love interest. He scowled at the thought.

"Why are you frowning?" she asked.

"Just thinking," he said and took another drink of water. He walked to the other side of the room then walked back. It wouldn't be a bad idea if Coco had someone looking out for her. She was a smart girl, but probably too sweet and trusting for her own good. If people knew they would have to deal with a protective man in her life, they might be less likely to try to take advantage of her.

He watched as Coco opened another card. She sighed.

He gave in to his curiosity. "What's that one?"

"A mother wants money for her sick child," she said, her voice miserable.

"It could be valid, but it may not be," he said.

She looked at him in shock. "You mean, you think someone would lie about that?"

He nodded. "Oh, yeah. Especially in this situation."

"That's—that's—horrible," she said. "I mean, what if I *were* a real princess and I got these kinds of requests?

"They would be screened by your staff," he said.

"I don't have staff," she said. *"I am staff."* She opened another envelope attached to a bouquet of roses. "Oh, goody, another invitation. This one from David Gordan in Dallas inviting me to a Christmas ball?" She lifted her hands helplessly.

He frowned. The name rang a bell. "Let me see that," he said and she handed him the typed note. "David Gordan. That's my stockbroker's son." He shook his head. "This is out of control." He sighed. "Well, damn. I guess I'm gonna have to be your fiancé."

Coco dropped her jaw. "What?"

"It won't be real," he said quickly, as much for himself as for her. After the debacle of his relationship with Brooke, the idea of an engagement nearly gave him hives. "It's just for the sake of appearances until the insanity dies down. This way it won't look like you're all alone and ready to have someone take advantage of you. If someone approaches you, they'll have to deal with me, too."

Her eyebrows furrowed. "I'm stronger than I seem," she said.

"I know you're strong. After what you went through for your mom and helping Emma to settle down, I know you're strong. But it's gotta be damn tiring to feel like you've always got to be on guard."

Coco sighed and her shoulders slumped. "You're right about that." She met his gaze with a wince. "Are you sure you don't mind doing this?"

"It's just for a little while," he said. "You mentioned that a fiancé would fix things a few minutes ago. I had to run it through my brain. It seems like the right thing to do."

She gave a slow nod and bit her lip. "Hmm. But it would cut into your dating time," she ventured.

He laughed. "That's not a big focus at the moment," he said.

"It would be a huge relief for me," she admitted. "If you're sure you don't mind. And we'll break it off the second you feel inconvenienced," she said with a firm nod.

"All right," he said. "I'll give Sarah the news in the morning. Should be all over the country by lunchtime."

Her lips twitched. "She seems pretty discreet to me."

"Trust me, if I tell her that she can share the information, she'll take off like a runaway horse. And she will love having this kind of scoop."

"Are you going to tell her the truth?"

He shook his head. "No one except you and I can know the truth. That's the only way it will work."

Coco took a deep breath and squished her eyes together as if she was preparing to take a jump into deep water. "Okay," she said and opened her eyes. "Let's do it."

Two days later, Benjamin, Emma and Coco boarded a flight with a connection in England that would land in Chantaine. Coco was so anxious that she feared she would explode during the flight. Plus she was hyper-aware of Benjamin now that they were supposedly engaged. She noticed that he treated her a little differently in front of people. Even in front of Sarah, he'd touched her arm and put his hand at her waist a couple of times. It had caught her off guard, but she realized they needed to appear as if they were romantically involved. She hadn't considered that when he'd offered to be her fiancé.

Coco had thought Benjamin was attractive before the engagement thing, but she'd pushed it aside and focused on Emma's adjustment. She would have to be blind to be totally immune to his tall, wide-shouldered frame and rugged masculine features. Now she was going to have to work twice as hard not to give in to her attraction to him. The fact that she'd been sitting mere inches away from him for hours wasn't helping her, either.

"Go to sleep," he said, cracking open one of his eyes.

"But Emma," she said, even though the baby was so deep in sleep she was drooling on Coco's sweater.

"She'll let us know if she wants something. Here," he said, extending his arms. "I'll take her."

Emma was out, so she probably wouldn't wake up even with the transition.

"Come on," he said. "You're wound way too tight. You need to close your eyes for a few moments."

Coco gingerly handed the baby to Benjamin, and saw that Emma barely stirred. She nestled against her daddy's chest and gave a soft baby sigh. The sight made Coco smile. "Maybe something good will come of this trip after all," she said.

"Go to—"

"Okay, okay," Coco said. "I'll rest my eyes, but I won't fall asleep."

One moment she was thinking about Benjamin. Then next she was thinking about meeting her half brothers and half sisters. The next moment, she heard a baby babbling. Blinking her eyes, she glanced over at Benjamin.

Emma, who was sitting on his lap, was having a baby conversation with him.

Shaking off her sleep, Coco stretched and smoothed over her hair. "How long was I asleep?"

He glanced at his wristwatch. "About two hours," he said.

"You're joking," she said.

"Nope," he said. "Emma woke up and started screaming bloody murder, so I had to walk her up and down the aisle."

Chagrined, she bit her lip. "And I slept through her screaming?"

"No," he said and his mouth stretched into a sly grin. "I was joking about that part, but I did walk her up and down the aisle a few times. She's gonna be a talker, isn't she?"

"I think so," Coco said, smiling at Emma and him. "I'll change her diaper. I'm sure she's due."

An hour later, they landed in Heathrow and grabbed a bite to eat. Soon enough, it was time to board the flight for Chantaine. Coco's nerves returned. She watched out the window as they drew close to the Chantaine airport. The island country was beautiful. The white sandy beach around the island was broken by jutting outcrops of rocks. The vivid blue of ocean contrasted sharply with the shore. She couldn't believe that she was connected to the island in any way. As the jet managed a three-point landing, she felt herself swell with anticipation. Soon, very soon, she would meet her half brothers and half sisters.

Benjamin carried Emma as they departed the plane, and after they collected their luggage, they left the airport to find a limo waiting for them. Coco met Benjamin's gaze. "Is this a big mistake?"

He chuckled. "We'll find out."

She smiled. "Thanks a lot."

"You wanted to come here," he pointed out.

"I know. I know," she said.

"Just think of it as a nice vacation," he said and leaned his head back against the seat.

"I'll try," she said and took a deep breath.

"Do you think they'll like me?" she asked him.

"If they don't, they're nuts," he said.

"Why?" she asked then shook her head. "Don't answer that. I'm just being weird and insecure."

"You're a damn good woman—princess or not," Benjamin said. "I'm not flattering you. Just telling the truth."

"Thank you," she said, but she was still nervous. "This is a little crazy."

"Roll with it," he told her. "When have you ever visited a Mediterranean island where the ruler was determined to meet and greet you?"

She took a deep breath. "Okay. I'll work on it. Our Emma sure was a good traveler, wasn't she?" she said in a low voice.

"Yeah, we'll see what happens tonight," he said. "The time change could be hell for all of us."

Coco was surprised when the limo drove past the palace gates. "I thought they would put us in a hotel outside the palace complex," she said to Benjamin.

"You underestimated yourself," he said.

She struggled with doubt. "We'll see."

Moments later, the chauffeur unloaded the luggage and carted it to a small villa with three bedrooms. Emma began to wake up as they stepped inside. Coco jiggled her as she walked into the villa.

The chauffeur guided her and Benjamin through the small building. "A cook is available to you. A nanny is available to you," he said. "Whatever you need, just dial this code," he said and wrote down a series of numbers. "Is there anything you need right now?" he asked.

Coco glanced at Benjamin.

"A few sandwiches would be nice," he said. "We need a little rest. Don't expect any of us to make an appearance before tomorrow."

The chauffeur nodded. "As you wish, sir."

The man left and Coco and Benjamin looked at the den of the villa. "This is nice," she said.

"Not bad. And we have a cook and a nanny at our disposal," Benjamin added.

"Yeah. Good luck with that nanny thing with Emma," she said and jiggled Emma again.

"You never know," he said. "She let me hold her for hours today."

"True," Coco said. "Sometimes babies grow and change when they visit different environments and have new experiences. So we'll see. Let's start with a blanket on the floor so she can stretch out and wiggle."

"Works for me," he said and pulled a blanket out of his backpack. He put it on the floor and she placed Emma on it. The baby immediately began to lift her head and feet. And wiggle. Emma made groaning sounds as if she were doing an aerobic workout.

"Go, girl," Benjamin said.

Coco laughed at his low-voiced cheer. "I just hope she'll expend enough energy to sleep in an hour or so."

"If she doesn't, we'll take turns," he said.

Coco wandered through the villa again, noticing the fine linens on the beds and in the bathrooms. "I'm surprised at how nice it is."

"What did you think? They would put you in the dungeon?" he asked.

"No," she said. "Well, maybe. After all, I'm the illegitimate spawn."

He chuckled and shook his head. "I know this is strange for you, but you may as well roll with it. In the scheme of things, how many people get a call telling them their father was a ruling prince?"

"True," she said. "I'll work on it. Which bedroom do you want?"

"Any room where my dear daughter is not sleeping," he said.

She laughed. "The good news is she can have her

own bedroom and I brought monitors so we know if she's crying."

"Works for me. I could use a beer. You could use some wine. Let me see if I can find something for both of us," he said and opened the refrigerator. "We're in luck. German beer," he said with a snicker. "White wine?" he asked her.

"I'm good with water. The flight was exhausting," she said. "I need to be ready when Emma wakes up after we put her to bed."

"You could call the nanny they offered," Benjamin said.

"Not tonight. Maybe another time," Coco said.

Moments later, sandwiches were delivered and Coco devoured hers. She diapered Emma, put her in the crib and fell asleep in the bedroom next to the nursery. With her clothes on.

Dead to the world, Coco awakened to the sound of a baby screaming. Blindly, she scrambled out of bed and rushed out of her bedroom toward the screaming. She bumped into a large, strong frame.

"Benjamin?" she murmured.

"Yeah," he muttered in return.

She stumbled into the nursery and pulled Emma up into her arms. "You're okay," Coco cooed.

Emma screamed in protest and Coco cuddled the baby closer. "You're okay," Coco said.

In short order, Emma calmed down. "Bet you need a diaper change," Coco said. "I can do that in no time."

Finding a flat surface, Coco set the baby down. Emma fussed, but Coco quickly changed her wet diaper and picked her up.

"Good girl," Coco said.

"That was fast," Benjamin said.

"It's all instinct when you do it every day," she said. "She's awake now. It may take a while for her to go back to sleep."

"I can stay up," he offered.

She shook her head. "I want you awake when I'm not," she said. "I'll take this shift."

"You're sure?" he asked.

"More than," she said. "Besides, you're due the rest since you walked her up and down the aisle while she was screaming on the plane," she said, lightly mocking him.

He chuckled. "Yeah. Well, let me know if you need me," he said and gently touched the tip of her nose. "Tomorrow's going to be a busy day for you."

Her stomach danced with nerves. "We'll see."

The next morning, a staff member from the kitchen delivered a basket of bread, butter and jellies along with coffee and hot tea. "This is breakfast?" Benjamin said, biting into a roll. "At least there's coffee," he said and poured a cup.

"Maybe this is all they eat for breakfast," she said as she gave Emma her bottle. "Or they're hoping they can starve us into leaving early."

He tossed her a sly look, and it occurred to her that the man was too good-looking for her own good anytime day or night. "No need for paranoia yet. You haven't even met them," he said. "You look tired. Did Emma go back to sleep?" he asked.

"After about an hour, but then I was wound up and couldn't. I think my internal clock is messed up."

He nodded. "Plus you're meeting your royal relations today."

"True," she said and the phone rang.

"I'll get it," he said and picked it up. "Benjamin Garner," he said. "Yes, Miss Jordan is here." He nodded. "Afternoon tea," he said, waggling his eyebrows in Coco's direction. "And this morning, a royal representative would like to take Miss Jordan for a tour of the palace grounds."

"What time?" she asked because she hadn't showered yet and knew she looked like something the cat dragged in.

"What time?" he repeated and waited for the answer. "In an hour?"

She nodded. "Yes," she said and put Emma on her shoulder to burp her.

Chapter Six

Promptly one hour later, a knock sounded on the front door of the villa. With Emma in one arm, Benjamin opened the door to a slim, middle-aged, balding man wearing a suit.

"Hello," the man said, his gaze sweeping the small foyer. "I'm Peter Bernard for Miss Coco Jordan. I presume you are Mr. Garner," Peter said. "You and the baby are more than welcome to join us."

"I'd like for her not to be distracted by the baby during the tour," Benjamin said, towering over the man as he extended his hand. "Miss Jordan is very important to me. I trust you'll take good care of her."

Coco grabbed her jacket and walked toward the door. Benjamin caught her arm before she could leave and she met his gaze. "Have fun, sweetheart. Emma and I will be waiting for you," he said and lowered his head to kiss her.

Coco stared at him for a long moment, stunned that he'd *kissed* her, then she reminded herself that this was part of their ruse. She finally managed to take a breath and nodded. "Thanks. I hope she'll take a little nap. I'll see you later, um, *honey.*" She nearly choked on the word. This was going to be more difficult than she'd anticipated.

"Miss Jordan," the man at the door prompted.

"Yes," she said, relieved to have her attention diverted from Benjamin. "Mr. Bernard."

He nodded and escorted her to a car parked in front of the villa. "We shall tour the grounds first and I'll provide you with a history of the Devereau family," he said as the driver opened the door for her and Mr. Bernard.

"Although our gardens and vegetation are always lovely here in Chantaine, unfortunately, due to the time of the year, most of our flowers are not in full bloom. As you can see, however, we have several green courtyards that provide the royal family with opportunities for moments to ponder and escape the pressures of their responsibilities."

Coco drank in the sight of the lush, green palace grounds. She could only imagine how stunning they would be with colorful flowers and foliage. As Mr. Bernard continued to give her a running commentary on the various buildings, including guest cottages, staff quarters and stables, she wondered what it would be like to grow up in a place like this. She thought of her own childhood home in a rural town in Texas and smiled.

"Do you have fishing ponds?" she asked.

Mr. Bernard blinked at her. "Fishing ponds?"

"Yes. Large ponds where you can swim and fish," she said.

Mr. Bernard gave a slight smile. "We have a pool and ocean for swimming. Likewise, the royal yacht can be used for fishing expeditions. There are a few stocked ponds on the property that feature mostly garibaldi fish and carp. Do you have more questions?"

She shook her head. "Not right now."

"Very well, we shall now proceed to the palace," he said.

Mr. Bernard began to share the history of the Deveraux family and Chantaine. The family, of course, went back centuries and representatives of the crown had conducted a series of negotiations with both France and Italy in order for the royal family to remain in power and for Chantaine to maintain its independence.

"Some men are born to rule and some are determined to make a difference. Chantaine is proud that with this new generation, the royal family actively seeks to improve the quality of life for all of Chantaine's people. Within the last several years, His Royal Highness, Stefan, has invited a limited number of cruise ships to our port. He and the rest of the royal family have instituted art, music and film events with percentages donated

to Chantaine's charities. And, of course, Her Highness
Bridget married a highly credentialed American doctor,
who now serves as our chief medical officer. Prince Stefan is always looking for ways to improve Chantaine."

The car slowed to a stop in front of the grand palace
entrance. White columns rose several stories high. A
man in uniform stood at the front door. The driver ushered her out of the car and she joined Mr. Bernard as
the huge heavy door opened to a grand two-story foyer
with curving staircases and marble floors. Above her
hung several chandeliers.

"Wow," she whispered.

Mr. Bernard continued his discourse as he led her
throughout the main floor of the palace, which held
numerous meeting rooms, two ballrooms and several
nooks with antique furniture where someone could
look out the window and enjoy the sight of the palace
grounds. As her guide commented on the origin of the
architecture of the palace, she couldn't contain her curiosity any longer.

"What was he like?" she asked. "Prince Edward?"

Mr. Bernard seemed slightly taken aback. "Prince
Edward was a sword master. His passion was yachting
and he was loyal in his duties as prince. He graduated
from university in France and provided Chantaine with
an excellent heir, along with a progeny that are a delight
to our citizens."

"And his—" she paused, wanting to repeat the word

he'd used, though it wasn't one she would dream of choosing "—his progeny. What are they like?"

"As I said, they are delightful."

But that didn't answer her question.

Coco ate half her sandwich with Emma on her lap while Benjamin wolfed down the meal delivered from the palace kitchen. He eyed her remaining half sandwich.

She shoved her plate toward him. "Take it. I'm not going to eat it. I have formal tea in a short while. Can we look that up on Google? I've never had a formal tea before."

"You're sure?" he asked, staring at her sandwich.

"I'm sure," she said and shoved her plate toward him.

He immediately scooped up her half sandwich. "Did you get any real information?" he asked before he took a bite.

"He was very nice and informative, but when I asked what the royal family was like, he said *delightful*."

He scowled. "No one is always delightful. He's a PR guy. You'll get a better feel for this after this afternoon."

"But I'm nervous now," she confessed. "I've *never* had a formal tea before and certainly never with royals. I really need to check Google. Am I supposed to curtsey?"

"It's a choice. You're not one of their subjects," he said. "You're not a citizen of their country."

"True," she said, feeling conflicted. "I just want to be respectful."

He snorted. "Let them be respectful to you."

His response made her smile.

Emma waved toward the plate she'd shoved in Benjamin's direction and protested as if she wanted what was on his plate.

"Uh-oh," he said.

"Yes. We have jars ready for her. As soon as you finish, can you give her some food while I look up *high tea* on the internet?"

He chuckled. "Yeah, I'm there," he said, reaching for Emma.

Emma hesitated.

"He's got the food," Coco said in a low voice and gave Emma a squeeze before she passed the baby to him.

"And that baby food is where?" he asked as Emma began to squawk.

"I'll get it," Coco said and found a jar in a backpack. "Here," she said, giving him a jar of strained peas.

He made a face. "This didn't end well the last time I fed her strained peas."

"Stop when she starts to spit. Don't continue to put food in when she is spitting it out," she said. "It's pretty logical."

He frowned. "Easy for you to say. You do this all the time."

"This is your opportunity to bond with your daughter," she said.

Emma began to fuss and lift her arms toward Coco. "Oops, I'll go into a different room and try to find out more about an afternoon tea. May I use your tablet?" Coco asked.

"Go right ahead," he said.

Emma let out a loud scream of protest that tugged at Coco's heart, but she forced herself to close the door behind her. She suffered during the next couple moments while Emma loudly voiced her displeasure. Finally, the baby quieted, and Coco's stomach unknotted just a bit. She was still tense about meeting her half siblings.

Pulling out the tablet, she ran a search on afternoon tea and scanned for proper etiquette. *No circular stirring. Move spoon from six o'clock position to twelve o'clock position. Never put your napkin in the seat. Don't slice your scone....*

Coco made a face. She didn't even like scones. She continued to cram for the tea when a knock sounded on the door. Her stomach jolted into her throat and she jumped to her feet.

Taking a deep breath, she walked through the kitchen where Emma grinned at her. Peas were smeared on her cheeks and in her hair. "I think she's done," she said in a low voice to Benjamin.

"Think so?" he said in a dry tone. "I made the mistake of giving her the spoon."

Coco watched Emma bang the spoon on the tray then toss it onto the floor. She winced. "Bad precedent. We'll need to distract her during her next mealtime."

Another knock sounded and Coco met Benjamin's gaze. He rose to walk her to the door. "Just remember what I told you. Even that Emily Post woman says Americans should not bow or curtsey to anyone."

"I'm pretty sure Emily Post never wrote a column about this particular situation," she muttered and opened the door.

Benjamin grabbed her arm and lowered his head to press his mouth against hers. "I've got your back," he said.

His reassurance gave her a warm feeling. "Thanks," she said and joined Mr. Bernard for the second time that day.

Mr. Bernard prepped her for the tea during the short drive to the palace. "I'll introduce each of the princesses to you individually. Prince Stefan will stop in later, due to his work schedule. Come this way," he said and guided her down the marble hallway to a small room furnished with a lush wool carpet, antique furniture and a small table set with a sterling tea set, china teacups and saucers, small plates and a small tower of the scones she was not supposed to slice, along with jellies and other treats.

Mr. Bernard stood next to the door while Coco waited and walked around the room. She didn't want to be suspicious, but she couldn't help wondering if he were remaining in the room because he thought she might lift a souvenir and try to pocket it. The notion made her fume. She might not have been raised in a palace, but she'd been taught the difference between right and wrong.

Coco took a deep breath and chided herself. *Be positive.*

Suddenly, she heard footsteps and three women walked through the doorway. Mr. Bernard bowed to each of them. After studying their photographs on the internet, Coco could name each of them. The blonde was Princess Fredericka. The stylish brunette was Princess Bridget and the woman with the sweet face and wild hair and who also appeared to be sporting a baby bump was Princess Phillipa.

"Princess Fredericka, may I present Miss Coco Jordan," Mr. Bernard said.

In the interest of erring on the side of politeness, Coco attempted a curtsey and briefly bowed her head.

Fredericka extended her hand. "My pleasure to meet you," she said and stepped aside for Mr. Bernard to introduce Princess Bridget. She also followed with, "My pleasure to meet you."

The icy formality strained her nerves as she prepared for her third curtsey. "Princess Phillipa, I present Miss Coco Jordan."

Princess Phillipa took Coco's hand with both of hers. "My pleasure to meet you. Thank you for coming such a long distance to meet us. Shall we sit and drink tea?"

Coco breathed a slight sigh of relief. At least Princess Phillipa seemed friendly.

A server appeared and poured the tea, asking each person. "Sugar or cream?"

"Just sugar, please," Coco said. "Thank you very much."

She watched the princesses do the vertical stirring motion she'd read on the internet and followed their example. A long silence followed.

The princesses exchanged expressions with each other. Bridget set down her teacup. "I understand you live in Texas. As you probably know, our family has associations with several Texans. My sister Princess Valentina lives in Texas with her husband and daughter, and my husband is originally from Texas. Do you like it there?"

"I don't really know anything else," Coco said. "I've lived there my entire life and haven't traveled all that much. My experience is that there are a lot of good people in Texas. Because of that, I consider myself pretty lucky."

Bridget nodded and glanced at Fredericka. "Texas has such charm. I'm not sure I could endure your summers. How do you do it?"

"Air-conditioning and iced tea and lemonade," she said.

Phillipa laughed. "That sounds like something Eve would say. Eve is our brother Prince Stefan's wife. She's also from Texas. I'm not sure how much Mr. Bernard has shared with you or what you may have gleaned from the internet about the family."

"Mr. Bernard gave me a tour this morning and gave me a brief history lesson on Chantaine and the Devereau family, but it was so much information, I may not be able to pass the quiz if I have to take it this afternoon," she confessed.

Bridget's lips lifted in a half smile that she quickly hid with her teacup. "Tell us about yourself."

Coco immediately felt at a loss. "Well, as you know, I'm from Texas. I'm studying for a degree in early childhood education. Well, I *was* studying, but my mother became ill." She noticed that she was cupping her teacup and remembered that was a no-no, so she put one of her hands in her lap.

"We're sorry for your loss," Phillipa said. "My husband has recently been through a similar experience with his mother."

"Oh, I'm sorry. My sympathies to both of you," Coco said.

"Did I understand correctly that you are working as a nanny?" Bridget asked.

"Yes," Coco said. "For Benjamin Garner's daughter, Emma. She's adorable."

"How old is she?" Bridget asked.

"Only five months old, but quite verbal."

Bridget's eyes rounded in surprise. "She's already talking?"

"In her special language," Coco said. "She's quite the magpie."

Phillipa laughed. "When you're not taking care of Emma, what do you like to do?"

"I have to be honest, most of my time has been spent

helping Emma adjust to living with her father. Emma's mother died suddenly less than two months ago. But when I get the chance, I like to fish."

All three of the princesses stared at her silently, and Coco wondered if she'd overshared.

"Fish?" Fredericka echoed.

Coco nodded. "With a pole and a worm or crawdads."

"Eve would love this," Bridget muttered under her breath. "She already thinks we're a bunch of sissies, so—"

The door to the room opened and Mr. Bernard announced, "His Royal Highness, Prince Stefan."

Coco's mind went blank, but she noticed the princesses rose, so she did the same. Clumsily. She knocked over her teacup, spilling the brown liquid onto the exquisite tablecloth.

"Oh, no! I'm so sorry. I—" She reached for her napkin and began to mop up the liquid. "How will you ever get this tea out of this beautiful material? I—"

"Miss Coco Jordan," another male voice said.

Coco glanced up to meet Prince Stefan's gaze. He didn't look friendly. She gave a quick curtsey, on the wrong foot, and dipped her head.

Prince Stefan extended his hand and she rose. "It is our pleasure to meet you. I trust Mr. Bernard has taken good care of you," he said.

"Yes, thank you."

"I must leave due to a meeting this afternoon. Please don't hesitate to call Mr. Bernard for anything you may need during your stay. Have a good day to all of you," he said, glancing at his sisters and he left the room.

Coco vaguely remembered that she was supposed to curtsey again, so she did, using the correct foot this time. As soon as the prince left, the servers changed the table-cloth in record time. Self-conscious, Coco glanced to-ward the princesses. Their expressions suddenly seemed cool and remote. Coco would almost swear someone had turned the temperature in the room down to freezing.

Sinking carefully into her chair, Coco pressed her lips together and made herself smile. None of the prin-cesses returned her forced grimace. A server asked her if she would like more tea and she shook her head. She didn't want to ruin any more antique linens.

Silence permeated the room like the most stifling heat and humidity in July. Coco was at a loss as to what to say, and it appeared the princesses felt no need to chat. She wondered if they were truly that upset about her spilling tea.

A clock sounded three times. Fredericka glanced at her watch and stood. Her sisters followed. Coco quickly rose to her feet.

"We've kept you long enough," Fredericka said. "It was a pleasure to meet you and we hope you'll enjoy your visit to our lovely country."

Blinking from the abrupt ending to the visit, Coco dipped a few times. The princesses exited the room and Mr. Bernard appeared. "I shall escort you to your villa now," he said.

Her mind whirled during the few moments it took to ride to the villa. *Was that it?* she wondered. She'd flown halfway around the world to have tea with her so-called half sisters and a few seconds with her so-called half brother.

She'd told herself to expect nothing. Her stomach began to turn and her heart hurt. Locking her fists together, she lectured herself. *Do not get upset. Do not get upset.*

Mr. Bernard ushered her out of the car. She felt him watching her as she walked toward the front door.

"I'm not disappointed," she whispered to herself. "I'm not disappointed. I'm not—"

The front door opened before she'd barely touched it and Benjamin—strong, wonderful Benjamin—studied her face. "How'd it go?" he asked.

Coco burst into tears.

"Not great," Benjamin muttered and gently pulled Coco into the small den. He helped her onto the love seat as she continued to cry.

"I—shouldn't—have—" She broke off and sobbed again.

The sound made his gut twist. Plus, he was starting to get real concerned that she would hyperventilate. "Hey," he said, taking her shoulders. "Take a breath."

She opened her mouth as if she were trying to comply, but another sob escaped. "I'm sorry," she managed. "I haven't—"

"Take a breath," he told her. "Really." He cupped her face. "Close your eyes. And breathe."

She closed her eyes and drew in a shaky breath. She shuddered as she exhaled.

"Another one," he told her.

She breathed again and her sigh was a little less shaky. "I'm sorry. I can't remember the last time I cried this much."

"Then I guess you've been holding it in. If you're okay, I'll get you some water," he said.

She nodded and rubbed at her wet cheeks. "Just embarrassed."

"Don't be," he said and got up to get her a glass of water. "You're in one hell of a strange situation."

Returning, he held the glass to her lips and noticed how plump and pink her mouth was. She sipped the water then took the glass with her own hands. "Thanks." She took another sip and another deep breath and shook her head. "I just feel so stupid."

"Why?"

"I don't know what I was thinking. I kept telling myself and you that they wouldn't have any interest in me, but some stupid part of me must have hoped they would." She closed her eyes. "It's not that I really believed there was any chance for a real sister-sister or sister-brother kind of relationship. I just hoped it would be a little more friendly."

"What did they do?"

"Nothing terrible," she said. "They were just horribly polite. The prince came into the room where we were having tea and I spilled my tea all over this beautiful tablecloth. I wondered if that was why they acted so cold after he arrived. He was only there for about a half minute." She shook her head in confusion. "Before that, Bridget and Phillipa were almost nice. They even smiled a couple times and laughed."

Benjamin frowned. Why would the royal chicks turn suddenly mean? "Did Prince Stuffy say anything to his sisters when he was there?"

"Stefan," Coco corrected, but laughed. "Never thought of that about his name, but—"

"Did he say anything to his sisters?" he repeated.

She shook her head. "No. He kinda glared at them, but he didn't say anything."

"Hmm," Benjamin said, wondering if the way the royals had behaved toward Coco was all part of a plan.

"What are you thinking?" she asked.

"Just thinking," he said.

"Well, I don't have to think about this situation one more minute," she said. "I'm ready to leave now."

Emma let out a cry from the room where she was sleeping. "Oh," Coco said. "I should get her. I hope I didn't wake her."

"Probably not. She's been asleep for a while," he said and thought about Coco's situation with the Devereaux. He hadn't expected them to fall all over themselves welcoming her, but something about it didn't smell right to Benjamin.

An hour later, after Coco gave Emma a bottle and her dinner, she put the baby on a big blanket on the floor of the den. Benjamin noticed Coco pacing restlessly. She was still upset about the Devereaux. He'd come up with a plan of his own, but he didn't want to tell her about it quite yet.

"It's still light out. You want to take her for a little stroll?" he asked.

Coco nodded, her face easing with relief. "Great idea. Do you want to go?"

"I think I'll stay inside. I need to go over some updates from the foreman," he said.

"Okay," she said and put a light jacket and a little hat on Emma. "We won't be gone long," she said and stopped suddenly. "Thank you for putting up with me this afternoon."

The expression in her blue eyes made his chest knot. "It wasn't anything. I just want you to feel better," he said and squeezed her shoulder.

She rose on tiptoe and surprised the heck out of him when she brushed her soft lips across his jaw. "It was a big something to me," she countered, then fastened the baby in the stroller and left.

Benjamin rubbed his jaw at the strange sensation where she'd kissed him. He wondered if the rest of her was as soft as her lips. He wondered what her lips would feel like on his body. He wondered what kind of sounds she would make if he kissed her and touched her all over.

His body heated and he shook his head at himself.

Crazy, he told himself. He had more important things to think about than the fact that he hadn't been with a woman in too long. If there was one woman he shouldn't even be thinking about taking to his bed, it was Coco. She was too important to him because of Emma. Coco was off-limits and he was damn determined to make sure he didn't forget that.

Benjamin walked toward the telephone in the villa and picked it up. He dialed the number for Mr. Bernard, who picked up after the first ring.

"Bernard. May I help you?"

"Yes, you may. I need to speak with Stefan Devereau."

Silence followed. "Pardon," Bernard said. "To whom am I speaking?"

"This is Benjamin Garner, Miss Coco Jordan's fiancé."

Bernard cleared his throat. "Mr. Garner, I'm afraid it will be impossible to arrange an audience with the prince. His schedule is arranged months in advance."

"I don't want an audience. I want a man-to-man chat," he said. "You can tell Stefan that the Devereaux family will be facing a public relations nightmare if he can't find time to talk with me. Understand?"

Bernard cleared his throat. "I will relay your message, Mr. Garner."

"You do that," Benjamin said and hung up the phone.

Chapter Seven

The phone in the villa rang two hours later. Benjamin picked up quickly since Coco had fallen asleep on the sofa.

"Benjamin Garner," he said in a low voice.

"Mr. Garner, this is Prince Stefan's assistant. He will see you for fifteen minutes this evening. Mr. Bernard will pick you up within five minutes."

Benjamin didn't like dancing to someone else's tune, but this wasn't about him. He was taking care of Coco. Even the phone hadn't awakened her. "I can do that," he said and hung up the phone.

He glanced in the den and saw that Coco was still asleep. Poor thing was completely tuckered out. He grabbed the baby monitor, put it next to her on the end table, scrawled a note about taking a walk, and went out the front door. Seconds later, the car slowed to a stop and Bernard popped out.

"Mr. Garner," he said and opened the door. "I'll brief you on proper etiquette with the Prince."

"No need," Benjamin said and got in the car. "He's not my prince."

"But, sir," Mr. Bernard sputtered. "I have instructions. I must brief you."

"Do what you have to do, but I won't be listening. I've got more important things to think about," Benjamin said. "I'll take responsibility for my own actions. I always have."

Mr. Bernard hesitated a half beat. "Very well, sir. The first rule is that you never turn your back on a royal and…"

Benjamin clicked Mr. Bernard's voice to the off position and planned his strategy with Stefan. Just a few moments later, he was led through a side door and upstairs to the second floor. He passed a plainclothes security man and was stopped outside a door by another security man.

"Monsieur, I will now inspect you before your meeting with His Highness," the man said.

Benjamin lifted his hands. He didn't need a gun in this situation. He knew his biggest weapon was tarnishing the precious image of the Devereaux. Seconds later, he was led into a large office furnished with rich woods and leather. He noticed a child's toy on the desk and was surprised. A photograph of a woman with dark hair and laughing eyes graced the mantel behind him, along with a picture of a little girl with ringlet curls and blue eyes.

Benjamin lifted his eyebrows, speculating. So maybe Stefan was human after all. A few moments later, a man entered the room. "His Royal Highness, Stefan Devereaux."

Benjamin stood as the man who was Stefan entered the room. Tall with black hair, cold eyes and a frown, he stalked into the room. "Mr. Garner," Stefan said more than asked.

"Yes. Evenin'," he said and waited for Stefan to take a seat at his desk before he sat down.

"My assistant tells me that you delivered a threat regarding your intent to attack the reputation of my family," Stefan said.

"That's a bit overdramatic," Benjamin said. "I just thought you would want to know what kind of impression your family is making on your newly revealed relative. Coco gets tons of calls every day from the media. All she needs to do is tell the truth about her visit and it won't be good for the royal family."

"What more does she want? She enjoyed tea with my sisters. I made a personal appearance," Stefan said, his jaw tightening. "Perhaps this is a monetary issue. Very well, how much does she want?"

Benjamin scowled in return. "That's insulting. Anyone ever tell you that you could use a little more compassion?"

The man at the door moved forward. "I shall remove Mr. Garner at once."

Stefan waved the man aside. "No, Peter. I'll handle this." He leaned forward. "What exactly does Miss Jordan want?"

Benjamin sighed. "This may be difficult for you, but try to imagine this. You're an only child. You're adopted. Your father is dead. Your mother just died of a terminal illness. You're all alone in the world with no relatives. What would you want?"

Silence followed. For three seconds. A woman burst into the office. "What are you doing working this late at night?" the woman demanded.

It took a moment, but Benjamin recognized her from the photograph, except her face was pale and she looked ill. The man at the door began to apologize.

Stefan immediately rose and crossed the room to take the woman in his arms. "Eve, you shouldn't be up. You've had a rough day. Go back to bed. I'll be there soon."

The woman frowned and glanced at Benjamin, who had also risen.

He gave a nod. "Ma'am."

She narrowed her eyes and returned her gaze to Stefan. "He's from Texas." She paused a half beat and her eyes widened in realization. "He's with Coco Jordan. Is she here? How did I miss her?"

"I told you I would handle this. You weren't feeling

well, so Bridget, Phillipa and Fredericka had tea with her today."

"Tea?" Eve echoed in disdain. "You gave a girl from Texas tea? And I bet it wasn't iced." She took a deep breath. "What's going on?"

"We can discuss this later," Stefan said.

"That's fine," she said. "In the meantime, I'd like to meet a fellow Texan." She moved toward Benjamin. "Hello. I'm Eve Devereaux," she said, extending her hand.

"My pleasure," Benjamin said. "I'm Benjamin Garner. Hate to see your sleep disturbed. I'm sure your husband and I can finish our talk."

"Bourbon or whiskey?" she asked with a faint smile and sank into a chair.

"Eve," Stefan said. "I insist that you return to our quarters."

"Only if you promise I can meet with both Benjamin and Coco tomorrow. And only if you promise to give Benjamin his choice of liquor. You must also take a drink with him," she said.

"As you request," he said, his mouth tight with impatience.

"And," she said.

"And that's enough," he said firmly.

She smiled and rose. "Had to try," she said and pursed her lips in a smooch before she exited the room.

Stefan gave a heavy sigh. "Please be seated. Peter, please get Mr. Garner something to drink."

The man stepped next to Stefan's desk. "Yes, sir. What would you like?"

"Whiskey will do," Benjamin said.

"I'll take the same," Stefan said. He met Benjamin's gaze. "Now that you've gained my wife's attention, I should warn you that I'll be ruthless if you take advantage of her kindness."

Benjamin lifted the glass of perfect single-barrel whiskey in a salute to Stefan. "Glad to hear it, Your Highness. Wouldn't want it any other way."

Stefan knocked back his whiskey. "Very well. There will be a family visit tomorrow. One of the advisors will also convey Miss Jordan's financial inheritance. I should warn you that the amount is meager. These days, royals earn their pay and are encouraged to live on the palace grounds."

Benjamin nodded. Although he would protect Coco's financial interests, he knew what she wanted most. "Make it as friendly as you can. You met her. She's no shark." He stood, leaving the rest of his drink on the desk. "I think we're about done. Your wife is waiting for you and I don't want to keep you."

Stefan stood and nodded. He offered his hand. "Good night," he said and left the room.

Benjamin was immediately led out of the palace to the waiting car. He suspected that Mr. Bernard would have liked to dump him on the curb once they reached the villa, but the man exited the car and held the door open. "'Night, Bernard," Benjamin said.

"Good night, sir," the man said.

Benjamin walked to the front door and found Coco where he'd left her. No sounds coming from the nursery monitor. All was good. He picked up Coco and carried her to the bedroom where she'd slept last night. His hands itched to carry her soft body to his bed, but he knew better.

He just hoped tomorrow would be better for her than today had been. He slid her down to the bed and pulled the covers over her. She wiggled as if she were on the edge of awakening. Then she sighed and pressed her face into the pillow.

He should have resisted, but he didn't. Benjamin leaned down and brushed her cheek with his lips. She was the softest, sweetest thing he'd ever felt against his mouth.

"God help us. *Another family meeting,*" Bridget said to her sister, Phillipa, affectionately known as Pippa as they walked down the palace hallway toward Stefan's office. "Do you think he found out that we smiled at Coco Jordan? I'm starting to wonder if he used a hidden camera in the room while we were having tea."

"That would explain why he scowled at us just before he left yesterday," Pippa said. "It's ridiculous that he insists that we can't be friendly with her."

"I know," Bridget said. "I felt like I was kicking a puppy. She seemed very nice. I have a hard time believing her goal is to bring down the House of Devereaux."

"Someone has got to get through to Stefan," Pippa said.

"Good luck," Bridget said with a sigh. "The only one who can reason with him when he's like this is Eve, and she's having so much nausea from her pregnancy right now, I can't bring myself to bother her."

"I know," Pippa said, placing her hand over her own pregnant belly. "I had a few bad weeks, but it seems to have passed. Eve's just seems to be getting worse. Stefan's terribly worried about her, and I can't say I blame him."

"Well, here we go," Bridget said and knocked on Stefan's office door. The door immediately swung open and she was surprised to see Eve sitting in the room, eating a piece of toast. Stefan was on the phone.

"Eve, how wonderful to see you. How are you feeling?"

"Fine," Eve said, clearly fibbing. "I'm just not used to being restrained from regular activities. Plus, according to all the books, the nausea is supposed to have passed."

"I'm so sorry," Pippa said, hugging her sister-in-law.

"I am, too," Bridget said, reaching down to brush a kiss over her sister-in-law's cheek.

"How's the ranch coming?" Eve asked.

Bridget smiled at the fact that Stefan's wife hadn't forgotten the outrageous project Bridget and her Texas-born husband were pursuing. A ranch on Chantaine. "Thank you for asking. As you know, we're in the house. The whole ranch and animal thing will take a while."

"I'll help when I stop feeling so terrible," Eve said.

"Concentrate on taking care of yourself," Bridget said.

Eve made a face. "So boring." She glanced at Stefan, who was still on the phone. "So what did you think of Coco? Is she a villain in disguise?"

"I'd be shocked," Pippa said. "She was refreshingly genuine. I think you would have loved her. She says she loves to go fishing in her spare time, although she rarely has any spare time since she's taking care of a mother-less baby. These are all clearly signs of a sociopath." Pippa scowled at her brother, who was too busy on his phone call to be aware of her.

"She did seem quite nice," Bridget said.

"What did Fredericka think?" Eve asked.

"Fredericka has more experience masking her emotions," Bridget said. "She's already gone back to Paris."

Eve's face fell. "What a shame. I would have liked her to meet Coco in better circumstances. That's why you're here. I insisted that Stefan allow you to meet Coco in a more natural, welcoming way. Her fiancé was ready to take her back to Texas. I think if dueling were still in style, he would have challenged Stefan."

Bridget gaped at Eve. "Engaged? I didn't know she was engaged."

"Apparently, she and her employer fell for each other. Easy to understand with the devotion she's showing to his daughter," Eve said.

"Hmm," Pippa said. "She didn't mention an engagement."

"We didn't exactly invite her to overshare, especially after Stefan showed up and gave us his devil glare," Bridget said.

"True," Pippa said and leaned toward Eve. "So what's the plan now?"

"We're going to have a family gathering today," Eve said. "With everyone. All the children."

"The twins?" Bridget echoed. Her beloved stepsons were sweet, but terribly active toddlers.

"Everyone. Even Stephenia," Eve said. "And we're inviting Coco and her fiancé and his baby. I believe her name is—"

"Emma," Pippa said. "I read the dossier," she added.

"Are husbands required to attend?" Bridget asked.

"It's not expected, at such short notice, but if you can coerce them, that would be wonderful," Eve said and munched on her toast.

"I'll try to tear Nic away from his satellite meetings," Pippa said doubtfully. "If he knows there's a time limit, I'm more likely to be successful."

"Ditto," Bridget said, thinking of her doctor husband's demanding schedule.

Stefan hung up his phone and turned to the group. "I have an announcement. We're going to have a family gathering this afternoon with Coco Jordan, her fiancé and his daughter."

"We already know," Bridget said. "We just need to know the start time."

Stefan frowned. "How would you know?"

"Did you really think we were going to sit here quietly while you talked on the phone?" Bridget asked.

Stefan narrowed his eyes. "There's no need to be disrespectful."

"There's no need to keep us waiting, Your Highness," she said, giving in to the need to needle her brother. She was the one most likely to push back besides Eve.

"Darling," Eve said, scrubbing her arm with a brush. "You were busy, so we already discussed the plans."

Stefan, clearly distracted by the way she scrubbed her arm, switched focus. "You're not feeling well, are you?"

"I'm fine," she said for the umpteenth time. "Your heir just likes sitting on my liver. Which makes me itch. It will end in a few months."

Stefan went to her side and cupped her cheek. "How can I make this up to you?"

"I'll think of something," Eve said and rubbed herself with the brush again.

After lunch, Coco, Benjamin and Emma entered the office of a palace advisor, George Singleton. "Welcome," he said, waving his hand to the two seats across from the desk. "It's my privilege to inform you of your inheritance from Prince Edward."

"Inheritance?" Coco echoed as she balanced Emma on her knee. She glanced at Benjamin in surprise.

"Just let Mr. Singleton bring you up to speed," he said.

She nodded. "Okay. Thank you, Mr. Singleton."

"Unfortunately, the prince's trust is set up to benefit the heirs who work for the benefit of the Devereaux. There is also a housing credit for all heirs who live on the palace grounds."

Coco nodded, but was having trouble taking it all in. Truth be told, she hadn't thought she'd inherit one penny from Prince Edward, since she was in her twenties when her paternity was revealed.

"Therefore you are due $103 American dollars per month after all taxes are removed. Additionally, you will receive an education stipend of $5,000 American dollars payable after your completion of an undergraduate degree."

"Oh," she murmured. "I couldn't finish my degree because my mother died."

Mr. Singleton cleared his throat. "Perhaps an exception could be made."

"Perhaps it could," Benjamin said.

Mr. Singleton nodded. "I'll discuss this with the other advisors. I must inform you that although it appears that royals lead an easy financial life, they must meet several criteria for financial support. The list of appearances they make is endless."

Coco nodded again. "I—"

Benjamin placed his hand over hers. "That doesn't alter any obligations toward Prince Edward's offspring— Coco."

Mr. Singleton sighed. "Very true, sir. I'll tell you the results of my discussion with the other royal advisors. Mr. Bernard shall now guide you to the family gathering. I understand you'll be meeting outside due to the favorable weather."

Mr. Singleton rose and extended his hand. "Miss Jordan," he said extending his hand. He turned to Benjamin. "Mr. Garner."

Benjamin shook the man's hand. "Nice meeting you."

"Thank you, sir," he said and Mr. Bernard arrived to lead them outside.

"It's a beautiful day. Princess Eve has determined that everyone would enjoy the warm sunshine. There will be a time at the playground so the children can release their energy. Princess Bridget's twins will especially enjoy the opportunity to play and explore, as will Princess Stephenia."

"Princess Stephenia?" Coco asked, trying to recall what she'd heard about the name.

"Princess Stephenia is Prince Stefan's daughter." He chuckled.

"Why do you laugh?" Coco asked.

Mr. Bernard frowned. "I'm not laughing."

"Yes, you did," Coco said. She sighed. "You're safe. We won't rat on you. Why did you laugh?"

Mr. Bernard slid her a sideways glance. "Princess Stephenia is quite the handful. When she arrived here, she screamed every time she encountered the prince."

"When she arrived?" Coco echoed.

Mr. Bernard pursed his lips. "That's all I have to say. Princess Stephenia is a delightful child."

Coco glanced at Benjamin. "Looks like you and Stefan may have more in common than you thought."

Benjamin glared at her.

The car stopped beside a playground with a slide, swings and climbing equipment. "It looks like a lot of fun for the children," Coco said.

"We are happy to please," Mr. Bernard said and moved outside the car to open the door. "A stroller will be brought to you for your convenience."

Surprised at the thoughtfulness, Coco automatically extended her hand to Mr. Bernard's arm. "Thank you. That is so very thoughtful."

Mr. Bernard looked at her in surprise then glanced away. "As I said, we're very happy to please. Call me for any need," he said and got back in the car.

She and Benjamin watched the car drive away.

"Weird guy," Benjamin said.

"But nice," she said. "I think the royal stuff keeps him from being too real."

Benjamin shrugged. "Maybe. Let's give Emma a try in the swing before everyone else shows up."

Coco smiled. "Great idea."

They strapped Emma into the baby swing and Benjamin gently pushed it from the front. Coco stood to the side and watched the baby's eyes grow round. Benjamin increased the force of the push and Emma began to laugh. With each successive swing, she let out a shriek of delight.

Seeing Benjamin with his baby girl in such a happy moment brought tears to Coco's eyes. When she'd first arrived at Benjamin's home, they'd both seemed terrified of each other. Now they were truly starting to bond. Coco knew that Emma was one lucky girl. Benjamin was on the road to becoming a terrific father. She was so caught up in watching Benjamin and Emma that she didn't notice Princess Phillipa until she appeared by her side.

"Oh, hello, Your Highness," Coco said and started to curtsey.

Phillipa shook her head. "Not necessary, and please call me Pippa." She pointed toward Benjamin and Emma on the swings. "He looks like excellent husband material. I hear congratulations are in order for your engagement."

Coco blinked for a few seconds then remembered the pretend agreement she and Benjamin had made. "Thank you," she said, uneasy with the deception. "It was nice of Prince Stefan to arrange this time on the playground for us."

Pippa chuckled. "You can thank Eve for that. Ah, here she comes, along with Stephenia, and the twins and Bridget bringing up the rear. When will Bridget learn not to wear heels when she's chasing toddlers?"

"Boys, Stephenia," Pippa said, stepping in front of the galloping toddlers. "Careful of the swing."

The three youngsters stared at the baby in the swing. The little girl with ringlet curls pointed at Emma. "Who?"

"That's Emma," Pippa said. "She belongs to Mr. Garner and Miss Jordan."

Benjamin waved at the kids and Pippa made the introductions. He continued to push Emma in the swing. The toddlers scrambled onto the various pieces of miniature playground equipment.

"I didn't realize there were so many children," Coco said, trying to recall what she'd read about the Devereaux offspring on the internet.

"And more on the way," Pippa said, touching her abdomen. "Eve is due before I am, but I'm having such an easy time compared to her that I feel guilty."

"Oh, I'm sorry to hear that," Coco said to the tall, dark-haired woman.

"It's not high-risk, just extremely uncomfortable," Eve said.

"How are you feeling today?" Pippa asked Eve.

"I'm fine. I slept longer than usual," Eve said then turned to Coco. "Coco, it's my pleasure to meet you and welcome you to where the wild things grow here in Chantaine," she said with a smile. "I hope you'll enjoy your time here."

Bridget glanced around the playground. "Where are my little darlings?" she muttered, narrowing her eyes. "Ah, in the hide-and-seek house. Should have known." She turned to Coco and smiled. "So nice to see you again. That's a darling baby in the swing. Hope the man is just as darling, too. The Devereaux seem to have a weakness for Texans."

A shriek of distress sounded from the other side of the hide-and-seek house. "Excuse me," Bridget said. "That's mine. I know his voice."

"I never would have believed what a great mother she's become," Pippa said.

"She fell for the doctor and his boys hook, line and sinker," Eve said. "A joy to watch. Bridget always gave the impression of being the royal fashion plate, and single forever. Turns out her heart was squishier than she thought."

At that moment, Coco began to feel a little hope that maybe she wasn't completely alone in the world after all. Maybe the Devereaux actually were a little bit like her. At least on the inside.

After playtime, which included Benjamin chasing the toddlers and making them laugh until they were breathless, everyone went inside for lunch. Nannies arrived to take the children when they grew restless. Stephenia, however, wanted to stay, and Eve permitted it.

Coco noticed that Benjamin talked very little. She could practically feel his mind clicking with all his observations. He put his hand over hers and her brain instantly stuttered. Even though she knew his touch was just for show, it still affected her. Bridget gave her apologies as she left for an event at a library. Pippa received a call from her husband and left the room to take it.

Eve had seemed to grow much more weary as the day proceeded. Coco feared that Eve's desire to make her feel welcome was making Eve stay longer than she should. "It's been wonderful having this opportunity to get to know all of you better. I can't tell you how much I've appreciated the time with you. We should probably get back so Emma can take a nap."

"Are you sure I can't do anything else for you?" Eve asked as she shared a small cookie with Stephenia while the toddler sat on her lap.

"Not a thing," Coco said and stood.

"Well, if you're sure," she said and set Stephenia on her feet. Eve stood, and the blood appeared to drain from her face. "Oh," she murmured and collapsed onto the floor.

Benjamin was by the woman's side in an instant. Stephenia began to cry, so Coco set Emma on a blanket and picked up the distressed toddler. "Is she okay?" Coco asked. "We need to get help," she said and stepped into the hallway where a man stood outside the door.

Moments later, the room was filled with a doctor, nurse, two guards and Pippa.

"I keep telling her she's doing too much, but she won't listen," Pippa said, wringing her hands. "She's just not used to sitting still for anything. She thinks it's a sign of weakness."

"True Texan spirit," Benjamin said, now holding Emma. "Good luck to her husband."

Stephenia was still upset, but quiet as she clung to

Coco with one hand and soothed herself with her thumb in her mouth. "She'll be okay," Coco said to the child resting on her hip. "See, she's sitting up."

"Already fussing at the doctor," Pippa said in a wry tone.

Eve waved aside the crowd around her and stood. The doctor and guards, however, stayed within arm's reach. "I'm fine. Completely fine."

"One of the top lies spoken every day," Benjamin said in a low voice.

Eve glanced across the room and spotted them. "Oh, no. I've frightened Stephenia," she said, walking toward Coco.

"She's okay," Coco said and set the toddler down onto her feet.

"Mamaeve," Stephenia wailed, lifting her arms for a hug.

Eve bent down and Benjamin pulled out a chair for her to sit down. Eve flashed a look of impatience. "Honestly, there's no need for a fuss."

"The fainting thing cancels out your denial. You know the old saying—actions speak louder than words," Benjamin said.

"I'm glad someone else said that," Pippa said.

Eve still looked irritated. "I don't like being forced to sit."

"You're not being forced," Coco said. "You're being helped."

Eve rolled her eyes in disbelief.

"It's true," Coco said. "You have a very important job to do. Probably one of the most important jobs of your life. You're nurturing a baby. There are two lives at stake and both are very important to many people. Even though it seems that sitting down or resting is being lazy, it's not. You probably think it's difficult and boring, but it's a necessary part of your job."

Eve stared at Coco for a long moment. "I guess I never thought of it that way. I just expected to take pregnancy in stride and keep doing what I've always done." She glanced at her doctor. "I guess it doesn't always work out that way."

"Quite true, Your Highness," he said.

"I'm just not the fainting type," Eve said.

"As long as you follow the doctor's direction, you won't become the fainting type," Pippa said. "Like you were today."

Eve bared her teeth slightly then sighed. "Okay, my job is to gestate. Hopefully someone will help amuse me."

"The line forms behind me," Pippa said with a smile.

Coco felt another invisible thread connecting her to Eve and Pippa.

That evening after Coco and Benjamin both bathed Emma, they sat on the love seat and propped their feet on pillows placed on the coffee table. Benjamin rotated between a soccer game and a television show on the BBC.

"I feel like I need subtitles. The British English is so different from Texas English," Benjamin said.

Coco laughed, and the sound made his chest tighten and expand.

"Does that mean you feel the same way?" he asked.

"I guess so. I just never thought of it that way," she said and met his gaze. "Thanks for being with me today. Between the meeting with the advisor and Eve fainting, it was a roller-coaster ride."

He nodded. "Yeah. What do you think of the Devereaux now?"

"I think they bleed," she said. "Like you and me."

He met her gaze and something inside him grew and expanded. Coco was deep, sometimes sad, but he could tell that she kept trying to be positive and hopeful. Despite everything she'd been through, she wanted to give people the benefit of the doubt. Being with her made him want to be less cynical.

"You did well today," he said.

She laced her fingers together then unlaced them. He covered her hand and her fidgeting stopped. She glanced up to meet his gaze. The moment stretched between them.

Fighting a massive internal debate, Benjamin lowered his mouth to hers. Slowly. Slowly enough that she could turn away if she wanted. But she didn't. Her gaze was locked with his. Her eyelids lowered with each millimeter he drew closer. He wanted to take her mouth, absorb her into him. He wanted to rush, but he made himself go slow.

Eons seemed to pass. He finally pressed his mouth against hers. Her lips were soft and sweet. There was a sense of waiting and wanting in the air. He inhaled briefly, wanting to focus on her mouth.

She responded, rubbing her lips against his.

The sensation of need ran through him like wildfire, and he felt a little of his self-control shatter. Clenching his hand into a fist, he tried to regain control. But then she rubbed her lips against him again and he felt it all the way down from his mouth to his chest to his gut to his groin.

Benjamin opened his mouth and slid his tongue into her mouth. She tasted sweet and wild. When she slipped her hands around his neck, he just wanted more.

Chapter Eight

Coco felt as if she were stuck on the top of a ferris wheel. She sank against Benjamin's chest as his mouth took hers. She hadn't allowed herself to want him. She'd scolded herself not to be attracted to him. He was her boss, and he was wounded from his experience with Emma's mother. A bad combination.

But now he felt strong and everything about him was too seductive to resist. The way he kissed her, the way he held her. He deepened the kiss further and her breath seemed to stop in her throat. She felt a terrible restlessness that invaded her from head to toe, with special emphasis in between. She wriggled against him to soothe the sensation, but that just seemed to make it worse.

Benjamin let out a low groan and the sound vibrated

inside her. Leaning backward, he dragged her on top of him. One of his hands slid to cup her breast while his other pressed her pelvis against him. His unmistakable hardness found the place between her legs where she began to ache.

She tugged at his shirt, wanting to feel his bare skin. He growled in approval and seconds later she felt her naked breasts against his chest. With her skirt and his jeans between them, she just wanted to get rid of everything keeping her from being as close as possible to him.

He must have heard her need. Benjamin found the zipper to her skirt and pushed it down, along with her panties. Finally, she was naked. All she needed was to help him get rid of his jeans and underwear and—

A muffled sound emanated from the baby monitor. Coco was so turned on she wasn't sure that she'd heard correctly. Benjamin continued to caress and kiss her, making her hotter with each passing stroke.

Another sound from the baby monitor. This one louder. Another that turned into a wail. Coco stilled as her heartbeat throbbed in her ears and throughout every pulse point in the body. Benjamin didn't seem to hear.

"It's Emma," she finally managed to say. "She's awake. And crying."

Benjamin pulled his mouth away from hers, his eyes dark with the same need she felt. When Emma let out another cry, realization crossed his face. He swore under his breath and helped both her and himself into a sitting position.

Coco was still aroused, but she suddenly felt self-conscious by the contrast of her complete nudity and Benjamin's half-dressed state. Fumbling with her blouse, she struggled to find the buttons. "I'll get her," she said. "I just need to put on my clothes."

"No, it's okay," he said as he stood. "I'll do it." He pulled on his shirt and left the room.

The blouse was turned half-inside-out, making the act of dressing herself that much more frustrating. She finally put it on, then pulled on her panties and skirt. When she stood, she suspected her panties were on backward.

Confused about what she should do next, she pushed her hair out of her face and walked toward the room where Emma was supposed to be sleeping. She glanced inside in the darkness and saw the outline of Benjamin standing as he rocked from side to side with Emma in his arms.

She didn't want to interrupt because it appeared he'd successfully quieted her. Her heart twisted. More progress between Dad and his daughter. A few moments ago, however, she'd thought of him as anything but a dad.

Coco stood there for a few moments to collect her breath and sense. What did it mean that they had nearly made love? What next? Should she stay awake or try to go to sleep?

Slowly, she walked to her bedroom and sank onto the bed, her head still spinning. Coco could hardly believe that Benjamin was really interested in *her*. She'd always viewed herself as very ordinary, but with determination. That determination had kept her sane during life's less sane moments. And this was one crazy moment. Coco knew that she was no bombshell, like the woman who had given birth to Benjamin's child.

Wash your face. Brush your teeth. Things will be clearer in the morning. How many times had her mother repeated those words to her? Coco followed her mother's advice, then crawled into bed and told herself to stop thinking about Benjamin. But then she turned on the baby monitor just in case Benjamin went to sleep and Emma awakened again.

In a low voice, more breath than song, Benjamin hummed a lullaby to Emma. Her heart swelled so much it hurt at the loving sound, and she closed her eyes at her odd instinct to cry. She was no crybaby. Why was this happening to her? She couldn't remember a man affecting her so deeply. It was as if he reached her on a cellular level. The possibility was disturbing. She took a deep breath to still the feelings rolling through her.

She tried counting backward from one hundred to fall asleep, but somehow Benjamin's lullaby made her drift off.

The next morning she awakened to the sound of Emma chattering through the nursery monitor. She allowed the baby to experience some time by herself. It was good for Emma to self-soothe for a short time.

Coco's mind wandered to thoughts about Benjamin. Something inside her had solidified. She knew she had strong feelings for him. She knew he was important to her. Coco smiled and bounced out of bed, ready for the day. Ready for her future with whatever happened between her and Benjamin.

She threw on some clothes and made a quick trip to wash her face and brush her teeth then raced into Emma's room. "Well, good mornin' darlin'," she said as the baby began to fuss.

Emma glanced at her and gave a welcoming chortle.

Coco changed the baby and picked her up. "Who wants a bottle and breakfast?"

Emma began her version of a morning chat with unintelligible, but happy sounds. "Bottle first?" A moment later, Coco warmed a bottle and sat on the sofa to feed the baby. Emma gave a few burps and Coco put her in the pack and play.

Coco grabbed a quick shower. When she walked out of her bedroom dressed, with wet hair, Benjamin greeted her in the hallway. "'Morning," he said.

Her heart hammered against her chest. "'Morning," she returned. "I've already given Emma her bottle. She should be ready for breakfast soon. Did she keep you awake too long last night?"

"Just awhile," he said, and raked his hand through his damp hair. "Listen, I'm sorry about last night. That shouldn't have happened. I shouldn't have—" He broke off.

Her heart felt as if it broke in half. "Shouldn't have?" she prompted.

"Shouldn't have kissed you. Shouldn't have gone after you like that," he said.

She worked hard to take a breath. "Are you saying you didn't want me?" she managed, confused and so hurt.

"Not want you," he echoed and looked away. "At that moment, I did," he said. "But it still shouldn't have happened. I don't want you to start thinking this engagement is real. Last night wouldn't have happened if we were still in Texas." He met her gaze. "I can't get into a relationship right now. I have too much going on."

Coco crossed her arms over her chest. "Is that the same way you felt about Brooke?"

He took a sharp breath and shook his head. "Brooke was a crazy impulse. I broke all my rules. I don't want to do that again."

She struggled to swallow over the lump in her throat. "Okay. I'll feed Emma."

She turned away and felt his hand on her arm. But she didn't turn to look at him because she wasn't sure she could control her facial expression. "I don't want to hurt you. That's why we can't do this."

She pulled her arm away from him. "I'll feed Emma."

Thank goodness for the baby. She demanded and received so much of Coco's attention that for the next several hours, she managed not to look Benjamin in the eye. It was for the best. What should have been a make-out session had turned into something far more for Coco. Crazy. Stupid. She would be more careful from this moment on. She wouldn't give in to silly secret feelings for Benjamin. She just wished she'd never given herself permission to even consider Benjamin as *her man*.

After spending most of the day inside, Coco was ready to scream. She needed to get out. She needed to get away from Benjamin. She called Mr. Bernard to ask about an outing. He suggested a few possibilities and Coco selected the beach. Slathering Emma with baby-safe sunscreen and dressing her in a protective baby bathing suit, Coco plopped a hat on the tot's head and got ready.

When Mr. Bernard knocked at the door, Coco was just about ready.

Benjamin answered the door and Coco grabbed Emma and raced to greet their guide. "Emma and I are going to the beach," she said breathlessly. "We'll see you later," she said and walked out the door, feeling a smidgeon of self-satisfaction that Benjamin was staring after her and the baby with a surprised look on his face.

Mr. Bernard told her a bit about Chantaine's beaches and warned her that the ocean temperature might be a little chilly for the baby. She appreciated his consideration. With help from him, she was quickly situated on the beach with an umbrella, chaise longue and an extra-large towel.

Coco put Emma in her infant carrier, and for once, the baby didn't struggle to escape. Emma sat, appearing relaxed, with her eyes half-open. Coco smiled at the sight of Emma, wondering if the sound of the ocean was soothing to the baby.

Sighing, she leaned back against her chair and let the breeze and surf sounds assuage her own riot of feelings and thoughts. With one eye on Emma, Coco watched the soft whitecaps as they gently met the shore. She wondered how often Prince Edward had taken solace at the sight of the sea. Everyone had told her how much he had loved yachting.

The last time Coco had been to the ocean had been three years ago—a too-brief trip with college friends. Her favorite part of that trip had been a walk on the beach by herself. Was that something she had in common with her birth father? Or was it just crazy to consider that she had anything in common with him except some genetic material?

Coco dismissed her debates and focused on the peace and relaxation of the moment. Emma was quietly content, the sun was shining, and Benjamin wasn't nearby to disrupt her—although his presence wasn't required to mess with her mind. Just a thought would do.

"Hello, hello," a voice called from behind her.

Coco glanced up to see Bridget walking toward her, wearing a bright pink hat, a pink suit and pink heels. In the sand? Coco stood and watched as a man followed after the princess carrying a chair. "Thanks so much, Anthony. I won't be long," she said to the man then turned to Coco. "Would you like a little cocktail?"

"I'm good with my water," Coco said. "What a surprise."

Bridget shot a sly look and sank onto the chair. "I'm good with those," she said. "I hope I'm not interrupting, but I heard you were having some beach time and since I was driving by, I thought it might be fun to make a little stop." She glanced down at Emma, who was regarding the princess with curiosity. "Do we have a little beach baby here?"

"I think this is her first ocean sighting and she seems to love it. The sound of the waves and the breeze. It affects me that way," Coco said. "It was nice of you to stop by."

"My pleasure. I'm in between appearances today. I'll turn into ranch frau tomorrow. The things I do to please my husband," she said, making a tsk-ing sound. "Well, he did give up his career in Dallas to move to my country and my brother immediately saddled him with a hugely challenging job. I would do anything for him, even though he drives me crazy," Bridget said. "I'm sure it the same with you and your Benjamin."

Coco clenched her teeth for a moment then produced a smile. "I wonder if all men make their women crazy."

"Oh, they must," Bridget said. "You've probably heard that whole Venus and Mars thing. Well, scientists have conducted a study on the differences between men and women, and they say we're so different we could be different species. Pippa the brainiac told me that. So now scientists are telling us what we've always known. Men are aliens."

Coco laughed despite the fact that her heart was still hurting. "And you have two little males, too," Coco said.

"I know. And I love all three of my men. The twins are always doing something that makes me laugh and sometimes cry. I suspect the same thing has happened with you and little Emma," Bridget said, glancing at the baby. "Oh, look, she's blowing bubbles. I miss those days."

"If you miss it that much, you could have a baby," Coco drawled.

"*Mon dieu,* no," Bridget said. "I'm sure I'll do it one day, but Ryder, the boys and this *ranch* keep me quite busy enough." She shot Coco a sideways smile. "Cheeky of you to suggest it, though. Sounds like something I might say to one of my sisters."

A throwaway comment, but the word *sisters* caught at Coco's heart.

"Well, enough about that subject," Bridget said. "The other reason I wanted to chat with you is because there's going to be a charity gala at the palace in a few days. And we would like you to join us."

Surprise raced through Coco. "Charity gala," she echoed and shook her head. "That's so nice of you, but I would need a babysitter. And I can't imagine I have anything to wear. And—"

"Excuses, excuses," Bridget said. "We have several wonderful nannies who would provide excellent care for

Emma. And although no one would accuse us of having runway fashions to rival Paris, we do have a few nice boutiques."

Coco could easily imagine that the price of a dress in one of those boutiques would require at least a month of her pay. "Oh, I don't know," she said, thinking the event sounded like the adult version of prom.

"Eve, Pippa and I will be very sad if you don't attend," Bridget said.

"And Stefan?" Coco asked, although she suspected she already knew the answer. Stefan would love for her to just disappear.

"Stefan is secretly grateful to you for telling Eve that she is doing a job by being pregnant. No one has been able to get her to slow down. *Slow down* and *Eve* don't belong in the same sentence. She's one of those save-the-world types," Bridget said.

"Like you?" Coco asked and took a sip of water.

Bridget twitched her lips. "There you go being cheeky again. We can go shopping for your dress tomorrow," Bridget said and rose to her feet. She waved for her chauffeur. "Time for me to go. Thanks for letting me join—"

Panic set in. "Bridget, I'm very honored by your invitation, but I don't think—"

"I don't want you to be honored. I want you to attend," Bridget said. "Don't tell me you don't like shopping. I had that trouble with Eve and Pippa," she said, shaking her head.

"That's it," Coco fibbed. "I'm just not much of a shopper."

"Well, I'll just have to pick something out for you and send it over. Will Benjamin need a suit?" Bridget asked.

"No, but—"

"But nothing. If he brought a suit, he's ready."

"I'm not sure this is his kind of party," Coco said.

"It won't be that bad. There will be beer available and Benjamin can chat with Ryder about sports. He misses that." She brushed her hands together. "There. All done. I'll talk to you soon. Ciao, darling."

A couple hours later, Coco strolled into the villa toting Emma.

"How was your time at the beach?" Benjamin asked.

"Great," Coco said. "I found out we're going to a charity gala sometime soon."

"What?" he said.

She felt a quick tension in her belly, but pushed it aside. "No problem. You have a suit, so you should be good. Plus, they'll serve beer, and Bridget's doctor husband is from Texas and he'll want to talk sports."

"What about Emma?" he asked.

"They have nannies galore," she said and foisted Emma into his arms. "I need a shower."

Coco headed straight for the bathroom, turned on the shower and hopped inside. She enjoyed the warm spray over her head and body and willed the water to wash away her worries.

* * *

Benjamin changed his daughter's diaper and gave her a bottle. He wondered if he should bathe her. He wondered when the hell Coco was going to come see him. He pulled some baby food from the counter, plunked Emma into her infant seat, and began to spoon some green substance into his daughter's mouth.

"Airplane flying through the sky," he said, feeding Emma.

"Nice technique," Coco said, walking into the room. She wore a white robe far larger than she was.

"I have to get creative," Benjamin said and sailed another foot into Emma's mouth. "Wanna take over?" he asked.

"But you're doing so well," she said.

Benjamin sighed.

Emma gave a raspberry, sending her green food all over Benjamin's chest.

"I think she's done with dinner," Coco said.

Benjamin shot Coco a dark look. "Ya think?"

Emma gave another raspberry and he would have sworn he heard Coco snicker, but he was too busy protecting himself from some vile puréed vegetable to check. He rubbed Emma with a cloth and she began to fuss.

"I'll take her then I'll go to bed," Coco said.

"TV is out here," he pointed out.

"I can read a book. G'night," she said.

"But—" Benjamin said as Coco lifted Emma from the baby seat.

"We're good," Coco said and took Benjamin's daughter to the bathroom.

"You sure I can't help?" he asked.

"No. We're taking a bath," Coco said.

Benjamin visualized Coco taking a bath and his body instantly tightened. He walked toward the bathroom and spied Emma in the bathtub. She gurgled at Coco, who encouraged her.

He paused before speaking. "Does she like this?"

"In the right conditions," Coco said. "Optimal temperature, etc..."

"How do you know all this?" he asked.

"Experiment and practice," Coco said, still not looking at him, which irritated him.

"You wanna give me a clue?" he asked.

"Soon enough," she said. "I'll write it all down, but there are a lot of particulars."

"Is that a woman thing?" he asked.

Coco rinsed Emma and pulled her from the tub. She shot him a sideways glance. "There are particulars for every baby. Male or female."

"But in my baby's case?"

"She likes berry-scented soap and her fave temp is almost hot. She loves a sip of apple juice while she's in the tub..."

"Hell, that sounds like an apple-tini," Benjamin said.

"No vodka needed for Miss Emma," she said. "Just good hugs and a lullaby."

"And what about the nanny?"

Coco paused for a long moment and bit her lip. "Not your problem."

"Why do I feel like it is?" he asked.

"Misplaced responsibility?" she asked and placed Emma in his arms. "Enjoy your sweetie pie. I'm going to bed."

"Whoa," Benjamin said. "She looks like she'll be gone for the night in just a few minutes. Flat-screen is available as soon as she's asleep."

"I need to protect myself," Coco said.

"What do you mean?" he asked.

"I mean that you are dangerous at night. I need to avoid you then," she said and turned away.

Benjamin held his daughter as he watched Coco walk away, and he suddenly felt alone. Regret filled him, tightening his chest and spreading outward.

"Hey," he said. "Are you sure you're okay?"

She glanced over her shoulder, but didn't meet his eyes. "I'm great. Let me know if you need help with Emma."

"I will," he said, feeling alone. Very alone. He knew he had made a mistake kissing Coco and undressing her as he had. On the other hand, he hadn't slept last night, either, and he'd thought about her all day.

Maybe another night would cure him, he hoped. If

not, another day would do it. He swore under his breath. If twenty-four hours didn't do it, then he would need help.

A couple hours later, Benjamin went to bed. It took a while for him to fall asleep. A vision swam before him. Coco appeared and lowered her mouth to his. Time passed in a millisecond and she was naked against him. He realized that he was also naked and her breasts felt delicious against his bare chest. Her nipples were taut and sensitive as he touched them.

Her moan made him unbearably aroused. *I want you,* he said.

I want you, she echoed.

Seconds later, he slid his hand between them to the top of her thighs where she was moist and swollen. He stroked her as he kissed her.

"You feel so good," he said, sinking into her kiss and the intimate sensation of being so close to her. His breath hitched in his throat and he stretched toward her, wanting to be inside her.

Finally, he thrust inside, where she was wet and warm. He pumped, feeling the sweat bead on his forehead. His heart hammered against his chest. He was so aroused he could explode.

Coco stretched her legs around him and held him close. "I love you," she whispered.

Her words stopped his heart. "Don't love me," he said. "I'm not the right man for you. Not right now."

"I love you anyway," she said.

He felt himself rise again inside her. Swearing, he couldn't hold himself back. Even though she'd told him she'd loved him. Even though she shouldn't love him, and he shouldn't let her.

But he couldn't control the way she made love to him with her body, and he couldn't stop the way he made love to her with his body, either. He began again the rhythm of sinking himself inside her. He felt himself grow closer and closer to release. He was almost there....

He woke up, sweating, his pulse racing, and he was as hard as a brick. It took him a few seconds to separate the dream from reality. Coco was not in his bed whispering alarming words in his ear while they made love to each other.

"Thank God," he muttered as he sat up, though his body was in complete disagreement. His body clamored for satisfaction, and his heart— His heart wasn't involved, he told himself. His heart had no room for the woman who was the nanny to his daughter and who had just learned she was part royal.

The next morning, Coco tried to avoid Benjamin, which was difficult because the villa wasn't that large. So she took Emma for walks in the stroller. Three of them. She was just about to leave for a walk on her own when Bridget called.

"Time for shopping," Bridget said. "Now don't turn

me down. I know you're not doing anything. Mr. Bernard reports that you've taken Emma on multiple walks."

"I don't know, Bridget," she said and decided to be honest. "These boutiques may be a bit out of my price range."

"Oh, don't worry about that. Eve wants to give this to you as a gift," Bridget said.

"Oh, no. I couldn't," she said, horrified at the prospect.

"She'll be terribly offended if you don't accept. Eve is so kind and wonderful. You wouldn't want to offend her, would you?" Bridget asked, and Coco couldn't help thinking she was being played.

"I'm sure she would get over it," Coco drawled.

"Oh, stop being so difficult. Even if you don't find anything you like, it will get you off the palace grounds, and you shouldn't miss Chantaine's downtown area. Some find it quite quaint."

Coco couldn't disagree with the idea of escaping Benjamin for a while. "All right," she said. "You're very kind to invite me, but don't count on coming back with anything for me."

Soon enough, Coco learned that Bridget was one pushy princess. "Oh, please," Bridget said after they'd cruised through the second boutique. "You're making this miserable. There's got to be something you like. There are so many dresses that would look wonderful on you."

Coco shrugged. All the prices had been out of her

range so far. "You know how it is when you can't find exactly the right dress," Coco said as she sifted through a rack of dresses. She wandered toward a sale rack in the back of the store.

"Trust me, there's nothing there," Bridget said. "Come back up front."

Coco continued to flip through the rack and found a simple sapphire-blue full-length dress. The price was still a little high, but...

Bridget came to her side. "Lovely color. A little plain, but with a little jewelry, it would do." She glanced at Coco and smiled. "You have Devereaux eyes, only a little sweeter."

"You're the sweet one," Coco said. "Putting up with me to do all this shopping."

"Oh, trust me," Bridget said. "This is a pleasure after playing ranch frau this morning. Now try on your plain dress. I'm ready to disapprove and we'll move on to the next shop."

Coco tried on the dress and loved it. She loved that the color was vibrant and the design simple, a V-neck with an A-line that flattered her slim frame.

Bridget crossed her arms over her chest and shook her head. "I want to veto it, but something about it is perfect. We can do something with your hair, give you some jewelry, the right shoes."

"Shoes?" Coco echoed. "I have black heels."

"We can do better than that," Bridget said.

Coco felt a sinking sensation. "Better than black heels?"

"Of course we can," Bridget said.

Coco wrestled with Bridget to pay the bill. For a moment there, it could have gotten bloody, but Coco pulled out the guilt screws. "This is embarrassing me," Coco said.

Bridget immediately backed off. For a full moment. "Fine," she said. "But I'm still getting your shoes."

Chapter Nine

Two nights later, Benjamin paced the front room, dressed in his suit, tugging at his shirt collar. What had possessed him to agree to go to this gala? He could have said no-how, no-way, but he'd thought his absence might look odd since he and Coco were supposed to be *engaged*.

Now he was stuck with what would likely be the most uncomfortable evening of his life. He took another gulp of water and paced the front room again.

Out of the corner of his eye, he spotted a vibrant blue color and he spun around. Coco entered the hallway, looking beautiful in a long evening gown with a sparkly headband and bracelet. Her hair was a mass of tousled waves, her face enhanced with a hint more makeup than usual. Her lips glistened and she licked them, making him wanting to kiss her.

"Do I look okay?" she asked.

He shook his head. "No. You look beautiful," he said.

Relief smoothed out her features. "Thanks. You didn't have to say that."

"It's true. That dress looks great on you. The color almost matches your eyes."

"Thanks. I found it on the sale rack."

"You didn't have to get a clearance dress," he said.

"I didn't want to overspend. And I didn't want the Devereaux to pay for it, even though Bridget insisted they would," she said and fiddled with her wrap.

"I would have bought you a dress. Heaven knows you're due a bonus after dealing with Emma nonstop," he said, chuckling.

She met his gaze and smiled. "Maybe, but I wanted to pay for this myself."

"You just didn't want to be one of those illegitimate moochers," he joked with her.

She laughed with him. "You've got that right. I know you can't wait to go tonight."

"Oh, I've been so excited all day that I can hardly stand it," he said in a dry tone. "I haven't been this excited since I went to the Super Bowl."

She swatted his chest. "Liar, liar, pants on fire," she said.

"Ouch, you have a mean right hook," he said.

"Again, liar, liar—"

He held up his hands, enjoying the fact that she was acting relaxed with him. Since the night they'd almost had sex, she'd frozen him out. He knew he deserved it, but it sure as hell didn't feel good.

"Okay, okay," he said. "When is the babysitter supposed to get here?" he asked.

As if on cue, a knock sounded at the door. Benjamin answered and a young woman entered.

"Please forgive me. I'm Natalie and I've been helping Princess Bridget's twins. I'm here to take care of your baby, Emma. Are there any specific instructions?" she asked.

"If the bottle doesn't work, you can give her a small amount of cereal," Coco said.

"She likes Cheerios, but hopefully she won't be awake long enough for that," Benjamin said. "If she wakes up after you've put her to bed, when all else fails, sing to her."

"But she loves to be rocked," Coco added.

And so it went for several moments. Natalie duly wrote down all of Benjamin and Coco's instructions and suggestions, which, after all was said and done, could have been the first chapter of a book.

"You'll call if you have any problems at all?" Coco asked, halfway wishing she could stay in the villa instead of going to the gala. She was growing more nervous with each passing moment.

"Enjoy the party," Natalie said. "Your baby will probably sleep all the way through. If she doesn't, I will rock her and sing to her."

Coco felt a surge of relief. "Thank you. But you'll call..."

"Yes, I will call. Please go and enjoy," Natalie said. "Your car is waiting."

Coco took a deep breath. "Then we should leave," she said and glanced at Benjamin.

"Yes, we should," he said and ushered her out of the villa to the car.

Benjamin looked amazing, Coco thought, as he helped her into the car. He was dressed Texan formal in a black suit, bolo tie and his black hat. He hadn't worn his hat in a while so he wouldn't frighten Emma. He looked sexy enough to kill. And it would take all she had not to be the victim of this murder.

She crossed her left leg over her right and pumped it.

"That's some shoe," Benjamin said.

Coco glanced down at the sparkly pump and smiled. "Yes, it is. Bridget insisted. I insisted that it was on sale, which it was." She pumped her foot again. "It almost looks like Cinderella's slipper, doesn't it?"

"Well, I never wore Cinderella's slipper, but yeah, I can see the resemblance," he said. "Nice legs."

Coco immediately pushed her dress over her leg. "Thank you," she murmured.

Seconds later, the limo stopped in front of the palace and the driver escorted them out of the car.

"Thank you," Benjamin said and slid his hand behind Coco's waist. "Nice that they let us in the front door this time," he said.

She glanced up at him and felt a camera flash, saw it in her peripheral vision. "This is going to be different," she managed, meeting his gaze.

"Get ready for the circus, darlin'," Benjamin said and they walked inside the palace.

A string orchestra played beautiful music and waiters served appetizers and champagne. The chandeliers sparkled like diamonds. The marble floors gleamed, making Coco fear she'd fall on her derriere! A girl needed tennis shoes, not heels, in this situation.

"It's so beautiful," Coco said. "Look at all the dresses."

"If you say so," Benjamin said. He nodded at a server. "Can you get me a beer?"

"Yes, sir. I'll be right back," the server said.

"Bet it won't take him long," Coco said.

"Why?" Benjamin asked.

"Because you're so threatening," Coco said.

"I'm not threatening," Benjamin protested. "I just want a beer."

Coco snickered. "You still scared him."

Benjamin shot her a mock frown. "Why aren't *you* more afraid of me?"

"Because I am magic for your daughter," she said.

Benjamin shrugged. "Can't deny that," he said and suddenly his beer appeared. He glanced at Coco

and lifted an eyebrow before he nodded at the server.
"Thanks."

"My pleasure, sir. Please let me know if you need
anything else," the server said and walked away.

A man in uniform appeared at the top of the double
staircase and rang a bell. "Please proceed to the ballroom to your right. The royal family will arrive soon."

The crowd moved toward the ballroom, and Coco became separated from Benjamin. She craned her neck to
find him in the crowd, but couldn't see him. She should
have been able to see him with his Stetson, but every
time she looked above the crowd, someone raised an
arm or a tall man walked in front of her.

"Lovely lady," a man said to her.

Coco glanced to her right and gazed at a middle-aged
man with piercing blue eyes. "Thank you," she said.
"Please excuse me…"

"A Yank," the man said in delight. "An American.
We're deluged with Italians and French. How did this
happen?"

Coco shrugged. "Lucky, I guess," she said.

A half beat later, she felt a tap on her shoulder and
she turned around, hoping it was Benjamin. Instead, it
was Bridget.

"How are your shoes?" Bridget asked with a beaming smile.

Coco paused then gave a mangled curtsey. "Your
Highness," she said.

Bridget waved the courtesy aside. "Oh, stop. Show me your shoes."

Coco obediently lifted her Cinderella pumps. Bridget clapped her hands and smiled. "Excellent. You look ravishing. I'll check in with you later." She looked past Coco and her smile fell. "Oh, hello, Rodney. *Ciao.*"

"You're good friends with the princess," Rodney said as Bridget walked away.

"No, not really," Coco said.

"You must be. She was quite friendly with you and knew about your shoes." Rodney squinted at her. "You have the Devereaux eyes," he exclaimed. "You have an American accent." His eyes widened in recognition. "I saw your photo on the internet. You're the illegitimate Devereaux. No wonder Princess Bridget was nice to you. I'm sure Stefan gave her instructions."

Dismayed, Coco stared at him.

"And I'm Rodney, your third or fourth cousin," he said, extending his hand. "I'm a black sheep of the family, too. You're safe with me," he said in a confidential tone.

But somehow she didn't feel so safe. Instead, Coco felt confused and uncomfortable. "I need to leave," she said.

"Stay with me. I can make introductions," Rodney said.

"Oh, no, that's okay," Coco said. "I need to find my date. A pleasure to meet you," she fibbed with a shrug and rushed away. Luckily enough, she ran far enough to run into Benjamin.

"Thank goodness," she said.

"Trouble?" he asked.

"Some distant cousin of the Devereaux started asking questions. I had a hard time getting away from him," she said.

"Then stay with me," he said and enclosed her arm inside hers. "No one is competing for my presence."

"Bet it's the hat or the bolo," she said, unable to keep herself from smiling.

"Who knows?" he asked, but clearly didn't care.

The throng of people formed a long line outside the ballroom. "I wonder why this line is moving so slowly," Coco said.

"Because one of the perks is the opportunity to meet the royal family just inside the door," Benjamin said in a dry tone.

"How do you know that?"

"One of the servers told me," he said.

Coco was tempted to bolt. She wasn't interested in having her bad curtsey viewed by so many people, and she could tell that Benjamin was bored out of his mind. "You're hating every minute of this, aren't you?"

"Well, it's not a ball game or a barbecue," Benjamin said. "I'm trying to look at it as a trip to the circus."

Coco laughed. "I like the idea of the circus."

"It's not just an idea," Benjamin said. "Look at how all these people are dressed. Feathers?"

"You could say the same about me," she said. "I. Sparkle. Kind of." She glanced down at the broach between her breasts.

He shook his head. "You look beautiful. No feathers. No way you look like a freak."

She smiled up at him. "Well, I guess that means I should thank you, though I'm not feeling overly flattered."

Benjamin leaned toward her. "You look damn good," he whispered in her ear.

"Thanks," she whispered. "You look pretty damn good yourself."

"It's the hat," he said.

"Yeah, and Emma would totally agree," Coco shot back.

He frowned at her.

"It's true," she said. "You and your Stetson. Scary."

"I'll make you change your mind," he said, ushering her closer to the doorway into the ballroom.

Finally, Coco was presented to Stefan and Eve. She curtsied. Again, awkwardly.

Stefan nodded and extended his hand. "I'm glad you could attend tonight. I hope you're enjoying yourself."

"Thank you for inviting me," Coco said.

"My pleasure. I'm grateful for your positive words to my wife," he said.

Coco nodded. "I wish you both the best," she said and was led to Eve.

"Good to see you," Eve said. "I love it that you curtsey the same way I did," she said with a chuckle.

"I suspect that's not a compliment on my form," Coco said.

Eve nodded. "But your advice to me was superior," she said.

"How are you feeling?" Coco asked.

"Good right now. I'm taking advantage of my good moments then resting during my other times. Thank you for coming tonight," Eve said and turned to Benjamin. "And you, too. You're a lucky man to have Coco."

Benjamin slid his hand around Coco's waist and nodded. "That, I am."

They were led away from Eve. Hating her instant emotional reaction to his touch, Coco moved away from him as soon as possible.

"You're going to need to pretend a little better," he said in a low voice next to her ear.

Again, his closeness made all her nerve endings jump. "I guess I'm not as good at pretending as I hoped I'd be."

"Looks like they have a good spread of food. Maybe that will make you feel better. I think there's even some chocolate. I'll get you a glass of champagne," he offered and walked toward a server.

Coco immediately felt a sliver of relief that he'd stepped away from her. She needed to get better control of her reactions to him. Coco didn't want to make a fool of herself over her boss. She tried to distract herself with the beautiful display of appetizers and desserts.

Benjamin returned with her champagne as she nibbled on a few bites of a crab cake. Seconds later, a band began to play. "Ladies and gentleman, I present Her Highness Bridget and her husband, Dr. Ryder McCall. Let the dancing commence."

Several couples immediately joined Princess Bridget and her husband on the dance floor. Coco watched, entranced by the scene. It was like something out of an enchanted story, more beautiful than any movie could capture. The women's dresses reflected the light from the chandeliers, and the men looked so handsome and sophisticated. Their reflections echoed off the mirrors on the walls of the ballroom.

"Wanna dance?" Benjamin asked.

Coco whipped her head around to look at him. "No," she immediately said.

"You look like you do," he said with a shrug.

"It's just so beautiful. All of it. The people, the women's dresses, the mirrors and the lights. Have you ever seen anything like it?"

He glanced at the dance floor. "It's a sight to see. I've been to a few charity events in Dallas where everyone was dressed in designer clothing and the rooms were decorated. Gotta say, though, I like the view from my backdoor on a spring morning better than this."

His comment took her by surprise, yet resonated inside her. For all the glamour and sophistication of her half siblings' lives, Coco felt so much more at ease back at the ranch. "You could be right," she said. "The flowers on the tables are beautiful, but nothing beats bluebells."

"Tough, but beautiful," Benjamin said. "Just like a Texan woman. C'mon and dance," he said, slipping his hand to her waist. "I'll never forgive myself if you didn't take your chance to dance at the palace."

She thought about refusing. Being close to Benjamin was hard on her. But how could she turn down the chance for this kind of memory? When would she ever get this opportunity again?

"Okay," she said and to her surprise, the band slid into a song just right for a Texas two-step. "A two-step," she said, stepping into Benjamin's arms and matching his rhythm. "How did that happen?"

"The international prompt," he said with a sly grin. "A tip to the right guy."

She couldn't help laughing at his confidence. Her heart shouldn't feel as if it was flying above her. She shouldn't feel as if she were ten feet off the ground. Shouldn't, shouldn't, shouldn't.

Just this once, Coco told her brain to stop and focused on the moment. Everyone and everything in the room was a blur to her except for Benjamin's deep gaze and his strong arms. She wondered if she would ever feel like this again.

After they danced, she indulged in a second glass of champagne. She allowed Benjamin to talk her into another head-spinning, heart-turning dance. Being held by him was addictive. She loved the scent of his soap and the sensation of his muscles beneath his jacket. His broad shoulders and slightly calloused hands provided a constant reminder that he was all male. And she was all female. His gaze was focused totally on her, and he drew her closer than was necessary.

Fighting giddiness, she excused herself to the powder room and washed her hands with cool water. She needed to dial down her reaction to him. He was just pretending, she reminded herself. Though true, the thought depressed her and she struggled with opposing feelings. Could he look at her that way, as if she were the most beautiful woman in the room, and truly feel nothing?

"Have you heard there's an illegitimate Devereaux here tonight?" one woman said to the other as they checked their makeup in the mirror.

Coco stopped cold and tried not to look in the women's direction.

"I'm surprised they're even recognizing her," the other woman said.

"She probably wants a handout. I heard it from a friend of Stefan's assistant that they're just being nice to her so she won't talk bad about them to the press. Any inheritance she receives will be a pittance."

"She's American, isn't she? I'll bet she'll try to get a reality show out of it. Low-class shows."

She looked in the mirror at herself and saw a woman with flushed cheeks and slightly tousled hair. A woman full of wishes and dreams she'd tried to deny. She'd been able to dismiss what was said by her distant cousin, Rodney. He'd seemed liked he delighted in scandalous news about the Devereaux. She supposed most people did, including the two women who'd just been talking about rumors. When more than one person was repeating the same rumor, though, maybe it wasn't a rumor. Maybe it was the truth. And maybe she was being a total fool to think that the Devereaux cared about her one little bit.

Suddenly, she couldn't bear to stay in the palace one more minute. It felt false and she felt silly. She had to get away. Leaving the powder room, she immediately caught sight of Benjamin and walked toward him.

"I'm ready to go, please," she said.

He studied her for a moment. "You're upset. What happened?"

"I just realized I don't belong here. The Devereaux aren't really my family, and they never will be."

"Are you sure?"

"Yes. Very sure," she said and pushed back the urge to cry. Her magical night at the palace was fake in every way. Since the Devereaux were all busy with guests, Coco thanked the official palace rep at the door. A car quickly arrived to take her and Benjamin back to the villa.

They arrived in no time and the nanny reported that Emma had easily fallen asleep. Coco felt like crap. All she wanted to do was ditch her dress and go to sleep. Maybe she could resell the dress on eBay. She felt weak and weepy and hated herself for it.

"I guess we should go to bed," she said and turned toward the hallway.

Benjamin caught her hand. "Come back."

"Not a good idea," she said in a voice that sounded husky to her own ears.

"You can trust me," he said and pulled her around to face him. "What's going on?"

She bit her lip, her stomach knotting. "It's all so fake. They don't want me here. You're not really my fiancé. It's too much."

He nodded and pulled her against him. "You've had a crazy time."

She buried her head in his chest and inhaled his wonderful scent that made her dizzy.

She forced herself to pull back. "I hate that it's all fake. The Devereaux want me to disappear. You don't really want me. I just want something real right now."

He paused a long moment, but kept her in his arms. "I want you," he confessed. "I just know I shouldn't."

"But you turn it off so easily," she said.

He lifted his forefinger to her lips. "Not really."

Her heart fluttered. "You could have fooled me."

His expression softened. "Sweetheart, you're easy to fool."

She took a deep breath. "Well, now, that really makes me feel better."

He lifted his hands to cradle her head. "Shut up," he whispered and lowered his head.

His lips landed on hers and she felt her consciousness begin to slide away. "I'm not sure," she said against his lips.

But he continued to kiss her, his tongue sliding past her lips. Tasting him, she had no inclination to pull away. Coco sank into him.

He slid his hand down her back to push her intimately against him.

"Oh, Benjamin, this is a bad—" She broke off when he rubbed against her. He was hard and wanting. Heat roared through her. Primitive need ricocheted through her bloodstream.

Coco craved more. She wanted all of him.

He squeezed her hips and groaned, undulating against her.

"Benjamin," she whispered. "Don't take me half-way this time."

He stopped and she could almost feel him debating. Seconds later, he gave her a French kiss that took her around the world and ground himself against her intimately. "I want you," he muttered.

A few breaths later, her dress was discarded on the floor, along with her underwear. She tugged at his bolo and shirt, then his black slacks. Benjamin shoved off his jacket. His skin was hot against hers. She craved his strength. His muscles flexed in an almost involuntary motion.

Coco couldn't get close enough. He continued to kiss her, pulling her down on the couch. She rubbed her breasts against his chest, drinking in his moan. "You're so sweet," he said. "I can't get enough."

He flipped her over on the couch and thrust inside her.

Coco gasped at the sensation.

"What?" he asked. "Don't tell me you're a virgin."

"No," she said. "It's just been a long time. And you're…"

"I'm what?" he prodded.

"Nothing," she managed. "Don't stop."

Benjamin couldn't seem to refuse the invitation. He began to pump and she echoed his movements. It was the most primitive, sensual experience she'd ever had. Coco just hoped it was more than physical for him, because it seemed to permeate her entire being. She was in deep trouble if this was just sex for him.

He thrust inside her and she could see his pleasure stamped on his face as he jerked and went over the top. It rocked her into another universe. She didn't climax, but something inside her would never be the same, and she curled around him and held him as tight as she could.

Chapter Ten

"You didn't come," he said, his eyes dark with sex and satisfaction.

"It's not important," she said because the experience had been so powerful for her. "Just being with you—"

Benjamin slid his hand between her legs and began to caress her.

"Oh," Coco said. "That feels—"

He found her sweet spot and she couldn't speak. It felt so good. She wriggled against his hand.

Moments later, he slid inside her again, hard and ready.

Coco stared at him in surprise. "What?"

"Yeah," he said and drove inside her.

Her breath caught and she left her inhibitions behind.

At this moment, Benjamin was everything. "Give yourself to me," he whispered. "All of you."

He continued to stroke her as he thrust inside her. Coco lost all concept of time. She gave herself totally to him.

She felt herself explode in a million sensations. Clinging to him, she pulled him into her.

She heard him swear six ways from Sunday. Finally, he slumped against her, still inside her.

"Lord help us," he said.

"Yeah," she whispered in response because she feared she would never get enough of him.

She felt Benjamin's release. A moment later, he began to stroke her in her most sensitive place. "Oh," she said. "I'm not sure—"

She broke off when she felt a twist of sensation.

"Give it to me," he said in a husky voice. "Give me all of you."

She couldn't refuse him. Between the way he touched her and the sound of his voice, she was all his. Coco gave herself to him and to the moment and went over the top.

Seconds, breaths later, she clung to him. "You're the most incredible woman in the world," he said, one hand cupping her jaw.

"Will you say that tomorrow?" she asked. "Or will you forget?"

His eyes blazed into hers. "I'll never forget."

* * *

Hours later, Emma cried out, waking both of them. Benjamin lifted his head. "I'll get her."

"No, I'll get her," Coco said, shaking her head and trying to clear her bleary vision.

"I can get her," he said and began to rise, naked from the bed.

"You might want to get a robe or something first," she managed.

He swore under his breath and groped around the room.

Coco found one of his shirts, and pulled it on. He was so much taller it almost reached to her knees. "Beat ya," she said and couldn't swallow a laugh.

She kissed him as Emma's cries grew louder. "Whatever you do, don't you dare tell me you regret this," she said, then rushed to Emma's room and grabbed a diaper and wipes. She found the baby howling and kicking.

"Well, good morning, sunshine," she said. "What's all this fussing for?" she asked as she changed Emma's diaper. Emma's cries faded as Coco chatted with her. Carrying the baby to the kitchen, she found Benjamin already warming a bottle. He'd pulled on a pair of jeans and a shirt he hadn't bothered to button. His hair was ruffled and when he looked at her, she wondered how a man holding a baby bottle could look so dangerously sexy.

"You get your shower. I'll take her," he said, extending his arms.

"Are you sure? She definitely woke up in a cranky-pants mood." She glanced at Emma who was studying Benjamin with a solemn gaze.

"She'll get over her reservations with me once I give her the bottle," he said in a dry tone. "Now go get your shower and get dressed, or I'll be tempted to take you back to bed."

Startled, she met his gaze and felt a rush of heat. "Is that a promise?"

He chuckled, taking the baby from her hands. "The first time I saw you, I thought you were the sweet, nurturing type. You looked so young I almost thought you were a teenager."

"But I'm not that young," she insisted.

"No. And you've got some fire underneath all that sweetness. I'll see you after you get dressed," he growled.

Delighted by the fact that he was finally seeing her as a woman, Coco hummed on her way to the shower. Benjamin couldn't deny that he had feelings for her now. He had shown her in a way no woman could mistake last night. They'd made no promises to each other, though. She needed to remember that. The thought almost made her stop humming, but Coco had never known a man like Benjamin and she suspected that she never would again. She just wouldn't count on anything between them lasting forever. That was okay, she told herself. No one in her life had been around forever.

Benjamin patted Emma's back after her feeding, and she let out a burp that would rival what he would expect from a truck driver. The fact that such a little being could let out such a loud sound never ceased to amaze him. "Bet you feel better, don't you?" he said, grinning at his daughter.

She giggled in return.

Her smile gave him a crazy little thrill. Thank goodness for Coco. He wondered if Emma would still be terrified of him if not for Coco. And now that he'd had Coco in his bed, things were definitely complicated. He couldn't deny a ferocious attraction for his daughter's nanny, but he also knew he wasn't in love. Even though Coco had insisted that he not voice his regrets, he knew he would have a hard time not thinking about her in a sexual way. And he feared that Coco, with her tender heart, might fall for him.

His phone rang, interrupting his worrisome thoughts. "Benjamin Garner," he said, propping Emma on his knee.

"This is Ray McAllister. Sorry to bother you, but I have some bad news. Foreman Hal broke his leg and had to have surgery. It will be a while before he'll be mobile again," he said. "Plus Jace quit yesterday."

Benjamin winced. "Damn. When it rains," he said and didn't need to finish the statement. "Is Hal okay?"

"More ticked off than anything else," he said.

"Okay. I'll make arrangements to get back to the ranch. Can you handle things until I get there?"

"Sure, boss."

"Okay, well, call if you have any problems. I'll be in touch," he said and turned off the phone.

Coco entered the room. "Problem?"

Benjamin nodded. "I have to get back to the ranch as soon as possible. My foreman broke his leg. You can stay here if you want."

She shook her head. "I think I've had enough of the Devereaux circus. I wouldn't have minded meeting my blood brother, but it looks like he doesn't care that much about meeting any of us. Maybe that's for the best. I'll pack."

Benjamin arranged for the flight and their palace rep took them to the airport. Coco had put together a carry-on bag to keep Emma fed, amused and happy, but he was hoping the baby would sleep.

He noticed that Coco stared out the window until the island of Chantaine disappeared from sight. "Are you sure you didn't want to stay?"

She shook her head. "No. My tie to the Devereaux is just an interesting story, and that's all."

"You keep saying that," Benjamin said. "I thought you and the princesses were starting to get along. They were nice to you, weren't they?"

"Yes, but I have reason to believe that the only reason they were nice is because they were afraid I would say bad things about them to the press."

"What makes you think that?"

"I overheard some ladies talking while I was in

the powder room," she said. "A man, he said he was a cousin. He pretty much said the same thing," she said.

"It doesn't matter why the Devereaux decided to be nice to you. It's important that they were. You wanted a chance to spend time with them and get to know them a little bit. So you got what you wanted," he said.

Coco frowned. "I would have preferred that they act more genuine to me."

"Not me. I wasn't going to let them be rude to you. You've gone through enough because of them. The least they could do is treat you with a little kindness."

Coco shook her head. "What do you mean *you* weren't going to let them be rude to me? You didn't have anything to do with how they acted toward me." Realization crossed her face. "Or did you?"

Benjamin shrugged. "It wasn't a big deal. I just had a little conversation with Stefan—"

Her eyes rounded. "Stefan," she echoed. "What kind of little conversation?"

"I just told him that you deserved better treatment than what you got at that tea party, and it could turn into a PR disaster if his family didn't act nicer," he said.

"So it's true?" she said. "The only reason they were friendly to me was because you threatened them."

"I didn't threaten," Benjamin said. "I just gave them facts. If they were snooty to you, and reporters asked about your time in Chantaine, you wouldn't have much good to say about the Devereaux."

"I can't believe you did that," she said in a harsh whisper.

"I can't believe you're getting all worked up over it," he said. "I was not going to allow them to make you feel like you're their daddy's dirt, because you're not. You're better than that."

Coco looked out the window. "I just wanted it to be as real as possible."

"Sweetheart, you're dealing with royals. They've spent most of their lives pretending."

"But I didn't want them to pretend with me."

Benjamin's gut twisted. Twice. She went silent and turned away from him.

Eleven long hours later, they arrived in Dallas, gritty-eyed and exhausted. One of his assistant foremen, Ray, greeted them after they picked up their luggage.

Benjamin sat in the front while Coco and Emma sat in the back of the SUV. Emma began to fuss and Coco gave her a bottle of diluted juice. Emma sucked it down in no time and gave one of her hearty burps. It must have been enough to tide her over, however, because she stopped whining.

"Fill me in," Benjamin said to his assistant foreman.

Ray did, and the news wasn't all that pretty. Benjamin had several full days of work ahead of him. Less than an hour later, they pulled into his ranch's driveway. Benjamin unfastened Emma's car seat and carried her inside.

"I'll take care of her," Coco said.

"The time change may have messed her up," he said.

"The time change will have us all messed up," she said with a tired smile.

"Yeah, I guess so," he said and lowered his head to kiss her. It wasn't a publicly necessary kiss. It was just something he was compelled to do. He felt her breathless surprise and took her mouth. It was an indulgence he allowed himself because he knew he would work nearly nonstop during the next few days.

He pulled back slightly. "Listen, about my talking to Stefan about you. No self-respecting fiancé would do less."

She studied his face. "I wouldn't know."

"Well, you do now," he said, and kissed her again.

It took over twenty-four hours for Coco and Emma to begin to recover from the time change. Half the time, when Emma was awake, Coco rested the baby on her chest. Two days later, she took Emma for a stroll around the house. Then another. And another.

At that point, it occurred to Coco that Emma needed exercise more than she did. She took the baby inside and set her down on a blanket for baby aerobics. Emma didn't enjoy the session. She cried until Coco rolled her onto her back and entertained her with toys. After several moments of more baby aerobics, Emma wailed for a few more moments.

Then Emma sank back against her baby pad and closed her gorgeous baby eyelids. "Well, that's my sign,"

Coco murmured and picked up the baby and carried her to her crib. Seconds later, Coco climbed into her own bed.

A few hours later, she awakened in the middle of the night. She rushed into the nursery to find Benjamin walking the floor with Emma.

Her heart leapt. "Sorry," she said. "I can take over now."

"I'm good," he said. "How has she been since we got back?"

"I took her for a long walk, but she needed a work-out," she said.

He looked at her as he jiggled her while he walked. She rested her mouth on his shoulder. "She's drooling. Is she teething?"

"Probably," Coco said. "You're good at that bobbing thing."

He shot her a wry glance. "Think so?"

"Yeah. How was life on the ranch today?" she asked.

"Coulda been worse. There's always catch-up when you go away. That's probably why my father never took a vacation."

"Do you regret the trip?" she asked.

"Not really," he said. "I danced with the most beau-tiful woman in the world in Chantaine."

She couldn't help smiling all over. "That's pretty darn nice."

"Just telling the truth. Go back to bed."

"I feel guilty," she said.

"You won't in the morning when she wakes up screaming for a bottle."

Well, it had been a long several days, especially over the Atlantic. Which had been Benjamin's indulgence of her. "Sure?" she asked.

He nodded. "Go to bed."

She did as he suggested because she knew the next several days would be uncertain at best. When Coco awakened in the morning, she waited for the sound of Emma screaming, but there was only silence. Coco wasn't sure whether to relax or panic. She sat up in her bed and listened as she took a deep breath. Silence. No sound of Emma screaming or unhappy.

Rising from her bed, and still listening, she cracked open her bedroom door, but she still heard nothing. She feared not taking the opportunity to take a shower, but couldn't stop herself from listening for Emma. It was instinctive.

After several more moments of silence, Coco dove into the shower and washed herself from head to toe. She scrubbed herself dry, pulled on her clothes and went downstairs to find Emma in a high chair in the kitchen and Sarah spilling more Cheerios on her tray.

Emma picked up as many of the cereal bits as she could and stuffed them into her mouth.

"Take it easy," Sarah said. "You're not that hungry, sweetie. You put that fist in your mouth and you'll choke. Fact of life."

Coco winced and went toward the kitchen. Emma

began to choke. "Sarah," Coco said. Both of them tugged Emma's fist from her mouth.

"Emma, don't do that to yourself," Coco said.

"Learn this lesson young," Sarah said. "You can't eat more than you can fit in your mouth."

Coco decided an outing was in order. After breakfast, she plunked Emma into the stroller, then into the car seat and drove into town. She wheeled Emma through a discount store then went to the diner where her friend was serving several guests.

Coco asked to be led to a booth in the back and requested hot cocoa with marshmallows. A moment later Kim plopped down her hot chocolate along with applesauce and a spoon. "Back in a minute," Kim said.

"I'll be here." Coco sipped her hot chocolate and spoon-fed Emma.

The baby accepted the applesauce. "Good girl," she said as she stole a sip of hot chocolate.

Kim slid into the booth seat across from her. "Hello? So you're a princess? Why didn't you tell me?"

"Trust me. I'm no princess," Coco said and gave Emma another spoonful of food.

"But you went to Champagne," Kim said.

"Chantaine," Coco corrected. "I'd never heard of it, either."

"What were they like?" Kim asked.

Coco took a deep breath. She had to decide what she was going to say about the Devereaux. Now. She decided to go with the truth. "They were very kind to me," Coco said. "They work hard. They have children and husbands and they worry just like you and I do."

Kim frowned. "No dirt?"

Coco shook her head. "No dirt. They were nice."

"Well, that's boring," Kim said.

Coco laughed. "Sorry. You wanted me to have a miserable time?"

Kim rolled her eyes. "Of course not. I just thought it would be more exciting. Wasn't there anything exciting about the trip?"

"The island was beautiful. The beach was lovely. I got a great pair of shoes that I left in the villa where we stayed."

"Villa?" Kim echoed.

"House," Coco said. "We didn't stay at the palace. I went to tea and spilled mine on the tablecloth. Benjamin and I attended a gala at the palace."

"Oh, the gala must have been fabulous," she said with a dreamy look in her eyes. "Speaking of Benjamin, though, I understand you're engaged. Tell me more."

Coco gave a tentative nod. "It just happened. We're taking it slow," she said.

"Hmm," Kim said, lifting her eyebrow. "That sounds mysterious."

"It's not," Coco said. Emma let out a yell, bless her heart. "Oops, I think she wants more applesauce," she said and shoved another spoonful into the baby's open mouth.

"She is so cute," Kim said. "Do you want anything else for her?"

"I'm packing cereal, so I'm good," she said.

"You're so smart. You could be a mom," Kim said. "Gotta go."

Coco sighed as Kim walked away. For now, she had decided not to think about her connection to the Devereaux. Before, she couldn't help hoping for some great connection with the family who shared her father's genes and blood. The truth, however, was that they were all just people and, in her case, they had no bonds of history. She was truly alone in the world now, and she needed to make her peace with that.

Emma opened her mouth for more applesauce. Coco fed the baby several more spoonfuls. "Yummy, huh?" she asked and wiped off Emma's face.

Emma squawked, but permitted the cleanup. "Time to go," she said and lifted her from the high chair. She left extra money on the table for the bill and tip and headed out the door, waving at Kim as she left.

As she stepped outside the door, several people greeted her with microphones and cameras. "Miss Jordan, tell us about your experience in Chantaine. How did your sisters and brothers treat you? When will you be seeing them again?"

Emma curled against her in fear. "The Devereaux were very kind and welcoming to me. They could not have treated me better. The royal family works hard for the people of Chantaine, and they are just lovely." She paused a half beat as she heard the cameras flash. "That is all I have to say."

"But, Miss Jordan, what about your relationship with the Devereaux? What about—"

"That is all I have to say. I've responded to you. Now, you're frightening Emma. Please respect my privacy," she said, and walked to her car and put Emma into her safety seat. She got into the driver's seat and headed back to the ranch, jittery all the way.

When she pulled to the side of the house, Emma was fully asleep. Coco was relieved that the baby had not been traumatized by the experience, but it bothered her that the paparazzi had surprised her. She was still upset by it.

Coco took Emma inside, set her down in her crib for a nap and went to her own bed for a rest. For the first thirty minutes, her mind whirled. She remembered how Emma's body had tensed against hers in fear as the reporters surrounded them. The memory made her sick. More than anything, she wanted Emma to feel secure. She hated the idea that she was causing any kind of stress for the baby who had already lost her mother. Although she was exhausted, she tossed and turned, but finally fell asleep.

It must have been five minutes later that she heard Emma screaming at the top of her lungs. Coco nearly levitated from the bed. She glanced at the clock. It hadn't been five minutes. It had been *nearly an hour*. She collided with Benjamin as she raced into the nursery. "Sorry," she murmured. "I guess I was sleepier than I thought."

"Understandable," Benjamin said. "We're all still adjusting to the time change."

"I guess," Coco said and reached for Emma. "How are you, sweetie? Are you still frightened from this afternoon?"

"What happened this afternoon?" Benjamin asked as Coco changed Emma's diaper.

"I went to town, stopped at the diner, and a bunch of reporters and photographers were waiting outside. I think they scared Emma because she was wrapping herself around me like a rubber band."

Benjamin frowned. "I would have thought the fuss would have died down by now."

"You and me both," Coco said and held Emma against her. "I decided to give a positive statement about the Devereaux. Nothing more, but of course, they wanted more."

Benjamin sighed. "I guess I'll just have to keep one of my men available for you."

Coco felt guilty. She knew that Benjamin had lost two of his top employees. "That doesn't seem fair," she said. "I don't think it's right that you should have to give up one of your employees because of me."

Benjamin shrugged. "You gotta do what you gotta do. Other than the scare today, how's she's doing?"

"She's getting more interested in sounds. I think she may try to communicate even more soon."

"Seems to me she communicates pretty strongly when she screams," Benjamin said in a wry voice. At the same time, he lifted his hand to the baby's hand. Emma curled her fist around his finger. "So tiny. So vulnerable. Keeping her safe scares the hell out of me sometimes."

"You're doing a pretty good job," Coco said as she slid her hand over his.

He met her gaze for a long moment. "So are you. I've missed you."

Her heart skipped over itself. "I've missed you, too," she whispered.

"Ranch demands have been crazy since I got back," he said.

"I know," she said. "It was a luxury for you to go to Chantaine with me. I still appreciate it."

"Even though you didn't want me talking to Stefan on your behalf," he said.

"Well," she said and took a deep breath, "I think you were operating in my best interests."

"I didn't want to have to beat him up for him to see the truth," he said, sliding his hand over her hair.

"You would have been arrested for that," she said.

Benjamin shrugged. "Sometimes you gotta do what you gotta do. Listen," he said. "Ask Sarah for help. She's okay with it, and Emma doesn't mind her."

Coco nodded. "I'll work on it. I just don't want to overwork Sarah. She has a lot to do, preparing meals for your staff."

"Yeah, but she took advantage of the time we were away. With a baby in the house, we all have to make adjustments and Sarah knows that, too."

"Okay," she said.

"And I'll assign one of my men to you," he said.

"That shouldn't be necessary," she said. "I don't go out that often and I don't like the idea of pulling someone away from their assignments just because I want to go into town."

"I'll give you a cell number. Let him know when you want to go out and he'll escort you. It won't be a big deal," Benjamin said.

"Are you sure?" she asked, skeptical.

"Yeah. Now don't argue with me. There are times when my guys are sitting around doing nothing. You're just making one of them earn his pay every now and then."

"If you say so," she said.

"I am," he said and lowered his mouth to hers, taking her in a long kiss that reminded her of the night they'd shared at the villa in Chantaine.

Chapter Eleven

Although it was a bit chilly outside, Coco bundled up the baby and took her for a stroll. Emma really seemed to enjoy the outdoors. After she returned it was dinnertime, and she fed the baby then bathed her and put her to bed after one more bottle. As much as Coco had needed that little nap she took earlier, she knew it would be a while before she would be tired enough to sleep tonight, so she put on a jacket and went for another walk around the house.

After she'd made two and a half circles, Benjamin appeared at her side. "So, what's bothering you now?"

"Nothing," she said, thinking she was most bothered by the warm pleasure she felt just having him by her side. "I guess I was caught off guard at the diner today, but I'm hoping the interest will die down now."

"It will," he said. "What else?"

"Nothing. I'm just trying to burn off some extra energy, so I'll be able to sleep tonight."

"I would have thought Emma would take care of burning off any extra energy," he said.

She chuckled. "She usually does, but since I took that late nap…"

He stepped in front of her and pulled her against him, and looked down at her from beneath his hat. He pushed a strand of hair from her face. "I can help you burn off your extra energy," he offered in a low voice that made her heart stutter.

His suggestion was unmistakably sexual. Her nerve endings hummed. "What about Sarah?" she asked because the housekeeper lived in a small suite downstairs.

"Sarah will be too busy watching her reality television to notice," he said. "I haven't stopped thinking about being with you."

Coco hadn't stopped thinking about him, either. "Okay," she whispered because her throat was tight with anticipation. "How— Where—" She shrugged.

"Your room," he said. "You go upstairs first. I'll be up in five minutes or less," he promised then lowered his head to kiss away any reservations.

Her heart hammering, she strode quickly to the house, then upstairs to her bedroom. Pulling off her jacket, she wondered if she should change clothes. She didn't have any sexy lingerie. She started to panic, but then he opened the door and closed it behind him.

"Nervous?" he asked as he walked toward her.

"A little," she admitted.

"Or excited," he said with a sexy grin.

"Maybe," she said, wishing she had half his confidence. "What about you?"

He gently pushed her down on the bed with his arm beneath her to cushion her fall. He followed her down. "I'm not at all nervous," he said and when she felt his hard lower body against hers, his arousal was unmistakable.

Then he kissed her and everything blurred deliciously together. He helped her remove her clothes. She awkwardly helped with his. His hands heated her skin everywhere he touched her. She relished the sensation of his muscular body entwined with hers. He touched and teased her and she did the same to him until they couldn't stand the anticipation one second longer. He drove her over the edge and he followed.

Benjamin rolled to his side, panting after his release. Pulling her against him, he nuzzled her head with his chin. "I can't get enough of you. How'd you do that?" he asked.

She smiled into his throat. "Same, same," she said. "I lo—" He stiffened and she broke off in horror because she'd almost said she *loved* him. "I—" She cleared her throat. "I really like being with you," she said. "In every way."

She felt his body relax against hers. "I feel the same way," he said and rubbed his mouth down her cheek to her lips.

The next morning, she awakened to the sound of Emma chatting through the baby monitor. And no Benjamin beside her. She felt an odd sense of loss and confusion but pushed it aside as she pulled on a long-sleeved T-shirt, underwear and a pair of jeans. Walking into the nursery, Coco found Emma batting at a stuffed bunny and chatting with it.

Coco's heart twisted in love. Emma had grown so much since the first day she'd taken over as nanny. "Hello, Miss Chatterbox. How are you this morning?"

Emma immediately turned her head to look at Coco and gave her a toothless smile.

"Aren't you the gorgeous one?" she said and changed the baby's diaper. She lifted her up from her crib and pointed to Benjamin's photograph on the chest of drawers. "That's your daddy. Can you say daddy?"

Emma made several unintelligible sounds.

"Da-da," Coco said. "Da-da, Da-da, Da-da." She'd coached the baby too many times to count.

Emma continued to make her sounds. Just as Coco began to turn away, the baby said, "Da-da."

Coco blinked. "Did you say Da-da?"

"Da-da-da-da," she repeated.

"You're saying Da-da," Coco said, so excited she couldn't stand it. "Da-da."

"Da-da-da-da," Emma said.

"Gotta find your daddy," Coco said and bolted for the stairs. She hoped Benjamin was in the office. Darting to the office door, she threw open the door, but he wasn't there. Her heart sank. "Dang." Searching her mind for a way to record the moment, she pulled her cell phone from her pocket and pushed record. "Say Da-da," she said holding the phone toward Emma's mouth.

Distracted by the phone, Emma leaned toward it and tried to lick it.

"No," Coco said and pulled the phone slightly away. "Da-da," she coached. "Da-da."

"Da-da," Emma whispered.

"Good girl," Coco said. "Again. Da-da."

"Da-da-da-da-da-da."

Coco saved the recording and kissed Emma on her cheek. "Yay."

After she gave Emma her bottle, Coco sent the voice recording to Benjamin's phone.

Moments later, he called her back. "Did I hear what I think I heard?"

"You did. Your daughter said Da-da. How does it feel?"

"Pretty damn good," he said. "Do you think she knows what she's saying?"

"Mostly," she said. "I point to your photo and say *Daddy*. She said it for the first time this morning. I'm excited."

Benjamin chuckled. "I can tell you are. Thanks for

the recording," he said. "And thanks for last night," he added.

"Sure," she said, her stomach taking a dip. "Sure. I'll talk to you later." She hung up the phone full of mixed feelings. Just hours ago, she and Benjamin had made love, but she could tell that he didn't want to hear her tell him she loved him. And just now, she was turning cartwheels because his daughter had uttered two identical syllables that may or may not identify him.

Her chest tightened with the realization that she was feeling too much for Benjamin. He might regard her as a fun lover, but he didn't truly want her as a fiancée, let alone as a wife.

She was his *employee*.

That knowledge stirred her uncertainties. How was she supposed to manage her growing feelings for Benjamin when they were living in the same house and he seemed more than happy to share her bed? On occasion, anyway. And what would happen to her when his desire for her waned?

Coco wasn't sure how to keep her heart safe. She was all alone in the world, and even though Benjamin had stepped up to help her, she shouldn't count on him. She shouldn't mistake his kindness and sexual interest for anything more.

The house phone began to ring again, calls for Coco, wanting her to make an appearance or give an interview. Coco could tell that Sarah was growing impatient with the interruptions.

After Emma's morning nap and lunch, Coco decided they could both use an outing. She knew of a park in town and although it was a little chilly, she thought she could bundle Emma well. And, heaven knew, she needed to get out. Her thoughts and feelings were ricocheting throughout her body and mind. She gave a call to the ranch hand Benjamin had assigned to her and left a message when he didn't answer.

She drove to the park, hauled out the stroller and plopped Emma into it. "Ready to go?" she said.

Emma, wrapped up with a hooded coat, looked around. Coco rose and found a group of photographers coming toward her. She held up her hand. "Whoa. Leave us alone."

"We just want to ask you more about your visit to Chantaine," a man said.

"I've already said all I'm going to say. The Devereaux were very kind to me and Chantaine is a beautiful island. I wish all of you would have the opportunity to visit. There's nothing else to say."

"There has to be more," a woman said, lifting a microphone in her direction.

"No, there's really nothing more to say," Coco said. "Now, please leave us alone."

"But—"

"But nothing," Coco said and shoved the stroller away from the paparazzi vultures. She practically ran and it wasn't a running stroller.

Emma giggled, and Coco wished she could laugh,

too, but she was so furious with the intrusion in her life. In Emma's life. In Benjamin's life. She would have thought all the craziness would have died down. But no. She wondered how long it would take. She wondered *what* it would take to make them stop.

Rounding a curve, a man leapt out in front of her. Coco screamed, and Emma began to cry.

"I just want an interview," the man said.

"Leave me and my—" She searched for the word, because they weren't her family. Brutal truth. Emma wasn't her baby. Benjamin and Sarah weren't her family, as much as she might want them to be. And Boomer wasn't her dog. "Leave my friends alone."

She ran away and prayed she wouldn't encounter anyone else.

Upset by the paparazzi, Coco struggled to figure out what she should do. It would be so much easier to just continue on her current path. Benjamin was more than happy with how she'd taken care of Emma. He was also happy to have her in his bed as long as deep emotions and true commitment weren't involved. That reality ripped at her.

So how did she take care of Benjamin and Emma and herself at the same time? Coco brooded over that question. What was best for Emma? What was best for Benjamin? What was best for Coco? The same answer kept coming back to her again and again, and Coco knew it would only cause her more pain. But it was all too necessary.

The next day, she advertised for a nanny.

Over the following week, she avoided Benjamin and interviewed her possible replacement. It sounded drastic, but Coco couldn't handle her feelings for Benjamin and she wanted the best for both Emma and her father. That meant she needed to leave. She would adjust to the change. She had to. She knew what it was to lose people she loved. Sometimes she wondered if that was her destiny.

Coco interviewed five women for her position. One was perfect. Coco insisted on two background checks that came back cleaner than a whistle. Susan Littleton was perfect. More perfect than Coco was, which made her feel oddly envious.

Despite her yuck feelings, she forged on and confronted Benjamin before he left one morning. "What's up?" he asked as she met him in the front room.

"I need to talk to you," she said.

"That's new," he said with a grumpy expression on his face. "You've been avoiding me."

"Yes. I'm sorry. I wanted to be with you, but—"

"Yeah, yeah," Benjamin said, clearly not believing her.

Coco took a deep breath. "I think it might be best if I leave."

Benjamin's eyes widened in alarm. "Why?"

"I can't stand the way the paparazzi are haunting

me, Emma, you," she said. "It's wrong. And I think the only way to make them go away is for me to go away."

"What?" he asked.

She bit her lip. "Yes, and then there's our so-called engagement," she said. "And the sex. I don't think I can handle sex and a nonengagement with you."

"Then we can stop," he said.

"Easy for you to turn off your emotions. Not for me," she said. "I really want to stay, but I want what's best for Emma. And you."

Benjamin's expression turned grim. "So what the hell do you think is *best* for Emma and me?"

Her stomach clenched at the hostility in his voice. She handed him the folder she'd held by her side. "I have found a wonderful replacement. She's probably even better than I am," she admitted reluctantly. "Her name is Susan Littleton and I've put her through numerous interviews and background checks."

"I don't have time for this," he said.

"She's already met Emma, and Emma loves her," Coco said.

"You're determined to do this," he said.

"I think it's best," she said, her heart breaking.

"I didn't think you would quit on us," he said and put his hat on his head. "I'll meet with her tomorrow," he said and walked out the front door.

The next day, the shoes Coco had left in Chantaine arrived with a note from Bridget. *I can't believe you left*

*without saying goodbye. I can't believe you left without
your Cinderella shoes. Yours truly, Bridget.*

Coco could almost believe Bridget was sincere. She
could almost believe Bridget cared about her.

That would be a mistake, wouldn't it? She looked at
the shoes and remembered dancing with Benjamin at
the palace. Her heart twisted at the memory. She took
the shoes to Emma's room and put them in the baby's
closet. Maybe when she was older, she could use them
when she played dress-up. It tore at her to know she
would miss the precious milestones of Emma's growth.

After his own background investigation and interview, Benjamin reluctantly approved Susan Littleton.
He was angry and upset that Coco was abandoning
him. He'd grown to care for her, and God knew Emma
adored her. He would have been far more terrified about
Coco leaving if he hadn't observed Susan and Emma.
He also knew, however, that Coco had been responsible
for bringing Emma to the place that she could accept
another caregiver.

His life was simple and the ranch could be boring for
a woman. He couldn't help wondering if Coco shared
some of his mother's qualities. Maybe she had a little
wanderlust. That would explain her determination to
leave.

Benjamin surrounded his heart and emotions with
barbed wire. That way, no one could wound him. He
helped Coco pack her small car. Reluctantly.

She placed one last box on her passenger seat and turned to face him.

"You're sure you want to do this?" he asked, shoving his hands into his pockets.

She took a deep breath and bit her lip. "I'm sure it's right for you and Emma."

He narrowed his eyes. "Is it that easy for you to leave?"

Her eyes turned dark with emotion. "Not at all. Just the right thing," she said. "Thank you for everything."

She hugged him and he couldn't quite resist embracing her in return. "Yeah," he said. "Don't be a stranger, princess."

She laughed. "That's such a joke," she said and pulled back. "Thank you again, for everything."

Coco got into her car and drove out of his life.

Coco didn't know where she was going. She just wanted to remove all the attention directed at her away from Benjamin and Coco. That was her goal. She should feel a great deal of satisfaction. And she did, she told herself. She really did.

So why did she also feel miserable?

Coco drove to Fort Worth and got a cheap hotel for the night. Although she'd carefully planned her exit, she hadn't planned what she would do next. Coco was at a loss. She considered making a trip to the Gulf Coast. With her car loaded with all her belongings, she wasn't sure that was practical.

When she awakened the next morning to silence and no baby sounds, sadness overwhelmed her. She missed Emma. She missed Benjamin. She glanced out the window at the gray day and fought tears. Trying to pull herself out of her misery, she took a shower then checked her phone. She'd received a voice message from a Valentina Devereaux Logan, telling her to call her back. To say the least, Coco was surprised by the message. During her continental breakfast provided by the hotel, she debated whether she should return the call.

Tossing a coin, she made the decision when tails won the call.

Coco dialed the number, braced for anything.

"Hello, Tina speaking," a woman said, as a child screamed in the background.

The sound of the screaming child somehow immediately put Coco at ease. After caring for Emma, it was such a familiar sound. "This is Coco Jordan."

"Oh, lovely," Tina said. "Pardon me for a moment. My daughter is being a tyrant. Katiana, you may not have cupcakes for breakfast, and if you continue to scream, you'll be sitting in the naughty chair."

Coco couldn't help smiling at Tina's words to her daughter.

"There now, again pardon me," Tina said. "I hear you're leaving your current position due to the paparazzi. You must come and stay with me."

Coco blinked. "Excuse me?"

"Yes, you must come here. After all, everyone, except one of my brothers and I, has met you. That's not at all fair, is it?"

"I wouldn't know," Coco said. "How did you know I'd left my job?"

"Bridget called and talked to the housekeeper. I would have called before, but Stefan was such a bear. Of course, now he thinks you walk on water since you got Eve to slow down a bit."

Coco took a deep breath, trying to stay on track with the conversation. "I really don't need your pity."

"Well, you've got it because I've suffered the paparazzi. But the real reason I want you to come is because I want to meet you. And I want to see your eyes. Bridget tells me you have the Devereaux eyes. But kinder."

"I don't know what to say," Coco said. She hadn't expected this at all.

"You should say, 'Yes, thank you very much. I'll accept your invitation,'" Tina said.

It wasn't as if she had anywhere else to go, Coco thought. "Maybe I could just visit for the day," she said, thinking out loud.

"Or longer," Tina said. "I'll give you the address so you can put it in your GPS, although you may have to call again once you get closer." Tina recited the address.

"If you're sure," Coco said.

"I'm quite sure and I look forward to meeting you," she said.

Coco followed the instructions to the ranch where

Valentina and her family lived. The main house was beautiful and there was a turkey wreath on the front door to add a homey touch. Standing on the front porch as she knocked on the door made her homesick for Benjamin's ranch.

She heard a rush of footsteps. "Katiana, heavens child," a woman said and opened the door. A middle-aged woman with iron-gray hair and a little girl with brown curly hair pulled into pigtails stood in front of Coco.

"You must be Coco Jordan. I'm Hildie and this is Katiana. Come on in. Her Highlyness is on the phone about another one of her charity projects. She's determined to save the world," the woman said as she led Coco inside the house to a den furnished with comfortable-looking furniture and toys on the floor. "She'll be right with you. In the meantime, Katiana, you can pick up your toys and get ready for lunch."

"But I'm still playin'," the little girl said.

"I'll help," Coco offered.

Hildie glanced at her. "Hmm. That's nice of you," she said and left the room.

"What do we have here?" Coco asked Katiana.

The child picked up one of the figurines on the floor. "This is Rose the Fairy Queen. She's the boss of the other fairies."

"I'll bet she's very smart," Coco said. "Where does she take her nap?"

"In the box," Katiana said and stroked the fairy figurine. "But I like to take them with me when I nap sometimes."

"It's probably easier for everyone to get their sleep if they go in the box. Is this a pony fairy?" she asked, picking up a horse figurine.

Katiana nodded and began to tell a story about how the pony likes to take everyone for a ride. Coco couldn't help wondering if Emma would play with fairy dolls and make up stories about them. Within a few moments, and a few extra stories, the two of them got all the toys put away in the box.

A young woman with wavy brown hair and dressed in casual clothes entered the room. "Oh, no. Have we already put you to work?" she asked. "I'm Tina."

Coco stood, wondering for a moment if she should curtsey.

"Don't you dare curtsey," Tina said as if she'd read her mind and moved toward her, extending both her hands. "It was so lovely of you to come, Coco. And Bridget and Phillipa were right. Devereaux eyes, but so kind. You've met my daughter, Katiana," Tina said.

"Yes, she told me all about her flower fairies," Coco said. "She's so verbal."

Tina ruffled her daughter's hair. "Yes, a blessing or a curse depending on the moment. Miss Hildie is going to give you lunch while Coco and I have a chat."

"I want to chat, too," Katiana said.

"Later, if you take a good nap. Run along," she said and dropped a kiss on her daughter's cheek. "Please have a seat. Would you like something to drink? Tea, coffee, apple cider?"

"Apple cider would be great," she said and Hildie delivered mugs to each of them within moments.

"Now, I've heard a bit about you. You lost both parents and your mother was ill for some time. Please accept my condolences," Tina said, covering Coco's hand with her own. "I'm also terribly sorry you felt you needed to quit your job. And weren't you engaged to the ranch owner?"

Coco felt her cheeks heat. "It was more of an arrangement than a real engagement. He just offered to pretend in order to protect me from the crazy offers I was receiving. I thought it would all die down, but I couldn't take Emma for a stroll in the park without being hounded by the paparazzi. Emma had been through so much with losing her mother and coming to live with her father, and they didn't get along very well in the beginning at all."

"He didn't like the baby?" Tina asked, clearly appalled.

"Oh, no, he loved her. She was terrified of him, screamed every time he came around. But that's all better now. She even said *Da-da* the other day," Coco said. Then she took a breath. "But the paparazzi were causing too much of a burden on the whole household. It just didn't seem right to me that Benjamin would assign one of his men as a guard."

"So you quit because of the press?" Tina asked.

"Mostly. There was also some confusion over pretending to be engaged, and I didn't want to get into that kind of situation with my employer. Especially since I lived in his house, and—" She broke off. "I'm sorry. I'm rambling."

"Not at all," Tina said. "It must have been hard to leave the baby."

Coco felt tears sting her eyes and her heart swell with a knot of emotion. Tina was so kind and seemed so genuine that Coco felt as if she could be herself with the woman. "Terribly. The only consolation I have is that I found a wonderful nanny. She'll probably be better than I was," she said.

"Oh, I doubt that. So what are your plans?"

"I don't know. Get a job. I've thought about finishing my education. I only had a year and a half left when my mother got so ill," she said. "I couldn't imagine going back right away. There was so much that had to be done afterward."

"Of course you couldn't. But maybe you're a bit more ready. Hildie's very big on education. She always says that once you have your degree, no one can take it away from you," Tina said.

"Hildie sounds like a smart woman," Coco said.

"She's a treasure. I can't imagine our lives without her. As soon as I put down Katiana, you and I can have lunch. Chicken noodle soup. Would you like to freshen up? I can ask one of the ranch hands to bring in your luggage."

"Oh, no, that won't be necessary," Coco said, although the thought was tempting. Tina seemed to infuse the house with warmth and comfort.

"Well, you must stay at least one night because I've already promised Katiana you'll be around this afternoon. We can't have you driving around these country roads in the dark."

Coco stayed for lunch and dinner and met Zachary Logan, Tina's husband, who looked at his wife and daughter with such adoring eyes that it made Coco's heart hurt. She wondered if a man would ever look at her the same way. Coco knew she should have left when she did, because she had begun to wish that Benjamin would make their engagement real, and that had been a very dangerous wish. Being at the Logan ranch soothed her at the same time it reminded her of what she'd left behind.

Two days later, Coco felt she had accepted as much of Tina's hospitality as she should. She headed toward Fort Worth to apply for jobs and, if she was lucky, entrance into a university to complete her degree.

Chapter Twelve

Two and a half weeks later, Benjamin sat in his office and stared into a glass of whiskey. A knock sounded at the door. It was nearly 8:00 p.m. He knew it was Sarah. He opened the door and there she stood with a tray in her hands bearing a sandwich and soup. "Hi, Sarah. Thanks."

"You haven't been eating well," she said with a disapproving glance. "And you're drinking too much, too."

"Sarah," he said in a warning voice as he returned to his chair.

"Well, you are. It's not healthy. You're upset. It's not good for the baby," she said.

"What do you mean it's not good for Emma? She's fine. Susan is doing a great job."

"How much time have you been spending with your daughter?" Sarah demanded.

Benjamin hung his head. He'd buried himself in his work ever since Coco had left.

"You should go after that woman and make her come back," Sarah said. "Coco was the best thing that's happened to this house in a long time."

"You didn't feel that way when the phone was ringing off the hook with calls for her," he said, looking up at her.

Sarah waved her hand. "A minor annoyance."

"She's the one who left. She was determined to go," he said, plunging his spoon into his soup. He lifted it to his mouth and scalded his tongue. "Damn."

"That's what you get for not doing the right thing. If you hadn't let her get away, you wouldn't be in this situation," Sarah said, crossing her arms over her chest.

"How was I supposed to keep her when she wanted to leave?" he asked.

"Maybe you could have told her you had feelings for her," Sarah said.

"I never said that," he said, stirring his soup.

"Well, maybe you should have," she retorted. "You were engaged to her. Or at least you said you were."

Benjamin frowned at his housekeeper's razor-sharp instincts. She clearly thought there'd been something fishy about the engagement. "How do you know she wasn't getting bored? Maybe she has signed up for one

of those reality TV shows or is taking all those interviews that she was offered," he said.

"She's in Fort Worth working as a waitress trying to
go back to school in January," Sarah scoffed.

He stared at her. "How do you know that?"

"I have my ways," she said. "You messed up," she
said, wagging her finger at him. "It's up to you to fix it."

He gave her his best scowl, but she was unmoved.
"I have work to do," he said and looked at his laptop.

"Yes, you do. In more ways than one," she said and
left the room.

Benjamin stared after her, then rose to close the door.
There were definite downsides to having long-time employees. A. They thought they knew you better than they
should know you. B. They thought they had the right to
speak their mind.

Benjamin snarled and returned to his desk. He took
bites of his sandwich and spoonfuls of soup. Thank
goodness, the soup had cooled. Excel files faded before his eyes. Images of Coco stood front and center.
He saw her smiling and laughing, kissing him. He saw
her kissing Emma's head as she rocked her to sleep. He
saw her falling for him.

Benjamin plunged his head into his hands. What
could he do? What *should* he do?

Two days before Thanksgiving, Coco hustled to de-
liver blueberry pancakes at a Fort Worth café. After an
afternoon break, she would serve T-bones at a popular

steakhouse. If she was lucky, she would be able to get a loan for her first semester at a state-supported school within a couple weeks.

She automatically delivered water and coffee to two tables, took orders and placed them. After delivering orders to another table and picking up ketchup, hot sauce and extra butter, she grabbed a cup of water for the table in the back. "Would you like coffee?" she asked, her pitcher poised above the customer's cup.

"Always," he said. His voice was too familiar. She'd heard it in her dreams. She glanced up and stared into the dark-eyed gaze of Benjamin Garner.

"Hi," she managed, her heart racing in an irregular beat. "What are you doing here?"

"Needed some breakfast," he said and glanced at the menu.

"Oh," she said and pulled out her pad. "What would you like?"

"What's good?"

"Most everything," she said. "Blueberry and pecan pancakes are popular, along with the meat-eaters omelet."

He nodded. "You like this job better than taking care of Emma?" he asked.

Her heart fell and so did her cheery facade, but she quickly pulled it back in place. "Not really, but I needed to go." She took a deep breath to calm herself and lifted her pencil to her pad. "What do you want?"

"Eggs, bacon and pecan pancakes," he said.

"Can do," she said and turned away. Her heart was tripping over itself. She just prayed she wouldn't trip over her own feet. She'd never expected Benjamin to show up here, but then, she'd never expected to see him again in her life. Coco resisted the urge to rush to the bathroom and fix her hair or put on some lipstick. She knew what she looked like, and it wasn't at all glamorous.

Forcing herself to focus, she delivered orders to other tables and when Benjamin's order was ready, she placed it on his table, along with extra butter, syrup and orange juice.

"I didn't order orange juice," he said.

"It comes with the pancakes. Can I get you anything else?" she asked.

"Yes, you can," he said, locking his gaze with hers. "You can come back to the ranch with me."

She almost dropped her carafe of coffee, but clenched her fist. "I—um—I can't do that."

He rose to his feet. "Why not?"

She sucked in a deep breath. "It just wouldn't work. I started to feel too much—" She broke off. "Want too—" She shook her head, not wanting to reveal how deep her feelings for him were.

"You started to want me. You started to love me," Benjamin said.

She closed her eyes, trying to keep herself under control. "Don't be cruel," she whispered.

"I'm not being cruel," he said. "I started loving you, too."

Coco opened her eyes and gaped at Benjamin. The carafe dropped from her hand. She stared at the coffee spilling on the floor. "Darn."

"It's just coffee," Benjamin said and pulled her into his arms. "I love you. I want you in my life forever. I want you to marry me."

Coco met his gaze and felt her knees weaken. "Marry you?"

"Yeah," he said. "I know I can be a pain in the butt, but being with you makes me happier than I ever thought I could be. I've been a miserable fool since you left."

Coco bit her lip, feeling overwhelmed with emotion. "But I thought you weren't ready. I thought you didn't want to make a commitment," she said and he covered her lips with his fingers.

"I was wrong," he said. "Don't expect me to say that a lot," he told her. "But you took me by surprise. I didn't expect you to get under my skin, but I'm glad you did. I want you under my skin and in my life forever. Starting now. Marry me," he said and pulled a box from his pocket. "This time, for real," he said, and flipped open the box to reveal a diamond ring.

Gasping, Coco couldn't fight the tears burning her eyes. She looked into the gaze of the man who was everything she'd ever hoped for. "Yes," she said. "I love you."

"And I love you," he said.

* * *

A month later, just before Christmas, she and Benjamin, along with the new nanny, and Sarah, traveled to Chantaine. Bridget had insisted that Coco and Benjamin get married in Chantaine. At first, they had protested, but then they had both seen the wisdom of combining their wedding with a honeymoon. Coco had also realized that the Devereaux were far more welcoming to her than she had previously thought.

Eve, in full bloom of pregnancy, and Pippa, with her baby bump, fussed at her dress.

"It's beautiful," Eve said of Coco's shoulder-grazing lace dress. "And I'm not the prissy type."

"Neither am I," Pippa said. "And I love it, too. Benjamin's a lucky guy."

"Damn lucky," Bridget said, entering the room in five-inch heels. "The nannies are taking care of our lovely demons, so we should get this show on the road, as you Americans say."

Soon after, Valentina and Katiana entered the room above the chapel where Coco and Benjamin would soon be married. Tina moved toward Coco and embraced her. "You look gorgeous."

"Like a princess flower fairy," Katiana said.

Coco bent down to kiss Tina's daughter. "You are so sweet."

"Time to move out, everyone," Bridget said, clapping her hands as she toddled in her Christian Louboutin heels. "Can't keep the groom waiting forever."

Each of the Devereaux women kissed her on the cheek before they left. Bridget lingered behind. "You're a wonderful addition to our family," she said. "We're so lucky to have you."

Tears wells in Coco's eyes. "I'm the lucky one."

"We would all argue that, but not now," Bridget said and gently pressed a handkerchief underneath Coco's eyes. "Are you okay?"

"Yes, it's just been a journey. Less than a year ago, my mother died of cancer, penniless, then I became a nanny. After that, I went back to waitressing. Now I'm getting married to a man I was afraid to dream of. It's been a crazy year."

"And it's only going to get better," Bridget said with a mysterious glint in her eyes.

Coco wrinkled her brow. "What do you mean?"

"You'll see soon enough," she said. "Do you need anything else?"

"Just a little help getting down the stairs," Coco said.

Bridget opened the door and the wedding assistant appeared. "I am at your service, miss."

The assistant guided her down the stairs and Coco waited in the foyer for her cue to enter the chapel. Her stomach danced with nerves as the doors were thrown open and she walked, by herself, down the aisle.

Benjamin stood, in his Western tux, waiting for her at the front of the church. The other guests disappeared before her eyes. At this moment, Benjamin was her everything, and he held her gaze every step of the way down the aisle.

Coco finally arrived by his side and he took her hands and kissed her. "You're safe with me," he whispered. "You'll always be safe with me."

He couldn't have said anything that moved her more. He couldn't have said anything that made her feel she'd finally found home. With him.

The minister called the service to order.

Benjamin recited his vows. Coco made hers, and they were pronounced man and wife. The small group in the chapel applauded in approval, and Benjamin took her mouth in a kiss that sealed their promises for a lifetime. Coco swooned. Oh, how could that happen to a modern-day nonprincess?

After the ceremony, there was a private reception in a palace ballroom. Stefan took the stage. "We have the unusual joy of sharing the marriage of our father's daughter, Coco Jordan, to Benjamin Garner. In this unusual and blessed situation, the Devereaux family wishes to convey a special, honorary title to Coco. She has already contributed in a unique way to our family. That said, Coco Jordan is now Honorary Princess of Chantaine," he said and dipped his head. "Bless you and yours and forever."

Coco looked at Benjamin. "Did he just say what I thought he said?" she asked.

He chuckled and nodded. "He did."

"So I'm a princess?"

"You always were royalty in my eyes," he joked, his gaze holding hers.

She laughed and shook her head. "I didn't need to be a princess. I just needed to belong to you."

He took her mouth in a kiss. "Looks like I'll have to hire an extra guy to protect my princess. No worries, darlin'. You're worth every penny."

Coco sank into him. "I'm the luckiest girl in the universe."

"Just one more thing," Bridget said, interrupting their kiss as she led a tall man toward her. "Eve helped. We did something similar for her."

Coco pulled back, studying Bridget and the tall man. Something about him seemed familiar. She stared at him and noticed that his eyes mirrored hers in color. Her heart reverberated in recognition.

"You're my brother, aren't you?" she asked.

"Yes. And you're my sister," he replied. "Maxwell Carter at your service, Your Highness," he said with a wry grin.

She laughed out loud. "Yes, just as you are a prince. Your Highness."

"Not me," he said with a shake of his head. "I wish I'd known you before."

A wisp of loss swept through her. "You know me now, and I'll be your pain-in-the-butt sister the rest of your life."

He gave a crooked grin. "Why do I feel like I suddenly won the genetic lottery?" Max asked.

"Because you did. In every way," Benjamin said and turned to his bride. "Just tell me you don't expect me to bow to you now."

"Only at certain moments," she said and laughed.

Benjamin took her mouth again, and Coco knew she had finally found home with the man of her heart and her dreams.

* * * * *

THE RANCHER'S HOUSEKEEPER

REBECCA WINTERS

Rebecca Winters, whose family of four children has now swelled to include five beautiful grandchildren, lives in Salt Lake City, Utah, in the land of the Rocky Mountains. With canyons and high alpine meadows full of wildflowers, she never runs out of places to explore. They, plus her favourite holiday spots in Europe, often end up as backgrounds for her romance novels, because writing is her passion, along with her family and church.

Rebecca loves to hear from readers.
If you wish to email her, please visit her website, www.cleanromances.com.

CHAPTER ONE

COLT Brannigan kissed his mother on the cheek. "I'll see you tonight." He turned to her caregiver. "I'm working with the nursing service in Sundance. They'll be sending someone out in the next few days to start helping you with Mom's care."

"I'll be fine. Hank's been able to give me some free time."

"That's good. See you tonight, Ina."

Colt's sixty-year-old mother didn't know anyone. She'd been diagnosed with Alzheimer's before his father's death sixteen months ago. It had grown much worse over the past year. She needed round-the-clock care.

"Hey, Colt?"

At the sound of his brother Hank's voice, Colt shut the bedroom door and strode down the hallway of the ranch house's main floor toward him.

"What's up?"

"Phone call for you from Warden James's office."

Warden James? "Must be a wrong number," he said, knowing full well it wasn't. He walked past his brother and headed for the back door, not needing another delay when he should be in the upper pasture.

Hank followed him at a slower pace due to his walking cast. "You *did* advertise for a housekeeper in the *Black Hills Sentinel*. They want to know if you've already filled the position."

Colt realized he should have indicated in the ad that they were looking for a female housekeeper. His mother would insist on it *if* she could express herself, but that time would never come again. "Tell them it's too late."

"But—"

"No buts!" He cut his brother off with a grimace. Before their father had passed away from blood clots in the lungs, he'd obliged the warden by granting him a favor, one he'd lived to regret.

The freed inmate had been taken on as a ranch hand on a provisional basis. He'd stayed only long enough for a few meals and a paycheck before he took off with the blanket from his bunk and some of the other hands' cash. To add injury to insult, he'd stolen one of the ranch's quarter horses.

Colt had tracked him down and recovered the stolen property. The ex-felon was once again behind bars. Unfortunately the percentage of freed inmates who ended up back in prison was high. Now that Colt ran the Floral Valley Ranch, he'd be damned if he would make the mistake his father had and invest any more time or money on an ex-con.

"I'll be checking fences all day. Won't be home until late. Call if there's an emergency." He jumped off the back porch and headed for the barn. After swinging into the saddle, he galloped away on Digger.

It took the right kind of female to run a household like theirs and manage the domestic help. In fact it took a *saint*, but those were in short supply since their previous housekeeper, Mary White Bird, had died. Colt realized their family could never replace her. The full-blooded Lakota had been their mother's right hand and an institution on the ranch.

He'd advertised in various newspapers throughout Wyoming and South Dakota, but so far none of the applicants had the qualifications he was looking for. Forget a released felon. Colt was getting desperate, but not *that* desperate.

Floral Valley Ranch 4 miles.

Geena Williams rode past the small highway sign and had to turn around. Eight miles back an old rancher at the Cattlemen's Stock and Feed Store in Sundance, Wyoming, had told her she might miss the turnoff if she weren't looking for it. He'd been right. From here on out it would be dirt road.

She stopped long enough to catch her breath and take a drink from her water bottle. During the day the temperature had been sixty-nine degrees, with some wind in the afternoon, typical for early June in northeastern Wyoming. But now it had dropped into the fifties and would go lower. Her second-hand parka provided little insulation.

Though the weather had cooperated, it was sheer will and adrenaline that had gotten her this far. Now desperation would have to get her the rest of the way. Her legs would probably turn to rubber before she reached her destination, but Geena couldn't quit now. She needed to make it to the ranch before it was too dark to see.

A half hour later she caught sight of a cluster of outbuildings, including the ranch house, but it was ten to ten and she didn't dare approach anyone this late.

She pedaled her road bike over to a stand of pines and propped it against one of the trunks.

Her backpack contained everything in the world she owned. No. That wasn't exactly true. There were some other items precious to her, but she had no idea where they were. Not yet anyway.

She undid the straps to eat some snacks. They tasted good. After she'd pulled out her space blanket, she more or less collapsed from exhaustion onto a soft nest of needles beneath the boughs of the biggest tree.

Using her pack for a pillow, she curled on her right side and covered up, still in shock that tonight the only roof she had over her head was a canopy of stars. She picked out the Big Dipper. Venus was the bright star to the west.

Heaven.

"Come on, Titus. Time to go home."

Colt shut the barn door. The border collie raced ahead of him with more energy than he knew what to do with. Titus led a dog's perfect life. He was loved. He ran and worked all day, ate the food he wanted and had no worries. That's why he went to sleep deliriously happy and woke up happy.

As for Colt, he wouldn't describe himself happy in the delirious sense. He'd been in that state only one time. Falling in love at twenty-one had been easy when you'd been on the steer-wrestling circuit, winning prize money and dazzling your girl.

It was the happily-ever-after part he didn't have time to work on before she wanted out because a married man had ranching duties and she wasn't having fun anymore. Their eleven-month marriage had to have been some kind of record for the shortest one in Crook County, Wyoming.

At thirty-four years of age now, he recognized his mistake. They'd been too young and immature. It simply didn't work. Since then he'd dated women from time to time, but unless he met one who enriched the busy life he already led, he didn't see himself in a rush to get married again.

Suddenly the dog switched directions away from the ranch house, barking his head off. He hadn't gone far when he made that low growling sound that let Colt know they had an intruder on the property. Whether animal or human he couldn't tell yet.

As he hurried to catch up, he heard a woman's voice say, "Easy, boy," trying her best to soothe the black-and-white beast who'd hunted her down. He weighed only forty-five pounds, but in the dark his terrifying growl had clearly made her nervous.

Closer now, Colt could see why. The female on her feet beneath their granddaddy's ponderosa was wrapped in a space blanket that covered her head. She probably couldn't see anything. Enveloped like that, she presented a tall silhouette to Titus who couldn't quite make her out. Any mystery caused the dog to bark with much more excitement.

Against the trunk Colt glimpsed a brand-new road bike. Next to her feet he saw a backpack. "Quiet, Titus," he commanded the dog, who made a keening sound for having to obey and walked over to Colt.

If she was a nature lover, she was going about it the wrong way. "Are you all right, ma'am?"

"Y-yes," she stammered. "Thank you for calling him off. He startled me." She had an appealing voice. The fact that she didn't sound hysterical came as another surprise.

"What in the devil do you think you're doing sleeping out here in the dark?" The women of his acquaintance wouldn't have dreamed of doing anything so foolhardy. "Any animal could bother you, especially a mountain lion on the prowl."

She pulled the edges of the blanket tighter. The motion revealed her face. "I got here too late to disturb anyone, so I thought I'd rest under the tree."

"You came to this ranch specifically?"

"Yes, but I realize I'm trespassing. I'm sorry."

Her apology sounded genuine and she spoke in a cultured voice. What in blazes? He was taken aback by the whole situation. After a glimpse into hauntingly lovely eyes that gave him no answers, he took in a quick breath before picking up her backpack. It was unexpectedly light and had seen better days.

"For whatever reason you've come, I can't allow you to stay out here. Leave the bike and follow me. It'll be safe where it is."

"I don't want to intrude."

She'd already done a good job of it and had gotten his attention in a big way, but that was beside the point. "Nevertheless, you'll have to come with me. Let's go."

The three of them made an odd trio as they entered the back door of the house. He showed her through the mudroom, past the bathroom to the kitchen. Titus headed for his bowls of food and water. After that he would go to his bed in the den. Colt's father had been gone a long time, but Colt had a hunch the loyal dog was still waiting for his return. Maybe Titus wasn't that happy after all.

Colt put the woman's backpack by one of the kitchen chairs. Out of the corner of his eye he watched her remove the space blanket. She *was* tall, probably five foot nine. He'd thought it might be the blanket above her head that had added the inches. After folding it, she laid it on the oblong wood table, then took off her insubstantial parka. He imagined she was in her mid-twenties.

Except for white sneakers, everything she wore, from her jeans to her long-sleeved navy crew neck, looked well-worn and hung off her. The clothes must have originally been bought for a larger woman. Her brunette hair had been pulled back with an elastic in an uninspiring ponytail. No makeup, no jewelry.

He thought he might have seen her before and tried to imagine her features and figure with a little more flesh on her. Had she been ill? In profile or frontal view, her mouth looked too drawn, the hollows in her cheeks too pronounced, but the fact still remained he felt an unwanted attraction.

Two physical characteristics about her were remarkable. Great bone structure and eyes of inky blue. They looked disturbingly sad as they peered at him through lashes as dark as her brows and hair. Why sad, he couldn't begin to imagine.

If she'd been running away from a traumatic situation, she bore no bruises or wounds he could see. She stood there proud and unafraid, reminding him of an unfinished painting that needed more work before she came to full life. That in itself added an intriguing element.

"You're welcome to use the bathroom we just passed."

"Thank you. I'll do that. Please excuse me."

After she disappeared, he walked over to the counter, bemused by her femininity. She'd been endowed with more of it than most women.

Hank had made a fresh pot of coffee and had probably gone to their mother's bedroom to sit with her for a while. As Colt reached for a couple of mugs from the shelf, his intruder returned. He told her to sit down. "I can offer coffee. Would you like some, or does tea sound better?"

"Coffee, please."

Colt poured two cups. "Sugar? Cream?" he called over his shoulder.

"Please don't go to any trouble. Black is fine."

He doctored both and brought them to the table where she'd sat down at the end. "I laced yours anyway. You look like you could use a pick-me-up."

"You're right. Thank you, Mr...."

"Colt Brannigan." He drank some of his coffee.

She cradled the cup. With her eyes closed, she took several sips, almost as if she were making a memory. This puzzled him. He stood looking down at her until she'd finished it. In his opinion she needed a good square meal three times a day for the foreseeable future.

"How about telling me who you are."

Her eyelids fluttered open, still heavy from fatigue. "Geena Williams." This time he thought he remembered that name from somewhere, too. Eventually it would come to him.

"Well, Geena—perhaps if I made you a ham sandwich, more information might be forthcoming about where you've come from and why you showed up on our property."

"Please forgive me. I'm still trying to wake up." He'd never heard anyone sound more apologetic. She got to her feet. "I was just freed from the women's prison in Pierre, South Dakota, today and came all the way to your ranch. I'd hoped to interview for the live-in house-keeper position for a temporary period of time, but it took longer for me to get here than I'd supposed."

With those words, Colt felt as if he'd just been kicked in the gut by a wild mustang. In an instant everything about her made sense, starting with the call from the prison warden this morning. He must have believed she was trustworthy, yet the new bike propped beneath the tree didn't match her used clothing. Had she stolen it?

She's an ex-felon. With the realization came an in-explicable sense of disappointment.

"Is the position still open?" The hope in that question, as if his answer meant life and death to her, almost got to him.

He had to harden himself against it. "I'm afraid not."

All people had baggage, but anyone who spent time in prison carried a different kind. Colt was looking for a housekeeper who was like Mary White Bird. A wise woman who'd raised a family of her own, a woman who'd helped his mom run the affairs of the ranch house since he was a boy without being obtrusive. She'd had an instinct for handling the staff and guests, not to mention the hothead personalities within the immediate and extended Brannigan clan.

As for Geena Williams, she was too young. She'd done time. He had no idea what crime she'd commit-ted, but he knew she could use counseling to rejoin the world outside prison walls. Who knew the battles going on inside her? Hiring her was out of the question.

Her eyes glazed, yet not one tear spilled from those dark lashes. "You've been very kind to me, but I realize I've made a big mistake in coming here without arranging for an appointment first."

He frowned. "As it happens, Warden James called here this morning hoping to make one for you. I asked my brother to tell him it had already been filled. It appears the two of you had a miscommunication. For your sake, I'm sorry the warden didn't say anything to you."

A look of confusion marred her features. "Warden James is a woman, but I didn't know she'd called you. After I was taken to her office yesterday morning, she informed me I'd be freed this morning. I guess she was trying to help me find work so I would have some place to stay.

"As soon as I could go to the prisoners' lounge last evening, I scanned the classified section of the *Rapid City Journal* looking for work and saw your ad. I noticed it had been listed a while ago and feared it might have already been filled, but I decided to take a chance anyway and came straight here."

Colt was astounded by everything she'd told him. His brother had said the warden had seen the ad in the *Black Hills Sentinel*. Even if this woman were telling the truth, it didn't matter. There was no job on the ranch available to her or any other inmate, but he was consumed by curiosity. Shifting his weight he asked, "Don't you have a spouse or a boyfriend who could help you?"

"I've never been married. One fellow I was dating before my imprisonment never came near or tried to reach me."

Colt surmised their relationship couldn't have been that solid in the first place. "You don't have relatives who could help you?"

A shadow darkened her features. "None."

None?

He raked his hair in bewilderment, unable to imagine it before he realized she could be lying about it. Maybe she was ashamed to go home. Colt hadn't been in her shoes, so it wasn't fair to judge.

"How did you know where to come?" The ad indicated only that the ranch was near Sundance, Wyoming. Twelve miles, in fact. He'd only listed a box number.

"I realize I was supposed to respond with an email, but I didn't have access to a computer. By the time the bus dropped me off this afternoon in Sundance where I'd decided to start looking for work, I figured that if someone knew where you lived, I'd just come straight here.

"So after I bought my bike at the shop, I rode over to the Cattlemen's Stock and Feed Store. Everyone working there said they knew Colt Brannigan, the head of the Floral Valley Ranch. The owner sang your praises for taking over after your father died and making it even more successful. Then this older rancher who was just leaving was kind enough to tell me where to find the turnoff for your ranch."

Colt was dumbfounded by her explanation and her resourcefulness, especially the fact that she'd bought a bike. He could always call there to verify she'd actually made the purchase. "You rode all the way here on the highway at night?"

"Yes, but it wasn't dark then. I need transportation to get around. Since I don't have a driver's license yet, I can't buy a junker car."

"Isn't a new bike expensive?"

"Yes, but the bike at the shop in Sundance was on sale for $530.00. They threw in the used helmet for ten dollars. I would have bought all new clothes, but after that I only had $160 left of the money I withdrew from my prison savings account. I spent some of it on food, the space blanket and my shoes."

He blinked. "You earned the money in prison, I presume."

"Yes. They pay twenty-five cents an hour. That resulted in forty dollars a month for the thirteen months I was incarcerated."

Thirteen months in hell. What crime had she committed?

Colt ran his thumb along his lower lip. "So you came out of there with $520.00?"

"Seven hundred actually. I worked some extra shifts and they also give you fifty dollars when you leave."

He would never again begrudge his taxpayer dollars going to an ex-felon who'd paid her debt to society and had been freed from prison. "So how much money do you have on you now to live on?"

"Ninety-two dollars. That's why I need a job so desperately. I'm a good cook. In prison I did every job from helping in the kitchen and cleaning to laundry and warehouse work, to hospital and dispensary duty and prison-ground cleanup. I'm a hard worker, Mr. Brannigan. If you called the prison, they'd tell you I put in forty-plus hours every week with no infractions. Do you know of anyone in this area who might be looking for help?"

Anyone?

She was looking at someone who needed a housekeeper and an additional caregiver for his mother as soon as yesterday!

He rubbed the back of his neck, pondering his shock that he would even consider the possibility of her working for him when he knew next to nothing about her except the worst. Though she was definitely a survivor, the culprit tugging at him was the vulnerability in those intense dark blue eyes.

Before he could formulate his thoughts, let alone give any kind of answer, Titus came flying through the kitchen to greet Hank, who'd just walked in the back door with Mandy. Their presence surprised Colt because he'd thought Hank was with their mother.

Colt had been so deep in conversation, he hadn't heard Mandy's car. Since Hank had broken his leg, she'd been the one chauffeuring him around.

She smiled. "Hey, Colt—"

"Hey yourself, Mandy." She was a cute smart blonde from Sundance who'd known Hank since high school, but as usual he had eyes for someone else. This time they'd ignited with interest after swerving to the very female stranger standing in the kitchen.

Taking the initiative, Colt said, "Geena Williams? This is my brother Hank and his friend Mandy Clark."

Everyone said hello and shook hands. Hank could see the backpack and space blanket. He was dying to ask questions, but Colt wasn't ready to answer them and said nothing to satisfy his brother's burning curiosity.

"We'll be in the family room," Hank eventually muttered before they disappeared with Titus at their heels.

Geena reached for her parka and put it on. "I know I'm intruding. If you wouldn't mind me sleeping in the back of one of those trucks parked outside, I'll be gone first thing in the morning."

Colt had already come to one decision. Ignoring her comment he said, "You've had a long day. Take the coat off, Geena. I'm going to fix you a sandwich and some soup before you go to bed in the guest room. Tomorrow will take care of itself."

He'd heard that saying all his life and wasn't exactly sure what it meant. However, he didn't want to do any more thinking tonight. What he ought to do was drive her into town and fix her up at a hotel, but he was bushed. At least that was the excuse he was telling himself for keeping her here. She could sleep in Mary's former quarters down the other hallway.

Geena had done a lot of dreaming in prison. It had been the only way to escape the bars confining her. But not even her imagination could have conjured the living reality of Colt Brannigan.

She didn't know such a man existed outside her fantasies. By the way the men at the Cattlemen's Store had described him, she'd thought he must have been older to be a legend already. But Geena estimated he was in his mid-thirties. There was no sign or mention of a wife.

When she'd first seen him beneath the kitchen light, the intelligence in those hazel eyes examining her came close to taking the last breath out of her. She stared back in disbelief at the ruggedly gorgeous male who was without question in total charge of his world. Tall, dark and handsome was a cliché women had used for years, but in her mind *he* could have been the one who'd inspired the words.

Yet, putting all of those qualities and attributes aside, it was his kindness to her that made him unique and set him above other men. Instead of throwing her off his property, he'd brought her inside and fed her, given her a beautiful room and bed to sleep in, even after she'd told him she'd just gotten out of prison.

In a daze over everything that had happened, Geena emerged from the bathroom wearing a clean bathrobe she'd found hanging on the back of the door. Smelling sweet and squeaky clean, she turned out the lights and padded over to the queen-sized bed. She'd taken a bath *and* a shower, luxuriating in the products he'd provided for her to use.

All day and evening she'd been doing things unassociated with prison for the first time in over a year. The taste of freedom was indescribable. No more feeling of doom. No more fear that every second of your life from now on would be lived in constant purgatory. No more prison smells, no more sounds during the night of other prisoners being sick, coughing, sobbing, raging or fighting with other inmates through the walls.

No more claustrophobic gray cell, no more clank of prison bars or guards telling you when, where and how you would live, how you would talk and answer. No more living in a enclave with women who wanted nothing to do with each other, who lived to be on the outside with a man again. If any of them could see Mr. Brannigan...

While she sat on the side of the bed to finish drying her hair with a fluffy yellow towel, she looked out the tall picture window. It took up close to a whole wall of the spacious bedroom with its cross-beamed ceiling. She'd purposely left the curtains open so she could see the full moon casting its light across the foot of the hand-carved wood bed.

The room was filled with Sioux artifacts; rugs of the Lakota tribe covered the hardwood floor. On one wall hung a Sioux tapestry in predominantly red colors. Over the bed was an authentic beaded Sioux tobacco bag.

After her host had accompanied her to the room and left, she'd walked over to study the dozen framed photographs placed on the dresser. They featured a short Lakota woman. In some she was alone, in others she stood surrounded by her native family, all of whom were in ceremonial dress. Whoever she was she held a place of great honor in this wonderful ranch house. Though modernized in parts, it had to have been built at least a hundred and fifty years ago.

When her hair was dry enough, Geena formed it into a braid that fell over one shoulder. Her last act was to set the clock-radio alarm for four in the morning. Then she was finally able to lie down on two comfy pillows and relax.

Mr. Brannigan had gone out of his way to feed her and make her comfortable for the night. Geena couldn't help but think of the man who'd been rescued by the Good Samaritan. His gratitude couldn't have been any greater than hers for Mr. Brannigan's goodness. As soon as she could, she would repay him.

For now her first priority was to get some sleep before she slipped out of the house at first light and pedaled back to Sundance. She'd wanted the housekeeper job here, but since that wasn't possible, she'd take any job that would give her a roof over her head. If nothing turned up in Sundance, she'd double back to Spearfish, South Dakota, and look there.

One way or the other she had to stay close to Rapid City, the place where she needed to begin the search for Janice Rigby, the woman who'd once lived with Geena's brother before disappearing. Before he'd died, he'd told Geena that Janice was expecting. If she'd had the baby, it might be Geena's only living relative. She ached for

the family she'd lost. To have a little nephew or niece…
Time was of the essence for Geena to find out.

Geena could probably get her old job back in Rapid
City with FossilMania, but she didn't dare. For the pres-
ent she needed to remain invisible to the people who'd
known her before she'd been arrested. One of them
might see her and alert Janice she was out of prison.
For some strange reason, Janice had never liked Geena.
She didn't want to frighten the other woman off before
Geena could catch up to her.

But she'd worry about all that tomorrow. For what
was left of the rest of the night she'd dream about Colt
Brannigan.

CHAPTER TWO

COLT entered the den and patted Titus's head. "I'm going to keep you company for a while." After closing the door, he moved over to the desk and sat down at the computer. Too wired to sleep right now, he typed the name *Gina Williams* in the search engine. She'd been in prison. There might be something about her from some old newspaper and magazine articles.

Nothing came up but a lot of other females whose profiles were online. He tried a different spelling. More of the same. On a whim he searched for a list of different spellings. Up came Jean, Geenah, Jeenah, Jina, Jeana, Geana, Ginah, Giena, Jiena, Gienah, Geena.

He tried each one. After putting in the last name on the list, he was ready to call it quits for the night when twenty entries popped up. All of them recounted the brutal slaying of Rupert Brown, an eighty-one-year-old widower of Rapid City, South Dakota. The collector of priceless Old West and Indian artifacts had been attacked and slain by *Geena* Williams, twenty-six, the tenant living in the basement apartment of his house.

Colt shot out of the chair, feeling as if he'd been the one stabbed. Geena had committed murder? *That* murder?

He rocked back on his cowboy boots, unable to believe it. While his mind and body were reeling, he grabbed the back of the chair until he could get a grip on his emotions, but adrenaline kept him on his feet.

He remembered hearing about the sensational murder on the evening news. The killer had been a beautiful young single woman. That's why she'd looked familiar to him.

Incredulous, he sank back down in the chair, damned if he read the rest, damned if he didn't. Compelled to finish, he read the entire article. Robbery had been the motive. It had happened soon after Colt's father had died and their family had been in deep mourning, but the story had been all over the media, so he had heard about it at the time.

He groaned loudly enough that Titus moved over and sat by him. Again Colt felt as though he'd been the one repeatedly bludgeoned with the Marshalltown trowel she'd plunged into the old man's chest numerous times.

Colt knew every human had a dark side, but to imagine that the woman sleeping in Mary's room had killed an old man in cold blood seemed beyond the realm of possibility to him.

There was a picture of her after she'd been taken into custody. She'd been fifteen to twenty pounds heavier then with hair to her shoulders. According to one of the reports, she'd been given sixty years. That was as good as a lifetime sentence.

But she'd served only thirteen months of it.... How could she be out on parole this fast? Had there been a mistrial? Some snag that had freed her because the evidence wasn't strong enough to hold her?

There had to be a flaw in Colt that had misread the

purity in her eyes. Geena had seemed like a shiny dime
gleaming pure silver he'd picked up from the ground.
But when he turned it over, he discovered rust had eaten
the silver away.

Her situation reminded him of the freed prisoner his
father had hired. His dad had felt sorry for the younger
man. Everyone makes mistakes, Colt. This man deserves a second chance.

But the second chance had turned into an opportunity for the ex-felon to take advantage and rob his father.

Colt's instincts had been right not to hire this woman,
but he wanted an explanation for Geena's release and
he wanted it now!

Grabbing his phone, he called South Dakota information for the women's prison in Pierre. In a minute he
was put through to the prison's voice mail. There was a
menu. He pressed the digit for an emergency.

When a voice answered he said, "This is Colt
Brannigan from the Floral Valley Ranch in Wyoming.
I have to speak to Warden James tonight. She called
me earlier today. I wasn't able to return it until now.
This is urgent."

"Hold the line please."

"Thank you."

The blood was still surging through his veins when
he heard a sound on the other end. "Mr. Brannigan?
This is Warden James."

"I appreciate your coming to the phone. I know it's
late, but this call is about one of the inmates, Geena
Williams. She came to my ranch tonight looking for
work, but she said she didn't talk to you about it."

"That's true. She must have seen your ad in the
prison newspaper. When she left our facility this morn-

ing, she indicated she'd go to a women's shelter for the night."

"Why was she released when she's supposed to be serving a sixty-year sentence for murder?" Whatever answer she gave him wouldn't help, but he still had to know.

"She didn't tell you?"

Colt took a shuddering breath. "Tell me what?" he bit out.

"Yesterday morning I got word from the governor of South Dakota that Ms. Williams had been wrongfully imprisoned and the real killer has been caught."

"What?"

For the second time since coming in the den, Colt was on his feet, but for an entirely different reason. With the warden's explanation, he felt as though he'd just been freed from his own hellish prison after reading the hideous details on the Internet.

He hadn't been wrong about Geena. After what she'd been through, no wonder he saw that vulnerable look in her eyes.

"Ms Williams has been fully exonerated. She was given her certificate."

"Certificate?" he muttered, still in shock.

"It's a legal document—her passport to freedom, for want of a better word."

He realized it must have been in her backpack. "She spent a whole year in prison for nothing?" he blurted. After sustaining the shock, he was outraged for her.

"Yes. Hers was a very unusual case, very cruel. When I realized she had nowhere to go, I thought I might be able to help her find work and tried several places without success. After I learned that the position at your ranch had been filled, there was no point in telling her. I didn't want her to get discouraged."

Colt felt shame for having blown off the warden's phone call so easily. If he'd bothered to speak to her himself, he would have learned the truth about Geena and would have given her a chance to apply for the position. "She took the news well," he admitted. Hell— she'd been incredible about it!

"That sounds like Geena. I'm glad to hear she made it to your ranch safely and hope she finds work soon. She was a model prisoner in every sense of the word. It pains me that she was ever incarcerated."

His mouth had gone so dry, he could hardly talk. "That's all I needed to know. I'm more grateful to you than you know for coming to the phone. Goodnight, Warden."

"Goodnight, Mr. Brannigan."

He was so wired he knew there'd be no sleep for him tonight. After leaving a note in the kitchen that he'd be out on the range if an emergency cropped up, he headed for the back door.

Titus was right there with him and climbed in the truck before they took off. For the rest of the night he drove around thinking. He could hear his father's voice. *Everyone makes mistakes, Colt. This man deserves a second chance.*

But in Geena's case, she *hadn't* made a mistake!

Shocked when it got to be four-fifteen, he turned around and headed home with his mind made up about what he wanted to do. Before he parked the truck, his headlights shone on the big ponderosa further down the drive.

Her bike was gone.

* * *

At ten to six, Geena rode into the full-service gas station in Sundance. She was glad the dog hadn't heard her
leave the ranch house. While Mr. Brannigan was still
asleep, she'd been able to slip away unnoticed and get
going. Her problem now was to wait it out until someone came to open the station so she could get a drink
and use the restroom.

There were several piles of rubber tires stacked outside the bay doors. She propped her bike against one.
Since no one was there, she pulled down two tires and
sat on them while she rested against the pile. Once she'd
covered herself with her space blanket, she was able to
relax and plan out her day.

Her first destination would be the library. She'd scan
the want ads online and find a job. If she ate only two
meals a day and bought her food at the grocery store,
she ought to stay afloat for a little while longer.

Tonight she'd sleep at the YWCA. She'd passed it
yesterday on her way to the bike shop. In fact, en route
to the library, she'd go over there and reserve a cot before they reached their quota for the day.

When it got to be seven-fifteen, she rolled off the
tires and put them back, then walked her bike over to
the restroom and rested it against the wall to wait. Pretty
soon a man drove in and opened up the office. She said
hello and followed him inside to get a soft drink. He
went around and unlocked the restroom for her.

Once she'd used the facility, she opened the door,
only to find her bike was gone! Geena had been in there
only a minute. Frantic because of her loss, she raced
around to the front, thinking she'd catch the culprit before he could get away.

"Relax, Geena."

At the sound of the deep, familiar voice, she swung around to face a clean-shaven Colt Brannigan standing at the side of the dark blue truck she'd seen parked outside the ranch house. His hard-boned features were shadowed beneath his black cowboy hat. This morning he was wearing a blue-and-green plaid shirt that covered his well-defined chest. Hip-hugging jeans molded to his powerful thighs.

Her thighs, in fact the whole length of her legs, wobbled just looking at him.

She'd never seen a sight like him and had the conviction she never would again, no matter how long she lived. When she'd left the ranch earlier, she'd determined to put all thoughts of him out of her mind. Geena had survived prison by shutting off her feelings. Surely she could do it again while she made a new life for herself, but this man was unforgettable.

"I was afraid someone would steal your bike, so I put it in the back of my truck for safekeeping."

Geena's heart was still racing too fast. She knew her upset over the stolen bike wasn't the only reason she couldn't seem to quell its tempo. Nervousness caused her to rub damp palms against her jeans-clad hips. "What are you doing here?"

He took a step toward her. "When I saw your bike was missing, I figured I'd find you in town. We have unfinished business this morning."

"Before I left, I put a thank-you note and a twenty-dollar bill on the kitchen table."

"I read it."

"I wish it were twenty times as much money. Last night I felt like a pampered princess. You could have no idea what it did for my spirits."

"I'm gratified to hear it." The way his gaze penetrated as he stared at her made her all fluttery inside. She folded her arms across her chest, not knowing how to contain her emotions.

"Most people wouldn't give a person like me the time of day. Last night at your hands I was treated to a taste of heaven. I won't forget. You're one in a million."

"You give me too much credit." The truth came out in a raspy voice. "Last night I couldn't restrain myself from looking on line to read the news articles about your imprisonment. They said you were supposed to be serving a sixty-year sentence for a capital one murder."

Geena eyed him calmly. "In that case I'm astounded you'd let a convicted killer stay through the night. Did you think I'd taken off with some of those authentic Sioux valuables and that's why you're here waiting to catch me with the goods? Or is it simply a question of morbid curiosity? You're welcome to search my backpack." She handed it to him.

His eyes narrowed before taking it. "If I'd thought you were untrustworthy, I would have driven you to town last night and dropped you off at the nearest shelter."

She had trouble breathing. "The housekeeping position hasn't been filled yet, has it?"

"No."

"I didn't think so. Thanks for being honest about that."

Colt didn't respond to her comment. Instead he opened her backpack and eventually drew out a brown envelope. She watched him reach inside and produce the certificate she'd read over and over again during her bus ride from Pierre, unable to believe she was free.

He studied it before his head reared. "Why didn't you show me this last night?"

"Because you told me the job had been filled. I didn't question it. You were incredibly kind to have brought me into the ranch house to sleep. In truth I was deathly tired last night."

"I noticed," he murmured.

"Before I fell asleep, I couldn't decide why you'd been so good to me. Was it out of an inborn sense of guilt and duty to one of your fellow creatures less fortunate than you? Or possibly even a modicum of faith in mankind? Whatever sentiment drove you, your mother would be proud of you. Now I'm afraid I have to get going to find a job."

He put everything back in her pack and handed it to her. "If you're still interested, I'm offering you the position of housekeeper. For a *temporary* period," he emphasized.

A small cry escaped her throat. Maybe she was hallucinating. "When did you make that decision?"

"After you went to bed last night, I called Warden James. Before I could ask her any questions, she told me you'd been exonerated and hoped you'd be able to find a job soon."

A tremor shook her body while she absorbed the revelation. "So—"

"So you see—" he interrupted her. "My mother wouldn't have been proud of me. In her mind, half a loaf doesn't cut it."

The blood pounded in her ears. "It cut it for me, so don't beat yourself. If I'd been in your shoes, I would have phoned the prison, too." She bit her lip. "Even if I'm innocent, why are you willing to take a chance on me?"

He put his hands on his hips, the ultimate male stance. "Besides your work ethic in prison which the warden praised, anyone who went through all you did yesterday to get the job deserves a chance. I came close to offering it to you before you went to bed, but the niggling thought that I'd seen or heard of you before propelled me to look on the internet first."

She paced a little, then stopped. "It was a hideous crime done to a dear friend. I spent thirteen months reliving the real killer's treachery to him. But I will always be a persona non grata in some people's eyes. Is that why your job offer is temporary? Because you know certain parties will refuse to believe the truth and it could cause trouble? Mind you, I'm not being ungrateful—just curious."

Lines bracketed his mouth. "To hell with what anyone else thinks. The position would be temporary to anyone I hired—a trial period, if you prefer. Both sides have to find out if the job is a good fit. You *did* say you only wanted it temporarily."

"Yes. What would you say if I work for you until the end of the summer? By then I have other plans and you'll have had time to find someone really suitable."

He studied her for a moment, then said, "End of summer it is. But when you've been with us a while, you might not want to stay that long, so your suggestion makes sense."

Mr. Brannigan was no one's fool. Being up front with him was the only honest thing to do. Then it wouldn't come as a surprise when she gave her notice to leave.

By then she ought to have a lead on the whereabouts of her brother's lover. And child. *If* it was his…

"Thank you for giving me this opportunity. How long have you been without a housekeeper?"

"A month. We've been hard hit by our previous housekeeper Mary White Bird's passing. You need to know she's been the only housekeeper on the ranch since my brothers and I were born."

"That long?"

He gave her a solemn nod. "Since her death, it's been hard even to contemplate someone else taking her place."

Geena's thoughts reeled. "She's the lovely Sioux woman in those pictures?"

"Yes," he said in what sounded like a reverent tone.

"You're right. No one could ever fill her shoes. I'm shocked that you'd let me sleep in her room among all her precious things. The tobacco bag is fabulous."

Emotion darkened his hazel eyes. "It belonged to her husband. I see you know your native American history."

Her throat swelled. "I learned a lot from Rupert." She eyed him directly. "Thank you for this wonderful opportunity. I realize Mary White Bird will never be forgotten, but for as long as I'm with you, I swear I'll work hard and not make you regret you hired me." Right now she felt she was the luckiest woman on the planet.

"In return I promise not to be too terrible a taskmaster, as my brothers continually remind me I am."

"Are you going to tell them I was in prison?" She hated the throb in her voice. They were standing close enough she could feel the warmth from his hard body.

"No. You've been exonerated for a crime you didn't commit, but that's up to you if you want to tell some-

one. As far as I'm concerned it's not information anyone needs to know."

She stole an extra breath. He was like a great bul-
wark in a storm. "You're a good man, Mr. Brannigan.
I'm so thankful for the job I could kiss your feet. But
not in front of the service-station attendant, who's been
watching us for some time."

The tautness in his expression relaxed. "I'll buy a
tank of gas, then we'll drive over to Tilly's and hash
out the details of your contract while we eat breakfast.
I'm in the mood for a big one. I don't know about you,
but I think better on a full stomach."

While he walked over to the gas pump, she climbed
in the cab of his Dodge Ram and held her backpack on
her lap. Through the back window she could see her
bike. She still couldn't believe he'd tracked her here in
order to offer her the housekeeping job. She was definitely being watched over.

In a few minutes they drove through the town of
1200-plus people to a spot he had to know well. Maybe
she was dreaming about the fabulous man who'd just
offered her a solid job on a ranch not more than seventy
miles from Rapid City. That's where she would begin
her investigation to recover her past.

The dreams just kept coming after they entered the
restaurant. Geena hadn't had waffles with strawberries
and whipped cream for over a year. With some slices of
ham added to the plate, she thought she'd never enjoyed
a meal so much. "You don't know how good this tastes."

"I can only imagine." He'd been watching her over
the rim of his coffee cup. "Are you up to some more
questions? Then you can fire away at me."

She sat back in the booth, already knowing the most

important thing about him. "Ask me anything you want, Mr. Brannigan."

"Call me Colt." When she nodded he said, "Where are you from?"

"I'll try to answer all your questions at once. I was born in Rapid City. My parents died young. My brother Todd and I were raised by our grandmother who lived on a fixed income and rented her home. I always did waitressing. After our grandmother died, I left for college in Laramie. Todd stayed at the house and worked laying pipeline."

"How did you manage financially when it was out-of-state tuition?"

"Through student loans and waiting on tables. I still owe $22,000. After graduation I went to work for a company in Rapid City called FossilMania."

"I've heard of it. What did you do there exactly?"

"We went out in teams in vans to find fossils. When we'd get to an area the owner felt contained dinosaur remains, we'd scour a certain section of land to begin a dig with our tools. I'm afraid that doesn't sound like a résumé for a housekeeper."

"Don't worry about it. Have you ever ridden a horse?"

"No."

"Then I'll teach you. Emergencies crop up from time to time. You'll be more useful in that kind of a situation if you can ride."

Geena wondered what circumstances he had in mind, but realized he was anxious to learn about her background. The questions she had for him could come later.

"In Rapid City I found an inexpensive basement apartment to rent from Rupert Brown."

She would have moved back to her grandmother's small house with Todd, but by then he had a girlfriend and she was living with him. Janice had disliked Geena on sight. She was so furtive, Geena knew the other woman had something to hide.

Her brother didn't have the best luck with women. Geena feared Janice was the wrong fit for him, but she'd never said anything to Todd because she loved her brother too much and didn't want to hurt him.

"Rupert and I shared an interest in artifacts and Native American memorabilia. Over the year I lived there we became good friends."

The next part sent a shudder through her. "One day when I came home from doing my field work, the police were there and arrested me for Rupert's murder. It had happened early in the morning and my fingerprints were all over the trowel I often used."

"You were framed!"

"Yes. A lot of his treasures had been stolen. Several of his irreplaceable books were found in my apartment along with my own small collection of fossils, all with my fingerprints."

"Someone had to know about your relationship with the victim."

"Definitely. It turned out to be a collector who'd come by his place when I'd been there with him. Various dealers interested in Western Americana often dropped in for a look at his things, hoping to get him to part with some of them, but his prices were too high. I think he did it purposely because he couldn't bear to part with anything. This angered the killer."

"If you were gone on long digs, the criminal had plenty of time to plant evidence in your apartment."

She nodded. "It gave me chills to think someone had been in there doing whatever. When I was put on trial, I couldn't afford an attorney, so a public defender was provided. I told him everything I could about the people who'd been to Rupert's apartment. I came up with a few names—any clues I could remember. But nothing came of it and the jury found me guilty."

"I don't know how you dealt with it," his voice grated.

"I think I was in shock the whole time. To be honest, I don't know why I didn't die on the spot. I wanted to. The thought of sixty years in that place, helpless to get out and do anything—"

A strange almost primitive sound came out of her new employer.

"Todd promised to find me a good attorney who could prove my innocence, but he didn't have any extra money. A month after I'd been put in prison, I got a message he'd been killed." Hot tears stung her eyelids.

"He was your only living relative?"

"Yes. I was notified through the warden's office by one of the executives at the pipeline company. He said there'd been an accident during an earth-removal incident, suffocating Todd and one of his co-workers. I was listed as the next of kin on his application. I swear the tragedy was more devastating to me than learning I'd be spending the rest of my life in prison."

Geena never knew what had happened to Janice. It was as if she'd vanished. More unconscionable, she'd never tried to get word to Geena about Todd. How anyone could be that heartless had almost destroyed her.

What made it so much worse was that the last time she'd ever spoken to Todd, he'd told her Janice was pregnant. He had hopes that a baby would settle Janice down and they could become a real family. Now that Todd was gone, Geena's only living relative might be the baby Janice would have delivered by now. But what if it wasn't Todd's?

While she was deep in her own tortured thoughts, lines had marred Colt's features until she almost didn't recognize him. "Who was the man from the pipeline?"

"A Mr. Phelps. He was decent enough to find out from me where my parents and grandparents were buried. I heard he made arrangements for Todd to be buried next to them at the cemetery."

Geena couldn't stop her voice from trembling and was unable to talk for a minute. One of the first things she wanted to do was go to the cemetery. After that she'd pay Mr. Phelps a visit and personally thank him for his kindness. She finally lifted her head. "But no more looking back. A miracle has happened."

She laid her napkin on the table. "Day before yesterday I was taken to the warden's office. She put me on the phone with the detective who'd been working on the investigation. He told me that some of Rupert's stolen artifacts had turned up. He found the real killer through new DNA evidence and arrested him. I almost did die right then. For *joy*."

She'd also talked to the public defender who'd represented her in court. He'd told her that within the month, the state would be reimbursing her some money for the time she'd been wrongfully incarcerated. The sum would be enough to help her carry out certain long-range plans. He gave her his number and told her to call him as soon as she had an address so he'd know where to send her the check.

When she looked up at Colt, his compassion-filled eyes were a sight she would never forget. "You've lived through something impossible for anyone else to comprehend. No platitudes could make up for the year you lost in there."

"That's true, but it's okay. It's over. You've offered me the job I wanted." It thrilled her to think that with the money she'd be receiving, she'd be able to pay Colt back for saving her life right now.

"Time will tell about that," he murmured.

She cleared her throat. "A minute ago you told me you used the word *temporary* in order for both sides to be ensured of a good fit, but I already know you're a good fit for me. That's because you were willing to be kind to me even after you knew I'd been in prison. There's a universe of difference between exoneration and a release for doing time."

Without his hat on, she thought he suddenly looked paler beneath the luxuriant wavy hair he wore medium-cropped. She couldn't decide if it was brown or black. Obviously it was a shade in between. "Are you all right? You look like you've seen a ghost," she murmured.

"Not even to be allowed to bury your own brother... You should never have spent one second in that prison," he whispered in a fierce tone without acknowledging her observation.

"But I'm free now, enjoying this delicious breakfast because of you!" she cried softly, still having to pinch herself. He represented a huge blessing in her life. Knowing she might have a niece or nephew out there filled her with the desire to work so hard for him, he would never complain.

In the process she'd try to find Janice and get a good

look at the baby. She'd know if it was Todd's. If it turned out to be his, then she hoped she could arrange for visits and keep their family connection alive. But there were still a lot of what-ifs....

Colt studied her as if trying to see into her soul. Geena could read his mind. She sensed that the guilty thoughts he'd entertained at the beginning, causing him to tell her the job had been filled, were going to weigh on him. She didn't want that for him.

"Stop running over yourself," she teased, warming to the side of him that had a strong social conscience. "When I showed up at your stable, you didn't tell me there was no room at the inn. That'll win you a lot of points in the next life. It's won them with me." The last came out in her husky voice.

CHAPTER THREE

"THAT'S gratifying to hear." Emotion seemed to have deepened the green flecks in Colt's eyes. "If you're through eating, we'll drive over to the bank and set up an account for you. Which reminds me we haven't discussed your salary yet. What were you making at FossilMania?"

"Fifteen hundred a month."

"Did you have savings from that job?"

"A little. When Todd closed out my bank account for me, I told him to give it to the attorney he was going to hire, but he never got the chance." For all Geena knew, Janice had gone off with it, too.

Colt's lips thinned before he put some bills on the table for their meal. "For starting pay, how does twenty-five hundred a month sound? That includes room and board, two days a week off, a truck for your use and medical benefits."

She was staggered. "I think you know how that sounds." For one thing, she could start paying back her student loan. Any extra she could save would help her to make inquiries about Janice. "In fact, I doubt anyone else you hired would be offered as much."

"Being the housekeeper on the Floral Valley Ranch

covers a lot of territory. Mary made considerably more than that. In time you will, too, depending on how you like the work." Geena was certain she'd like the work, but she'd be working there only three months. That was their bargain. "Let's go."

They left Tilly's to walk to the bank located in the next block. By the time business had concluded, he'd arranged for an account to be opened in her name. The bank officer handed her a bank card and an envelope with a hundred dollars cash.

Colt took her elbow and ushered her out the doors. On the sidewalk he paused. "I've advanced you your first month's pay. You need a wardrobe and all the extras that go with it. You ought to be able to find what you want in the stores along here, so I'll leave you to get your shopping done. Bradford's is on the corner over there. I'll meet you out in front in say, two hours. If you need more time, we'll take it."

"I won't need two hours. You're too generous, Colt."

"When you've been with us a month, you'll realize you earned every penny of it and will be asking for a raise."

Some people had difficulty accepting gratitude. He seemed to fit in that category. "What am I supposed to wear during my work day?"

His eyes swept over her, but she couldn't read their expression. "Not a uniform. That's for sure."

"Thank you for that," she half laughed, putting a hand to her throat. His lips twitched in reaction. When he did that, her heart jumped.

"Put on whatever is comfortable."

She knew she looked pathetic in the hand-me-down clothes provided at the prison. Day before yesterday she'd been ecstatic to exchange the prison uniform for them. But today the knowledge that she could walk into a shop and pick out some new outfits made her so thrilled, she was close to being sick with excitement.

"I've never had the experience of buying a whole new wardrobe at once. You may regret you gave me this get-out-of-jail-free card. I might go hog wild."

He shoved his hat back on his dark head. "Frankly, ma'am, I hope you do."

With that remark, she knew she looked awful and didn't feel half as guilty while she spent the next couple of hours choosing clothes to wear, starting from the skin out. She went a little crazy on cosmetics and makeup. In the last store she tried on designer jeans and a white, form fitting Western shirt with pearl snaps and extended tails.

She loved the spread collar, not to mention the brown embroidery on the sleeves and yoke. The guy waiting on her brought out cowboy boots and a white cowboy hat to match. She'd never worn Western clothes like this in her life.

Geena put everything on and stood in front of the full-length mirror. Though she needed to gain ten pounds, the gleam in the clerk's eyes when he told her she looked fantastic made her feel better about herself and settled one matter for her. She would wear the whole outfit back home.

Yesterday she'd learned that the head of the Floral Valley Ranch was held in the highest regard in this part of Wyoming. If she was going to work for him, she needed to present herself in the best light.

Before she left the fitting room, she tossed her old clothes in the wastebasket. They'd been used by enough other women that she didn't feel guilty about discarding them. No doubt her new boss would be happy to know she'd gotten rid of them. To her relief the clerk, who'd been chatting her up, offered to help her out of the store with her all her bags.

She'd bought a lot of things, yet she knew he didn't normally offer to carry a client's purchases to the car for them. It had been a long time since she'd been around men. The attention from this nice-looking guy was fun and flattering. "Thanks for your help, Steve." It said Steve Wright on his name tag. "I really like my new clothes."

"On you, so do I. If you're going to be in town later, we could have dinner after I close up. How about it?"

"Afraid not" sounded a voice behind them with an underlying hint of steel. "She'll be at work."

Geena swung around to look at Colt. In the background she could see his truck double-parked. The piercing yellow-green of his eyes sent a tiny shiver down her spine. Was the transformation too much? She turned to the clerk. "Steve? This is my employer, Mr. Brannigan."

"Nice to meet you, sir."

While Colt nodded, Geena smiled at the clerk. "The next time I'm in town, I'll come by."

"Good. I'll be watching for you."

"Let me relieve you." Colt took care of all the bags before putting them in the back of the truck.

When the clerk went inside the store, Colt walked to the passenger side of the truck and opened the door for her. The boots made her a little taller, putting her on a better footing with him. Before she climbed in, she eyed him beneath the brim of her hat.

"You're probably upset about the purchase of this outfit. Tell me now if I've done something wrong. The only reason I decided to buy it was because you said I needed to learn how to horseback-ride. I want to look the part and fit in."

"What you buy is your business," he muttered.

"But there *is* a problem."

"There could be" came his cryptic answer. His gaze roved over her features visible beneath her cowboy hat. "It's not your fault," he added, as if it cost him to admit it.

Oh. Now she got it.

"You mean that I'm a woman?" It was absurd for Colt to think she was a femme fatale. She climbed in the truck so he could close the door. When he came around and got behind the wheel she turned to him. "He was just being a guy."

"I noticed."

"Look, Colt. I realize you employ a small army of men on your ranch. Sometimes a woman can cause trouble without meaning to. Todd told me stories about the problems with a few women who came out to see the men while they were laying pipe." That's where he'd met Janice. "But you have my promise that while I work for you, I'll keep everything professional. If there's a problem with any of them, I'll come to you immediately."

"I can't ask for more than that." There were invisible layers to this issue, but he wasn't willing to explain. They could be professional or personal. Maybe both. When she got to know him better, she'd find out.

He turned on the engine and joined the mainstream of traffic. "Before we head out of town, I'll take you over to the supermarket where we do our grocery shopping and introduce you to Bart, the manager. You'll be cooking for those of us in the ranch house. But he's worked with Mary and knows how to fill the lists for the food prepared by the cooks feeding the stockmen out on the range. The cooks come to the house to pick up from you once a week."

She averted her eyes. "You're right. There's a lot to learn. Who actually lives at the ranch house besides you and Hank?"

"Our mother and her caregiver, Ina. Then there's my brother Travis and his wife Lindsey. They live in the house close by, but eat their meals with us. She's pregnant and close to her delivery date. After the baby's here, they'll probably stay at the ranch house for a week, maybe more. Mary had been looking forward to taking care of the baby."

That meant Geena would be helping with its care. The idea excited her, but Colt had sounded far away just then. She had an idea that when they'd lost Mary, they'd lost a great deal more than a housekeeper. For Geena to think she could just step in and fill Mary's shoes was ludicrous, but she'd do her best not to disappoint him.

"Is Hank serious about the girl he brought home?"

"No. They've been friends since high school."

Geena smiled. "I don't think there is such a thing between a man and woman."

"No?"

"I saw the way she looked at him." Mandy was crazy about Hank. "But thanks for the information so I don't say something wrong. Tell me about my schedule."

"You work Monday through Friday. Your weekends are your own. Breakfast at seven, dinner at seven and lunch for our mother and Ina at one o'clock. The rest of us fix our own lunches if we come in. Most of the time we're out on the range and eat with the hands.

"When extended family and guests come for visits, they stay in the ranch house if there's room, or occupy a couple of the cabins nearby and join us for meals. Lindsey's mother will probably come and live at the house for some of the time. Occasionally business people fly in and stay over."

"I see."

"Mid morning Mary came to the post office in town to pick up the mail and left it on the desk in the den. Before we leave Sundance, I'll drive you over there to show you and give you a key to the box."

"I'll remember that." She glanced at him. "Tell me about your mother."

He grimaced. "She has full-fledged Alzheimer's and isn't going to get better."

"Oh no—how old is she?"

"Sixty."

"So young? I'm sorry, Colt. My grandmother's best friend had it toward the end." It was an awful disease. "Is Ina good to her?"

"Yes, but she needs help. Lately mother has been more restless and jumps up to walk around without warning. She needs more watching. After we leave the supermarket, I'm going to drop by the nursing service and see if I can't speed things up to get another caregiver to help spell off Ina."

Geena stirred in the seat. She was about to say she'd be glad to help out, but since she didn't know the full scope of her own responsibilities yet, she thought the better of it. As head of the family, Colt Brannigan had a lot of emotional worries to juggle along with running a big ranch. She was amazed at his capacity.

Bart turned out to be friendly to her and as respectful of Colt as the men she'd met at the Cattlemen's Store the other day. He went out of his way to assure her there would be help to load the truck when she came for large orders. All she had to do was pull around back to the docking area.

After kitchen duty for three hundred and fifty women in the prison, feeding six people twice a day didn't sound too daunting. Her biggest concern was to plan enjoyable, hearty meals for the men who were out in the saddle all day.

After they got back in the truck, Colt swung his head toward her. "Make that your second conquest of the day. It's a good thing he's happily married with four children."

How come you're not, Colt? Geena was dying to ask him that question, but he would have to tell her when he was good and ready. *If* he was ever ready.

"After being behind bars for a year with an all-female population, you have no idea how good it feels to be appreciated instead of being hated for being a woman. Right now I'm so thankful to be free and so thankful for my new job I can't even begin to tell you."

His gaze held hers for a moment. "I'm not unhappy about heading back to the ranch with a new housekeeper in tow. For the last month we've had to subsist on Hank's cooking. It hasn't been pretty."

She laughed before he started the engine and drove them to the medical center. Geena couldn't remember the last time she'd felt like laughing. Between her imprisonment and Todd's death, she'd thought there could be no state of happiness for her ever again. But sitting here in the cab waiting for Colt, she realized she'd been given a second chance to find it. All of it would be due to the striking, hard-muscled rancher entering the building and turning female heads left and right.

Gutted by the knowledge that Geena had been wrongfully imprisoned under the worst of circumstances, Colt could hardly concentrate on the nursing supervisor's words. To think she'd lived thirteen months behind bars for a crime she didn't commit! With the assurance that an aide would be available in another two weeks, he walked back outside and got in the truck. His cab had never smelled so fragrant.

Last night Colt had noticed the interest in Hank's eyes when he'd glimpsed Geena in the kitchen. The trouble was, that was before Colt had seen Geena turned out like *this*. In that outfit, she knocked every beautiful rodeo queen right out of the arena. He had no doubt Hank would fall all over himself trying to work his considerable charm on her. But Hank had enough problems. Colt didn't want him getting involved with Geena. Time would tell how well she fended him off.

The fact that she'd read Colt's mind after introducing him to the salesclerk a little while ago meant she understood some of his concerns. By her teens, men would have started coming on to her in droves. The way she'd handled the spiky-haired guy who'd called him sir, proved she knew how to deal with male attention.

Her assurance that the job was all that mattered to her right now gave him another reason to feel justified in hiring her, but unfortunately that promise wouldn't prevent his ranch hands from proving they were going to be the first to break through her defenses. And if one of them did, she planned to be gone by fall, so it didn't matter.

Naturally Geena's personal life in her free time was her own business. On that score Colt had no right to an opinion one way or the other. He glanced at her. "After we run by the post office, are there any more stops we need to make before leaving Sundance?"

An amused smile appeared on her face that already looked more relieved of tension. "Have you glanced out your rear window to see all the bags stashed back there?"

He chuckled. "I was thinking more along the lines of a rest stop or another meal."

"I think you're the one who's hungry again. How about we pull in to the Hungry Horse drive-in before going back to the ranch?" She could read his thoughts all right. "Do you know in prison I would dream about consuming a fresh limeade? I used to pay extra for half a dozen cherries to go with it. The combination of the two flavors can't be beaten. Crazy, huh?"

"Not crazy at all." He equated a fresh limeade with summer. Since his mother's illness, his father's death and Mary's passing, he'd forgotten what summer felt like. Geena's thoughts were attuned to his at unexpected moments.

What she didn't know was that he agreed with her about friendship between a man and a woman. It needed to exist alongside passion in a tight marriage, but outside of it, he didn't buy it any more than Geena did. His brother used Mandy, whose feelings for him were far from platonic.

To her credit she had a masterful way of covering

them up, but there would come a point when Mandy would wake up to the fact that his brother's interest lay in another woman and to waste any more time with him was futile.

With the mail collected, he headed for the drive-in. When it came their turn in the line of tourists, he ordered a steak burrito and two fresh limeades with additional cherries. Once they were on the road again he said, "I'm going to drive us back along the fire-break road. It'll circle around the ranch and take us up on some vista points so you can view the whole layout."

"Wonderful. How big is it?"

"Seventeen thousand acres. Eight thousand of them are deeded land."

"While I was riding my bike along here this morning, I yearned to get up on that mountain casting its long shadow over the valley. What's it called?"

"Inyan Kara. Some historians call it Hollow Mountain and others Stone-Made Mountain, but Mary said it comes from her language meaning 'mountain over mountain.'"

"I envy you having learned so much from her."

"The first Brannigan bought the property in 1872 and built the original part of the ranch house. We've survived five generations starting with the Sioux, then the U.S. Cavalry, followed by frontiersmen, pioneers, settlers, cowboys and outlaws."

She flashed him an infectious smile. "Oh, yes. The Sundance Kid. He and I have something in common, except I understand he was kept eighteen months in the Sundance jail before he was released and left the country. That's five months longer than yours truly out in Pierre's all-women prison."

Colt was glad she could be lighthearted about an experience that would have destroyed most people.

"One of my mother's ancestors was a pioneer from Scotland, but he didn't create an empire like your family has done," she volunteered. "What about your ancestry?"

"We're mostly English with a little Scotch-Irish thrown in."

"Our family has English blood too. How did your ranch get its name?"

Naturally the new housekeeper wanted to learn all she could. "General George Armstrong Custer rode through this area in early summer and saw the flowers in the high meadows. He called it Floral Valley and the name stuck."

"That's beautiful. In fact the beauty of this whole place takes my breath away."

She'd just put her finger on what was wrong with Colt. Since this morning when he'd found her at the gas station, he'd been in that condition and hadn't caught it yet. He drove them higher until they came to the first lookout where she could see the out buildings and the cattle grazing. Colt heard sounds of appreciation coming out of her before she started firing more questions. The woman had an inquisitive mind.

"We have a five-hundred-animal unit operation and bring in cattle on a rental basis over eighteen pastures. Sixteen of them have live water from the creeks and springs. For the other two, we've put in four wells and banks, along with earthen reservoirs."

She shook her head. "This is a huge enterprise."

"A lot goes on here, but it's manageable, although I'm a little short-staffed at the moment. Travis has had to stay close to Lindsey lately and Hank's broken leg has put him out of commission. Mac and the hands have been doing double duty."

"And you probably triple." This woman said all the right things. "Tell me what's beyond this vantage point."

"We have six hundred acres of wheat, and some other acreage of alfalfa and grass hay mix for use year round. We also have an income source from pasture lease, farmland crop-sharing and hunting fees."

"What do people hunt here?"

"Elk, deer, antelope and wild turkeys."

He heard a sigh. "Thank you for taking your time to give me a bird's-eye view of the ranch. I know there's a ton to learn and it will take me ages, but at least I can picture all this in my mind now. Otherwise I'd be like the proverbial deer in the headlights. It's an absolute paradise, Colt."

Not everyone felt that way if they weren't raised on a ranch. His ex-wife had come from San Francisco. Their two lifestyles had never mixed. He understood that. In Geena's case she'd be leaving in the fall, so it didn't matter if she took to the ranching life or not.

"In a few days when I have to inspect the herd, I'll take you with me so you can see the flowers Custer described. Now *that's* paradise."

"I'd love it," she murmured before he realized what had just come out of him. This was how you got in trouble. Geena was the new housekeeper. Her job was temporary. Period! She couldn't even ride a horse, and here he was planning an outing with her under the guise of work.

Yet hiring her had solved two problems. She needed a job and had provided a stopgap for him while he hunted for the right person to become another fixture on the ranch. Since Mary's passing a month ago, he hadn't had enough time to find that special person.

As for Geena, she had other plans. You didn't expect a woman like her to stay with the housekeeper position a long time, even if there were no contract. With her college degree she could make a whole new career for herself.

There were men out there—single, divorced, widowed—who were dying to link up with such an attractive woman. He'd already seen evidence of that today. She'd put prison behind her, and she expected to move on by the first snowfall. For the time being, the family needed Geena's services and she needed a few paychecks behind her before she left. But to his chagrin, the thought of her leaving didn't sit well with him, which was ridiculous.

He started the engine and drove them on a short cut through the pines to reach the house. Alice, one of the house cleaners, had parked her green pickup truck next to Hank's black one. Now would be as good a time as any for Geena to meet her.

After the truck was parked, she got down while he reached for the bags in the back. They entered the house and walked through to Mary's old room, except that from now on it would be known as Geena's.

Alice was in the bathroom scouring it, but stopped her work to see who'd entered the bedroom. "Hi, Colt."

"Hi, Alice. I'd like you to meet Mary's replacement." He put the bags down on the rug. "This is Geena Williams. She's from Rapid City, South Dakota. Geena? Alice White Eagle is a younger cousin of Mary's."

The pretty, fortyish mother of three was five feet one,

as Mary had been. Since Colt had known her, she'd kept her thoughts to herself, but clearly she was shocked by Mary's young replacement. The difference had to be astonishing to say the least. "Hello, Geena."

His new housekeeper removed her cowboy hat and put it on one of the two leather armchairs. Both women wore a braid. He'd discovered Geena looked sensational no matter how she did her hair.

"Hi, Alice. It's very nice to meet you." She shook the woman's hand. "I'm sorry Colt and I didn't come in sooner. I scoured that bathroom this morning. Now it has made extra work for you. Have you changed the sheets on the bed already?"

"Not yet."

"That's good because I found fresh sheets in the cupboard and changed them earlier."

"No problem." Alice's smile included Colt as she said it.

It might not be a problem for Alice, but Geena had known a different kind of hard work day in and day out for over a year. Colt hadn't realized she'd done those things to the room before creeping out of the house at dawn. She continued to surprise him in pleasant, elemental ways. It was as if she already knew the password to infiltrate the secret recesses of his psyche.

Geena glanced at the pictures on the dresser. "Those photos of your cousin are lovely, Alice. So is this room. You must miss her very much."

"Yes."

Colt's gaze flicked to Geena. "Alice is one of the three women who keep the ranch house spotless. We couldn't get along without them. They work a rotation. She comes in every third day. You'll meet Elaine tomorrow and Trish on Friday. They're usually here by eight-thirty and work till eleven, though Alice asked to start work later today. It'll interest you to know Alice's husband, Ben White Eagle, is our chief stockman."

Geena nodded. "I know that has to be hard work, but if you love animals it would be a pleasure."

Alice stared at her. "He's a man of the earth, like Colt."

"Who wouldn't love it in this beautiful place? Do you have children?"

"Three."

"What are their ages?"

"Thirteen, eleven and eight."

"How wonderful. I'd love to meet them. I hope you'll bring them sometime."

"Sometime I will. They're in school."

"Maybe bring them afterward for cookies and milk? My grandmother always made that for me."

Alice only smiled, but Colt knew that Geena wanting to include her children was a sure way to win her friendship. Geena had a way.

"Alice's family lives in one of the cabins further up the hillside, so occasionally you'll see them playing," he explained. "The other two women are married and live in Sundance with their families."

Geena nodded. "Have you worked here long, Alice?"

"Ten years."

"Then you're the person to come to if I have a question when Colt isn't available."

"Alice knows everything, but I'll go over the housecleaning duties with you later," Colt interjected. "From then on you can meet with them if you have a special request or they need something from you."

"That sounds good to me. How about you, Alice?"

"It's good."

The soft-spoken woman couldn't help but be positively affected by Geena's friendliness. Had she always been easy to get along with? Or had she learned to deal with other women in prison and now had it down to an art form? Alice nodded in agreement and left the bedroom with her cleaning supplies.

"I'm sure you want to freshen up, then I'd like to introduce you to my mother. Will ten minutes give you enough time?"

"Plenty."

"Then I'll be by for you shortly."

CHAPTER FOUR

GEENA watched both of them leave the room. It excited her that Alice was also Lakota. Geena had a strong interest in native American history and would enjoy getting to know her better. No doubt it would be difficult for Alice to see someone else taking over the housekeeping duties that had been Mary's domain for several decades. Geena hoped in time they could become friends, but it wouldn't happen overnight.

Her mind flicked back to Colt. She went into the bathroom, only needing a minute before she was ready for him. Mrs. Brannigan might not recognize her loved ones any more, but she was Colt's mother, the one who wouldn't have approved of a half loaf.

There was a definite streak of cynicism running through her oldest son, though he kept it hidden for the most part. Like Achilles, the most handsome of all the heroes during the Trojan War, Colt appeared to be invulnerable in every part of his magnificent body *except* his heel. Achilles had died from a small wound received there.

Geena believed it was a woman who'd become Colt's only weakness. The fact that there was no mention of a woman in his life meant he still fought that weakness with all the breath he possessed. She'd sensed that much out under the ponderosa tree when his demeanor had sent out an aura that said *trespass at your own risk*.

She'd gotten the point instantly. Not that it was any of her concern. She was here to help keep order in Colt's house. Right now she wanted to look and be at her best for the woman who'd given birth to him. Anxious because she'd like to live up to all the things he expected of her, she expended some excess energy by going out into the hall while she waited.

The walls were lined with generations of family pictures. You name it and it was all there. She feasted her eyes on them. They dated from more than a hundred years ago to the present. Babies, little boys and girls, teenagers and adults. Parents, grandparents, great-grandparents. Some on horseback, rodeo shots, groups hiking, skiing, fishing.

The pictures of a younger, painfully handsome Colt winning prizes for steer-wrestling captured her attention. A young handsome Achilles all right. She found herself looking for every picture of him she could find from infancy to the age he was now. While she feasted her eyes on him with his family or alone, she heard footsteps in the hall and turned in that direction. It was his brother Hank.

"Well, hello again," he spoke first.

"Hi, Hank."

He moved toward her on his walking cast. His hair, a little overly long, had more brown in it than Colt's. Wearing jeans and a Western shirt, he was another good-looking Brannigan. She'd thought so last night. He had softer edges than Colt and was probably an inch shorter than his brother, who had to be six foot three.

"I didn't know you were still here." In his voice were all the questions she'd seen in his eyes last night, yet hadn't uttered. As his gaze swept over her, his pure green irises lit up in male appreciation. "It's the best news I've heard since the doc told me my leg was only broken in one place."

"Considering I can see you in the grouping of bull riders in these pictures, I suppose that *was* good news."

He let go with a hearty laugh. "Don't tell me you're a helper from the nursing service. I never saw one who looked like she was queen of the Sundance rodeo before."

That's what she looked like to him? How funny. Last night she'd resembled a bag lady. Geena didn't know what Colt would want her to say, but since he hadn't arrived yet, all she could do was be honest. "I came here to apply for the housekeeping position."

The charming flirt looked blown away. "You've got to be kidding! Who let you in the house?"

"Your brother."

His brows lifted. "How come you're still here?"

With that one question, Hank had just told her a mouthful about the hard inner facing of his older brother, who would never have hired her under normal circumstances. But there'd been nothing normal about her meeting with Colt. What Hank didn't realize was that his brother was suffering from a surfeit of guilt about her. In order to assuage it, he'd hired her for a *temporary* period.

No one knew that better than she did. It was just as well, because she was on a mission to find Todd's girlfriend, wherever it took her. "He decided to try me out on a probationary basis."

Looking stunned, Hank muttered something unintelligible under his breath.

"I'm very happy about it and hope your family will be too." She was more thankful than ever for the new clothes she was wearing as well as the other things she'd bought. Besides lingerie she now had jeans, tops, a few skirts and blouses, some sandals and a new purse and wallet. All things she'd once taken for granted, but prison had changed her perspective and priorities.

"Where are you from?"

"Rapid City."

After a long pause he said, "Since you're new to Wyoming, keep Saturday night open and I'll show you around Sundance. We'll do some line-dancing. How does that sound?"

"It sounds fun and I'm flattered," she said without having to think about it. "But whenever I'm employed, I have rules. No socializing within the company. In the case of the Brannigans, no fraternizing with the family or those employed on the Floral Valley Ranch. Besides, you can't dance until that cast comes off."

The playfulness left his eyes. "Did Colt tell you to say that?"

"I've been a working girl for a long time, Hank. I set my own rules." She'd learned how to protect herself in prison in order to survive.

He studied her for a minute, clearly stymied. "What are you doing out here in the hall alone?"

"Your brother should be along any second. He's taking me to meet your mother."

"He might be a while. When I passed him, he was on the phone with Sheila making his plans for the weekend. Come with me. Ina's probably taken Mom outside."

Had she been completely wrong about Colt? Silly how her heart pounded harder because she thought this Sheila could be someone important to him. *It's none of your business, Geena.* It couldn't be!

She followed Hank to the master bedroom. In truth it was an apartment with a fireplace and a den. She loved the vaulted ceiling and Western motif. The double doors were open onto a covered veranda.

Geena picked out their slim mother immediately. She was dressed in jeans and a blouse and was probably five feet four. Instead of boots, she wore sneakers and sat on a covered swing with her hands on her knees, as if she was getting ready to stand up and go. She resembled Hank in coloring, but there were sprinklings of silver in her short brown hair and some of the facial features were reminiscent of Colt's.

"Hi, Mom." Hank bent down to kiss her cheek. "Someone's come to see you. Laura Brannigan, meet Geena Williams, our new housekeeper." Eyes more brown than hazel stared at Geena without animation. There was no recognition before Hank finished the introductions. "Geena, meet her caregiver Ina Maynes."

"How do you do?" They shook hands. Ina was a bigger woman with blond hair, probably in her early fifties. She sat on a chair next to the swing. On the coffee table were a lot of books and magazines.

"How's she been doing since lunch?" he asked Ina.

"The same. Restless. She roamed the house this afternoon."

"That medicine the doctor prescribed should start to work by morning."

Geena glanced at Hank. "What kind does she take?"

"It's a new prescription for her anxiety."

Their mother continued to use her right foot to push off.

"Here you all are." Colt had come out on the veranda. Geena wished her body didn't quicken at the sound of his deep voice. His gaze flicked to her. "I see you've met mother and Ina."

"Yes. Hank caught me in the hall looking at the pictures. We're just getting acquainted."

"That's good." He turned to Ina. "Why don't you take a break until dinner? Geena and I will go for a walk with her."

"Thanks. I've got a letter to write."

Somehow Geena needed to keep reminding herself there was nothing personal in Colt's suggestion. For him it was vital she get to know the inner workings of the family so life on the ranch could get back to some kind of normal for them.

He reached for his mother's hand and helped her up from the swing. Still holding it, he waited until she'd stepped to the grass before he let go. Geena walked on her other side, enjoying the lush greenery surrounding the house.

"We'll head for the stream in the distance. It's one of our favorite places. When we were little tykes, she'd make picnics and teach us boys how to fish there, didn't you, Mom?"

Geena fought the tears smarting her eyelids as she noticed Laura make a beeline for the cottonwood trees lining the water's edge. All the memories of her life were locked up inside, but she seemed to know instinctively where she wanted to go. Every so often Geena eyed Colt with a covert glance. This had to be so hard for him and his brothers. She was touched by their love and devotion.

When they reached the rippling brook, his mother stood there quietly and stared. "What are the things she used to like?"

Colt angled his head toward her. "She loved to cook and garden. Now that she's at this stage, I have no idea. All we do is try to replicate what she used to enjoy— play her favorite music and read to her from the books she loved. She likes walks."

"What about horseback-riding?" His dark brows lifted in surprise. "From the pictures, she looked like an accomplished rider."

"She was a top barrel racer from her late teens on. That's how she and Dad met. He was a bull rider."

"That sounds like a magical beginning for them. Is there a reason she can't still ride if it's with supervision?"

He looked taken aback by her question. "I don't know. It's food for thought." She saw the love in his eyes as he looked at his mother through his black lashes. "Speaking of food, I bet you're hungry, Mom. Hank ought to have dinner ready for us pretty soon. Let's start back."

Colt took her hand and the three of them headed for the house. The mention of his mother's interests had Geena's mind racing with an idea. She couldn't wait to try it out once she was used to her official duties.

He took them around the house to the front drive where they could enter through the front door. This way he gave Geena a tour of the rustically decorated main floor. A marvelous hand-carved staircase rose from the center of the massive foyer. On the right it was flanked by a spacious living room, all vaulted with timbers. Beyond it lay a family room with a stone fireplace and furniture upholstered in red-and-green plaid.

On the left of the main hall was a dining room with a carved oak table and matching hutch. She counted twelve chairs. Down one hall she saw a study with display cases filled with trophies of all kinds and a large rack of antlers over the lintel. The other hall led to the big kitchen and another hall where Geena would be living.

"Lindsey's not feeling well, so I'm going to run dinner up to them," Hank announced when they entered the kitchen. The food was on the table ready to be served.

"I'll do it," Colt offered. "Be right back."

"I don't mind."

"With your leg in a cast, you'd have to walk. I can drive there in two seconds." She heard that same voice of authority she'd heard him use with the salesclerk. Already she was learning that Colt was by nature a fixer and took it upon himself to help everyone. Again she was impressed by that caring.

Hank gave up the argument but Geena noticed he wasn't happy about it. When Colt's logic couldn't be faulted, she wondered why it seemed so important to Hank. By now Ina had joined them at the table.

Geena started eating. "This spaghetti's delicious." He'd served canned fruit cocktail and store-bought bread.

"Thanks." He was still upset. "I can cook three things and the family's sick of them all."

Ina chuckled. "That's not true, Hank. We've enjoyed your meals." She helped Laura eat while she ate. Colt's mother appeared to have a good appetite and didn't turn away any food. She was such a lovely woman. Too young for this. Todd had been too young to die. Life could be cruel.

Hank's eyes focused on Geena. "I hope you can cook because I'm living for tomorrow when I don't have to eat any more of my...stuff." He'd almost said something else, reminding her of her brother Todd when he'd been in a grumpy mood. Hank appeared to be around thirty years of age, the same as Todd would be now if he were alive. She missed her brother so much, she still felt deep pain when she thought of him.

"I promise I won't make spaghetti for a month."

His dour expression didn't change. "That's a comforting thought." Hank had a big chip on his shoulder. She suspected her negative response to his invitation to go dancing hadn't helped his mood this evening.

"I would imagine you'll feel a lot better once that cast comes off. How much longer for you?"

"Next Monday. It's been a royal pain."

She was about to ask him how he'd broken it when Colt came back in the kitchen. He shot her a glance as he sat down at his place. "Have you been talking about me again?"

Ina chuckled, but Hank countered with another question. "What's wrong with Lindsey?"

"She's been having some contractions, but Travis said the doctor didn't think they'd last. They've stopped for now." His spaghetti disappeared fast. Geena would have to fix a lot of food to keep him satisfied.

Hank didn't move a muscle, but she could tell he was disturbed about something. Colt on the other hand went on eating as if nothing in the world could possibly be wrong. On impulse she got up from the table.

"I'm going to get myself some more coffee. Anyone else want some?"

"You can fill mine again," Colt answered.

She poured him another cup, realizing this was going to be her job from now on. It felt good to be useful again, especially in this household with all its dynamics and tensions, the kind that existed in a normal home. She'd missed the feeling of family.

It hadn't been the same after Todd had brought Janice home to live. Geena had wanted her brother to find the right woman and get married. She thought about the way Janice treated him and shuddered when she tried to imagine Janice with a baby. If Janice couldn't remain true to one man, the baby would suffer from the instability.

Geena had to stop thinking that way and sat down to finish her fresh cup of coffee. When she was through, she'd come to a decision and got to her feet once more. After picking up her plate, she walked around the table to remove Hank's, hoping to improve his cranky disposition.

"I take it you've been chief cook and bottle washer around here for a month, Hank, but no longer. Naturally I don't know where everything goes yet, but if I do the dishes myself, I'll find out. By tomorrow morning I'll be ready to tackle the meals."

The frown on his face turned to one of surprise before his chair shot back. Despite his cast, he stood up in a hurry. "Glory hallelujah!" was all he said before disappearing down the hall.

Ina took her cue and got up to walk Laura back to her room. That left Colt who started clearing the rest of the table. Even though the kitchen was roomy, his tall, powerful body seemed to fill it. He eyed Geena. "Two pairs of hands make the work go faster. Don't you agree? While we work, ask me all the questions you want."

She took him up on his offer, loving the cozy, domestic feeling now that they were alone. Around him her heart rate ran at a higher speed and there wasn't a thing she could do about it.

"Where's Titus?"

"He's sleeping up at Mac's place tonight. Mac Saunders is the ranch foreman. I'll introduce you to him and his wife, Leah, when it's convenient. Their family adopted Titus a long time ago. Everyone misses Dad and the dog is a reminder."

"That's so sweet. What kind of food do you feed him?"

"It's right here." He opened one of the cupboards and showed her everything, including his doggie treats.

"What about your mother? Does she require a special diet?"

"No. The doctor only said her meals should be well-balanced."

"Everyone needs that."

"We kind of fell down in that department this last month. As you noticed, Hank's been a limping time bomb." He flashed her a grin before emptying the dishwasher. She hadn't seen that particular look before. It made him too appealing.

While she loaded it, she watched where he put the clean dishes and utensils. After wiping off the counter, she cleaned the oven top. Colt took care of the table. Before she knew it they were done.

"Follow me to the walk-in pantry. The laundry room

is through that other door on the right." She did his bidding, marveling at the amount of food storage. The pantry was really another room.

"The big freezer is out in the mudroom. You'll find all the cuts of beef, pork and lamb you want. Everything's labeled. The freezer side of this fridge has chicken, ham, bacon, sausage. The rest is usually full of vegetables, fruits, salad, eggs, milk, cheese, yeast. The flour and sugar are kept in the bins on the right side of the dishwasher."

He'd mentioned all those items for a reason and Geena tried not to laugh out loud. "Thank you for the grand tour." She had an idea they hadn't eaten like they used to since Hank had taken over in the kitchen. Colt had put his point across big-time. Now it was up to her to produce those meals he was definitely salivating about. No worries there. Her grandmother had been a great cook and Geena had learned everything from her.

"Okay," he said, lounging against the counter with his strong arms crossed. "Ask me the question that's been bothering you since we came into the kitchen with mother."

The man had radar. "I don't know what you mean."

"That's the first lie you've told me since we met."

"What I'm thinking or wondering while I get to know your family is private and not important, Colt."

"It is to me. Out with it."

"This is about Hank," Geena whispered.

"I knew it. He needs to apologize for his rudeness. I'll talk to him. Let's go for a ride where we can be private. You won't need your purse unless you want it."

Alone with Colt. Excitement chased through her like the cool breeze she'd felt at the service station when she'd heard his voice and had discovered he'd followed her.

They left out the back door. He walked her past the other trucks and cars to a smaller, two-door white Ford pickup. "This is yours from here on out. The last person to drive it was Mary, but she didn't have long legs like yours." While she quivered from his personal comment, he opened the driver's side for her. "Go ahead and get in so you can adjust the seat the way you want."

Her arm accidentally brushed against his shoulder as she climbed in. It sent arcs of electricity through her nervous system. Her body was still reacting to his touch and made her clumsy as she tried several times to position the seat at the proper distance. He'd opened the door on the other side to watch. His action didn't help.

Finally she got it right. "There." As soon as she said the word, his masculine frame climbed in next to her. She couldn't help but be aware of his long, rock-hard legs. "Did you ever drive around in this with Mary?"

"No."

"I didn't think so."

They both chuckled before he handed her the truck keys on a ring. "Go ahead and take us up the road."

She started the engine. The tank was three-quarters full. "It's been a long time for me."

He slanted her a glance. "You rode your bike all those miles, so I don't see a problem."

The automatic transmission made it easy. After backing out, she headed up the hillside past the outbuildings. He pointed out Travis's place and Ben and Alice's cabin. Farther on, Mac and Leah's house. With him giving her directions, they reached another area of the property featuring open rolling grasslands.

"I dreamed about times like this in prison. You have no idea what it means to be free." Her voice shook. "I'm sorry if I talk about it so much. I'll try to stop."

His profile took on a chiseled cast in the semi-darkness. "Three nights ago you were still behind bars. Like a returning war vet, you'll always have that memory with you. But hopefully in time, the experience won't traumatize you."

"Are you speaking from personal experience?"

"Not exactly. I have a cousin, Robert, who's my age and lives in Casper, Wyoming. He was in the military, but he hasn't been the same since he got home last year. Though he's in therapy and doing better, he still has occasional flashbacks and flies up to the ranch for a few days every so often to talk to me."

"The poor thing. PTSD?"

"Yes."

"There was a woman in my cell block who'd served in Iraq. When she got back, she torched her stepfather's warehouse because he beat up her mother. She didn't know he was inside. His death sent her to prison. Sometimes at night we'd hear her screams and have to listen to things that made my skin crawl. She needs help."

Colt shot her another glance. "After what you've been through, you could benefit from some professional therapy yourself."

"Warden James told me the same thing," she admitted.

"The insurance I pay for you would cover a psychiatrist. Robert's is one of the best around."

"But if he's in Casper, that's pretty far away."

"No problem. I do regular business there with my uncle and will fly you in our Cessna from Taylor Field.

If you'd like, I'll leave the doctor's name and phone number for you on the kitchen counter by the phone."

Panic enveloped her because she sensed Colt was already worried about his new housekeeper. Part of her hoped he cared for her in a more personal way, but maybe she was deceiving herself. After all, that is what he did: he cared for people and took care of them.

It was natural for him to be concerned over everyone on the ranch. He carried their problems on his back. Since she needed this job desperately, she'd better go along with his suggestion. Not that she'd find herself out of work if she didn't. He wasn't like that. But she wanted harmony between them.

"Thank you." What else could she say? Deep down, she knew she needed help from an outside source and was grateful. "If you'll do that, I'll make an appointment."

"Good." He sounded relieved. "At the next rise, there's a lookout where you can pull to a stop."

She drove a little further till she came to it. Evening had fallen. The surroundings of rough hills with steep ravines beyond them was surreal. Geena shut off the engine and got out of the cab. He joined her as they took in the vista.

"After his release, the Sundance Kid was a fool to leave Wyoming," she said. "He could have redeemed his life by starting all over again right here, on a spread just like yours."

A chuckle escaped Colt's lips before he sobered. "It looks beautiful, but it has its headaches. Tell me what happened with Hank today."

Colt was a natural-born leader who took on the man-

tle of the ranch and everyone's problems without thinking about it. He really was a breed apart from other
men, and he already had a tentacle hold on her heart.

CHAPTER FIVE

"HE asked me to go dancing on Saturday night," she answered without pretending to misunderstand. Colt knew it had to be something like that. "Naturally I turned him down."

"On what grounds?"

"That I have a rule never to combine the personal side of my life with business. I thought he'd handled the rejection just fine, but later at dinner he seemed upset."

"No man likes to be turned down, but Hank had more than your rejection on his mind, trust me." He cocked his head, feeling very protective of her. "I'll have a talk with him." His brother was a bit of a player.

"Maybe you shouldn't. I don't want to hurt his feelings."

Her caring stirred Colt's emotions. "Anything else you'd like to ask me?"

"I wondered how he broke his leg in the first place."

"At the rodeo in Laramie. The bull stomped on him before he could roll out from under him."

"Oh no— Is Hank a champion?"

Colt nodded. "He's won a lot of prize money. This year he was hoping to win the world championship in Las Vegas coming up in December, but this broken leg has cost him a lot in practice time. He could go for it next year, but he's not getting any younger. That's a demon he can't fight."

"What will happen if he doesn't compete any more this year?"

"He'll keep doing his work here on the ranch."

"That explains a lot of his pent-up frustration." She flicked him another glance. "In the hall I saw pictures of you steer-wrestling. When did you stop competing?"

He hadn't expected that, but she deserved an answer. "After I got married. By the time we were divorced, I had too many ranch responsibilities to consider going back to competition."

"I see."

Colt waited for the inevitable fallout questions, but they never came. She wasn't like any woman he'd known before. She'd gotten under his skin, all right. If he felt this way right now, how would he handle her leaving at the end of the summer? Before more time passed, he intended to ask her about her future plans.

"Before we go back, there's something else you should know. Lindsey's going to have that baby any minute. She's very good-looking and high maintenance. So's her mother. After she gets out of the hospital, don't let either of them order you around."

"Being the new inmate on the block, I learned the hard way about bullying. The trick is not to let them get away with it the first time." Geena's smile revealed a hint of toughness. She had grit, all right.

"That goes for headstrong animals, too."

"Thanks for talking to me, Colt. I think I'm ready to face tomorrow."

He shifted his weight. "One more reality check. Are you feeling overwhelmed yet?"

She took her time before answering. "I'd be lying if I didn't tell you I'm nervous that I won't be able to live up to your expectations. But having said that, you don't know how nice it is to be around a real family where I can try to help make things easier. Your load is huge. I could ask you the same question about feeling overwhelmed."

"I admit sometimes I am. When everyone needs you at once, it can be a little suffocating, but that feeling passes. We were talking about your problems." She had the ability to draw him out when he least expected it.

"In prison I learned about work. It's the great panacea."

Work had always been his panacea, but lately he'd found out it wasn't nearly enough. That appeared to be Geena's fault. Fighting her charisma was like battling a force of nature.

"If there's any advice I can give you as your employer, treat the ranch house as your own home. Make it yours."

"Thank you."

"If you want to change the decor in Mary's old room, you have my permission to do whatever you want with it."

"I couldn't!" she emoted. "It's like living inside a fabulous museum. I love it."

"You'd make her happy if she heard that. The entertainment center is in your bedroom armoire but keep in mind we have a family room you saw off the living room. It's there for your use any time. And something else." He pulled a cell phone out of his pocket. "I bought you this and a laptop today while you were shopping."

She took it from him. Though brief, he felt her touch like a white-hot brand. "You've thought of everything!"

"We need to be able to keep in touch. I've programmed my cell phone number on two, and put your number in my phone. You can phone long distance or out of the country. Later you can program in the other phone numbers you want.

"I also loaded the laptop and left it in your room. Look through it when you have time. If you have problems navigating, I'll help you. It contains all the information you need on the staff. Phone numbers, addresses. That includes the hands and stockmen. Emergency numbers.

"As for the house inventory, once you have a grasp, it'll make a difference in what supplies you order and how much will be needed at one time. You're welcome to use the computer in the den too."

"All I do is say thank you." She put the phone in her front pocket. "Now there's something I have to say to you."

"That sounds serious."

"It is. Don't ever hold back if you've discovered I've done something wrong or overstepped my bounds or dealt with something in a way that made things worse. The only way I can learn is for you to tell me straight up, Colt. No lies, no tiptoeing around the truth to spare hurt feelings."

Her earnestness brought out more of her natural beauty. "In other words, no quarter asked."

"None. I'm a big girl going on twenty-eight. I grew up after I was put in prison."

Prison was the word that came up in her conversation more than any other. Colt decided he was the one who needed therapy if he was going to be able to handle it. "Then I would say we understand each other."

"Yes."

She beat him back to the truck and started the engine. They returned to the ranch house while another amazing full moon started its ascent. She poked her head out the window. "Can you believe we actually went up there?"

"One of our hands thinks it was a hoax."

"Several inmates were convinced it was a conspiracy, too. To be honest, I really don't care what they believe. How could anyone care on a night like this? Umm. Fresh mountain air. There's nothing like it."

"I agree with you."

"I know one thing. I'll never take anything for granted again."

Almost to the house, his cell phone rang. He checked the caller ID and picked up. "Hank?"

"Travis left me a message that Lindsey's water broke. The doctor told him to drive her to the hospital."

Colt was afraid he knew why his brother sounded so anxious. "This is what we've all been waiting for."

"Where are you? Haven't you checked your messages?"

For once Colt had been too involved in his conversation with Geena to think about anything else. "I was busy."

"Shouldn't we do something?"

"Not until Travis asks us. I'll see you in a few minutes."

After he clicked off Geena said, "I take it the baby is coming. Is it a boy or a girl?"

"A girl."

"You're going to be an uncle before you know it. That's exciting."

It should be. But having both his brothers in love with the same woman clouded the picture for Colt. "Now that we're back, you go to bed, Geena. It's been a long day. I'll see you in the morning."

"Thank you for giving me a new start. I'll always be indebted to you." She jumped down from the truck and hurried into the house without drawing out their conversation. Was she a little spooked by Colt? He'd gotten the impression she was a very private person, but maybe he made her nervous. By the time he walked through the back door, she'd disappeared.

He moved through the house to check on his mother. She was in bed asleep. All was quiet from Ina's room. After locking up and turning out lights, Colt climbed the stairs. Hank met him at the top and followed him into his bedroom.

"Where in the hell have you been?"

"I gave Mary's truck to Geena. She drove us a ways while she got used to it."

"That's quite a transformation from the woman I met in the kitchen last night. What's the story on her? I didn't see a car."

"She didn't have one. Geena arrived on her bike to interview for the position." Straight from prison.

"She's a biker?"

"Not in the sense you mean. She has a road bike. I put it inside the storage shed for safekeeping."

"So where did she sleep last night?"

Colt was getting tired of answering his questions. "In Mary's old room."

"You're kidding! You mean you hired her on the spot?"

No, but for reasons he still hadn't examined, he hadn't want to see her leave. "Not until today. With Ina occupying the guest room on the main floor, I had to put her somewhere last night." Certainly not upstairs in the other guest room across from Hank's bedroom.

His brother might take it on himself to get more acquainted with her and start asking questions. Geena would rather no one knew about her time in prison. Colt didn't want his brother making her uncomfortable.

"Can she even cook?"

Geena's looks had knocked his brother sideways. Obviously, so had her rejection. But his brother was so mixed up emotionally, it was hard to read him. "I guess we'll find out tomorrow. At least you're off the hook. She's temporary until fall. By then I'll find a woman like Mary to replace her."

"Fat chance."

Colt agreed, yet he had to honor the contract he'd made with Geena. That meant he needed to put out more feelers for a permanent housekeeper, but the idea of her leaving was growing unacceptable to him.

"Let's just be thankful that with the baby coming, someone will be here to help out. A word of warning, Hank. Let's respect her boundaries, hmm?"

His brother sighed. "I'm going to have to, since she turned me down for a date."

Good. The resignation in Hank's voice told him all he needed to know. "That makes for less complications around here. Go to bed, Hank. We'll hear from Travis

before long. I don't know about you, but I'm whacked."
Except that Colt knew he'd have another sleepless night.

When the alarm clock went off at five-thirty, Geena
jumped out of bed to get ready for her first day of work.
She'd showered last night, so all she had to do was put
on a fresh pair of jeans and a plum-colored cotton crew
neck sweater with short sleeves. While she rebraided
her hair and put it on top of her head, she wondered if
the baby had been born yet.

After applying a pink lipgloss, she slipped on sandals
and hurried through the house to the mudroom. Tonight
she would serve leg of lamb with all the trimmings.

Once she'd taken it out of the freezer and put it aside
in the kitchen to thaw, she made coffee, then got bacon
and sausage from the fridge. They'd taste good with
scrambled eggs. For an added treat, she made milk
gravy and baking powder biscuits. She'd forgotten how
much fun it was to cook. Her grandmother's recipes
were the best.

By five to seven, everything was ready and she'd
poured the orange juice. As she added two kinds of jam
to the table, her employer entered the kitchen in a tan
Western shirt and jeans. He could have no idea how his
incomparable masculinity affected the opposite sex.

"Good morning, Geena. Something in here smells
fabulous."

He smelled marvelous himself. "I hope it tastes as
good." Colt was so striking, she busied herself pouring
him some coffee at the place where he'd sat last night.
"Do I take it you have a new niece?"

Before he sat down, his hazel gaze appraised her so
thoroughly, she could hardly breathe. "Not yet, but I

suspect it won't be long now. After breakfast Hank and I will drive to Sundance and see how things are going. By the way, I spoke to Hank last night. He gets it."

Geena's heart warmed to him even more for being concerned. "Thank you for telling me." While he drained his glass of juice, she went over to the stove and made up a plate for him. "Do you like milk gravy on your biscuits?"

"I like everything. Bring it on."

"You sound like my brother Todd."

"How old was he when he died?"

"I'd say Hank's age."

"Were you close?"

"Very." Until Janice moved in with him. She was probably living with another guy by now. And what about the baby? Was it even alive?

Stifling another shudder, she brought his plate over and set it in front of him. "Before I serve anyone else, does anyone in the house have allergies I should know about? Or foods they truly don't like? Especially your mom?"

He ate two sausage links before he flashed her a sideward glance. "Not to my knowledge, but I appreciate you asking. Won't you join me?"

"Not yet. I'm waiting for everyone to come." In truth she derived pure pleasure from watching him eat while she propped herself against the counter to drink her coffee. Anticipating his desire for more biscuits, she took a plate of them to the table. In a minute they disappeared.

Soon a guest she hadn't thought of came flying into the kitchen. He plopped his head on Colt's leg.

"Hey, Titus." He rubbed his fur. "Mac must have

brought you home." His presence reminded Geena to put out dog food for him.

After feeding the dog a sausage, Colt got up from the chair and left and, before she knew it, he came back into the kitchen with a dark-blond man who had to be in his mid forties. "Mac Saunders? Meet Geena Williams, our new housekeeper."

Mac removed his cowboy hat and shook her hand. "Pleased to make your acquaintance, ma'am."

"Sit down and have breakfast with us," Colt insisted. "These biscuits and milk gravy are to die for." Colt sounded like he'd meant it.

"Yeah?" the foreman grinned. His blue eyes lingered on Geena before he complied.

"Let me take your hat." She put it over on one of the other counters before she served him a plate.

"Yup," he said a minute later. "I think I just died and went to heaven."

Colt eyed her briefly. "Did you hear that, Geena?"

"If it's food, men love it," she teased.

"*This* is food—" Mac blurted with such enthusiasm it warmed her heart. While the two men discussed the day's work schedule, she heard other voices.

Hank came in, making record time with that cast on his leg. He was followed by Ina and their mother. Geena was kept busy serving everyone. She buttered a hot biscuit for Laura and put blackberry jam on it.

"No word from Travis yet?" Ina inquired. Colt shook his head. "A first baby usually takes a long time."

"We're going to see him after we eat," Hank muttered. The other two men continued to talk business. Geena poured everyone a second cup of coffee and kept the food coming. Before long a restless Hank got up from the table. "Coming, Colt?"

"As soon as I've had one more of Geena's biscuits. I think I've eaten half a dozen."

Mac laughed. "With food like this, you're going to gain weight fast. Much obliged, Geena." He got up and walked over to the counter for his hat.

Hank wheeled around and left the kitchen in a temper Geena could feel. Colt eyed her briefly before he got to his feet. Though Colt had explained some of Hank's problems to do with his broken leg and his rodeo career, he hadn't told her everything. Nor had Colt explained about his own wife or his marriage. "See you later."

After the men left, Ina stood up. "That was a delicious meal, Geena."

"Thank you. I'm glad to see Laura enjoyed it too."

"She surely did."

"Colt said you eat lunch at one o'clock."

"Yes, but after all this, I'm not sure we'll be hungry. Don't go to a lot of trouble. Make something light. See you later."

Once they'd gone, Geena put more food and water out for Titus, then cleared the table and did the dishes. Before long she heard a female voice call out hello. It turned out to be Elaine Ruff, one of the house cleaners coming into in the kitchen. Evidently all three women had keys. They chatted for a few minutes. Elaine informed Geena that today was the day she washed windows.

Geena told her to go about her usual business, then she changed clothes and drove into town. She needed to pick up the mail. After that she renewed her driver's license and then bought produce. Ina had said she wanted something light for lunch so Geena decided to pick up some fresh crab for a salad.

Before she started back to the ranch, she made one more quick stop near the town center.

Colt entered the back of the house with no time to spare before dinner. He'd planned it this way on purpose. After leaving the hospital at eleven that morning, he'd seen the white truck parked in front of the police station on his way out of town. Hank hadn't noticed or he would have said something.

At the sight of it there, any relief Colt felt now that the long nine-month wait was over and mother and daughter were doing well had gone up in smoke. He could speculate till doomsday about Geena's skittishness, but it wouldn't do any good until she told him what she'd been doing there. The hell of it was, he knew it was none of his business.

But he wanted it to be his business because he was growing more attracted to her all the time. The fact that she was planning to leave the ranch at the end of the summer was the very reason he should have no personal interest in her. Unfortunately, he'd already become emotionally involved with her.

She was the first woman to get to him like this since his divorce. He hadn't thought he could feel like this again. But alongside the attraction was the frustration that she hadn't opened up to him emotionally. Not being able to know her private thoughts and feelings was driving him crazy.

When he'd dropped off a taciturn Hank at the house, he'd gone straight to the barn for his horse. Since then, he'd been in the saddle close to eight hours repairing fence line. Hard work should have brought some semblance of calm to his mind, but nothing could have been further from the truth.

He walked into the mudroom to wash the dust off his face and hands. After drying himself, he stepped into the kitchen and was assaulted by the smell of roast lamb and homemade cinnamon rolls. The aroma knocked him back on his heels. It smelled like his mother's cooking before she'd come down with Alzheimer's. Since then Mary had taken over in the food department. Her meals had been good, but nothing like this.

His gaze moved to Geena, who was wearing a denim skirt and striped blouse her figure did wonders for. Her back was turned to him while she tossed a green salad. Everything was in order. The table set. *So what were you expecting, Brannigan?*

She turned to put the bowl on the table and saw him. "I didn't realize you were back. Congratulations on becoming an uncle!" Her cheery attitude got under his skin. Whatever she was hiding wasn't visible on the surface. "How does it feel?"

Geena had done nothing wrong. In fact, so far she'd done everything right. That was the problem.

"I'm still getting used to the idea." It was Hank who had the problem dealing with his emotions where Lindsey was concerned. "Where's everyone?"

Something flickered in the depths of her eyes, as if she didn't know what to make of his state of mind. "Hank said he was going out with a friend and left the house hours ago." That didn't surprise Colt. With the birth of the baby, his pain had intensified. "I'm sure Ina will be bringing your mother shortly. Would you like to eat now, or wait for them?"

He rubbed the back of his neck. "I'll see what's holding them up." But no sooner had he started for the hallway than they appeared. He smiled at Ina before grasping his mother's hand to lead her to the table.

For a moment Colt felt as though he was on the wrong side of a looking glass. When he peered in, he was in the same house he'd always lived in with the same delicious smells from the kitchen wafting through the air. But the mother he kissed showed no recognition of him or her surroundings, while the woman at the stove— He couldn't finish the thought.

Colt helped his mother to the table and Geena started to serve them.

Who was she?

He knew certain basic facts about her, but he didn't know *her* or what made her tick. She would have had women and men friends before her imprisonment. His stomach muscles tightened when he realized she might have had a lover at the time she was incarcerated. Hadn't she mentioned a boyfriend from before prison? In one morning she'd been torn away from everything she knew.

No matter what her circumstances were now, he couldn't figure out why she would need to talk to the police. If this had something to do with her imprisonment, she should be making inquiries with the authorities in Rapid City, not Sundance.

"This is another wonderful meal, Geena," Ina raved as she bit into another slice of roast lamb.

"Thank you."

"How did you learn to cook like this?"

"My grandmother." Colt was certain that was true. You'd never eat food like this in prison.

The new development with Geena had robbed him of his appetite. He ate a little, but was unable to do justice to the meal. After thanking her, he got up from the table. "If you'll excuse me, I need to make some phone calls for Travis I can't put off any longer. If someone asks, I'll be in the study."

It wasn't a lie. He'd told his brother he'd inform everyone about the baby, but he couldn't sit there in front of Geena and pretend everything was fine when it wasn't.

An hour later he went back to the kitchen for coffee. Before he reached it he heard voices and discovered Travis sitting at the table talking quietly with Geena while he finished his dinner. He must have been here for a while.

She'd done the dishes and stood at the counter drinking coffee with him as if they were old friends. Travis knew Colt had hired a new housekeeper. Judging by the way he was looking at her, his brother more than approved.

His glance lit on Colt. "I decided to take your advice and come home for a meal and some sleep before I go back to the hospital." His eyes returned to Geena. "This is a housekeeper worth keeping."

"Time will tell," she murmured, reminding Colt of their conversation about her position being temporary. She already had her life planned out once she left the ranch. But what was it? "Could I get you some coffee, Colt?"

"No thanks." Caffeine was the last thing he needed if he hoped to get any sleep tonight.

"I was just about to ask Travis where he fits in the family line," she volunteered.

His brother's tired face broke out in a smile before he got to his feet. "It's like this. Colt's our big brother. I was born three years later, and Hank came along eleven months after that."

"And now you have a darling baby daughter of your own," she commented. "I can't wait to get a peek at her."

"If all goes well, I'll be bringing them home before dinner tomorrow." He cleared his own dishes and put them on the counter. "After hospital food, that meal saved my life. I'm going to the cabin and will see both of you later." He left the house through the back door.

While Colt watched her, Geena promptly put the dishes in the dishwasher and turned it on before wiping off the table. She'd made the kitchen spotless.

"Geena?" He couldn't take any more of her seeming nonchalance. She looked up with those innocent eyes. "If you'd come to Travis's bedroom with me please." He needed to talk to her and didn't want Hank walking in on them unexpectedly.

CHAPTER SIX

GEENA followed Colt through the house to the upstairs, having felt tension from him the second he'd walked in the kitchen. He wasn't the same man who'd left for the hospital earlier that morning with Hank.

For that matter, Hank hadn't been in a mood to talk when he'd returned before going out again. Once he'd gone, there'd been no sign of Colt for the rest of the day and no appetite from him at dinner. She couldn't begin to understand the undercurrents in this house. The arrival of a new baby should have generated a certain amount of talk and excitement.

Colt took a left at the top of the stairs and led her to a spacious bedroom with an en suite bathroom at the end of the hall. An unmade baby crib with a mattress stood in the middle of the rustic room. Her gaze went to some sacks piled on the colorful quilt of the king-sized bed.

"They have a nursery set up at their house, but as long as Lindsey will be staying here for a few weeks, I called and had this delivered on Monday. Tell me…if you were a new mother just home from the hospital, I'd like you to look around with your woman's eye and see what else needs doing. Alice cleaned in here yesterday."

The man in charge of his ranching empire could do

anything, but a new baby in the house presented a challenge no one, including Geena, was prepared for. Her heart went out to Colt because in the Brannigan household, the buck stopped with him.

"Why don't we make up the crib first?" She walked over to the bed and emptied the sacks. The first thing that came out was a little pink tub. "This is perfect for bathing the baby."

Colt put it in the bathroom then helped her undo the packaging. Before long the crib looked like a dream with its pink and white padded bumper pad tied in place. "The pink hearts on that eyelet quilt are adorable. How did you know to pick anything so gorgeous?"

"I didn't," he said in a deep voice. "I ordered everything over the phone and said it was for a girl."

"Well the baby will love it. What's her name?" She'd been waiting to hear from someone.

"I don't know. They're still deciding."

That explained why Travis hadn't said anything. "Is Lindsey from a prominent family?"

"Yes."

"Here in Sundance?"

"No. Gillette."

"Since I heard from the men at the Cattlemen's Store that Brannigan is a revered name in Wyoming, she and Travis must be having a difficult time trying to decide which names from both family trees should be retained." For the first time tonight she glimpsed mirth in his hazel eyes. That was an improvement from his earlier mood and made her breathing come a little easier. "Let's put the crib against the wall out of the way."

Together they rolled it across the Oriental rug covering the hardwood flooring. Their arms and hips brushed against each other. Being in touching distance made it impossible to keep certain thoughts from filling her head. Like how would she feel if Colt were her husband and they were bringing home their baby.

Angry with herself for letting her mind wander, she hurried back to the bed. "She's a lucky little girl to have these cute stretchy suits and shirts. Where shall we put the clothes?"

"How about the dresser next to the crib? There's nothing in it."

"Perfect. We'll stack the diapers on top." In another few minutes everything was done. "When a girlfriend of mine had a baby a few years ago, the hospital sent her home with everything she'd need. If Lindsey's missing anything else, it won't be a crucial item. I'd say this room was ready. Let me just check the bathroom for towels. You can never have enough of them."

There were several on the racks. A quick check in the cupboards and she discovered half a dozen more. "Everything looks in great shape," she announced after walking back in the bedroom. "With a wastebasket in both rooms, Lindsey will want for nothing."

Colt had gathered up the mess into one bag to be thrown out. "Want to make a bet?"

A gentle laugh escaped her lips. He had a heightened sense of responsibility for everyone in his family and all living on the ranch. Maybe too much? Besides a marriage that had clearly ended, was this one of the reasons he didn't find the time to play or develop a relationship of his own?

"You work too hard, Colt Brannigan. Don't you ever take time off?"

He eyed her narrowly. "Probably not as much as I should," he admitted in a rare moment of truth.

"There must be times when you feel stifled by all there is to do around here."

Colt nodded. "Someone has to do it."

Like finding a new housekeeper for instance? The thought that his hiring her had been part of those things contributing to his feeling of suffocation haunted her.

With her work done here, she started to leave, but he called her back. "Was I mistaken, or were you parked in front of the police station this morning?"

Ah... He'd seen her. Naturally that raised questions and explained a lot. She turned around. "After going to the store and the post office, I stopped there on my way back to the ranch."

"Are you in some kind of trouble where *I* could help?" There it came again. That concern for her. If it was because he was personally interested in her, she'd have been thrilled. But she feared his natural drive to be in charge put her on his list of things to tend to.

Earlier she'd asked Colt to tell her if she did something wrong or stepped over the line. Now he deserved an answer. "No trouble at all, but since I'm freshly out of prison and work for you, I can understand your concern and realize you deserve an explanation."

He cast her a speculative glance. "As long as you're not in harm's way, you don't have to tell me anything." His sincerity made her pulse race harder.

True. She didn't have to, but this man had been so good to her, she'd never be able to repay him. The least she could do was put his mind at rest where her activities were concerned.

"I'm looking for someone who disappeared from

Rapid City without a trace. While I was in prison, I asked Kellie Tyre, a waitress friend of mine, if she could find out any information about someone I'm looking for. Kellie and I corresponded a few times, but she couldn't tell me anything.

"I never dreamed I'd get out of prison, but now that I'm free, I decided to stop at the police station to ask if they knew a good private investigator I could contact who would make inquiries for me. They told me I'd have better luck phoning a reputable attorney who could give me the name of one."

Shadows crept over his arresting facial features. "Is this person you're looking for a man?"

"No. As I told you earlier, the man I'd been dating at the time of my arrest, Kevin Starr, dropped me faster than he would have done a hot potato. Rupert's death was a hideous crime. Kevin has probably had nightmares over the fact that he ever dated me. The fact that he didn't once try to talk to me about it, or hear my side of the story isn't unusual. It would take a remarkable man who loved me deeply to at least make a few gestures." Someone like Colt...

"I'm sorry for that, Geena."

"Don't be. I expected nothing. Only a rare human being like you would ever have let me go into prison without at least wanting to know the facts from my lips. It's because of the way you're made." Geena loved him for that compassionate attribute.

"You don't know that."

"Oh but I do. You took me in, remember? As for the answer to your question, I'm looking for the woman who was living with my brother when he was killed. Her name is Janice Rigby. She'd moved into my grandmother's house with Todd while I was still in college at Laramie. When I came back to Rapid City for good, my brother told me I could stay with them while I was looking for a job.

"But Janice made me so uncomfortable, I went apartment-hunting and ended up renting from Rupert Brown. I didn't want to cause trouble for my brother. He loved Janice, so I never told him I thought she might be seeing another man when Todd was out working the pipeline. I have no proof, of course, but when I would go over there, she wouldn't let me inside and that made me wonder.

"Once in a while he and I met for lunch, but I didn't go near Janice because I knew she resented me. I'm sure he knew it too. Each time I was with my brother, I sensed he wasn't happy, but he didn't tell me why. We'd always been close. After I was put in prison, he tried to do everything to help me."

Colt came closer.

"When I heard he'd been killed, I thought, of course, that in her grief Janice would get in touch with me so we could mourn together. But she didn't. Not one word." Geena couldn't stop the trembling in her voice. "I need to see her and ask her about Todd. I don't know any details."

I don't even know if she had the baby.

"Kellie's last letter said Janice no longer lived in my grandmother's house. The landlord kicked her out along with some guy who'd moved in with her. I'd had my suspicions she'd been unfaithful to Todd. Apparently she left still owing the landlord rent and didn't leave a forwarding address."

His mouth became a taut line of anger. "I'm assuming she took off with all your possessions."

Geena bit her lip. "After I was locked up, Todd took all the things in my apartment back to the house. I'm sure Janice got away with the lot and probably sold everything to settle somewhere else. The furniture wasn't that important, but the mementos and pictures are priceless."

Instead of saying anything, she heard a groan from Colt before he pulled her into his arms. She knew it was a gesture of comfort. The milk of human kindness was instinctive in him. Though she should have eased away, he had no idea how much she needed this and slowly she felt her stiff body relax against his hard-muscled strength. While her body shook with silent tears, he rubbed his hands over her back.

She would never have expected this kind of intimacy from a man who held his emotions so close to his heart. Geena was totally unprepared for the feelings every stroke of his fingers evoked against her arms and neck.

When she realized he'd aroused her desire, she was appalled by her response and needed to stop this before she got in too deep and found herself clamoring for his mouth. How mortifying that would be when all he'd meant to do was lend her a shoulder to cry on. She'd known other men's arms around her in the past, but this was different. Entirely different.

Through sheer strength of will she took a step away from him. "I was afraid I might break down if I told you about Janice." Avoiding his eyes she said, "Thank you for being a wonderful listener. If I had to fall apart, I'm glad it was with you. The head of the Floral Valley Ranch has an unequaled reputation for handling the unexpected. I ought to know since I've already created several problems you didn't ask for." She moved to the door. "Goodnight."

Unasked for was right.

And you couldn't leave it alone, Brannigan.

Colt had thought her visit to the police station had been motivated by her involvement with a man prior to her imprisonment. Once again he'd gotten things wrong. Damn, damn and damn. But her explanation about this Kevin Starr explained why she kept so much to herself.

He'd thought he'd been wired last night....

Turning off the bedroom light, Colt headed down the hall to his room for a shower. A long cold one that would put out the fire her body had ignited in him like bolt lightning. When he'd doused every lick of flame, he would be ready to call Sheila.

Sheila was an attractive forest ranger recently stationed in Sundance. He'd met her a few weeks ago when a bunch of local ranchers had been called on by the forest service to help build a fire break. A fire in the western Black Hills needed to be contained. When it was out, Sheila had asked him to a party in town for this Saturday night given by the rangers. He'd told her he'd have to let her know later on because he wasn't certain when the baby would arrive and he might be needed.

But he had no excuse to turn her down now. The baby was here and the ranch had a new housekeeper who was more than holding her own. Colt ground his teeth. He would tell Sheila yes and have a good time, even if it killed him.

* * *

While the family had been assembled for breakfast
Geena had been secretly relieved that Colt behaved as
if nothing had happened last night. That was because
the explosion of desire had all been on her part, not his.
This morning he'd devoured his steak and eggs with
relish before announcing that Lindsey's parents would
be arriving any time now.

"Put them in the guest bedroom at the other end of
the hall upstairs on the left. I'll try to get back to welcome them."

Geena nodded. She noticed Hank didn't say anything. Once Colt had left the table, he'd disappeared too.

After Ina and Laura had gone, Geena made up a
batch of sugar cookie dough. As she was putting it in the
freezer to get cold, someone else had joined her in the
kitchen. This time Geena wasn't surprised. She turned
to the woman in her mid thirties, "You must be Trish
Hayward. I'm the new housekeeper, Geena Williams."

"Hi. Alice told me. She said you were very nice."

"Thank you, Trish." They shook hands. "I know you
work around a schedule you've developed with Colt,
but before you make beds and do the wash, will you
come upstairs with me to the guest room? Lindsey had
her baby."

"I heard it was a little girl."

"Yes. She and Travis will be staying here for a while
and her parents will be arriving today. I want to make
sure that the guest room and bathroom are ready for
Mr. and Mrs. Cunningham."

"Sure."

They went upstairs and down the hall past Colt's
and Hank's bedrooms. Both beds were unmade. Colt's
looked thrashed, reminding her she was a restless

sleeper too. Much as she would love to take a closer
look at the pictures she could see on Colt's dresser from
the doorway, she would never go in there unless she
was given a reason.

His ex-wife must have been unforgettable for him not
to have married again. Maybe this Sheila his brother
had mentioned was someone important to him now.
Geena didn't want to be jealous, but the mere thought
of him holding another woman the way he'd held her
last night sent a strange pain through her heart. This
was what came from being locked away from men for
such a long time.

Tomorrow was her day off. When she went to town
to find an attorney, she'd drop by the store where she'd
bought her Western gear and say hello to the guy who'd
waited on her. If Steve was there and asked her out,
she'd go and have a good time. She needed to do something to get Colt out of her system.

She and Trish went through the guest room to get
it ready. The bathroom needed more towels and some
things from the pantry such as hand soap and tissues.
The closet had plenty of hangers and extra pillows.
They'd need clean pillow cases. The bed needed fresh
linens and the bedspread needed to be fluffed.

After leaving Trish to her duties, Geena went back
downstairs in search of Ina and Laura. She found them
taking a walk around the back of the house and joined
them.

"Ina? I want to try an experiment with Laura. When
you're through with your walk, would you bring her to
the kitchen? I'm making some cookies to have on hand
and thought Laura might enjoy helping me."

"That's an interesting idea. I'll bring her in a few minutes."

"Good."

When they appeared in the kitchen, Geena had made a place at the table to roll out a portion of the dough. She'd found a drawer full of cookie cutters and brought out the heart and the clover leaf along with a cookie sheet.

"Let's seat Laura right here. Colt told me she loved to cook. Maybe if she does a cutout and likes it, she'll do another one."

"It's certainly worth a try."

Geena got to work using the heart cutter first. It had a little knob that was easy to hold. She pressed it into the dough, then eased the cookie off the floured board with a knife and put it on the cookie sheet.

"Do you remember making these, Laura?" She put the cutter in the woman's hand and helped her press it down in the dough. After Geena lifted her own hand, Laura kept the cutter there and gave it another little thrust before lifting the cutter.

"That's perfect!" Geena cried. Before she could remove the cookie, Laura had found another spot and pressed all on her own.

"Well, what do you know," Ina marveled.

Laura was like a machine. Geena put the pan of cookies in the oven, then hurried to the freezer and brought out the other half of the dough to roll out. When she handed Laura the clover leaf to try, she hung on to the heart, her cutter of choice.

"It looks like you're having fun, Mom." Colt had come in the kitchen without them being aware of it and leaned between Geena and Laura to kiss her forehead. "Do you remember I like almond icing, too?"

Ina smiled. "Geena's idea is pure genius. I've never seen your mother enjoy anything this much."

Afraid the cookies were burning, Geena pushed herself away from Colt and rushed over to the oven to take them out. In truth, she'd felt the heat from his hard jaw searing hers. To her dismay he followed her and grabbed a paper towel so he could pick up a hot one.

"I haven't had a homemade sugar cookie in years." His gaze found hers and clung while he ate it in one go. "Mom used to make hearts and put our names on them."

"I tried to get her to use the clover leaf, but she didn't want it."

His eyes narrowed on her mouth. "That's because the leaves came unattached while we boys iced them. Wouldn't it be something if she still remembered?"

"If only more of her memories could come back," she whispered. If only Colt had met Geena under different circumstances and had asked her out because he couldn't help himself. Then she'd know that he had personal feelings for her. But she was the housekeeper, and she knew he was wonderful to everyone.

His eyes darkened with some unnamed emotion. "These cookies are delicious, by the way. Try one." He picked up another heart and put it to her lips, forcing her to take a bite. His fingers against her mouth sent curling heat to every atom of her body. While she munched he said, "Thank you for including her like this."

"It was an experiment. Since she liked it so much, she'd probably love some modelling clay. She could cut out cookies for hours."

"I'll pick some up and we'll try it with her." Maybe

it was a slip of the tongue, but his choice of words gave her heart a severe pounding. "I'm going to shower and change. By then the Cunninghams will have arrived. I'll settle them in their room and then drive them over to the hospital."

"Will they want a meal first?"

"Not until tonight."

She nodded. "I've planned dinner around food that should taste good to Lindsey."

"If it doesn't, it's Travis's problem." Meaning he'd have to deal with his wife in princess mode. Colt's tone had brooked no argument from Geena.

After he left the kitchen, she worked steadily to prepare everything and ice the cookies in Colt's favorite flavor. For dessert she made a lemon supreme pie. Anything chocolate might not be good if Lindsey was nursing.

Later, with no sign of anyone around, she went into the main dining room. The buffet yielded a drawer full of tablecloths. She found one in pale yellow and put it on the table. Since this was to be a welcome-home celebration for the baby, she went outside and picked some white daisies growing in the west garden.

She filled her arms with a large bunch and arranged them in two different vases from the china cabinet. One for the foyer table and one for the dining room. When she set it on the table with the china and crystal, it looked perfect. Now to get herself ready.

Once dressed in another skirt and top in dusky blue, she put her hair back in a French twist and fastened it with a clip. On her walk back through the foyer to the kitchen, she heard voices outside and opened the front door. Two cars had pulled up in the front drive.

Colt and Hank walked with Lindsey's smartly dressed parents, carrying flowers, suitcases and several bags of supplies sent home from the hospital. Travis helped his blond wife from the other car. Then he reached for the baby carrier.

When Lindsey's mother saw Geena inside the door, her gaze flew to Colt. "Who's this?"

"Our new housekeeper, Geena Williams."

She half laughed. "You're joking, of course."

Colt ignored her rudeness. "Geena? Please meet Martha and Jim Cunningham, Lindsey's parents."

"How do you do?" Geena smiled. "What a great day for all of you having a new baby in the family."

Mr. Cunningham eyed her with interest. "Indeed it is."

"Let me relieve you of some of this." She took the bags and flower arrangement he was holding. "I'll run these upstairs."

In Travis's room, she put the flowers on the bedside table and emptied the bags in the bathroom. They could arrange things the way they wanted. She took the empty bags with her and headed back downstairs, passing Colt on the stairs bringing up the suitcases. In a soft black shirt and tan trousers, he had an urban sophistication that showed her a whole new side of him.

His eyes penetrated hers. "The dining room looks amazing."

She couldn't stop her heart from thudding. "I hope it was all right."

"What do you think?" His question sounded fierce. "I told you to make this house your own. Everyone's speechless. The place hasn't looked like this since be-

fore Mother became ill and couldn't remember anything."

His compliment meant so much to Geena, she
couldn't form words. Instead, she murmured her thanks
and hurried on down. On her way to the kitchen, she
saw that everyone had assembled in the living room.
Travis had his arm around Lindsey, who was a beauty.
She looked flushed and exhausted. Hank, not saying
anything, sat across from Jim with his cast extended.

Martha held the baby, who, so far as Geena could
tell, hadn't made a peep. She was all pink with fuzzy
brown hair. So precious.

Ina sat on the loveseat with Laura. One grandmother
stared into space while the other one took over. Geena
felt a wrench in her heart before she moved to the other
part of the house.

While she was making coffee, Colt entered the
kitchen. "Lindsey's tired, so I think we'll eat now. She
might not last through the whole meal."

"No problem."

After pouring ice water, she put all the food on the
table where everyone could help themselves. Throughout the meal she poured coffee for those who wanted it.

At one point Lindsey's father glanced up at her while
he was eating. "This is the best fried chicken dinner
I've ever tasted."

"Amen," Colt agreed.

"Thank you."

Following their compliments Martha said, "Lindsey
needs to go upstairs." With those words, the dinner ended
and Geena could start clearing the table.

When all her duties were done, she put the dish towels and cloths in the washer. The tablecloth needed to go

to the cleaners to be laundered and ironed. She'd take care of that tomorrow.

Geena came out of the laundry room at the same time Lindsey's mother entered the kitchen. "There you are." She sounded put out.

"You wanted to see me?"

"Yes. Tomorrow I'd like you to serve breakfast upstairs in my daughter's room at eight o'clock."

"For the four of you?"

"Yes. She'll want juice, bacon and toast. My husband likes his eggs over easy. I'll only eat a little cereal with milk and a grapefruit. Travis will want scrambled eggs."

"I'd love to accommodate you, Mrs. Cunningham, but Saturday and Sunday are my days off and I'll be away for most of it." The older woman's eyes rounded in surprise. "Fortunately I went to the store and there's plenty of food for you to help yourselves. When I'm back on Monday, I'll be happy to prepare your breakfasts the way you want."

She lifted her chin. "Mary was always on hand."

"I understand she was a paragon and is sorely missed. Before I go to bed, is there anything Lindsey needs for the baby or herself? A little snack maybe? I made some sugar cookies that might taste good. They're in that canister next to the toaster."

"I think not."

"Then if you'll excuse me, I'll say goodnight."

Geena had barely reached her room when she heard a knock on the door. She opened it to find Colt standing there. She guessed her heart would never get used to the sight of him.

"I saw Martha leave the kitchen like she was hurrying to a fire. Any problems?"

"None."

The hint of a smile hovered on his lips. "Tell me what happened."

"She didn't know I don't work on the weekend."

"That explains it." His eyes swept over her. "I know you've been waiting for tomorrow so you can visit your brother's grave."

Colt knew her well, but he still didn't know everything. If she told him, then he'd just take it on. She couldn't let him do that. He had more than enough on his plate.

"I was just about to phone you and talk to you about it. I don't feel good about taking the truck to Rapid City. Would it be all right if I drive it as far as Sundance? I could leave it in the parking opposite the bus station. After my return from Rapid City later in the day, I'll stop at the post office on my way back to the ranch."

He lounged against the doorjamb. "I have a better idea. Tomorrow I have some errands to run and want to get away early, so I'll drive you. We'll find a place to eat breakfast in Rapid City and spend as much time there as you want. On our way back through Sundance we'll grab lunch and I'll do my errands. How does that sound?"

Geena *knew* how it sounded. His asking to spend the day with her fed into her fantasy about them. If she agreed, it would be stepping over that line between boss and employee into more personal territory. Maybe that was what he wanted. Did he? Did she dare dream?

"It sounds like you're going out of your way for me again when I know you're needed in a dozen places at once here on the ranch. I'd feel better about it if there were some way to repay you."

"So far no one has any complaints about the new housekeeper. You've freed me to get on with ranch business, a luxury I haven't known for a long time and feared I might never have again. That's payment over and above what I expected."

Geena might have mapped out a long-term plan for herself for after she left his employ, but she hadn't counted on this attraction to Colt that was deepening by the minute. "Thank you," she whispered.

He stood straighter. "Meet me at my truck at seven-thirty in the morning and we'll escape before Martha comes looking for you."

Geena laughed quietly. "It seems rather cowardly just to slip away."

His eyes gleamed with devilment. "In some instances it's better to run for your life, don't you think?"

"If you say so," she teased. "You're the boss."

She'd said it without thinking because she was enjoying their conversation so much. But maybe it had been the wrong thing to say because the amusement unexpectedly left his eyes. In its place she felt tension.

"Is there anything you'd like to ask me before I go upstairs?" His polite question verified her suspicions.

"No." For some reason she'd offended him without meaning to. After he'd offered to drive her to Rapid City in the morning, she didn't want any misunderstanding between them.

But maybe she'd misread him.

Maybe she was being paranoid.

If so, it was because she was crazy in love with him. It shouldn't have happened. It was too soon for anything like this to happen, but there was no other explanation for why he lit her up like an explosion of fireworks just thinking about him.

"Then I'll say goodnight." He turned and strode down on the hall on those long, rock-hard legs. How would it be not to have to say goodnight to him? Oh, what she'd give.

CHAPTER SEVEN

FLOWERS decorated many of the graves at the Mountain View and Mount Calvary Cemetery. When they'd reached Rapid City, Colt had stopped at a florist so Geena could get the flowers she wanted. She ended up buying five baskets of spring flowers. Once they were off again, she directed him to the cemetery and found the family plot.

Her parents and her grandparents each had a joint headstone. Colt helped her carry the baskets to place against them. The last basket she put at the head of the unmarked grave. But when she leaned over, she sank to her knees as if her elegant jeans-clad legs would no longer support her.

"Todd."

That one name was said in such a heart-wrenching tone, Colt's throat almost closed off with emotion. Without conscious thought his hands closed over her blouse-covered shoulders from behind. He rubbed them gently while her body shook with quiet sobs he could feel resonate through him. All he could do was hold on to her while she unloaded her grief.

Colt had never met her family, but they had to have been remarkable people to have produced a daughter and granddaughter like Geena. He felt a terrible sorrow for her that she'd lost her only sibling. There was something about this woman that brought out his need to comfort her. *Face it, Colt. You want to love her.*

Though Colt had lost his father, his death had been easier to handle because he'd lived a full life. Todd Williams's life had been cut short, depriving Geena of her last relative, denying her that solace. She'd been in prison at the time, unable to do anything. Her pain had to have been unbearable.

Colt knew he couldn't relieve it, but there were other things he could do. When Geena finally stood up, he kept his arm around her shoulders. "Before we leave," he whispered against her cheek, "we'll talk to the sextant and arrange for a headstone to be made for your brother."

"I was just going to ask if we could do that. Thank you."

Still holding her, they walked slowly across the grass to his truck. He helped her inside and drove them to the office where she was able to order one. She put down a deposit using her credit card. They told her to expect a wait of a couple of weeks. When it was ready, they'd phone her.

After they were in the truck once more, he turned to her, struck once again by the stunning picture she made. A woman had to have been born with a soft curving jaw and classic features like Geena's to carry off the French braid she wore. "Have you tried to reach the man from the pipeline office?"

"Yes, but I learned Mr. Phelps has been out of town this whole week and won't be back until Monday." Her tears may have stopped, but she was still in an emotional state.

"I know you want to see him in person. When you've made an appointment, I'll bring you again. While we're at it, maybe you and I can track down this Janice together and you won't need a PI."

Her head jerked around in alarm. "No—I-I mean I couldn't ask you to do that," she stammered. "Please—you've already done too much for me."

Whoa. For Geena to have such a strong reaction meant she was still keeping something from him. "You didn't ask. I offered."

"But I'm only an employee."

He blinked. Last night she'd reminded him he was the boss. At the time it had gotten under his skin, which was absurd because it was only the truth. And yet he didn't feel like her employer. The lines separating them had been blurred from the beginning and they were getting more blurred all the time.

She wasn't like the help he employed on the ranch—not like a friend or relative. Geena had arrived on the ranch during the night and had gone to sleep beneath a pine tree. Titus had found her first. She was something else entirely different and growing on him in ways he couldn't explain. Colt only knew he was craving her company more and more.

He started the engine. "Before we leave Rapid City, would you like to run by your grandmother's house?"

She averted her eyes. "I don't think I could handle that today. I've done enough crying already, but thank you for being willing. You've been wonderful to bring me here. It's meant everything, but now I feel emotionally drained. If you don't mind, I'd like to get back to the ranch and I am sure you would too."

Colt had no doubts this had been a big morning for her, but he knew in his gut there was more to the story about Janice than she was willing to divulge. He wanted to help her, but he needed a way to gain her confidence.

"You wouldn't have any way of knowing I've taken the whole day off. Hank's in charge. Since you and I could both do with a break from our problems, how would you feel about going for a horseback ride with me when we return? I could give you a few pointers. We'd only stay out as long as you feel comfortable."

She glanced at him with a worried expression. "It's part of my job, isn't it?"

His hands gripped the steering wheel tighter. "No. Only if you want it to be."

He watched her bite her succulent-looking lower lip. "To be honest, I'm scared of them."

The bands around his lungs relaxed. "Why?"

"When I was little, my friend's father had horses. We'd go in the stable to look at them. One day I tried to feed this horse some hay, but I got too close and it kicked me in the ankle. I never went near horses again and still have a small scar."

Colt had to suppress the urge to pull her into his arms. He could hardly keep his hands off her.

"Then it's time you learned to feel comfortable around them, but only if you want to. We have a mare named Carrot Top who's gentle and patient. I could introduce you. The two of you could take a long look at each other and decide whether you want to take the relationship any further."

"Colt—" She half laughed.

He liked the smile on that gorgeous mouth of hers. It was her first one of the day. "By the time we've had lunch in Sundance and get back to the ranch, let me know your answer and it can be arranged."

"Up over this next rise you're going to see something spectacular."

While Carrot Top followed Colt's gelding, Digger, over terrain only a horse could traverse, Geena watched the play of muscles across Colt's back and shoulders. To her he represented masculine beauty in action.

After being in the saddle for a half hour, she wasn't nearly as nervous as she'd been. The grandeur of the scenery made this first effort of hers worth every second. And of course there was Colt, who'd been incredibly patient and gentle with her while he taught her the fundamentals of horsemanship. Earlier, when he'd unexpectedly pulled off her cowboy boot to see and touch her ankle scar with his fingers, the sensation had felt so erotic, she'd almost fallen out of the saddle.

She loved him with an ache that would never go away, but she was playing with fire and knew it. There was a price to pay for every minute she spent with him. Though she admitted they had chemistry between them, for her to think he had feelings for her beyond a moment's pleasure was ludicrous. Colt had been married once and since then had stayed single for a reason. That wasn't going to change. She was his housekeeper, for heaven's sake!

This day with him had gotten away from her, but if there weren't any more days off that included him, then she could prevent mistakes from happening.

"Oh—" she cried when her horse drew alongside

Colt's. She lowered her cowboy hat to the back of her neck and took in the scene before her. "It's absolutely glorious! Those wildflowers swaying in the high meadow—they're beautiful beyond description. No wonder Custer wrote about it. You have to be the luckiest man on earth to have all this in your backyard."

Beneath his hat he eyed her speculatively. "So you're not sorry I got you on a horse?"

"How could I be?" she answered in a breathless voice. "This makes you want to go up there and roll around in them." She regretted those words the second they escaped her lips. He probably thought she meant rolling around in them with him. He wouldn't have been wrong.

"You're a good sport, Geena Williams, but I think you've had enough for your first day. If I keep you out here any longer, you'll be cursing me tonight when you're too sore to walk."

Her lips curved. "Maybe, but I don't feel it yet."

"You will," he answered with a heartbreaking half smile of his own. "Next Saturday we'll ride clear to the top."

No. They wouldn't, because she wouldn't let there be a next time. Every outing with him would make it harder to be separated from him. If there came the day when he asked her to stay on the ranch because he wanted to marry her, well that would be different. But she couldn't imagine that happening and needed to keep her plans firmly in mind.

With a mental sigh, she urged her horse to turn around and follow Colt down the mountain. Neither of them were inclined to talk. Her thoughts were too full of him as she relived every moment of their day together.

By the time they reached the stable, she dreaded their separation. In fact she couldn't stand the thought of it, but to spend any more time with him was dangerous.

Another time today at the cemetery when she'd felt his hands kneading her shoulders, she'd come close to turning around and crushing herself against him. That would have been a serious error on her part considering he'd driven her to Rapid City out of his innate generosity and concern.

Before he could come around to help her, she got off her horse by herself. No more touching. Not any. "Shall I brush down Carrot Top?"

His gaze took in all of her, sending curling warmth through her from head to toe. "That's my job right now. What you need is a good soak in the tub."

At the mention of a soak, a picture of the two of them luxuriating together refused to leave her mind. "That sounds like a marvelous idea. Thank you for this, for everything. I'll see you later."

She practically ran down the hill to the ranch house. Once inside she hurried through to her bedroom, thankful she didn't see any of the family. After a quick shower, she changed into fresh jeans and a short-sleeved, filmy, melon-colored blouse. Donning her sandals, she was ready to leave again.

She hoped Colt was still at the barn and wouldn't see her drive away. Naturally when he walked down to the house, he'd notice the white truck was gone. But that was okay. She'd be back in Sundance, having put twelve miles between them.

When they'd been in the downtown section earlier today, she'd remembered seeing a beauty salon. After finding it now, she parked in front. The ad in the window explained they accepted walk-ins as well as appointments. She approached the girl at the counter who told her it would be a ten-minute wait.

No problem. Geena grabbed a magazine and thumbed through it, not really seeing anything. The day spent with Colt had been too memorable for too many reasons.

When one of the beauticians called to her, she put the magazine back and took a seat in the chair. "What can I do for you today?"

Geena looked at herself in the mirror. "I need a haircut." She hadn't worn it short since she was in middle school. "In my job I do a lot of cooking and always have to wear it in a braid like this or swept up. I used to have semi-curly hair. How about a tousled wavy bob to the neck with a part on the side so I don't have to think about it?"

"You have the perfect facial shape for it. Leave it to me."

A half hour later Geena left the shop feeling pounds lighter. It wasn't the weight of the hair gone, but the image. She liked her new look that had no association with the past and her prison photos. Communing with Todd this morning had helped free her of a lot of pain she'd been carrying around because she hadn't been able to say goodbye to him.

Again, it was Colt who'd been her fairy godfather. He'd done everything for her. She didn't know how she'd repay him, but one day she would figure out a way.

Until that time, she needed to concentrate on finding Janice without Colt's help. When she met with Mr. Phelps next Saturday, she'd ask him if he knew a good attorney who could steer her in the right direction. She'd ride her bike to Sundance. From there she'd take the bus to Rapid City. It had a bike rack so she'd be able to get around once she was there.

With her plan solidly in mind, she gathered the mail from the post office, then decided to drop by Bradford's Department Store where she'd purchased her Western clothes. If Steve was working, she'd say hello and see what happened.

But when she parked near the corner and walked to the store, she saw that it closed at five-thirty on Saturday. She checked her watch. It was quarter to six. As she walked away she heard a voice call to her. "Ms. Williams?"

Geena spun around. To her shock, there he was. "Hi! I'm surprised you would remember my name."

He grinned. "Are you kidding? I've been hoping you'd walk in one of these days. Are you with your boss?"

She chuckled. Steve could be forgiven for asking that question. "No. This is my day off. I had some shopping to do and thought I'd grab a quick dinner."

"What a nice coincidence. I was just leaving the store to do the same thing when I saw you through the doors. But I wasn't sure if it was really you. You've cut your hair. It gives you an entirely new look. I like it."

"Thanks. This style makes a nice change."

"How about walking around the corner with me to get a pizza? They're pretty good. There's a theater next door. We could catch a movie if you'd like."

"That sounds great."

Three hours later they left the theater. As he walked her to her truck he said, "I've been invited to a private party at the Lariat Club tonight. Some of the forest rangers are throwing it for the guys who helped them fight a fire a few weeks ago. Besides free appetizers, there's going to be a live band and line dancing. Come with me. Whenever you want to leave, I'll follow you back to the ranch to make certain you get home safely."

Steve was a very nice guy from Sheridan. She found out that since college he'd been working his way up in business management after being assigned to this store. Even if she was beginning to feel the aches and pains from her first horseback ride, why not spend a few more hours having fun with him? Anything to put thoughts of Colt out of her mind for tonight.

He asked her to follow his car to the other side of town. After she'd parked across the street from the bar and got out, she could hear the music coming from inside. Steve caught up to her. "Sounds like the party's in full swing."

The place appeared to be packed. He ushered her through the crowd to the dance floor. "Let's do this before the band takes a break."

Geena hadn't been line dancing since her last date with Kevin Starr from FossilMania. Steve knew all the moves. His energy infected her. For a little while she simply went with the country-and-western sound, hardly able to believe she was a free agent instead of wasting away at the prison in Pierre.

When the music stopped, Steve's smiled faded and he got the oddest look on his face. "Maybe I'm seeing things, but I think the ranger who invited me to the party is coming this way with *your* boss."

Colt was here?

Geena's heart thudded so fast, it almost suffocated her.

"Hey, Steve—I'm glad you could make it. Who's your friend?"

Of necessity Geena had to turn around. Her gaze collided with Colt's. The gold flecks among the green of his eyes flashed molten as he took in her new haircut. She could feel the tension emanating from him to her bones. Unless his feelings for her ran deeper than she'd supposed, it made no sense. Oh Colt…if that was true…

"This is Geena Williams. She's the new housekeeper on the Floral Valley Ranch. Geena? Meet Sheila Wilson, one of the forest rangers assigned to Sundance."

The blonde woman nudged Colt in the ribs. "You didn't tell me that job had been filled. You're a dark one, you know that?" She turned back to Geena with an alluring smile. The ranger was good at covering up her feelings, but Geena had witnessed her shock knowing that she lived under the same roof with the man Sheila had invited to the party.

"It's nice to meet you, Sheila."

"I'm glad you could come. The more the merrier." Her blue-eyed gaze swerved to Steve. "How did you two meet?"

Steve moved closer to Geena, as if he were establishing his territory, but there was no contest for going up against Colt. In the coffee-colored shirt and jeans he was wearing, no man would ever compare. "I helped her buy a new outfit."

Colt studied Geena for a moment longer, but she couldn't read the expression in his eyes. "I take it you bought something else this afternoon." His voice sounded an octave lower than usual.

She shook her head. "No. I told Steve that the next time I came to town, I'd stop by and say hello. We've just come from a movie." She'd decided to tell the whole truth because Colt deserved nothing less. And if that bothered him, then why didn't Colt ask her out?

"If you'll excuse us, we're going to grab some hors d'oeuvres." Steve put a hand at the back of her waist and led her to a table near the front. Even in the crowded room Geena felt those piercing hazel eyes staring at her back. Colt would be able to tell she was having some difficulty walking after their horseback ride.

"Let's get out of here, shall we?" Steve whispered at last. She nodded. Seeing Colt here tonight had shattered her plan to try to forget him for one night. The whole evening had been ruined. She knew it. Steve knew it.

They walked across the street to her truck. The cool air met her hot cheeks. When they reached the driver's side, he put a hand against the door to prevent her from getting in. "Do you want to tell me what's going on with your boss? If looks could kill—"

"He didn't look at you like that!" she cried.

"I'm talking about the way the big rancher was looking at *you*, as if you were his property." Steve really thought that? "It was the same way he acted the other day. Tell me the truth, because I don't like to play games. Are you two involved?"

She lowered her head. "Not in the way you're thinking. I'm just his employee, but it's complicated."

If she explained about her false imprisonment, she had no doubt Steve would understand why Colt came off so protective around her. Todd would have been the same way. But Steve wasn't the man she loved, so there was no point in leading him on, let alone telling him about the horror of the past year.

"You're telling me," he muttered. "Do me a favor. If it ever gets uncomplicated, you know I'm interested."

"I'm sorry, Steve. I never meant for this to happen tonight. I'd hoped to spend an evening with you and was shocked when I saw Colt with Sheila."

"The other day she told me she's had a crush on him since she first met him. I think seeing you pretty well explained why their relationship has never gotten off the ground."

"I've only been at the ranch a week."

"Sheila fights fires and would tell you it only takes a single spark to ignite one."

That's what it had felt like that night in his kitchen. Colt had taken pity on her and had offered his hospitality. When she'd looked at him, something had leaped between them. Call it a spark. Whatever it was, she'd been on fire since then.

She sucked in her breath. "Thank you for the dinner and the movie. No matter what you think, I had a great time and enjoyed your company very much. Otherwise I wouldn't have come by in the first place."

"I believe you." He nodded and opened the door so she could get in. "I'll follow you home."

"No. It's only nine-thirty. Not that late. I only have twelve miles to go. Steve—I saw quite a few girls inside without partners. Go back in the bar and have a good time."

"Don't worry about me. See you around, Geena."

She'd hurt him, darn it.

Jabbing her key into the ignition, she started the engine and took off for the ranch. Colt had turned her whole world around today. Maybe she should give her notice, then work for the next three weeks to earn the money he'd already put in her account. After that she'd get on her bike and ride out of his life. Thanks to him she had some new clothes and a little money to find work somewhere else. In time there'd be more money. She just had to wait.

Once she'd turned off the highway onto the dirt road, she saw headlights behind her. It appeared Steve had decided to follow her home anyway. She wished he hadn't, but he was one of those nice guys who didn't deserve a situation like this.

She pulled in next to Hank's truck and got out of the cab. To her dismay she walked right into a wall of steel. "*Colt*—I thought it was Steve behind me."

His mouth had flattened into a thin white line. "Sorry to disappoint you."

Her brows furrowed. "I'm not disappointed. In fact I asked him not to follow me, but I *am* shocked to see you here when I know you were Sheila's date."

"Let's just say everyone's night was pretty well ruined."

"Because of me?" Her voice shook. "Is *that* what you drove all this way to tell me?"

"No," he said in a wintry tone.

"Then what's wrong?"

"I wish to heaven I knew."

"I think you were precipitous in hiring me. While you find the right housekeeper, I'll finish out my first month before I leave. How does that sound?"

A bleakness stole over his chiseled features. "I thought you wanted the job."

"I do, but you were the one who stated the arrangement was temporary in case one of the parties wasn't happy about it. As I see it, you already find me the wrong fit."

"Did I say that?" he challenged in a grim voice.

"In a way. You're angry as blazes right now."

His hands shot out to cup her hot face. "Maybe it's because after the day we spent together, it shocked me to see you enjoying yourself with someone else."

She'd asked him for honesty. He deserved it back. "You think I felt any different when I saw you there with *her*? On the day you hired me, Hank said you were busy on the phone with a woman named Sheila. That's why he took me to your mother's room to meet her instead of waiting for you. I wondered if she was someone important to you."

His fingers tightened in her hair. "I've never been out with her. The only reason I told her I would meet her at the party was to be polite. But as you can see, I couldn't even spend a whole evening with her once I saw you." His eyes lit everywhere. "You've cut your hair."

"I've wanted to change it since I got out of prison."

"Either way, you're a beautiful woman, Geena, and I have to have this before I take another breath."

His mouth closed over hers before she could stop him. Her hunger for him was so great she didn't want to stop him. He pressed her body against the truck with his and kissed her in so many different ways she groaned in ecstasy. Geena forgot where they were. She wrapped her arms around his neck in order to get closer. For a while she went where he led, giving him kiss for kiss, wanting to merge with him.

Her body literally trembled with desire. He had to have felt it and eventually relinquished her mouth. While she tried to catch her breath, he covered her

throat with kisses before burying his face in her hair.
"Tell me what really happened after you were arrested.
When Kevin didn't make contact, are you afraid he ran
off with your brother's lover?"

What? She couldn't believe what he'd just asked her.

"No, Cole—" He had the wrong idea completely. "I
never felt that way about Kevin. When I was away at
college, I fell in love with a man and thought we would
get married. We had several classes together and it was
a wonderful time in my life. But I found out through a
friend that he'd been lying to me all along and was only
separated from his wife, not divorced."

Cole held her tighter.

"He told me it was only a matter of time and begged
me not to leave him, but I was too devastated by his lie
to consider going back to him. I eventually got over it
and dated other guys, including Kevin, after returning
to Rapid City, but there was no one special. It's hard to
get your trust back after you've been betrayed."

His hands slid up her arms and he shook her gently, forcing her to look up at him. "You don't feel you
can trust me?"

"You know I do!"

"Then explain to me why you won't let me help you
find the woman who stole your possessions."

"Because it's not your problem and I don't want to
be any more of a liability than I already am. You've felt
sorry for me and have done more for me than anyone
else would have done. You told me you've been overwhelmed at times by all the responsibility."

"What are you talking about?"

"I'm not your typical woman who answered an ad
for a housekeeper. You think I don't know your family

has questions about me? You may not be harboring a fugitive, but if they knew who I was, I'd be a person of interest to them in the wrong way."

His jaw hardened. "I was right," he said in a savage whisper. "You need counseling to help you. Have you called that psychiatrist yet?"

"No, and I'm not going to. I'll find my own closer to home when I'm ready." She'd look for a P.I. online, too, and go from there.

"You're not telling me something," he ground out. "It means you're afraid."

"I could accuse you of the same thing," she threw back at him.

His dark brows furrowed into a bar above his eyes. "Explain that to me."

"Except for one reference about you giving up steer-wrestling after you got married, that's all I know about your personal life. I never asked questions about your former wife because I didn't feel it was my right."

After a long silence he muttered, "Touché," and let go of her arms.

She fought for composure because it appeared he still wasn't ready to confide in her about the most crucial time in his life. "Why don't we both agree this isn't the right fit for either of us? I'll work hard for the next three weeks before I leave. Hopefully you won't have any complaints."

In the semidark she thought his features had taken on a gaunt cast. She imagined her own complexion was probably the color of paste.

"Before I forget, here's your mail." She opened her bag and handed the bundle to him. "Goodnight, Colt."

Geena couldn't get away from him fast enough.

When she entered the kitchen, Hank was there drinking coffee. She flew past him, returning his "Hi" over her shoulder, and kept on going to her bedroom.

Shaken by the passion that had flared between them, Colt stood there for a few minutes in order to recover. When he could finally move, his legs felt as heavy as that vital organ pumping blood through him—blood that needed to cool so he could think rationally.

He'd blown it, but there was no way in hell he would let her leave the ranch in another three weeks. They both had trust issues, but after a year behind bars, hers had to be worse. Unfortunately he'd come off acting like her bodyguard, pushing everyone else away while he kept her close. In the process he feared he'd alienated her.

Determined to set things right between them, he stormed into the house. Ignoring Hank, who stared at him in astonishment, he strode down the hall to her bedroom and knocked on the door.

"Geena? It's Colt. I need to talk to you for a minute."

After a pause he heard, "If you don't mind, I'm exhausted. Could we do it in the morning at breakfast?"

Colt exhaled a heavy breath. "Tomorrow's your day off."

"I'm not going anywhere, so I'm planning to make the breakfast Martha asked me to make for everyone this morning."

His hand absently made furrows through his hair. "You don't have to do that."

"I know. I want to. Maybe Lindsey will let me hold her baby. I've been dying to do that." He heard a wobble in her voice that got to him. Everything about her got to him.

"If you'd told me, I could have arranged it."

"I know. You can arrange anything."

There he went again, trying to micromanage her life. The last thing he wanted was her resentment. *So what do you want, Brannigan?*

The answer terrified him for fear she didn't want the same thing.

His eyes closed tightly. "Get some sleep, Geena."

He turned on his heel and walked away, making a tour of the house to lock doors and turn off lights. Only by sheer strength of will did he eventually head up the stairs instead of finding his way back to Geena's room.

Hank was there, sitting on one side of Colt's bed with his legs extended. The two looked at each other. "What's going on with you and Geena?" his brother asked, point-blank.

Colt shut the door before backing against it. "I'll answer that question when you tell me what's been happening to you? I thought whatever went on between you and Lindsey was over before she started dating Travis."

Lines marred Hank's face. "It was over—for *her*."

That answered one of Colt's questions anyway. "What are you going to do about it?"

"Listen, Colt. I know you've needed me for the last six weeks. But after I get my cast off on Monday, would you care if I flew straight to Casper? Robert called here earlier to ask about the baby. We got talking about other things. Before I knew it he invited me to come for a visit if I wanted to. How about if I stay there until Travis and Lindsey have moved back to their house? Some time away might help me to get my head on straight."

Colt walked over to the desk and tossed the bundle

of mail on it. Then turned to his brother. "I think it's a great idea. He'll like having you around, too."

A look of relief crossed over his face. "Thanks, bro." Hank got to his feet and hobbled over to give him a hug. Colt hugged him back hard, wanting Hank to get past this. If he met the right girl in Casper… No doubt Robert was thinking the same thing.

"Our cousin is the best friend a man could have next to his own brothers." Colt's thoughts flew to Geena, who needed her brother. Colt wanted to be there for her, but *not* as a brother. Kissing her tonight had turned the fire into a near conflagration.

When Hank reached the door, he turned to him. "Maybe after I get back, you should do the same thing and spend some time with Robert. Geena has you more fired up than the bull that went after me."

His brother had *that* right!

CHAPTER EIGHT

GEENA glanced at the wall phone in the kitchen. She picked up the receiver and pressed the digit for the upstairs guest bedroom. Martha answered on the third ring. "Lindsey?" she asked in an anxious voice.

"No, Mrs. Cunningham. It's Geena. I have breakfast ready for all of you. Would you like me to serve it in your room or your daughter's?"

"Oh—I thought you'd be away like you were yesterday, but no matter. Bring it to our room. We'll eat around the table. Be sure there's sugar for my cereal."

For a moment Geena felt like Cinderella being given her instructions for the day. "I'll be there shortly."

After clicking off, she found one of the largest trays and stacked it while Ina and Laura ate their breakfast. On her way up the stairs she prayed she could manage the feat as well as Cinderella had done in the feature film.

Jim stood at their open door in pajamas and a robe with a big smile on his face. "Aren't you a sight for sore eyes! I hardly recognize you with that new hairdo. It's very very becoming."

"Thank you, Mr. Cunningham."

"I'll let Lindsey and Travis know breakfast has arrived. I've been salivating for more of your food since dinner the other evening."

"That's so nice of you to say." She swept past him and put the tray on the coffee table. Martha was also dressed in a robe, brushing her hair. Her eyes swept over Geena but she made no comment.

"I hope you brought enough food for me." *Colt's voice.* She swung around. Unlike the others, he'd already gotten dressed. In jeans and a white polo, he was so handsome in his rugged way, she could hardly take her eyes off him, but she *had* to.

"If not, there's more downstairs."

He grabbed a piece of bacon off the plate. "Um. Crispy, just the way I like it. Why don't I pop next door and see what I can do to get everyone assembled while this food is still hot?"

It was a good thing she hadn't seen him as she was coming up the stairs or her body would have gone weak, causing her to drop the tray. While she was still trying to recover, Colt came back in the room holding Travis's daughter. Her heart leaped at the sight of him with a baby in his arms.

He walked over to her. "Geena? Meet Abigail Cunningham Brannigan, my niece and newest member of both families. Abigail was Lindsey's grandmother's name," Colt informed her.

"How wonderful to have that connection."

Geena's gaze fastened hungrily on the baby wearing a tiny pink stretchy suit. She was wrapped in a receiving blanket. "Oh—she's absolutely adorable." When he handed the sweet-smelling baby over, Geena heard a muffled sound of protest from Martha, but it was too late. Colt had made certain Geena got the opportunity to hold the baby. She loved him for it.

The baby's eyes were open. Her mouth had formed into a perfect O. "You dear little thing. Welcome to the world, Abby." Unable to resist, she kissed her cheek, then held her against her neck and shoulder. The warmth of her little body tugged on all Geena's motherly instincts. She wanted one like this of her own.

With Colt for the daddy.

She couldn't stop thinking like that and started walking around the room, wondering what had happened to Janice. Had she delivered a healthy baby? Was it Todd's? Had he made Geena an aunt? Or was it another man's child? With this baby in her arms, Geena knew she had to find out the answers and she needed to do it soon.

Fighting the tears that had already moistened her eyelashes, she turned to Colt and handed the baby back to him. "Thank you for letting me hold her." Her voice was so thick with emotion she needed to get out of there.

"If there's anything else you want, phone me in the kitchen," she announced to the room, then hurried out the door. Lindsey and Travis were just leaving the other room in their robes. Geena kept going. They'd already met her. She was the hired help after all.

When she reached the kitchen, she discovered Hank at the table. She'd made plenty of food and he'd helped himself. His eyes brightened when he saw her. "I think I'm going to have to marry you to keep all this fabulous food in the family."

Her laugh was bittersweet. If Colt had said that to her…

"You seem happier today."

"I am. My cast comes off tomorrow and then I'm taking a short vacation."

"Where are you going?"

"Casper."

At the mention of it, guilt swamped her because she'd turned down Colt's suggestion to speak to the therapist there. To make things worse, he unexpectedly strode into the kitchen. "Did you save any food for me?"

"There's plenty," Geena assured him. "Sit down and I'll serve you."

She made him a big plate and poured both of them coffee. While he and Hank talked, she cleaned up the kitchen. In a minute Hank brought his dishes over to the sink. "If anyone wants to know, I'm leaving for the day. Danny's picking me up."

During her horseback ride with Colt, she'd learned Danny worked as Hank's hazer when they did the rodeo circuit. "Have a good time. Just think—tomorrow you'll be given your get-out-of-jail-free card."

"After what you survived for a year, I can't complain about six weeks' deprivation."

She stared at Hank in shock while Colt looked at both of them stone-faced. "You know?"

He nodded. "I sensed something was fishy the night Mandy and I walked into the kitchen. The next day when you told me you'd been hired, I wondered if it had anything to do with that call from the warden. So I called Warden James back." The expression in his eyes softened. "She told me what'd happened to you."

So Colt had kept his word. His good deeds just kept mounting up to the most marvelous man in the entire world. "And you didn't mind too much?"

"Sometimes innocent people get blamed for doing

bad things. What was there to mind? I told you the other day you're the best thing to happen to this ranch in years! The warden told me she was relieved to hear Colt had hired you. She's been worried about you and hopes you'll get all the help you need after what you've been through."

He flashed her a sly grin. "It was one decision I'm thankful my big brother made. By the way, I love your hair. See ya later." Hank gave her a kiss on the cheek before he left the kitchen.

"Geena," Colt murmured, "will you please sit down for a minute? I'd like to talk to you."

"All right." Last night he'd been upset. This morning his mood was completely different. Benign, for want of a better word.

"Can we start over again?"

Her head went back. "What do you mean?"

"Exactly what I said. The warden had the right instincts from the beginning. You do need all the help you can get in order to pick up the strings of your life again. I'm afraid I've tried to solve them for you all at once."

Colt was breaking her heart. This was probably the closest thing to an apology she would ever hear from his lips, but he didn't owe her any apology. Quite the opposite. She owed him everything!

Her fear now was that he was apologizing for those minutes in his arms last night. She'd wanted it to go on and on. The thought of it never happening again was too terrible to contemplate.

"You can't help it," she teased with a quick smile. "That's why you're the head of the ranch. Everyone loves you and looks to you. This place would fall apart without you. I admire you more than you know." *I love you more than you know.*

Lines bracketed his mouth. She'd forgotten he didn't like compliments. "Nevertheless, to make up for my heavy-handed behavior, I'd like to do something you'd enjoy. I feel like playing." He winked at her, reminding her of that other conversation they'd had. "Have you ever been to Devil's Tower National Monument?"

"No, but I've heard about it all my life." The idea of doing anything with him was so exciting she couldn't sit still and got up from the table to clear his dishes.

"It's a sacred place to the Lakotas where they perform the Sun Dance. June in particular is a time when most tourists are encouraged to honor their tribal traditions and don't try to climb it. But we're free to visit. Since it's a beautiful Sunday and we both have the day off, how about we put our bikes in the back of my truck and drive there?"

"You have a bike?" She sounded excited by the possibility.

He nodded. "I think mine still works. We'll pedal around and see the sights, then move on to other places and eat as we go." She heard his chair scrape as he got up from the table. "If that doesn't appeal, then tell me now and I'll get busy working on the books for the accountant who'll be here next week."

A whole day with Colt? It's what she'd been wanting all along. *Quick, Geena, before he withdraws his invitation and leaves.* After she'd turned on the dishwasher, she flashed him a glance. "I'd love it."

Eleven hours later, after doing the whole tourist-attraction loop through the Black Hills, Colt drove them into

Hulett, a town nine miles from Sundance. He parked near the White Pine Inn before ushering Geena inside for the best steak dinner this side of the Continental Divide, according to the sign. They had a great live band and dancing. He'd been waiting all day for this. If he had to wait five more minutes to get her into his arms, he was going to explode.

Once they'd been shown to a table and had given their orders, Colt asked her if she wanted to dance. The old Colt would have swept her into his arms without getting her permission, but he was on his best behavior and it was paying dividends. He felt they'd passed the point of no return today, they were no longer just boss and employee, but something more.

"I'd like that. It all depends on if my legs can handle it. We must have pedaled miles and you don't even show it. That has to come from working in the outdoors from sunup to sundown."

He hadn't been doing a lot of that since Geena had come into his life. Mac told him the ranch hands were beginning to wonder where he'd disappeared to. "Which exercise was more painful for you? Riding Carrot Top or your bike?"

"My bike, I think." She chuckled. "But if you're willing to take a chance on me, I won't say no."

The news was getting better and better. He moved around the table and walked her to the dance floor. No line-dancing here. With the soft rock playing in the background, Colt could get close to her so he felt every line and curve of her body. That's what he needed. To feel her molded to him and to breathe in her fragrance. She intoxicated him.

After several dances, he looked into her face, trapping her eyes so she wouldn't look away, but he caught her tearing up. "Are you too sore for this and haven't told me?"

"No," she answered quickly. "A week ago I was lying on my prison cot trying to figure out how to make my life count for something. I just didn't know how. If someone had told me that before long the Good Samaritan would rescue me and show me the time of my life, I would have known I'd gone insane."

He cocked his dark head. "Good Samaritan?"

"Yes. That's you."

Intrigued by the analogy he said, "In that case, what prevents you from allowing me to do something else good for you? I'm trying to improve my image as a whole-loaf guy. You could help me with that by letting me into your confidence a little more. You're fighting tears. I noticed you doing the same thing earlier while you were holding the baby. What did Abby's presence trigger in you?"

Her body quivered. That reaction told him he was getting closer to the secret she was keeping from him.

"When I saw you holding her, Colt, it reminded me that Todd's life had been cut short and he was denied the privilege of becoming a family man."

Colt felt she was telling him the truth, just not all of it. "Do you know, when I picked her up out of her crib, the first thing I wanted to do was show her to Mom and Dad? My divorce took its toll on the family. I think they despaired over any of their sons producing grandchildren."

"Oh Colt—" One lone tear trickled down her flushed cheek. "I'm being so selfish thinking only of myself and my sadness. I'm sorry." Their mouths were mere inches apart. She gave him a brief kiss on the lips before easing herself out of his arms. "Our dinner's waiting for us."

The touch of her mouth stayed with him after they settled down to enjoy their meal. Once the waitress brought dessert, Geena shot him a question he hadn't anticipated. Not tonight anyway. "Did you ever bring your wife here?"

He put down his fork. "No."

"Tell me about her. I've seen the family pictures on the walls, but you're always with family or friends, not one special woman. I'm filled with curiosity. How long were you married? What was her name? Where did you meet her?"

Colt lounged back in the chair. "Why do you want to know?"

"Why do you think?" she fired right back, then grinned. It was the grin that caused him to cave. "I'm a typical woman who wants to know everything. It's the way *we're* made."

He couldn't refuse her. "Maybe on the drive home."

"Good. I'm going to hold you to that. It's a woman's prerogative and this woman wants to know what makes the great Colt Brannigan tick."

He danced with her a few more times, but the direction of their conversation had changed the tenor of the evening. Though he could tell by the way she nestled against him that she loved moving to the music with him, she wanted something else from him. When the band took a break, he asked her if she'd like to stay.

Geena shook her head. "I'm ready to go."

Halfway back to Sundance, they reached the turnoff for the ranch. He drove them past the house to another road that took them up through a ravine lush with summer grass and foliage. No one would bother them here.

He parked at the side of the dirt road and shut off the engine. "I brought you to this spot because it's darker here. If you look up at the sky, you'll see the constellations better."

"My first night out of prison beneath your ponderosa, the Big Dipper seemed so close I could reach up and touch it. It was a heavenly night."

Colt stirred restlessly while he studied her profile. "Until Titus and I came along and ruined it for you."

She turned to him with the hint of a smile. "Once my heart rate settled back to normal, I didn't mind. Especially after you invited me inside the house when you could have ordered me off your property. The way the ranchers at the feed store talked, I assumed you were a man of probably fifty or so.

"Instead I was confronted by this much younger, attractive, modern-day knight in boots and jeans who'd rescued me from a dragon. You took my breath away. I kept wondering why you couldn't have come sooner and stormed my prison in Pierre."

Geena.

"I think I've been very patient waiting a whole week to hear about the woman who captured your heart. Naturally she would have been beautiful. Probably small and delicate, the kind that brings out a man's protective instincts. Blond maybe, with warm chocolate-brown eyes and a complexion like porcelain. How am I doing?"

"Make it strawberry blond and you've described Cheryl."

"Ah. You have to watch out for those strawberry varieties. Nature endowed them with that particular advantage over the rest of the female population. How young was she?"

"Twenty. I was twenty-one."

"And you were both smitten at first sight."

He examined her features in the moonlight. "That's the word for it," he said, concentrating on the woman next to him. "Nothing cerebral. Just pure hormones raging out of control."

"I'm sure there was more to it than that."

"Not really. It was the proverbial case of opposites attracting."

She eyed him speculatively. "Then she wasn't a farming girl?"

"No. The daughter of a surgeon from San Francisco."

"I see. How did you meet?"

"It was June. She was on vacation with several of her college friends. They'd driven to Reno for some fun and decided to take in a rodeo. Their first. I won my event that night and they were in the crowd to congratulate me. I stayed over to spend the next day with her."

"How long before you got married?"

"Six weeks."

"That fast—"

"Yes, ma'am. She followed me to some other rodeos on the circuit. By the time we reached Elko, I couldn't concentrate on anything. We decided to get married in San Francisco. My family flew out for the wedding. We took a two-week honeymoon in Hawaii on my latest winnings, then I brought her home to the ranch. We lived in the house Travis and Lindsey are in now."

"I can guess the rest," Geena murmured. "She hated the isolation and missed her friends."

Colt's gut twisted because he realized Geena had to

be feeling the same way since her imprisonment. She'd been uprooted from everything. He cringed to remember she'd had her life literally torn away from her.

"Cheryl wanted us to move to California so I could find a good job."

Geena gave a caustic laugh. "She certainly didn't know the real Colt Brannigan, did she? You could no more turn your back on your family and your Wyoming heritage than fly."

Neither could Geena forget her heritage when she was a South Dakota girl through and through.

He'd offered to drive her by her grandmother's home, but she'd refused because it would be too painful. More than ever he understood why she'd insisted on the housekeeper job being temporary. In time she hoped to recover certain mementos from the past and make her permanent home in Rapid City.

If anyone deserved to get her life back it was Geena. Haunted by what she'd lived through, Colt was going to help her whether she wanted it or not.

He started the truck and found a spot where he could turn around. She was silent all the way back to the house. Before they got out of the cab he turned to her.

"Tomorrow morning I'll be driving Hank to the clinic early so the doctor can remove his cast. We won't be eating breakfast. After that I'll fly him to Casper. He's going to spend some time with our cousin Robert. I probably won't be back until Wednesday. If an emergency should arise, Mac's in charge, but you can always phone me. If all else fails, there's Travis."

"Thanks for telling me." She opened the passenger door. "I'm glad for Hank. He needs to get away."

Colt grimaced. "In case you didn't guess that too, he thinks he's still in love with Lindsey."

After a pause, "They have a history?"

"Two dates only before she refused him a third one. Later on in the year she met Travis at a party by accident and they fell in love."

Geena nodded. "That explains his moroseness. The poor guy needs to settle down with a woman who has loved him for years. Like Mandy perhaps?"

His eyes squinted at her. "What are you saying?"

"Well, you have to admit she's been a good sport to chauffeur him around with his foul disposition since the cast was put on. It isn't friendship she wants. Hopefully one day soon he'll realize a relationship with Lindsey was never meant to be and he'll take off the blinders. Mandy hasn't been biding her time for nothing over the years you know."

Colt burst into laughter. "How do you know so much about everyone in such a short time?"

"That's easy. I've been in prison observing women for over a year. Somehow Mandy has learned to appreciate all Hank's wonderful qualities lying beneath that sinfully good-looking exterior of his. In the looks department all three of you Brannigan men were given more than your fair share," she added.

So saying, she jumped to the ground. "Have a good flight both ways and come home safely," she whispered. "The Floral Valley Ranch couldn't go on without you."

The last thing he saw were her imploring inky blue eyes shimmering in the moonlight. They put a stranglehold on him before she closed the door and vanished.

CHAPTER NINE

WEDNESDAY morning Colt left his uncle's ranch and flew from Casper to Rapid City to see Lieutenant Crowther, the detective who'd broken the case for Geena.

Colt sat across from him at his desk. "As I told you on the phone, Geena's brother, Todd Williams, passed away while she was in prison. I'm trying to help her find the woman who was living with her brother at the time of Geena's arrest. She'd like to recover some of her possessions. Do you know anything about her?"

The detective nodded. "Geena insisted she'd been framed and gave the public defender the names of everyone she could think of. Janice Rigby was among the list of suspects I compiled while I was trying to reconstruct the facts of the murder. I'll let you look at the rap sheet on her. She has an alias." He printed out a form on his computer and handed it to Colt to read.

Five years ago Janice had been arrested and served a one-year jail sentence for possession of marijuana in Leadville under the name Angie Rigby. After that there was a list of petty thefts throughout towns in the Black Hills area. Her last arrest had put her in jail for fifteen days. It had happened while Geena herself was in prison.

Colt raised his head. Somehow this woman had hooked up with Todd and used him like a bank because he'd been willing. Geena had loved her brother. He dreaded the thought of telling her what he'd found.

"When Geena first met Janice, she thought the other woman was involved with a man besides her brother, but a rap sheet like this means she had an addiction to drugs that started years earlier and this is only the tip of the iceberg. She probably sold every possession of Geena's and Todd's to support her habit."

The lieutenant's brows lifted. "I'm afraid so. I doubt she's in Rapid City now, but I'll tell you what I'll do. I'll run a search through the national database and see if there's new activity on her reported in other counties or states. If I find out anything, I'll let you know in case Geena is still interested in finding her. Give me your phone number."

They traded information.

"One more thing," the other man said. "There's a piece of news not included on the rap sheet. With this last arrest, they did a physical on her. She was six months pregnant."

Pregnant?

Colt shot out of the chair. Geena had to have known, but she'd never said anything to him about it. "I had no idea."

"Given the woman's record, maybe the baby wasn't her brother's and that's why Geena never told you."

"True." But maybe the baby *was* Todd's. If there'd been a live birth, Geena might have a niece or nephew out there somewhere. Getting back her mementos was one thing, but the possibility that the baby was Todd's would explain her desperation to catch up with Janice. Suddenly it was all clear to him.

"Thank you, Lieutenant. You've helped me more than you know."

Colt called a taxi to take him to the airport for the short flight back to Sundance. After being away from the ranch for any reason, home always called to him. But as he set down the Cessna and started up the truck, he forgot there was a speed limit. It felt like months, not days, since he'd last been with Geena.

To prove to himself she didn't matter to him, he'd purposely refrained from phoning her and had stayed in touch with Travis and Ina instead. But his experiment had backfired on him and he could hardly breathe as he parked the truck and hurried inside the ranch house to find her.

The house looked immaculate and was quiet as a tomb. He strode down the hall to his mother's room and heard voices coming from the veranda. When he stepped outside he found Travis and Lindsey eating lunch with Ina and their mother. Colt greeted everyone and kissed his mom who was still enjoying her food. "Where are your parents, Lindsey?"

"They drove to Gillette for a big party, but they'll be back this weekend."

Jim had probably gotten antsy sitting around.

"You're looking good. Where's the baby?"

"After Geena made lunch for us, she volunteered to tend her until her next feeding in order to give us a breather."

Travis eyed him. "Geena's amazing! As you can see, there's still plenty of food here. Sit down and tell us how Robert's doing."

"Actually I've had lunch and there are some things I need to do, so I'll fill you in at dinner."

He left the veranda and hurried through the house to the staircase. Taking the steps two at a time, he raced down the hall to Travis's old room expecting to find Geena, but she wasn't there. Colt checked the other upstairs rooms to no avail.

That meant she was in her room.

With his heart pounding like a sledgehammer, he went back down and took a few deep breaths outside her door. Afraid to knock for fear he'd wake the baby if she was asleep, he carefully turned the handle and looked inside.

Geena lay in the center of the bed facing the door. The carrycot sat on the floor. She'd put the baby next to her and was studying her the way a mother would do. Her face was awash in tears. He might have been mystified if he hadn't talked to the lieutenant. Moved by her pain and the tenderness she showed the baby, he entered the room and closed the door, then tiptoed over to the bed.

Abby was sound asleep. When Geena saw him, he heard her quick intake of breath.

"Lindsey told me you were watching her," he whispered, "so I thought I'd let you know I'm back. I hope it's all right I came in."

"Of course. Everyone must be glad you're home safely."

And you, Geena?

He leaned over. "She's beautiful, just like her mother."

Geena's wet midnight-blue eyes looked haunted. "I don't think I've ever seen a more perfect baby."

There was someone else Colt had never seen anyone

more perfect than. She was within touching distance. Unable to help himself, he picked up the baby and settled her in the carrycot, then he stretched out on the bed next to Geena. When she would have gotten up, he put out his arm and rolled her back into him.

He buried his face in her hair. "I've just come from police headquarters in Rapid City and know about Janice's pregnancy. Why didn't you tell me?"

She eased away enough so she could look at him. "I thought you were in Casper."

"I left there this morning and took a detour before coming home. I know you wanted to hunt for Janice on your own, but it's too late for that. After seeing her rap sheet, we're in this together from now on. There are some things you need to know about her."

"Besides her being involved with another man?"

He sucked in his breath. There was only one way to say it. "She spent a year in prison five years ago for possession of marijuana. Since then she's been in and out of jail several times for petty theft. If you think I'm going to let you go without me to look for her, then you don't know me at all."

"Yes, I do," she said on a moan, clutching him to her. "Only too well. That's why I hoped you'd never find out. When you hired me, you didn't know you'd be taking on so much responsibility. It isn't fair to you."

"Stop talking about fair, Geena. I want to help you, and the detective's going to do what he can to locate her. He'll be phoning me by the end of the week."

She shook her head. "I wish this hadn't happened. Now you feel a new obligation to help me. It's all you do and I don't want to be any more of a burden than I already am."

"If you're a burden, then it's news to me. Right now I'm going to kiss you, Geena. If you don't want me to, that's tough. No quarter asked or given you said. Remember? Your mouth is all I've been able to think about since you kissed me on the dance floor in Hulett."

His hand spanned her tender throat, positioning her face so he could plunder her mouth. He'd been starving for her. It was ecstasy to feel her crushed in his arms like this. He tangled her long gorgeous legs with his and kissed her over and over again. They rolled from side to side on the bed, finding new ways to bring pleasure to each other.

Ages later he pulled her on top of him. "I want to make love to you, Geena, and I know you want it, too."

"I don't deny it," she cried softly, kissing him back with a passion he'd never known in his life. This woman didn't have a selfish bone in her body. When she gave, she did it so completely he felt transformed.

Colt traced the voluptuous line of her lips with his finger. "Maybe some Friday night we could ride up into the mountains and camp out where we can be alone and look at the stars. We wouldn't come back till Monday morning."

She kissed every centimeter of his face. "Who would look after your mother and Ina?"

"Travis."

"How easily you say that when we know I was hired for that very job and more."

He bit her earlobe gently. "Your job is what I decide it is," he growled. "If that shocks you, I can't help it. You bring out the primitive in me. It's your fault. Ben White Eagle calls it 'woman magic,' sent down from the gods when a man is searching for his vision. According to him such magic can make him whole and guide his path."

She kissed his hair where she'd been running her hands through it. "Do the Lakota women have visions of 'man magic'?"

Her question delighted him. "I don't know. Why don't you ask Alice?" he asked against her lips before feasting from her mouth once more.

"I think I will. She's going to help me clean the pantry shelves on Friday."

"After that you'll need a nap. I can help you out with that, too." Once again he was lost in euphoria and forgot everything else. "You smell and taste divine, Geena. Did you know that? I think I'm never going to let you leave this bed."

"Not even to return Abby to her mommy? In case you didn't notice, she woke up a minute ago and wants to be fed."

If Colt had heard the baby, he'd been too entranced by Geena to think about anything else. But Abby's cries were growing louder, bringing an end to rapture he couldn't get enough of.

The tap on the door brought Geena to her feet. Colt was slower to respond and didn't get off the bed fast enough before Travis popped his head inside the room. Their eyes met in an unspoken message while Geena ran around the end of the bed. "Abby's been asleep until just now. I'll change her first."

"There's no need," Travis said. "I'll do it. We really appreciated the help. Lindsey was able to take a little nap." He lifted the carrycot from the floor.

A blush had swept up Geena's face. Travis wasn't blind and would see she'd been kissed senseless. Her blouse was no longer tucked into the slim waist of her jeans. It was all Colt's doing, but he didn't care. Slowly he got to his feet. "Looks like it's your shift, bro."

"Yup," Travis answered with a grin. "Thanks. You make a great babysitter, *bro*." He left, pulling the door shut.

Geena glanced at her watch. "I-I can't believe it's almost five," she stammered. "The baby slept for such a long time."

"She's a Brannigan and knows when to keep quiet for her uncle."

"Colt—" She laughed, but he knew she was embarrassed.

"Whatever you're thinking, just remember Travis knows I came looking for you and will realize I'm the one who took advantage. Your reputation is still impeccable."

The animation left her eyes. "As long as he knows we don't make a habit of this."

"Now, there's a thought." Colt didn't like being brought back to reality so fast. "What are we having for dinner?"

"Barbecued ribs and scalloped potatoes."

"In that case, I'll be back in two hours." He forced himself to walk to the door without grabbing her in the process. "After we eat, I'd like to spend time with Mom. I picked up some clay in Casper and thought we'd try out your idea."

"I'd love to see what she does with it. Yesterday I put her to work shucking corn."

There was no one like Geena. "Did she do it?"

"Oh yes. Perfectly. I gave her eight ears. I think she

got upset when there weren't any more to do. Tomorrow I'm going to see how she does shelling peas."

Colt knew he had to get out of her room before he threw Geena over his shoulder and took off to the mountains with her.

Geena went into the bathroom to freshen up. Abby had made the perfect chaperone. Her cry had brought Geena to her senses barely in time before Travis was at the door. Her tiny presence had prevented Geena from making the biggest mistake of her life. If she slept with Colt, she would be the one who ended up with a heartache that would never go away.

Colt had married the woman who'd stolen his heart. When it didn't work out, he'd retired it. There was no plan for another marriage in his future, but since he had a housekeeper who was madly in love with him, they could indulge in lovemaking whenever the opportunity presented itself.

Nope. That wasn't the way it was going to happen while she worked for him. She was the temporary help and didn't want him in the role of rescuer-lover. Her white woman's vision was more spectacular than that.

If by some miracle she caught up with Janice and found out she'd had the baby, Geena would go from there. No matter the outcome, she couldn't stay at Colt's and live off his generosity. Hopefully by the time her first month was up, she would have received the money from the state and would be able to leave his employ having fulfilled her contract. For now she'd make certain he didn't regret hiring her.

After she'd served dinner, Colt said, "Ina? I'll take

care of Mom and put her to bed. Feel free to do whatever you want."

The other woman looked thrilled. "Thanks, Colt. I'll be on the phone with my sister in Gillette if you need me."

Once she left the kitchen, he brought the modeling clay to the table for his mother and rolled out the red color with a glass. Once Geena had done the dishes, he asked her to sit down and play with them. She got three cookie cutters out of the drawer and put them in front of Laura. When his mom picked up her favorite and kept making hearts, he lifted eyes full of gratitude to Geena. She knew what he was trying to tell her.

Still trembling from the look he'd given her, Geena rolled out the blue dough. Without missing a heartbeat, Laura started in on it. Colt quickly rolled out the yellow. "I don't think Mom has had this much fun since the onset of her disease."

"She does it all with such perfection. What a wonderful woman she must have been to raise such devoted sons."

"Mom was the best." His husky tone spoke volumes.

They worked on until ten o'clock. He finally put his hands over his mother's. "Come on, Mom. I'm sure you're tired. Let's go to bed."

"I'll clean this up," Geena volunteered. "Goodnight, Laura."

He flashed her a penetrating glance. "Thanks for making this a memorable evening for her and me. The ribs were fabulous, by the way." With a kiss to Geena's unsuspecting lips, he took hold of his mother's hand. She got up from the table and he walked her out of the kitchen, taking Geena's heart with him.

Over the next two days she saw little of Colt and felt the loss. To handle it, she kept busy with her normal routine and spelled Ina off by taking Laura for walks around the ranch house. The new assistant, named Joyce, came on Thursday. Geena liked her upbeat disposition. She would work two days a week, plus one weekend a month. This would be a huge help to Ina.

On Friday morning Alice arrived and they went into the pantry to get to work. Halfway through their project Alice smiled at Geena. "You work hard like Laura used to."

"I do?"

"Yes. Colt's the same way. He's a great spirit."

"I agree," Geena said in a quiet voice. "I'm very lucky to work for such a generous man."

"That's because he has the soul of a Lakota inside him. He walks in harmony with Mother Earth where all things are related. Colt respects nature and is in balance with it."

"Those are beautiful words, Alice." *For a beautiful man.*

After they'd finished their work, Geena thanked Alice and then left for town. On the drive she thought about Colt's ex-wife. How little she'd understood him. You couldn't uproot Colt. It would be unthinkable. This was a man who matched his mountains—solid and forever. Her whole body ached with love for him. That was why she needed to leave his employ soon.

Once she'd done the grocery shopping, she stopped to pick up the mail. There was an envelope for her in the pile! Her hands shook as she opened the letter sent to her from the state of South Dakota. Inside was a check for $75,000.

The letter said, "This is reimbursement for your thirteen months of false imprisonment. It could never replace what you've lost, but it's my hope it will bring you some solace. Good luck to you in the future, Ms. Williams." It was signed by the governor.

She hugged it to her chest. This money would help her begin a new life independent of Colt, who'd saved her life up to now. After depositing it in the bank, she drove back to the ranch full of plans. Tomorrow she'd ride her bike to Sundance and catch the bus for Rapid City. There were people she needed to see.

For one thing she could pay Todd's back rent to the landlord. For another, she wanted to talk to her waitress friend Kellie. Maybe she knew someone who'd known Janice and could help track her down. Colt had told her the detective was looking into it, but Geena could do it too now that she had the means.

She returned in time to fix lunch for Laura and Ina. Dinner came and went, but there was no sign of Colt. They were moving the herd to the higher pasture. He probably wouldn't be home until time for bed.

Geena had just settled down for the night under her covers when the phone rang. "Colt?" she said after seeing the caller ID. "If you're hungry, I put your dinner on a plate in the fridge wrapped in foil."

"That's music to this starving man's ears. I'm on my way back to the house, but wanted to catch you before you went to sleep. Tomorrow morning I'm driving us to Rapid City. We have two appointments. Mr. Phelps is going to meet us at ten in his office. Afterwards Detective Crowther is expecting us to come to police headquarters."

Her heart raced. "Then he must have news about Janice—"

"I'm sure of it."

"But he didn't say if it was good or bad?"

"No. Since we're going that far, why don't you pack an overnight bag? We'll stay at a hotel so that we can have dinner and take in a film tomorrow night."

She moaned at the dangerous thought of being alone with him like that. "Colt—I—"

"I'll book separate bedrooms if that's what's bothering you."

"It's not!" she cried, but that wasn't entirely true. "I happen to know you have other things to do with your time and—"

"Goodnight, Geena. I'll see you out at my truck at eight o'clock. Don't take off early on your bike and force me to track you down like I had to do last time." He clicked off.

She bit her lip. He read her mind with frightening ease.

After breakfast at the hotel restaurant in Rapid City where Colt had checked them in to adjoining suites, they drove to the pipeline company. Mr. Phelps, who looked to be in his fifties, greeted them at the door of his office. Geena caught his hand in both of hers.

"Thank you for meeting with us when I know you don't have office hours today."

"I'm happy to do it, Ms. Williams. Won't you and Mr. Brannigan be seated?"

"Thank you."

The other man eyed her kindly from behind his desk. "When I heard you'd been exonerated, nothing could have made me happier. A great wrong was committed at a time when you were grieving for your brother."

Her throat almost closed with tears. "You have no idea how long I've been wanting to visit you. There aren't enough thanks in this world for what you did for him. To know you gave him a decent burial next to my family—" Moisture glazed her eyes. "It was the only thing that helped me through that dark time. You're a wonderful person, Mr. Phelps, and I'm going to pay you back every penny."

He shook his graying head. "I wouldn't accept it. Todd's accident happened on the job he was doing for us. Of course we paid for his burial. It was the least we could do. He was one of the hardest workers in our company and a very fine man, totally dependable and reliable."

"That was Todd."

"Everyone liked him and has missed him."

"I've missed him too." She felt Colt's hand grasp hers.

"In his file you were listed as the next of kin."

"One who was in prison," she whispered, "but you found me and made everything right. I'm very grateful."

"I wish I could have done more. Mr. Brannigan told me all your possessions are gone, even mementos and pictures. In light of that, I had this made up for you." He handed her a file folder from the top of his desk. "It's the picture he gave us when he made out his application for work. It's been blown up in color."

Geena opened the folder. A small cry escaped to see her smiling brother the way he'd looked a few years ago. "Oh—this is a wonderful picture of him!"

"He was a very handsome man. Obviously good looks abound in the Williams family."

She smiled, but could hardly see Mr. Phelps through the tears. "I'll treasure this forever. Bless you, Mr. Phelps." She cleared her throat. "We won't take up any more of your time."

As she got to her feet, he came around and gave her a fatherly hug. "I hope you can put this behind you now and get on with your life."

Geena looked at Colt. "With Mr. Brannigan's help, that's exactly what I'm doing. I'm finding out there are many Good Samaritans in this world."

Colt gave her arm a squeeze before escorting her out to the truck. The second they were inside, he leaned across the seat and put his arms around her. For a few minutes she had a good cry. "Sorry. I've gotten your shirt all wet."

"Do you really think I care?" He kissed her cheek, then with seeming reluctance he let her go before starting the engine. "Would you like to head back to the hotel before we drive to the police station?"

"No, but thank you for offering. This picture of Todd has made everything so real again. I have to know about Janice one way or the other."

CHAPTER TEN

No ONE was more aware of Geena's need to find out about the baby than Colt. He drove over the speed limit to reach police headquarters. The tall, rangy detective was waiting for them. Geena's eyes fastened on him. "You're the one responsible for my freedom, Lieutenant Crowther. Do you mind if I give you a hug?"

Colt saw the male admiration in the man's eyes before he said, "Not at all." He hugged Geena back. "I only wish the DNA evidence had turned up sooner to spare you more grief."

"Looking at it from my perspective now, thirteen months compared to sixty years doesn't sound like much."

"Only enough to change your life," he added on a perceptive note.

Geena eased away and sat down in front of his desk. "Colt says you have news for me about Janice."

His expression didn't reveal anything. "That's right."

"I need to find her and the baby if it's possible."

He sat forward in his chair. "It's possible, but you won't have to go looking."

"Why not?"

"After running her name through the database, I

discovered she'd been taken into custody some time ago and is now imprisoned at the women's facility in Pierre."

"What?" Geena's gaze swerved to Colt in shock.

"In January of this year eight members of a gang were arrested in Sturges, South Dakota, in a drug bust. She and her boyfriend were among that gang. The charges against her included theft of cash, possession of drugs, operating in a cocaine facility, distributing cocaine inside a school zone to name a few. Because of her prior felonies, she was sentenced to twenty years."

"Oh, how awful—" she blurted in pain. "What about the baby?"

"She delivered a girl born at Mercy Hospital here in Rapid City on November the sixth."

"A little girl?"

"Yes. She was born prematurely and kept in the hospital due to complications of drug addiction."

"I was afraid of that."

"Two months later Janice was arrested."

Geena groaned. "Where's the baby now?"

"At a group home here in Rapid City."

"So close? But what about visitation? It's a long way to Pierre from here. Who takes the baby to her?"

"There's been no visitation because she signed away her parental rights. When she declared that the father was deceased, she named you as the one remaining relative who might be interested in the baby. But she said that you were in prison and it seemed unlikely you would make a custody claim, since you'd been sentenced to sixty years."

The detective sent Colt a look. "In anticipation of our meeting, I ordered DNA testing done on her. As for your brother, the hospital took a sample of his DNA when he was flown to the hospital after his accident. They ran the tests for me and both came out a match, Geena. She's *your* niece. I've already alerted Mrs. Wharton at social services who's involved in this case. She now has all the particulars."

Geena's ecstatic squeal filled the whole room. She leaped out of the chair straight into Colt's arms. He caught her to him while she sobbed for the second time that day. He knew what this news meant to her.

When she'd recovered, she turned to the detective. "Can I see her?"

"Of course. I told the person in charge to expect you. The baby is in a facility run by the St. Francis convent as part of their outreach program. I've written down the address for you." He handed it to her.

"I know where this is." She lifted star-filled eyes to Colt. "We're only five miles from there."

"Then let's go."

The detective saw them to the door. "Good luck to you, Geena."

Tears streamed down her face. "Thank you for being you, for being there at the right time and the right place for me. I'll never forget you for as long as I live."

Colt watched the detective swallow hard. "Days like this make it worth it."

He'd taken the words right out of Colt's mouth. To see Geena this happy on the inside changed her entire countenance. If Colt himself could ever make her this happy...

They hurried out to the truck and she told him where to drive. It wasn't long before they reached the grounds of the convent and pulled around to the main doors

marked for visitors. Once they went inside, there were
arrows pointing the way to the group-home area. Colt
grasped her hand while they walked down a hallway
to the glassed-in reception room.

A sister looked up from the desk. "May I help you?"

"My name is Geena Williams, and this is my friend,
Mr. Colt Brannigan." At least Geena hadn't called him
her employer, but the word *friend* didn't cover what
he felt for her. "I'm here to see a little girl Lieutenant
Crowther told me you have. I just found out she's my
niece."

The older woman smiled. "Oh yes. He phoned to
tell me you were coming and he has alerted the social
worker working on this case. Please sit down."

"I understand the baby was sick after she was born."

"I'm afraid so. Because she came two months prematurely, her lungs were underdeveloped and the drugs in
her system almost took her life. It was a fight for quite a
while, but she finally started to do a little better. She's
still not thriving the way the doctor would like to see.
For a seven-month-old, she seems closer to five."

Geena looked stricken by the news. "Are you saying
her mental capacity has been affected, too?"

"No, no. But she's taking longer to catch up physically. The doctor said it was normal in these situations.
We try to pay as much attention to all the children as we
can, but we have a full nursery. Most people wanting to
adopt are searching for a healthy newborn."

Colt knew Geena couldn't take any more waiting.
"Could we see the baby, Sister?"

"Of course. I'll bring her to you."

Geena's complexion had taken on a pallor he didn't
like. "You heard the sister. The baby is fine. She just

needs some good old TLC. Sometimes a new colt struggles at first, so you baby it and talk to it, feed it more often and pretty soon it's prancing around like all the others."

A glimmer of a smile appeared. "You're right. I'm so thankful you're with me, Colt." She reached for his hand and clung. His pulse raced because it was one of the few times she'd taken the initiative with him. He'd been waiting for her to act on her own with him. "I couldn't have done this alone."

"I'm glad you didn't have to."

Before long the sister appeared with what did look like a five-month-old infant dressed in clean unisex overalls and a shirt too big for her thin frame. He watched Geena's eyes clap on her niece.

"I don't believe it," she cried softly when the sister lowered her into Geena's arms. "Oh, you darling little thing. You've got your daddy's brown hair and blue eyes, but the rest of you is Janice."

Not all. There was enough of Geena's beautiful mouth and chin thrown in the mix to tug at Colt's heart. The baby's lower lip quivered and she started to cry.

"Have I frightened you? I'm so sorry. I'm your Aunt Geena and I love you to death."

Colt knew that.

She put the baby against her shoulder and rocked her until she calmed down a little. "Sister? What's her name?"

"We have no idea, but we've called her Lori."

"That was my mother's name! How did she come by it?"

"I'm told that when the baby was taken to the hospital, this was wrapped in the blanket." She handed her a tiny gold charm with the name Lori inscribed.

"This is my charm, the one my grandmother gave to me to remember my mother!" She showed it to Colt. "Todd must have found it among my things."

Colt nodded. "Janice may have sold off everything else, but she had enough of a conscience to save this when she gave up her baby and mentioned you."

Tearing up like crazy, Geena got to her feet and started walking around the room while she cuddled her niece. "Lori is the perfect name for you, my little darling. Lori Louise Williams." She turned a beaming face to Colt. "Louise was my grandmother's name. The one who raised me."

By now Colt had joined them. He kissed Lori's nose. "She's a real beauty, just like her aunt." He pressed a kiss to the side of Geena's neck so she wouldn't forget all about him. Her answering quiver meant she was still aware of him.

"Sister? Would it be possible to keep her for the weekend?" The pleading in Geena's voice was too much for Colt. "We'll be staying at a hotel tonight. I want to get to know my niece."

"You don't live here?"

"No," Colt asserted. "Geena makes her permanent home with my family as housekeeper on the Floral Valley Ranch outside Sundance. It's just over the South Dakota/Wyoming border less than two hours from here.

"Since Geena is Lori's only living relative and plans to adopt her, she'd like to take her home immediately so the bonding can begin. We have our own doctors in Sundance and the ranch is already equipped with a nursery. Is there any reason why we can't take her with us right now?"

A big smile lit up the sister's face. "None at all. When the detective called, I told him I hoped this would be the result. If you'll drive over to social services now, you can make formal arrangements for the adoption with Mrs. Wharton. Then you can come back and pick up the baby."

"We'll do it!" He turned to Geena. She looked as if she'd gone into shock. The good kind. "After we meet with Mrs. Wharton, we'll check out of the hotel and run by a store to buy a car seat and carrycot for Lori. The rest we'll figure out when we stop for dinner in Sundance with our new little bundle." He kissed her mouth.

"Colt—" He could see the gratitude brimming over in her eyes. But he also heard the worry in her voice. This was one time he didn't want to listen to all the reasons she couldn't let him do this for her.

In three weeks Lori was blossoming. Now that Travis and Lindsey had moved back to their house, Lori had inherited the crib. She loved the pink hearts and reached for them and the figures hanging from the Mother Goose mobile Colt had bought.

Geena was delighted to see her little body had started to fill out. She wiggled and smiled all the time, especially when Colt was around. He was supposed to be the hard-working head of the ranch, but Geena swore he spent more time with her and Lori in her bedroom than anywhere else.

She would never forget what he'd told her about nurturing a sickly colt. Hands down he made the perfect father. Whether it was feeding Lori her bottle, holding her over his shoulder when she threw up, diapering her, walking her at night when she cried, he was right there to help. Clearly there were two women in Geena's bedroom who worshipped the ground he walked on.

When the next Wednesday rolled around, he took over feeding Lori while Geena prepared breakfast for the family. After everyone had eaten and disappeared, he got up and put the baby over his shoulder to get out any burps.

"Geena? I'm flying to Casper on business in a few minutes. I won't be back before Friday. I'll be bringing Hank home with me."

"I'm sure you can't wait for his help again."

"That goes without saying." He looked tired. That was because he did everyone else's work plus his own. It was too much. "Mandy's going to be happy, too. You know you can call me any time, and Travis is here for you day or night."

She'd been loading the dishwasher. It was a good thing her back was turned to him because she was afraid to look at him right then. He'd done more for her than any human being could be expected to do, but there was just one thing wrong with this picture.

He's not your husband, Geena, and he never will be.

"I know," she said without turning around. "Be sure to fly safely."

"I plan to take extra care. Lori's going to miss me, aren't you, sweetheart?"

"Of course she will. You've spoiled her."

"She shouldn't be so beautiful. That's because she takes after you. It's a good thing she's too young for me to worry about boys flocking around her," he said before leaving the kitchen.

Geena couldn't take his banter any longer, not when he wasn't the marrying kind. The time had come to carry out her plan. She'd been thinking about it since the day they'd brought Lori home, but it had never seemed the right time to leave his employ until now. The only way she could consider doing it was because Lori had given her the one reason to go on living without Colt.

She'd taken the housekeeping job not knowing what the future would hold. But the reality of the baby had changed everything. Geena had already signed the necessary papers and was waiting for the adoption to go through. Even if Colt were to tell her he'd like her to stay on indefinitely as the housekeeper, he hadn't expected her to bring a baby under his roof. No, no.

Once he'd left the house, she picked up the carrycot and took Lori to her bedroom. She had just enough time to pack up and write him a letter before Alice arrived to clean. But Geena had another job for Alice to do as soon as she got there.

"Where's the fire, bro?"

Colt made a grunting sound. "I've been gone two days." Once they left the airfield, he drove the truck faster.

"If there were something wrong, Mac would have phoned," Hank reasoned. "I thought you said everything was fine when you talked to Geena last night."

"That's what she said, but I'm not so sure."

"You think Mom's sick? Or Lori, and she's not telling you?"

"I don't know, but I'm sure as hell going to find out." Geena had said all the right things during his two conversations with her. And yet something had been missing and he didn't like the vibes he was getting.

When they reached the ranch house, Colt levered himself from the cab and rushed inside the house. He headed straight for his mother's room with Hank trailing. They found her and Ina out on the veranda. All seemed well.

After he kissed her and had a small chat with Ina, Colt walked through the house to find Geena. The first red flag went up when he saw Alice going up the stairs. This wasn't her day to work.

"Hi, Alice."

She turned around. "Hey, Colt."

"What are you doing here today?"

"Helping out."

Her non-answer made him totally suspicious and he headed straight for Geena's bedroom. When he walked in, he realized it had been vacated. Everything looked exactly as it had before Geena had arrived on the scene. No remnants of the baby or Geena. Nothing...

Sick to the core of his being, his eyes darted to the dresser where he saw an envelope propped next to some keys. Hardly able to breathe, he took the steps necessary to reach for it, then sank down on the side of the bed. When he opened the envelope and withdrew the letter, a wad of money fell out. The sight of it produced pain more excruciating than the horns of any rogue steer that had ever gored him.

Dear Colt—
How do I begin to thank you for all you've done for me? I had a talk with Alice a few weeks ago. She said you were a great man born with the soul

of a Lakota. Your life is in harmony with the earth and all things living, giving you balance.

I agree with her. Everyone comes to you because you're wise and generous, and so good it makes me cry. It's been my privilege to know you. As we said in the beginning, the contract was temporary. But things got out of balance when I found Lori and she was able to come home with me. You told the sister I had a permanent home with you, but it wasn't true. That wasn't part of the contract, so I've moved on.

Alice said she would fill in as housekeeper until you can find a permanent one. I hope you won't be upset with me for that. She loves you and she's wonderful. Best of all, she knows how to take care of your home and your family better than anyone else.

The money is payment for the two months' salary you've given me along with all the extras. I was no housekeeper and didn't earn a dime of it. You took me in out of the kindness of your heart. You let me play house and cook. You clothed and fed me in my hour of need. All of it brought me joy beyond description.

I wish you great joy in the future. Above all people, you deserve it.

God bless you, dearest Colt.

Geena.

Colt crushed the letter in his hand before he flew from the room out of breath. *"Alice?"*

He checked his movements when he saw her standing at the other end of the hall. "Yes, Colt?"

"Where is she?"

"The last time I saw her was in Sundance at the used-car dealership," she answered, calm as the summer day outside.

Geena had sworn Alice to secrecy.

His pain escalated because he knew Alice would never lie to him. "Do you think she went to Rapid City?"

She stared at him for a full minute. "I would not look for her in South Dakota. Perhaps Lindsey knows the truth."

Her Lakota soul had spoken to his, sending him a sign. He covered the distance between them and kissed her forehead before he set out to talk to his sister-in-law.

After being gone several hours on Saturday morning, Geena pulled up in front of her room at the Sleepy Time Motel in Laramie. It catered to families by providing rooms with a kitchenette and a crib, all the comforts of home for her and Lori.

She pulled the baby from the new car seat of her used Toyota and put her in the fold-up stroller she'd bought in Sundance with her own money. After grabbing the sack of ready-made formula from the front seat, she hurried inside the room to put Lori down for a nap with her bottle.

Geena had bought a newspaper and planned to look for live-in housekeeper jobs here. If there was no response in a few days, she'd head south to Fort Collins, Colorado. So far she'd found out nobody wanted a housekeeper with a baby.

Thanks to Alice, who'd driven her and Lori to the used-car dealership in Sundance on Wednesday, she'd been able to buy a second-hand car. She'd only brought their luggage and the carrycot with her. After thanking Alice profusely and waving her off, she was able to drive to the bank and withdraw some of her money. The rest she left in the account until she reached her final destination and had it transferred to a new bank.

Back at the ranch she'd left the keys on the dresser along with an envelope containing a letter to Colt and $7,000.00 in cash to repay him for everything. Alice had agreed to take over as temporary housekeeper until Colt found a new one. With that resolved, she'd set out to establish her new life with Lori away from the Floral Valley Ranch. Only distance and time would help heal the pain she'd been living through at the thought of never seeing Colt again.

While she scanned the want-ads, she heard a rap on the door. It was probably the maid bringing her some fresh towels. But when she opened it, she saw a tall man in a black cowboy hat who resembled Colt blocking the entrance. Yet he didn't look exactly like him because this man had a forbidding countenance and his eyes looked a furious black rather than a piercing hazel. His fists opened and closed at his sides.

"Colt—" Her hand went to her throat. She took a step back. "H-how did you find me?" Her voice faltered.

"Process of elimination," he bit out in a voice she wouldn't have recognized if she hadn't watched him say the words. "The man at the dealership in Sundance gave me a description of the car you bought and the license plate number. Lindsey told me you'd come to Laramie and were staying at a family-friendly motel. I figured as much, since you attended four years of college here. So I flew here and rented a car."

She shivered, because he would make a terrifying

adversary. "You shouldn't have come. I'm so sorry this has taken you away from the ranch unnecessarily. I told you everything in the letter and have tried to repay you in all the ways I could."

"You lied to me, Geena." His delivery was like a whiplash against her body. He hadn't heard anything she'd said.

"I've never lied to you—" she cried in defense. "I revere you too much to do that."

His mouth twisted cruelly. "What about my phone calls to you? 'Everything's fine,' you said. 'Don't worry about anything,' you insisted."

"But it was true!"

"No—" He almost spat the word. "You broke our contract. I trusted you. Now that trust is gone."

By now she was trembling, but she had to remain strong. "We agreed that my job was temporary while we determined if I was a good fit. But bringing Lori into your household changed the situation. You need a housekeeper, not a woman with a baby niece who requires extra attention and care. I became a burden, the last thing you asked for or deserved. Don't you understand how terrible I felt about doing that to you?"

His eyes narrowed to slits. "After assuring me on the phone that everything was fine, you left without saying one word to me," he accused her. "That's called a sin of omission. The worst kind." His voice grated with menace.

He wheeled around and headed for his rental car. She heard the tires squeal all the way out of the motel parking area.

She bit her teeth into the index finger of her hand.

Colt—what have I done?

This had to do with Cheryl, but she'd thought he and his ex-wife had come to an agreement before they'd divorced. He'd played it down when he'd told Geena about their problems and separation. But the white-faced rancher who'd just laid her out on the pavement had a lot more going on inside him than he'd allowed her to see until now.

Colt was in agony. Both Alice and Lindsey had seen that he'd been so affected by it, they'd told him the truth even though Geena had sworn them to secrecy. But she understood why because she was terrified by the change in him.

There was only one thing to do about it, and that was to go back and make him tell her exactly what was wrong.

To her relief, Lori had been a great little traveler on the way here. Geena had to hope her darling niece could handle the trip home. It would be a long drive. They probably wouldn't get to the ranch before late in the day, but it didn't matter. She needed to talk to Colt tonight!

Quick as she could, she packed them up and checked out at the motel office. Once on the road she headed north. Maybe Lori sensed something important was going on because she was an angel throughout the return trip. By the time they reached the ranch house, Geena was a complete wreck because she feared she wouldn't find Colt there. When she saw his truck, she practically passed out in relief.

But once she grabbed Lori and ran inside, he was nowhere to be found. The place was quiet as a tomb. She hurried back to her car with Lori and drove to Travis's house. He answered her knock and looked shocked to see her standing there with Lori in her arms.

"I thought you were in Laramie."

Lindsey joined him, equally surprised to find her at their door. "Geena?"

"I came home to talk to Colt, but he's not in the house. Do you know where he is?"

Travis eyed her speculatively. "I do, but—"

"I have to find him—" she broke in, cutting him off. One brow lifted. "How badly?"

They weren't brothers for nothing. He knew his big brother was hurting. Right then her love for Travis grew in leaps. "It's a matter of life and death to me."

He stared at her. "Life and death, huh?"

"Yes. We've had a terrible misunderstanding. I—I'm in love with him."

His eyes flickered. "If you'd said anything else…" He gave her a hug. "After he flew back from Laramie, I heard him tell Hank he was headed for the sheepherder's shelter in the high meadow and he didn't care what in the devil happened while he was away. No one was to know where he'd gone or when he'd be back. You'll have to get there on horseback."

"I know. When we went riding, he pointed it out to me. Do you think if I called Alice, she'd tend Lori for me tonight?"

"Why do that when you've got me?" Lindsey questioned. Geena could hardly believe what she'd just heard. "I can take care of her tonight. Abby often sleeps in her carrycot. We'll put Lori in the crib."

"You'd do that for me?"

"After the way you've been waiting on me, it's my chance to pay you back." She reached for Lori. "We'll take good care of her till you get back."

"You're terrific." She hugged Lindsey and gave the

baby a kiss. "I've got plenty of ready-made formula and diapers in the car."

"I'll get everything. Travis, honey? Will you saddle Carrot Top for her? There's enough daylight left for her to make it without problem."

"Sure I will. Come on. Let's get you on your way. I've only seen Colt bad one other time, but it was nothing compared to today. I hardly recognized him as my own flesh and blood."

Geena could top that. She didn't know the fierce stranger who'd left the motel in such turmoil.

"Thank you both for this."

Lindsey put an arm around her. In a whisper she said, "Colt can be scary when he's upset, but since you survived prison, I'm backing you."

Geena hugged her hard before hurrying after Travis.

"What in the hell are you making all that racket for, Titus? You've sniffed mountain lions and coyotes before."

Colt was trying to get the lantern to work. If it was broken, then he'd have no light until morning, but it didn't matter. The shelter was nothing more than a lean-to for when a hand got stranded in a blizzard. You could barely turn around in it.

He couldn't remember the last time the furnishings had been replaced, but that didn't matter either. Colt liked it this way. The tiny camp stove still worked and there was a pan to fry fish. What more could a man want with a mountain stream full of trout at his door?

All he required at the moment was the cot. One of these days it was going to collapse, but he'd worry about that when it happened.

By now Titus was at the door, yelping and scratching his paws against the wood in desperation. Colt knew he didn't need to go out any more tonight. "What in blazes has gotten into you?" He put the lantern on the floor and walked over to him. That's when he heard the neigh from more than one horse.

Anger consumed him that someone had ridden all the way up here. Unless an emergency had happened to his mother, he'd warned Travis to keep everyone away! Without taking care, he flung the door open. In the process the top hinge gave way so the door hung on a slant, but by now he was distracted because he'd seen someone dismounting the other horse.

Carrot Top?

Titus took off. Colt let him go because all of a sudden Geena came striding toward him, sending every thought flying. She was dressed in her designer jeans and cowboy boots. Outlining her beautiful body was the white Western shirt she'd bought in Sundance. The night breeze fluttered the ends of her hair and carried her fragrance. It almost knocked him over with recent memories of holding her in his arms while he buried his face in her dark brown mane.

He swallowed hard, thinking this might be a hallucination. "What are you doing here?"

"What do you think?"

This was the same female who'd faced him in the kitchen on that first night, but there were differences. This woman was the finished version. Complete. Full of confidence.

"How did you get here so fast?"

"I drove over the speed limit, just like you do."

Colt couldn't fathom it. "But that means you and Lori would've had to leave Laramie right after I did—"

"Yup. My niece is a fantastic traveler."

"Where is she?"

"Lindsey's tending her overnight."

His heart raced. He was too astounded to see Geena standing in front of him to question anything else. She'd come all the way on horseback and now darkness was falling over the mountainside. "You shouldn't have made the trip."

She put her hands on womanly hips, defeating him with her feminine charm. "Then I've come in vain?"

"I didn't say that."

"You called me a liar. I was called that once before and spent thirteen months confined before the truth was uncovered. I'm not about to spend one more night in pain for something I didn't do. Not when I've been accused by a man I admire more than any man in existence. So explain to me what you meant."

Colt couldn't take much more of this. "Let's just say you're not the person I thought you were."

"That's interesting. What kind of a person am I? I tried to do my best as your housekeeper. When I got the money the state gave me, I was able to pay you back. Of course there's no way to recompense you for your kindness, but I returned everything I could. As I told you in the letter, Alice only agreed to pinch hit. I hoped you wouldn't disapprove and thought she was a good choice for a replacem—"

"Why did you leave without discussing it with me first?" he broke in without apology.

Geena took a step closer to him. "Because I was

afraid that generous streak in your nature would prompt you to ask me to stay on longer."

"Would that be such a terrible penance?"

"Yes."

He bit down so hard he came close to slicing his tongue off. "I should have realized that after prison, the isolation of the ranch would be too much for you, too."

"You mean like it was for Cheryl? Come on, Colt. You don't really put me in the same category with her. What else did she do to you I don't know about? It's truth time."

"She lied from the moment we met."

"How?"

"By telling me she wanted to be a rancher's wife. I bought it and ended up paying for it."

"She didn't lie, Colt. She loved you and wanted you. I have no doubt she intended to be the wife of your dreams, but she found out it was a lifestyle she couldn't handle. She was a city girl, and deep down you knew it!"

He couldn't fight her logic.

"I, on the other hand, can't get enough of the ranch or the owner. Didn't you listen to a word I said the other night? I told you I thought the Sundance Kid was a fool not to have settled down right here."

Colt shook his head, afraid to believe her. "I never asked you to leave, Geena. I didn't want that damned contract in the first place."

Her breath was coming faster. He could hear it. "So what are you saying? That you want me to stay on as your permanent housekeeper and keep Lori with me until I've died of old age? That's what you told the sister at the convent."

"I said that so she wouldn't give you any grief about taking Lori home with us that day."

"Even though your ploy worked, you didn't mean any of it, did you?"

"You know damn well I did."

"You swear too much, do you know that?"

"Geena—"

"Well, as grateful as I am to you for everything, I'm sorry, because the answer is still no."

"That's what I thought. So why in the hell did you come back?"

"You really don't get it, do you?" she said in an emotional voice.

"Get what?" He'd had as much as he could take.

"Ooh— Sometimes you build those walls so high around you, nobody can climb over them. I'll say this once.

"I love everything and everyone on the Floral Valley Ranch. Everyone! Did you hear that? I mean *you*, Colt Brannigan. I'm madly, desperately in love with you! Don't you see that being your housekeeper would only be half a loaf? I want the whole thing with a wedding ring, nights under the stars like this, babies, grandchildren.

"You'll probably think I'm crazy, but from the moment I saw your ad in the paper, it seemed to have special meaning for me. But I'm afraid your heart died with Cheryl. If you think I'm going to stay around here for any other reason, then you don't know me at all. If I did that, then my heart would die, too, so I'm not going to let that happen.

"I want love in my life. I found out in prison that I need it. If it can't be you, then I have to believe there's someone else out there for me and Lori. I refuse to let my heart turn into a dried-up prune like yours."

Before he could think, she turned and dashed toward her horse, but Colt was faster and caught her in his arms before she could put her foot in the stirrup. "Feel *this*." He grasped her hand and pressed it against his heart. "Now tell me it's dried up."

"Colt—"

"I've been in love with you from the beginning, Geena. You know I have."

"I wanted to believe it."

"Then believe this." He molded her to his body and kissed that mouth he craved. "For weeks I've wanted to tell you, but I thought I'd give you more time to adapt to the ranch so you'd never want to leave."

"I always dreamed of living on a ranch. I'm a South Dakota girl. Don't you know it almost killed me to leave you?" she admitted, finding every part of his face and throat to devour. They clung with a ferocity that told him this time was forever for both of them.

"I want you for my wife. The family—everyone— adores you. I should have asked you to marry me when we brought Lori home. I've wasted too much time. I want us both to adopt her so we can be her legal parents. I'm crazy about her, too." He kissed her long and thoroughly. "Forgive me for today."

"If you'll forgive me for leaving without telling you. I never meant to hurt you, Colt. You're my very life. I poured out my heart to you in that letter."

"I know. I felt it and was humbled by the words. Marry me soon, Geena. We don't have time to waste."

She flashed him a seducing half smile. "I agree. Let's go somewhere private and discuss it."

"I'd invite you in, but this lean-to is ready to cave at any second. While you ride on Digger with me, we'll discuss wedding plans until we reach the house. But after we arrive, there'll be no more talk. I love you, Geena. When I got home and found you gone…well, you don't want to know what it did to me."

"Oh darling—don't ever stop loving me," she begged. "No quarter asked, remember?"

"None given, my love. That's a promise."

EPILOGUE

"AND SO, by the power vested in me, I now pronounce you man and wife. What God has joined together, let no man put asunder."

In the next breath Colt kissed Geena with such hunger, she was blushing by the time she heard the pastor clear his throat.

"Darling—"

"I heard him," Colt murmured against her lips, "but I have the right to kiss my new wife for as long as I want in my own house. I swear I'll love you forever, Geena."

"You think I don't love you the same way?" she cried softly, out of breath.

His brothers surrounded them. "Time to break this up, bro, so we can kiss the bride." There was laughter from the guests as Hank and Travis welcomed her into the family. Pretty soon everyone gathered round and Geena had never been so happy in her life. Pictures were taken.

The ranch house, decorated with fall flowers for the three o'clock ceremony, was filled with at least a hundred friends that included the ranch hands, staff and relatives. Everyone milled around eating the delicious food, laughing and talking.

Geena had invited Kellie, who'd struck up a conversation with Mandy over in the corner. Colt's mother sat near the fireplace with Ina. She looked stunning in an off-white lace suit Geena had picked out for her. Geena wore a white chiffon-and-lace dress that fell to the knee.

Lindsey wore a soft blue suit and took over tending Lori in the stroller while her baby was upstairs in bed asleep. Their two little girls would grow up together. Nothing could have thrilled Geena more. The fact that Hank had invited Mandy to the ceremony gave Geena hope there might be another wedding one day soon.

Lieutenant Crowther was the last to come up and congratulate Geena. His eyes looked suspiciously bright. "This is the kind of ending you wish for every person who's ever been wrongfully accused."

Tears trickled from Geena's eyes as she kissed his cheek. "If there's ever anything I can do for you, you know where to find me."

"I'll remember that."

"We both mean it," Colt said in an emotional voice, shaking the detective's hand. "Because of you, we've found our happiness."

After he left, Colt grasped Geena's shoulders. "The car is packed. Let's go while Lori is being distracted. If she sees us leave, she'll have a meltdown."

"You're right."

Without anyone being prepared for it, Colt edged Geena toward the hallway. At the last second, Geena tossed her bouquet to a surprised Mandy before they slipped out the front door and hurried to the car Laura Brannigan had driven before she became ill.

Colt started the engine and they took off down the drive. He reached for Geena's hand and squeezed it all the way to the highway. "Only a few more miles until we're alone."

"You're driving over the speed limit, darling."

His eyes blazed with love for her. "Henpecking me already?"

"Yes. I want us to live for a long time."

"I want that, too, since I'm planning on us having another baby by next year. Let's hope our beach honeymoon is productive."

Geena blushed while her heart leaped. "Boy or girl?"

"It doesn't matter. Lori Lou has made me hungry for more."

"She's crazy about you, Colt."

"The feeling's mutual. I was praying she was your niece."

"Why?"

"Besides making you happy, I knew it would alter your plans for the future. That was good, because I intended your future to be with me. I could see you and me together as husband and wife, with more family to come besides Lori. For the first time since I can remember, my life feels complete. That's your doing, darling."

To her surprise, he pulled to the side of the road and drew her into his arms. They kissed long and hard.

When he finally relinquished her lips, she said, "You know the old saying that when God closes a door, he always opens a window? That year in prison was my window because it led me to you. Those thirteen months weren't a waste. They taught me that every moment of life is precious. You're precious to me, Colt."

He crushed her to him. "Welcome to the Floral Valley Ranch and my heart, Mrs. Brannigan."

* * * * *

PRINCE DADDY
& THE NANNY

BRENDA HARLEN

Brenda Harlen is a former attorney who once had the privilege of appearing before the Supreme Court of Canada. The practice of law taught her a lot about the world and reinforced her determination to become a writer — because in fiction, she could promise a happy ending! Now she is an award-winning, national bestselling author of more than thirty titles. You can keep up-to-date with Brenda on Facebook and Twitter or through her website, www.brendaharlen.com.

Chapter One

So this is how the other half lives.

Hannah Castillo's eyes widened as she drove through the gates into the upscale neighborhood of Verde Colinas.

Actually, she knew it was more likely how half of one percent of the population lived, and she couldn't help wondering what it would be like to grow up in a place like this. Having spent the first eight years of her life moving from village to village with her missionary parents, she hadn't realized there was anything different until her uncle Phillip had brought her to his home in Tesoro del Mar.

And even then, she wouldn't have imagined that there was anything like *this*. She hadn't known that real people lived in such luxury. Not regular people, of course, but billionaires and business tycoons, musicians and movie stars, philanthropists and princes. Well, at least one prince.

Prince Michael Leandres was the thirty-eight-year-old president of a multimedia advertising company, cousin of the prince regent, widowed father of Tesoro del Mar's youngest

princess, and the first man who had ever made her heart go
pitter-patter.

As she slowed to wait for another set of gates to open so
that she could enter the drive that led to the prince's home,
she couldn't help but smile at the memory. She'd been twelve
at the time, and as flustered as she was flattered when Uncle
Phillip asked her to accompany him to the by-invitation-only
Gala Opening of the Port Augustine Art Gallery.

She'd been so preoccupied thinking about what she would
wear (she would have to get a new dress, because a gala
event surely required a gown) and whether she might be allowed to wear makeup (at least a little bit of eyeliner and
a touch of lip gloss) that she hadn't given a thought to the
other guests who might be in attendance at the event. And
then she'd walked through the doors on her uncle's arm and
spotted Prince Michael.

To a preteen girl who was just starting to take note of the
male species, he was a full six feet of masculine perfection.
He was also a dozen years older than she, and already there
were rumors swirling about his plans to marry his longtime
sweetheart, Samantha Chandelle. But Hannah's enamored
heart hadn't cared. She'd been content to admire him from
afar, her blood racing through her veins just because he was
in the same room with her.

Since then, she'd met a lot of other men, dated some of
them and even had intimate relationships with a few. But not
one of them had ever made her feel the same kind of pulse-
pounding, spine-tingling excitement that she'd felt simply
by being in the presence of Prince Michael—not even Harrison Parker, the earl who had been her fiancé for a short
time.

Now, fourteen years after her first meeting with the
prince, she was going to come face-to-face with him again.
She might even have a conversation with him—if she
could manage to untie her tongue long enough to form any

coherent words—and hopefully persuade him that she was the perfect woman to take care of his adorable daughter. Of course, it might be easier to convince him if she believed it herself, but truthfully, she wasn't sure how she'd let Uncle Phillip convince *her* that the idea of working as a nanny for the summer wasn't a completely ridiculous one.

Or maybe she did know. Maybe it was as simple as the fact that she was in desperate need of an income and a place to stay for the summer, and working as a nanny at Cielo del Norte—a royal estate on the northern coast—would provide her with both. But on top of that, her uncle claimed that he "would be most grateful" if she would at least meet with the prince—as if it would be doing him some kind of favor, which made the request impossible for Hannah to deny. That the salary the prince was offering was more than enough to finally pay off the last of her student loans was a bonus.

As for responsibilities, she would be providing primary care for the widowed prince's almost-four-year-old daughter. She didn't figure that should be too difficult for someone with a master's degree, but still her stomach was twisted in knots of both excitement and apprehension as she turned her ancient secondhand compact into the winding drive that led toward the prince's home.

Having grown up in tents and mud huts and, on very rare occasions, bedding down on an actual mattress in a cheap hotel room, she was unprepared for life in Tesoro del Mar. When she moved into her uncle's home, she had not just a bed but a whole room to herself. She had clothes in an actual closet, books on a shelf and a hot meal on the table every night. It took her a long time to get used to living in such luxurious surroundings, but pulling up in front of the prince's home now, she knew she was about to discover the real definition of luxury.

The hand-carved double front doors were opened by a uniformed butler who welcomed her into a spacious marble-tiled foyer above which an enormous crystal chandelier was suspended. As she followed him down a long hallway, their footsteps muted by the antique Aubusson carpet, she noted the paintings on the walls. She had enough knowledge of and appreciation for art to recognize that the works that hung in gilded frames were not reproductions but original pieces by various European masters.

The butler led her through an open doorway and into what was apparently the prince's office. Prince Michael himself was seated behind a wide desk. Bookcases filled with leather-bound volumes lined the wall behind him. The adjoining wall boasted floor-to-ceiling windows set off by textured velvet curtains. It even smelled rich, she thought, noting the scents of lemon polish, aged leather and fresh flowers.

"Miss Castillo, Your Highness." The butler announced her presence in a formal tone, then bowed as he retreated from the room.

The nerves continued to twist and knot in her stomach. Was she supposed to bow? Curtsy? She should have asked her uncle about the appropriate etiquette, but she'd had so many other questions and concerns about his proposition that the intricacies of royal protocol had never crossed her mind.

She debated for about ten seconds, then realized the prince hadn't looked away from his computer screen long enough to even glance in her direction. She could have bowed *and* curtsied *and* done a tap dance and he wouldn't even have noticed. Instead, she focused on her breathing and tried to relax, reminding herself that Michael Leandres might be a prince, but he was still just a man.

Then he pushed away from his desk and rose to his feet, and she realized that she was wrong.

This man wasn't "just" anything. He was taller than she'd remembered, broader across the shoulders and so much more handsome in person than he appeared in newspaper photos and on magazine covers. And her heart, already racing, leaped again.

He gestured to the chairs in front of his desk. "Please, have a seat."

His voice was deep and cultured, and with each word, little tingles danced over her skin. She couldn't be sure if her reaction to him was that of a girl so long enamored of a prince or of a woman instinctively responding to an undeniably attractive man, but she did know that it was wholly inappropriate under the circumstances. She was here to interview for a job, not ogle the man, she sternly reminded herself as she lowered herself into the Queen Anne–style chair and murmured, "Thank you."

"I understand that you're interested in working as my daughter's nanny for the summer," the prince said without further preamble.

"I am," she agreed, then felt compelled to add, "although I have to confess that I've never actually worked as a nanny before."

He nodded, seemingly unconcerned by this fact. "Your uncle told me that you're a teacher."

"That's correct."

"How long have you been teaching?"

"Six years," she told him.

"Do you enjoy it?"

"Of course," she agreed.

He frowned, and she wondered if her response was somehow the wrong one. But then she realized that his gaze had dropped to the BlackBerry on his desk. He punched a few buttons before he looked up at her again.

"And I understand that you've met Riley," he prompted.

"Only once, a few months ago. I was with a friend at the art gallery—" coincidentally, the same art gallery where she'd first seen him so many years earlier, though it was unlikely that he had any recollection of that earlier meeting "—and Princess Riley was there with her nanny."

Phillip had explained to her that the nanny—Brigitte Francoeur—had been caring for the princess since she was a baby, and that Prince Michael had been having more difficulty than he'd anticipated in his efforts to find a replacement for the woman who was leaving his employ to get married.

"The way Brigitte told it to me was that my daughter ran away from her, out of the café—and straight into you, dumping her ice cream cone into your lap."

Hannah waited, wondering about the relevance of his recounting of the event.

"I kept expecting to read about it in the paper," he explained. *"Princess Riley Accosts Museum Guest with Scoop of Strawberry."*

She couldn't help but smile. "I'm sure, even if there had been reporters in the vicinity, they would not have found the moment newsworthy, Your Highness."

"I've learned, over the years, that a public figure doesn't only need to worry about the legitimate media but anyone who feels they have a story to tell. A lot of ordinary citizens would have happily sold that little tale to *El Informador* for a tidy sum. Not only did you not run to the press to sell the story of the out-of-control princess, but you bought her a new ice cream cone to replace the one she'd lost."

"It wasn't her fault that the strawberry went splat," she said lightly.

"A gracious interpretation of the event," he noted. "And one that gives me hope you might finally be someone who could fill the hole that Brigitte's absence will leave in Riley's life."

"For the summer, you mean," Hannah sought to clarify.

"For the summer," he agreed. "Although I was originally hoping to find a permanent replacement, the situation has changed. The current nanny is leaving at the end of this week to finalize preparations for her wedding, and my daughter and I are scheduled to be at Cielo del Norte by the beginning of next. None of the applicants I've interviewed have been suitable, and your uncle has managed to convince me to settle for an interim solution to the problem."

She wasn't sure if she should be amused or insulted. "Is that why I'm here? Am I—"

"Excuse me," he interrupted, picking up the BlackBerry again. He frowned as he read the message, then typed a quick response. "You were saying?" he prompted when he was done.

"I was wondering if I'm supposed to be your 'interim solution.'"

His lips curved, just a little, in response to her dry tone. "I hope so. Although my royal duties are minimal, my responsibilities to my business are not," he explained. "I spend the summers at Cielo del Norte because it is a tradition that began when Samantha—"

His hesitation was brief, but the shadows that momentarily clouded his dark eyes confirmed her uncle's suspicion that the prince was still grieving for the wife he'd lost only hours after the birth of their daughter, and Hannah's heart couldn't help but ache for a man who would have faced such an indescribable loss so quickly on the heels of intense joy.

"—when Samantha and I first got married. A tradition that she wanted to carry on with our children." He cleared his throat, dropping his gaze to reshuffle some papers on his desk. "But the truth is that I still have a company to run. Thankfully I can do that from the beach almost as easily as I can do it from my office downtown. I just need to know that Riley is in good hands so that I can focus on what I need to do."

Be a good girl and stay out of the way so that Daddy can do his work.

The words, long forgotten, echoed in the back of Hannah's mind and sliced through her heart.

Maybe they had been born into completely different worlds, but Hannah suddenly wondered if she and Princess Riley might have a lot more in common than she ever would have suspected.

Her own father had rarely had any time for her, and then, when she was eight years old, her mother had died. She still felt the void in her heart. She still missed her. And she wanted to believe that in some small way, she might be able to fill that void for the prince's daughter. If he would give her the chance.

"Are you offering me the job, Your Highness?" she asked him now.

"Yes, I am," he affirmed with a nod.

"Then I accept."

Michael knew he should be relieved. He'd needed to hire a nanny for the summer, and now he'd done so. But there was something about Hannah Castillo that made him uneasy. Or maybe he was simply regretting the fact that his daughter would have to say goodbye to her long-term caregiver. Brigitte had been a constant in Riley's life almost from the very beginning, and he knew it would take his daughter some time to adjust to her absence.

He wished he could believe that being at Cielo del Norte with him would give Riley comfort, but the truth was, his daughter was much closer to her nanny than she was to her father. It was a truth that filled him with grief and regret, but a truth nonetheless.

He and Sam had long ago agreed that they would both play an active role in raising their child. Of course, that agreement had been made before Sam died, so soon after giving birth to their baby girl. How was one man supposed to care for an infant daughter, grieve for the wife he'd lost and continue to run the company they'd built together?

It hadn't taken him long to realize that there was no way that he could do it on his own, so he'd hired Brigitte. She'd been a child studies student at the local university who Sam had interviewed as a potential mother's helper when the expectation was that his wife would be around to raise their daughter.

For the first couple years, Brigitte had tended to Riley during the day and continued her studies at night, with Michael's sister, Marissa, taking over the baby's care afterhours. Then when Brigitte finished university and Michael's sister took on additional responsibilities elsewhere, the young woman had become Riley's full-time nanny.

I don't want our child raised by a series of nannies.

Sam's voice echoed in the back of his mind, so clearly that he almost expected to turn around and see her standing there.

He understood why she'd felt that way and he'd shared her concerns, but he convinced himself that a wonderful and energetic caregiver like Brigitte was the exception to the rule. She certainly wasn't like any of the harsh disciplinarians who had been hired to ensure that he and his siblings grew up to become proper royals.

Still, he knew his failure wasn't in hiring Brigitte—or even in hiring Hannah Castillo. His failure was in abdicating his own responsibilities as a father.

He'd wanted to do more, to be more involved in Riley's life. But the first few months after Sam's death had been a blur. He'd barely been able to focus on getting up every morning, never mind putting a diaper on a baby, so those tasks had fallen to Brigitte or Marissa.

At six months of age, Riley had broken through the veil of grief that had surrounded him. He'd been drinking his morning coffee and scanning the headlines of the newspaper when Marissa had carried her into the kitchen. He'd glanced up, and when he did, the little girl's big brown eyes widened. "Da!" she said, and clapped her hands.

He didn't know enough about a baby's developmental milestones to know that she was speaking her first word several months ahead of schedule. All he knew was that the single word and the smile on her face completely melted his heart.

Sam had given him the precious gift of this baby girl, and somehow he had missed most of the first six months of her life. He vowed then and there to make more of an effort, to spend more time with her, to make sure she knew how much she was loved. But he was still awkward with her—she was so tiny and delicate, and he felt so big and clumsy whenever he held her. Thankfully, she was tolerant of his ineptitude, and her smiles and giggles gave him confidence and comfort.

And then, shortly after Riley's second birthday, Brigitte made a discovery. Riley had been an early talker—not just speaking a few words or occasional phrases but in complete sentences—and she often repeated the words when the nanny read her a story. But on this particular day, Brigitte opened a book that they'd never read before, and Riley began to read the words without any help or prompting.

A few months after that, Brigitte had been playing in the music room with the little girl, showing her how she could make sounds by pressing down on the piano's ivory keys, and Riley had quickly started to put the sounds together to make music.

Before she turned three, Riley had been examined by more doctors and teachers than Michael could count, and the results had been unequivocal—his daughter was intellectually gifted.

He was proud, of course, and more than a little baffled. As if he hadn't struggled enough trying to relate to the tiny little person when he'd believed that she was a normal child, learning that she was of superior intelligence made him worry all the more. Thankfully, Brigitte had known what to do. She'd met with specialists and interviewed teachers and made all of the arrangements to ensure that Riley's talents were being nurtured. And when the advertising company he and Sam had established ran into difficulties because an associate stole several key clients, Michael refocused his attention on the business, confident his daughter was in much more capable hands than his own.

It had taken a while, but the business was finally back on solid ground, Riley was happy and healthy, Brigitte was getting married and moving to Iceland, and he had a new nanny for the summer.

So why was he suddenly worried that hiring Hannah Castillo had set him upon a path that would change his life?

He didn't want anything to change. He was content with the status quo. Maybe it wasn't what he'd envisioned for his life half a dozen years earlier, and maybe there was an empty place in his heart since Samantha had died, but he knew that he could never fill that void. Because there would never be anyone he would love as he'd loved Sam. There was no way anyone else could ever take her place.

Each day that had passed in the years since Sam's death had cemented that conviction. He had no difficulty turning away from the flirtatious glances that were sent in his direction, and even the more blatant invitations did nothing to stir his interest.

Then Hannah Castillo had walked into his office and he'd felt a definite stir of…something.

The morning weather reports had warned of a storm on the horizon, and he'd tried to convince himself that the change in the weather was responsible for the crackle in the air. But he knew that there was no meteorological explanation for the jolt that went through his system when he'd taken the hand she offered, no logical reason for the rush of blood through his veins when she smiled at him.

And he'd felt an uneasiness in the pit of his belly, a tiny suspicion that maybe hiring a young, attractive woman as his daughter's temporary nanny wasn't the best idea he'd ever had.

Because as much as he'd kept the tone of the interview strictly professional, he hadn't failed to notice that the doctor's niece was quite beautiful. She wasn't very tall—probably not more than five feet four inches without the two-inch heels on her feet. And while the tailored pants and matching jacket she wore weren't provocative by any stretch of the imagination, they failed to disguise her distinctly feminine curves. Her honey-blond hair had been scraped away from her face and secured in a tight knot at the back of her head in a way that might have made her look prim, but the effect was softened by warm blue eyes and sweetly shaped lips that were quick to smile.

Even as he'd offered her the job, he'd wondered if he was making a mistake. But he'd reassured himself that it was only for two months.

Now that she was gone and he was thinking a little more clearly, he suspected that it was going to be a very long summer.

Chapter Two

Hannah went through her closet, tossing items into one of two separate piles on her bed. The first was for anything she might need at Cielo del Norte, and the other was for everything else, which would go into storage. Thankfully, she didn't have a lot of stuff, but she still had to sort and pack everything before she handed over her keys, and the task was much more time-consuming than she would have imagined.

Subletting her apartment had seemed like a good idea when she'd planned to spend the summer in China as an ESL teacher. Unfortunately the job offer had fallen through when she'd declined to share a tiny one-bedroom apartment with the coworker who'd made it clear that he wanted her in his bed. She felt like such a fool. She should have realized that Ian had ulterior motives when he first offered to take her to China, but she honestly hadn't had a clue.

Yes, they'd been dating for a few months, but only casually and certainly not exclusively. When she'd sidestepped his advances, he'd seemed to accept that she didn't want to take their relationship to the next level. So when he'd presented her with the opportunity to teach in China during the summer break, she'd trusted that he was making the offer as a colleague and a professional. Finding out that he expected them to share an apartment put a different spin on things.

Ian's ultimatum was further evidence that she had poor judgment with respect to romantic entanglements, a truth first revealed by her broken engagement three years earlier. Now she had additional confirmation in the fact that she was fighting an attraction to a man who wasn't just a prince but grieving the death of his wife. With a sigh, Hannah taped up yet another box and pushed it aside.

When she finished in the bedroom, she packed up the contents of the bathroom. By the time she got to the kitchen, her legs were protesting all the bending and her shoulders were aching from all the lifting. But she still had to empty the pantry of boxed food and canned goods, which she was in the process of doing when the downstairs buzzer sounded.

She stopped packing only long enough to press the button that released the exterior door locks. It was six o'clock on a Friday night, so she knew it was her uncle Phillip at the door. Weekly dinners had become their way of keeping in touch when Hannah moved out of his house, and she sincerely regretted that she would have to skip the ritual for the next couple of months.

"It's unlocked," she said in response to his knock.

"A woman living alone in the city should lock her doors," her uncle chided, passing through the portal with a large flat box in his hand and the sweet and spicy aroma of sausage pizza enveloping him. "Didn't I ever teach you that?"

"You tried to teach me so many things," she teased, standing up and wiping her hands on her jeans. "I thought I'd seen more than enough boxes today, but that one just changed my mind."

"Packing is hard work." He set the pizza on the counter

and gave her a quick hug. He smelled of clean soap with subtle hints of sandalwood—a scent that was as warm and dependable as everything else about him.

"I'm almost done." She moved out of his embrace to retrieve plates from the cupboard. "Finally."

"How long have you been at it?" He opened the refrigerator, pulled a couple of cans of soda from the nearly empty shelves.

"It seems like forever. Probably about seven hours. But I've already moved a lot of stuff into a storage locker downstairs, so it shouldn't take me too much longer."

Hannah took a seat on the opposite side of the table from him and helped herself to a slice of pizza. She hadn't realized how hungry she was until she took the first bite. Of course, she'd been too nervous about her interview with Prince Michael to eat lunch earlier, which reminded her that she hadn't yet told her uncle about the new job.

But he spoke before she could, saying, "I heard you're heading up to Cielo del Norte on Monday."

Phillip was a highly regarded doctor in the community and his network of contacts was legendary, but she still didn't see how he could have learned the outcome of her interview with the prince already. "How did you hear that?"

He smiled, recognizing the pique in her tone. "The prince called to thank me for the recommendation."

"Oh." She should have considered that possibility. "Well, his appreciation might be a little premature."

"I have every confidence that you're just what his daughter needs," Phillip said.

She wasn't so sure. She was a teacher, and she loved being a teacher, but that didn't mean she was qualified to work as a nanny.

And yet that wasn't her greatest worry. A far bigger concern, and one she was reluctant to admit even to herself, was that she now knew she'd never completely let go of her childhood infatuation with Prince Michael Leandres.

She should have outgrown that silly crush years ago. And she'd thought she had—until she stood in front of him with her heart beating so loudly inside of her chest she was amazed that he couldn't hear it.

So now she was trying *not* to think about the fact that she would be spending the next two months at Cielo del Norte with the sexy prince who was still grieving the loss of his wife, and attempting to focus instead on the challenges of spending her days with an almost-four-year-old princess.

"I wish I shared your faith," Hannah said to her uncle now.

"Why would you have doubts?"

"I'm just not sure that hiring a temporary replacement is the best thing for a young child who has just lost her primary caregiver." It was the only concern she felt comfortable offering her uncle, because she knew that confiding in him about her childhood crush would only worry him.

"Your compassion is only one of the reasons I know you'll be perfect for the job," Phillip said. "As for Riley, I think she'll surprise you. She is remarkably mature for her age and very well-adjusted."

"Then why does the prince even need a nanny? Why can't he just enjoy a summer at the beach with his daughter without pawning off the responsibility of her care on someone else?"

"Prince Michael is doing the best that he can," her uncle said. "He's had to make a lot of adjustments in his life, too, since losing his wife."

Hannah used to wonder why people referred to a death as a loss—as if the person was only missing. She'd been there when her mother died, so she knew that she wasn't "lost" but gone. Forever.

And after her death her husband had handed their daughter over to his brother-in-law, happy to relinquish to someone else the responsibility of raising his only child. Just as the prince was doing.

Was she judging him too harshly? Possibly. Certainly she was judging him prematurely. There were a lot of professionals who hired caregivers for their children, and although Prince Michael kept a fairly low profile in comparison to other members of his family, she knew that he had occasional royal duties to perform in addition to being president and CEO of his own company. And he was a widower trying to raise a young daughter on his own after the unexpected death of his wife from severe hypoglycemia only hours after childbirth.

Maybe her uncle was right and he was doing the best that he could. In any event, she would be at Cielo del Norte in a few days with the prince and his daughter. No doubt her questions would be answered then.

"So what are you going to do with your Friday nights while I'm gone this summer?" she asked her uncle, hoping a change in the topic of conversation would also succeed in changing the direction of her thoughts.

"I'm sure there will be occasional medical emergencies to keep me occupied," Phillip told her.

She smiled, because she knew it was true. "Will you come to visit me?"

"If I can get away. But you really shouldn't worry about me—there's enough going on with the Juno project at the hospital to keep me busy over the next several months."

"Okay, I won't worry," she promised. "But I will miss you."

"You'll be too busy rubbing elbows with royalty to think about anyone else," he teased.

She got up to clear their empty plates away, not wanting him to see the flush in her cheeks. Because the idea of rubbing anything of hers against anything of Prince

Michael's—even something as innocuous as elbows—made
her feel hot and tingly inside.

Heading up to Cielo del Norte on Saturday afternoon had
seemed like a good idea to Michael while he was packing
up the car. And Riley had been excited to start their summer vacation. Certainly she'd given him no reason to an-
ticipate any problems, but if there was one thing he should
have learned by now about parenting, it was to always expect the unexpected.

The trip itself had been uneventful enough. Estavan
Fuentes, the groundskeeper and general maintenance man,
had been waiting when they arrived to unload the vehicle;
and Caridad, Estavan's wife and the longtime housekeeper
of the estate, had the beds all made up and dinner ready in
the oven.

As Michael had enjoyed a glass of his favorite cabernet
along with the hot meal, he'd felt the tensions of the city
melt away. It was several hours later before he recognized
that peaceful interlude as the calm before the storm.

Now it was after midnight, and as he slipped out onto the
back terrace and into the blissful quiet of the night, he exhaled a long, weary sigh. It was the only sound aside from
the rhythmic lap of the waves against the shore in the distance, and he took a moment to absorb—and appreciate—
the silence.

With another sigh, he sank onto the end of a lounge chair
and let the peacefulness of the night settle like a blanket
across his shoulders. Tipping his head back, he marveled
at the array of stars that sparkled like an exquisite selection
of diamonds spread out on a black jeweler's cloth.

He jolted when he heard the French door slide open again.

"Relax—she's sleeping like a baby." His sister's voice
was little more than a whisper, as if she was also reluctant
to disturb the quiet.

He settled into his chair again. "I thought you'd be asleep, too. You said you wanted to get an early start back in the morning."

"I do," Marissa agreed. "But the stars were calling to me."

He smiled, remembering that those were the same words their father used to say whenever they found him out on this same terrace late at night. They'd spent a lot of time at Cielo del Norte when they were kids, and Michael had a lot of fond memories of their family vacations, particularly in the earlier years, before their father passed away. Their mother had continued the tradition for a while, but it was never the same afterward and they all knew it.

Gaetan Leandres had been raised with a deep appreciation for not just the earth but the seas and the skies, too. He'd been a farmer by trade and a stargazer by choice. He'd spent hours sitting out here, searching for various constellations and pointing them out to his children. He'd once told Michael that whenever he felt overwhelmed by earthly burdens, he just had to look up at the sky and remember how much bigger the world was in comparison to his problems.

Marissa sat down on the end of a lounger, her gaze on something far off in the distance. "I know they're the same stars I can see from my windows in the city, but they look so different out here. So much brighter."

"Why don't you stay for a few days?" he offered, feeling more than a little guilty that she'd driven all the way from Port Augustine in response to his distress call.

"I wish I could, but I've got three full days of meetings scheduled this week."

"Which you should have told me when I got you on the phone."

She lifted a shoulder. "I couldn't not come, not when I heard Riley sobbing in the background."

And that was why he'd called. His daughter, tired from

the journey, had fallen asleep earlier than usual. A few hours later, she'd awakened screaming like a banshee and nothing he said or did seemed to console her. She'd been in an unfamiliar bed in an unfamiliar room and Brigitte—her primary caregiver—was on a plane halfway to Iceland. Michael had tried to console Riley, he'd cuddled her, rocked her, put on music for her to listen to, tried to read stories to her, but nothing had worked.

It hadn't occurred to him to call his mother—the princess royal wouldn't know what to do any more than he did. It wasn't in her nature to offer comfort or support. In fact, the only things he'd ever been able to count on his mother to do were interfere and manipulate. So he'd picked up the phone and dialed his sister's number. During the first year and a half after Sam's death, before he'd hired Brigitte full-time, Marissa had been there, taking care of both him and his daughter. And, once again, she'd come through when he needed her.

"Do you think I should have stayed in Port Augustine with her?" he asked his sister now.

"That would have meant a much shorter trip for me," she teased, "but no. I'm glad you're maintaining the family tradition."

Except that he didn't have a family anymore—for the past four summers, it had been just him and Riley. And Brigitte, of course.

"When does the new nanny arrive?"

Marissa's question drew him back to the present—and to more immediate concerns.

"Tomorrow."

She tilted her head. "Why do you sound wary?"

"Do I?" he countered.

"Are you having second thoughts about her qualifications?"

"No," he said, then reconsidered his response. "Yes."

Her brows rose.

No, because it wasn't anything on Hannah's résumé that gave him cause for concern. Yes, because he wasn't completely convinced that a teacher would be a suitable caregiver for his daughter—even on a temporary basis.

"No," he decided. "Dr. Marotta would never have recommended her if he didn't believe she was capable of caring for Riley."

"Of course not," his sister agreed. "So what are you worried about?"

He didn't say anything. He didn't even deny that he was worried, because his sister knew him too well to believe it. Worse, she would probably see right through the lie to the true origin of his concern. And he was concerned, mostly about the fact that he'd been thinking of Hannah Castillo far too frequently since their first meeting.

He'd had no preconceptions when he'd agreed to interview her. His only concern had been to find someone suitable to oversee the care of his daughter during the summer— because after conducting more than a dozen interviews, he'd been shocked to realize how *un*suitable so many of the applicants had been.

Almost half of them he'd automatically rejected because of their advanced age. Logically, he knew that was unfair, but he had too many unhappy memories of strict, gray-haired disciplinarians from his own childhood. Another few he'd disregarded when it became apparent that they were more interested in flirting with him than caring for his daughter. Two more had been shown the door when they'd been caught snapping photos of his home with the cameras on their cell phones.

At the conclusion of those interviews, he'd almost given up hope of finding a replacement for Brigitte. Then, during a casual conversation with Riley's doctor, he'd mentioned his dilemma and Phillip had suggested that his niece might be interested in the job—but only for the summer.

So Michael had agreed to interview her and crossed his fingers that she would be suitable. Then Hannah had walked into his office, and *suitable* was the last thought on his mind.

"Oh," Marissa said, and sat back, a smile playing at the corners of her lips.

He scowled. "What is that supposed to mean?"

"She's very attractive, isn't she?"

His scowl deepened.

"I should have guessed. Nothing ever flusters you—okay, nothing except anything to do with Riley," she clarified. "But this woman has you completely flustered."

"I am not flustered," he denied.

"This is good," Marissa continued as if he hadn't spoken. "And it's time."

"Mar—"

She put her hands up in a gesture of surrender. "Okay, okay. I won't push for any details."

"There are no details," he insisted.

"Not yet," she said, and smiled.

His sister always liked to get in the last word, and this time he let her. It would serve no purpose to tell her that he wasn't interested in any kind of relationship with Riley's temporary nanny—it only mattered that it was true.

And he would repeat it to himself as many times as necessary until he actually believed it.

With every mile that Hannah got closer to Cielo del Norte, her excitement and apprehension increased. If she'd been nervous before her previous meeting with the prince—simply at the thought of meeting him—that was nothing compared to the tension that filled her now. Because now she was actually going to live with him—and his daughter, of course.

She could tell herself that it was a temporary position, that she was only committing two months of her time. But two months was a heck of a long time to maintain her objectivity with respect to a man she'd fallen head over heels for when she was only twelve years old, and a little girl who had taken hold of her heart the very first time she'd met her.

Hannah cranked up the radio in the hope that the pulsing music would push the thoughts out of her head. It didn't.

She wrapped her fingers around the steering wheel, her palms sliding over the smooth leather, and was reminded of the feel of his hand against hers. Warm. Strong. Solid.

She really was pathetic.

She really should have said no when her uncle first suggested that she could be anyone's nanny. But as she drove through the gates toward the prince's summer home, after showing her identification to the guard on duty, she knew that she'd passed the point of no return.

Cielo del Norte was even more impressive than the prince's home in Verde Colinas. Of course, it had once been the royal family's official summer residence, bequeathed to the princess royal by her father upon the occasion of her marriage to Gaetan Leandres.

Hannah had been advised that there were two full-time employees who lived in a guest cottage on the property, the groundskeeper and his wife. Hannah had been thrilled to hear that Caridad, the housekeeper, also cooked and served the meals, because she knew that if she'd been put in charge of food preparation as well as child care, they might all starve before the end of the summer.

She parked her aging little car beside a gleaming black Mercedes SUV and made her way to the door. An older woman in a neatly pressed uniform responded to the bell.

"Mrs. Fuentes?"

"Sí. Caridad Fuentes." She bowed formally. "You are Miss Castillo?"

"Hannah," she said, stepping into the foyer.

"The prince has been expecting you." There was the slightest hint of disapproval beneath the words.

"I was a little late getting away this morning," she explained. "And then traffic was heavier than I expected. Of course, taking a wrong turn at Highway Six didn't help, either, but at least I didn't travel too far out of my way."

The housekeeper didn't comment in any way except to ask, "Are your bags in the car?"

"Yes, I'll get them later."

"Estavan—my husband—will bring them in for you," Mrs. Fuentes told her.

"Okay. That would be great. Thanks." She paused, just taking a minute to absorb the scene.

She'd thought passing through the gates at Verde Colinas had been a culture shock, but now she felt even more like a country mouse set loose in the big city. The house, probably three times the size of the prince's primary residence in Port Augustine, almost seemed as big as a city—a very prosperous and exquisite one.

"There's a powder room down the hall, if you would like to freshen up before meeting with Prince Michael," the housekeeper told her.

Hannah nodded. "I would."

"First door on the right."

"And the prince's office?"

"The third door on the left down the west corridor."

Michael sensed her presence even before he saw her standing in the open doorway. When he looked up, he noticed that she'd dressed less formally today than at their first meeting, and that the jeans and T-shirt she wore made her look even younger than he'd originally guessed. He'd told her that casual attire was acceptable, and there was nothing inappropriate about what she was wearing. But he couldn't help noticing how the denim hugged her thighs and molded to her slim hips. The V-neck of her T-shirt wasn't low enough to give even a glimpse of cleavage, but the soft cotton clung to undeniably feminine curves. She wore silver hoops in her ears, and her hair was in a loose ponytail rather than a tight knot, making her look more approachable and even more beautiful, and he felt the distinct hum of sexual attraction through his veins.

Uncomfortable with the stirring of feelings so long dormant, his voice was a little harsher than he'd intended when he said, "You're late."

Still, his tone didn't seem to faze her. "I told you that I would come as soon as possible, and I did."

"I had a conference call at 8:00 a.m. this morning that I had to reschedule because you weren't here."

He expected that she would apologize or show some sign of remorse. Instead she surprised him by asking, "Why on earth would you schedule a conference call so early on the first morning of your vacation?"

"I told you that I would be conducting business from here," he reminded her. "And your job is to take care of my daughter so that I can focus on doing so."

"A job I'm looking forward to," she assured him.

"I appreciate your enthusiasm," he said. "I would expect that someone who spends ten months out of the year with kids would want a break."

"Spending the summer with a four-year-old is a welcome break from senior advanced English and history," she told him.

Senior English and history? The implications of her statement left him momentarily speechless. "You're a *high school* teacher?" he finally said.

Now it was her turn to frown. "I thought you knew that."

He shook his head. "Phillip said you would be perfect for

the job because you were a teacher—I assumed he meant elementary school."

"Well, you assumed wrong." She shrugged, the casual gesture drawing his attention to the rise and fall of her breasts beneath her T-shirt and very nearly making him forget the reason for his concern.

"So what kind of experience do you have with preschool children, Miss Castillo?" he asked, forcing his gaze back to her face.

"Other than the fact that I was one?" she asked lightly.

"Other than that," he agreed.

"None," she admitted.

"None?" Dios! How could this have happened? He was the consummate planner. He scheduled appointment reminders in his BlackBerry; he took detailed notes at every meeting; he checked and double-checked all correspondence before he signed anything. And yet he'd somehow managed to hire a nanny who knew absolutely nothing about being a nanny.

"Well, my friend Karen has a couple of kids, and I've spent a lot of time with them," Hannah continued.

He shook his head, trying to find solace in the fact that their agreement was for only two months, but he was beginning to question why he'd been in such a hurry to replace Brigitte. Had he been thinking of Riley—or had he been more concerned about maintaining the status quo in his own life? Or maybe he'd been spellbound by Miss Castillo's sparkling eyes and warm smile. Regardless of his reasons, he knew it wasn't her fault that he'd hired her on the basis of some mistaken assumptions. But if she was going to spend the summer with Riley, she had a lot to learn—and fast.

"You'll need this," he said, passing a sheaf of papers across the desk.

In the transfer of the pages, her fingers brushed against his. It was a brief and incidental contact, but he felt the jolt sizzle in his veins. Her gaze shot to meet his, and the widening of her eyes confirmed that she'd felt it, too. That undeniable tug of a distinctly sexual attraction.

As he looked into her eyes, he realized he'd made another mistake in thinking that they were blue—they were actually more gray than blue, the color of the sky before a storm, and just as mesmerizing.

Then she glanced away, down at the papers he'd given to her, and he wondered if maybe he'd imagined both her reaction and his own.

"What is this?" she asked him.

"It's Riley's schedule."

She looked back at him, then at the papers again. "You're kidding."

"A child needs consistency," he said firmly, because it was something Brigitte had always insisted upon, and he usually deferred to the nanny with respect to decisions about his daughter's care.

"If you're referring to a prescribed bedtime, I would absolutely agree," Hannah said. "But a child also needs a chance to be spontaneous and creative, and this—" she glanced at the chart again, obviously appalled "—this even schedules her bathroom breaks."

Maybe the charts Brigitte had prepared for the new nanny did provide a little too much detail, but he understood that she'd only wanted to ease the transition for both Riley and her temporary caregiver. "Brigitte found that taking Riley to the bathroom at prescribed times greatly simplified the toilet-training process."

"But she's almost four years old now," Hannah noted. "I'm sure…" Her words trailed off, her cheeks flushed. "I'm sorry—I just didn't expect that there would be so much to occupy her time."

He'd had some concerns initially, too, but Brigitte had made him see the benefits for Riley. Maybe she was young, but she was so mature for her age, so focused, and she was learning so much. She had a natural musical talent, an artistic touch and a gift for languages, and there was no way he was going to let this temporary nanny upset the status quo with questions and criticisms on her first day on the job. Even if her doubts echoed his own.

"It is now almost eleven o'clock, Miss Castillo," he pointed out to her.

She glanced at the page in her hand. "I guess that means it's almost time for the princess's piano lesson."

"The music room is at the end of the hall."

She folded the schedule and dropped a curtsy.

He deliberately refocused his attention back on the papers on his desk so that he wouldn't watch her walk away.

But he couldn't deny that she tempted him in more ways than he was ready to acknowledge.

Chapter Three

Well, that hadn't gone quite as she'd expected, Hannah thought as she exited Prince Michael's office. And she couldn't help but feel a little disappointed, not just with their meeting but in the man himself. She'd thought he might want to talk to her about Riley's favorite activities at the beach, give her some suggestions on how to keep the little girl busy and happy, but she'd gotten the impression he only wanted her to keep the child occupied and out of his way.

As she made her way down the hall in search of the princess, she realized that she'd never actually seen him with his daughter. The first time she'd met Riley—the day of the ice cream mishap at the art gallery—the little girl had been in the care of her nanny. When Hannah had arrived at the prince's house to interview for the position, Riley had been out with Brigitte. She'd gone back for a second visit, to spend some time with the child so that she wouldn't be a complete stranger to her when she showed up at Cielo del Norte, but she hadn't seen the prince at all on that occasion.

Now he was in his office, and the princess was apparently somewhere else in this labyrinth of rooms preparing for a piano lesson. Did they always lead such separate lives? Did the prince really intend to spend most of his supposed holiday at his desk?

Once she'd gotten over her wariness about taking a job for which she had no experience, she'd actually found herself looking forward to spending the summer with the young princess. She'd imagined that they would play in the water and have picnics on the beach. She hadn't anticipated that the little girl wouldn't have time for fun and frivolity. Yes, she'd been born royal and would someday have duties and obligations as a result, but she wasn't even four years old yet.

Brigitte had made a point of telling Hannah—several times—that Riley was an exceptionally bright and gifted child who was already reading at a second-grade level—in French. She'd encouraged the young princess to demonstrate her talents at the piano, and Riley had done so willingly enough. Hannah couldn't help but be impressed, but in the back of her mind, she wondered why the child didn't seem happy.

Somehow that question had Hannah thinking about what she'd been doing as a four-year-old. Her own childhood had hardly been traditional, but it had been fun. In whatever village had been their current home, she'd always had lots of local children to play with. She'd raced over the hills and played hide-and-seek in the trees. She'd gone swimming in watering holes and rivers and streams. She'd created rudimentary sculptures out of riverbank clay and built houses and castles from mud and grass.

Her parents had never worried about the lack of formal education, insisting that the life skills she was learning were far more important than reading and writing. While the teacher in her cringed at that philosophy now, she did understand the importance of balance between life and learning.

At the princess's age, she'd picked up some words and phrases in Swahili and Hausa and Manyika, enough to communicate with the other kids on a basic level; Riley was studying French, Italian and German out of textbooks. And whereas Hannah had learned music by banging on tribal drums or shaking and rattling dried seed pods, Riley had lessons from professional instructors.

She could hear the piano now, and followed the sound of the sharp, crisp notes to the music room to find the prince's daughter practicing scales on a glossy white Steinway.

She was sitting in the middle of the piano bench, her feet—clad in ruffled ankle socks and white patent Mary Janes—dangling several inches above the polished marble floor. Her long, dark hair was neatly plaited and tied with a pink bow. Her dress was the same shade of cotton candy, with ruffles at the bottoms of the sleeves and skirt. The housekeeper was in the corner, dusting some knickknacks on a shelf and surreptitiously keeping an eye on the princess.

The soaring ceiling was set off with an enormous chandelier dripping with crystals, but the light was unnecessary as the late-morning sun spilled through the tall, arched windows that faced the ocean. The other walls were hung with gorgeous woven tapestries, and while Hannah guessed that their placement was more likely for acoustics than aesthetics, the effect was no less breathtaking.

Suddenly, the fingers moving so smoothly over the ivory keys stopped abruptly. Riley swiveled on the bench, a dark scowl on her pretty face. "What are you doing in here?"

"Hello, Riley," Hannah said pleasantly.

"What are you doing in here?" the princess asked again.

"I wanted to hear you practice."

"I like to be alone when I practice," she said, demonstrat-

ing that she'd inherited her father's mood as well as his
dark eyes.

Hannah just shrugged, refusing to let the little girl's attitude affect her own. "I can wait in the hall until you're
finished."

"I have my French lesson after piano."

Hannah referred to the schedule she'd been given, which
confirmed Riley's statement. "I'll see you at lunch, then."

The princess's nod dismissed her as definitively as the
prince had done only a few minutes earlier.

On her way out, Hannah passed the piano teacher coming in.

The older woman had a leather bag over her shoulder
and determination in her step. Clearly *she* had a purpose
for being here. Hannah had yet to figure out her own.

The conference call that Michael had rescheduled came
through at precisely eleven o'clock and concluded twenty
minutes later. A long time after that, he was still struggling to accept what he'd learned about Miss Castillo—high
school teacher turned temporary nanny.

Phillip Marotta had said only that she was a teacher;
Michael had assumed that meant she had experience with
children. Because he trusted the royal physician implicitly,
he had taken the doctor's recommendation without question.
Apparently he should have asked some questions, but he
acknowledged that the mistake had been his own.

Still, despite the new nanny's apparent lack of experience,
he knew that the doctor had stronger reasons than nepotism
for suggesting his niece for the job. And from what Brigitte
had told him, Riley seemed to accept her easily enough. Of
course, his daughter had had so many doctors and teachers
and instructors in and out of her life that she accepted most
newcomers without any difficulty.

So why was he uneasy about Miss Castillo's presence at

Cielo del Norte? Was he really concerned about Riley—or himself?

When Sam died, he'd thought he would never stop grieving the loss. He was certain he would never stop missing her. But over the years, the pain had gradually started to fade, and Riley's easy affection had begun to fill the emptiness in his heart. He'd been grateful for that, and confident that the love of his little girl was enough.

He didn't need romance or companionship—or so he'd believed until Hannah walked into his life. But he couldn't deny that the new nanny affected him in a way that no woman had done in a very long time.

A brisk knock at the door gave him a reprieve from these melancholy thoughts.

"Lunch will be served on the terrace as soon as you're ready," Caridad told him.

He nodded his thanks as he checked his watch, surprised that so much time had passed. Twenty minutes on the phone followed by an hour and a half of futile introspection. Maybe he did need a vacation.

The housekeeper dropped a quick curtsy before she turned back toward the door.

"Caridad—"

"Yes, Your Highness?"

"What is your impression of Miss Castillo?"

Her eyes widened. "I'm not sure I understand why you'd be asking that, sir."

"Because I value your opinion," he told her honestly. "During the summers that I spent here as a kid, you were always a lot more of a mother to me than my own mother was—which makes you Riley's honorary grandmother and, as such, I'd expect you to have an opinion of her new nanny."

"We've only spoken briefly, sir, I'm certainly not in any position—"

"Quick first impressions," he suggested.

"Well, she's not quite what I expected," Caridad finally admitted.

"In what way?"

"She's very young and…quite attractive."

He didn't think Hannah was as young as Brigitte's twenty-four years, though he could see why the housekeeper might have thought so. Brigitte had dressed more conservatively and she hadn't been nearly as outspoken as the doctor's niece.

"Not that Brigitte wasn't attractive," she clarified. "But she was more…subtle."

She was right. There was absolutely nothing subtle about Hannah Castillo. While she certainly didn't play up her natural attributes, there was something about her—an energy or an aura—that made it impossible for her to fade into the background.

"But I'm sure that neither her age nor her appearance has any relevance to her ability to do her job," she hastened to add.

No—the most relevant factor was her employment history, which he decided not to mention to the housekeeper. No doubt Caridad would wonder how he'd ended up hiring someone with a complete lack of experience, and he was still trying to figure that one out himself.

"If I may speak freely…" Caridad ventured.

"Of course," he assured her.

"You should spend more time around young and beautiful women and less behind your desk."

"Like the young and beautiful woman you 'hired' to help in the kitchen when you sprained your wrist last summer?" he guessed.

"I wasn't sure you'd even noticed," she admitted.

"How could I not when every time I turned around she was in my way?" he grumbled good-naturedly.

"Maybe she was a little obvious, but I thought if I had to

hire someone, it wouldn't hurt to hire someone who might catch your eye."

"Caridad," he said warningly.

"Your daughter needs more than a nanny—she needs a mother."

The quick stab that went through his heart whenever anyone made reference to Samantha's passing—even a reference as veiled as Caridad's—was no longer a surprise, and no longer quite so painful.

"And in a perfect world, she would still have her mother and I would still have my wife," he stated matter-of-factly. "Unfortunately, this is not a perfect world."

"Four years is a long time to grieve," she said in a gentler tone.

"When Sam and I got married, I promised to love her forever. Is that time frame supposed to change just because she's gone?"

"Unless your vows were different than mine, they didn't require you to remain faithful forever but only 'till death do us part.'"

"Could you ever imagine loving anyone other than Estavan?" he countered.

"No," she admitted softly. "But we have been together forty-one years and I am an old woman now. You are still young—you have many years to live and much love to give."

He glanced at the calendar on his desk. "I also have another quick call to make before lunch."

"Of course, Your Highness." She curtsied again, but paused at the door. "I just have one more thing to say."

He knew it was his own fault. Once he'd opened the door, he had no right to stop her from walking through. "What is it?"

"No one questions how much you loved your wife," she told him. "Just as no one would raise an eyebrow now if you decided it was time to stop grieving and start living again."

He hadn't been with anyone since Sam had died, almost four years ago. And he hadn't been with anyone but Sam for the fourteen years before that. He'd loved his wife for most of his life. After meeting her, he'd never wanted anyone else—he'd never even looked twice at any other woman.

But Caridad was right—Hannah Castillo was beautiful, and he'd found himself looking at her and seeing not just his daughter's new nanny but a desirable woman.

Thankfully the buzz of his BlackBerry prevented him from having to respond to the housekeeper. Acknowledging the signal with a nod, she slipped out of the room, closing the door behind her.

Michael picked up the phone, forcing all thoughts of Hannah from his mind.

Lunch for the adults was pan-seared red snapper served with couscous and steamed vegetables. For Riley, it was chicken nuggets and fries with a few vegetables on the side. She eagerly ate the nuggets, alternately played with or nibbled on the fries and carefully rearranged the vegetables on her plate.

Throughout the meal, Hannah was conscious—almost painfully so—of the prince seated across the table. She'd pretty much decided that she didn't really like him, at least not what she'd seen of him so far, but for some inexplicable reason, that didn't stop her pulse from racing whenever he was near. Remnants of her childhood crush? Or the shallow desires of a long-celibate woman? Whatever the explanation, the man sure did interfere with her equilibrium.

Thankfully, he paid little attention to her, seeming content to make conversation with his daughter. Hannah found it interesting to observe their interaction, noting how alive and animated the princess was with her father. Certainly there was no evidence of the moody child who had banished her from the music room earlier.

"Is there something wrong with your fish?"

Hannah was so caught up in her introspection that it took her a moment to realize that the prince had actually deigned to speak to her. She looked down at her plate now, startled to notice that her meal had barely been touched.

"Oh. No." She picked up her fork, speared a chunk of red snapper. "It's wonderful."

"Are you not hungry?"

She *was* hungry. The muffin and coffee that had been her breakfast en route were little more than a distant memory, and the meal the housekeeper had prepared was scrumptious. But not nearly as scrumptious as the man seated across from her—

She felt her cheeks flush in response to the errant thought. "I'm a little nervous," she finally admitted.

"About seafood?"

The teasing note in his voice surprised her, and the corners of her mouth automatically tilted in response to his question. "No. About being here…with you."

"With me," he echoed, his brows drawing together. "Why?"

"Because you're a prince," she admitted. "And I'm not accustomed to dining with royalty."

"I'm a princess," Riley interjected, lest anyone forget her presence at the table.

"It's only a title," her father told both of them.

"That's easy to say when you're the one with the title," Hannah noted.

"Maybe," he agreed. "But the matter of anyone's birthright seems a strange reason to miss out on a delicious meal."

She scooped up a forkful of vegetables, dutifully slid it between her lips. "You're right—and it is delicious."

She managed to eat a few more bites before she noticed the princess was yawning. "Someone looks like she's ready for a nap," she noted.

"I don't nap," Riley informed her primly. "I have quiet time."

"Right, I saw that on the schedule," Hannah recalled, noting that Brigitte had indicated "nap" in parentheses.

And then, as if on schedule, the little girl yawned again.

"I think you're ready for that quiet time," the prince said, glancing at his watch.

His daughter shook her head. "I want ice cream."

He hesitated.

"Please, Daddy." She looked up at him with her big brown eyes.

"Actually, Caridad said something about crème caramel for dessert tonight," he said, attempting to put off her request.

"I want ice cream now," Riley insisted.

"One scoop or two?" Caridad asked, clearing the luncheon plates from the table.

"Two," the princess said enthusiastically. "With chocolate sauce and cherries."

The housekeeper brought out the little girl's dessert, but as eagerly as the child dug in to her sundae, Hannah didn't believe she would finish it. Sure enough, Riley's enthusiasm began to wane about halfway through, but she surprised Hannah by continuing to move her spoon from the bowl to her mouth until it was all gone.

"Could I please have some more?" Riley asked when Caridad came back out to the terrace, looking up at the housekeeper with the same big eyes and sweet smile that she'd used so effectively on her father.

"You can have more after dinner," the housekeeper promised.

The upward curve of Riley's lips immediately turned down. "But I'm still hungry."

"If you were really still hungry, you should have asked

for some more chicken, not more ice cream," the prince told his daughter.

"I didn't want more chicken," she said with infallible logic.

Hannah pushed away from the table. "Come on, Riley. Let's go get you washed up."

"I'm not a baby—I don't need help washing up."

It seemed to Hannah that the young princess didn't need help with much of anything—certainly not with manipulating the adults in her life, a talent which she had definitely mastered.

But she kept that thought to herself, at least for now.

She didn't want to lose her job on the first day.

"Riley," Michael chastised, embarrassed by his daughter's belligerent response. "Hannah is only trying to help."

"Actually," Hannah interjected, speaking to Riley, "maybe you could help me."

The little girl's eyes narrowed suspiciously. "With what?"

"Finding my way around this place," the new nanny said. "I've only been here a few hours and I've gotten lost three times already. Maybe you could show me where you spend your quiet time."

Riley pushed away from the table, dramatically rolling her eyes as she did so. If Hannah noticed his daughter's theatrics, she chose to ignore them.

"If you'll excuse us, Your Highness," she said.

"Of course." He rose with her, and watched as she followed Riley into the house.

He wasn't pleased by his daughter's behavior, but he didn't know what to do about it. As much as he loved Riley, he wasn't blind to her faults. But the adolescent attitude in the preschooler's body was just one more of the challenges of parenting a gifted child, or so he'd been told. Was Riley's behavior atypical—or did he just not know what was typical for a child of her age?

Surely any four-year-old going through a period of adjustment would need some time, and losing her longtime nanny was definitely an adjustment. He hoped that within a few days, after Riley had a chance to get to know Hannah and settle into new routines with her, her usual sunny disposition would return.

After all, it was a new situation for all of them, and it was only day one.

But as he made his way back to his office, he found himself thinking that he probably missed Brigitte even more than his daughter did. Everything had run smoothly when Brigitte was around.

More importantly, he'd never felt any tugs of attraction for the former nanny like the ones he was feeling now for Hannah.

Chapter Four

According to Brigitte's schedule, Riley's quiet time was from two o'clock until three-thirty. When that time came and went, Hannah didn't worry. She figured the little girl wouldn't still be sleeping if she wasn't tired, and since there wasn't anything else on her schedule until an art class at four-thirty, she opted not to disturb her before then.

Hannah was staring at her laptop screen when she heard, through the open door across the hallway, what sounded like drawers being pulled open and shut. She immediately closed the lid on her computer, wishing she could as easily shut down the shock and betrayal evoked by her father's email announcement.

He'd gotten married, without ever telling her of his plans, without even letting her meet the woman who was now his wife. But she forced herself to push those emotions aside and crossed the hall to the princess's room, a ready smile on her lips, determined to start the afternoon with Riley on a better foot.

Riley didn't smile back. Instead, she scowled again and her lower lip trembled.

"I want Brigitte," she demanded.

"You know Brigitte isn't here," Hannah said, attempting to keep her tone gentle and soothing.

"I want Brigitte," Riley said again.

"Maybe I can help with whatever you need," she suggested.

The young princess shook her head mutinously, big tears welling in her eyes. "It's your fault."

"What's my fault?"

"You made me wet the bed."

Only then did Hannah notice that the little girl wasn't wearing the same dress she'd had on when she'd settled on her bed for quiet time. She was wearing a short-sleeved white blouse with a blue chiffon skirt now, and the lovely pink dress was in a heap on the floor beside her dresser. A quick glance at the unmade bed revealed a damp circle.

"Accidents happen," Hannah said lightly, pulling back the covers to strip away the wet sheet. "It will only—"

"It wasn't an accident," Riley insisted. "It was your fault."

Hannah knew the child was probably upset and embarrassed and looking to blame anyone else, but she couldn't help asking, "How, exactly, is it my fault?"

"You're supposed to get me up at three-thirty—when the big hand is on the six and the little hand is halfway between the three and the four," Riley explained. "But now it's after four o'clock."

She probably shouldn't have been surprised that the child knew how to tell time—that basic skill was hardly on par with speaking foreign languages—and she began to suspect that the next two months with Riley would be more of a challenge than she'd imagined.

"Brigitte would have woke me up," Riley said, swiping at the tears that spilled onto her cheeks.

"*Woken,*" Hannah corrected automatically as she dropped the sheet into the hamper beside Riley's closet. "And I know you miss Brigitte a lot, but hopefully we can be friends while I'm here."

"You're not my friend, you're the new nanny, and I hate you."

"I promise that you and I will have lots of fun together this summer. We can go—"

"I don't want to go anywhere with you. I just want *you* to go *away!*" Riley demanded with such fierce insistence that Hannah felt her own eyes fill with tears.

She knew that she shouldn't take the little girl's rejection personally. Despite her extensive vocabulary and adolescent attitude, Riley was only a child, reacting to her feelings of loss and abandonment. But Hannah understood those feelings well—maybe too well, with the news of her father's recent marriage still fresh in her mind—and she hated that she couldn't take away her pain.

"What's going on in here?" a familiar, masculine voice asked from the doorway.

Riley flew across the room and into her father's arms, sobbing as if the whole world had fallen down around her.

The prince lifted her easily. "What's with the tears?"

"I want Brigitte to come back." She wrapped her arms around his neck and buried her face against his throat, crying softly.

He frowned at Hannah over her daughter's head, as if the new nanny was somehow responsible for the child's tears.

"She's feeling abandoned," she told him.

His brows lifted. "Is she?"

She couldn't help but bristle at the obvious amusement in his tone. Maybe she didn't know his daughter very well yet, but she understood at least some of what the little girl was feeling, and she wasn't going to let him disregard the depth of those feelings.

"Yes, she is," she insisted. "She was upset when she woke up and the only person who was anywhere around was me—a virtual stranger."

The prince rubbed his daughter's back in an easy way that suggested he'd done so countless times before. "She'll get used to being here and to being with you," he insisted.

Hannah wished she could believe it was true, but she sensed that the princess would resist at every turn. "Maybe, eventually," she allowed. "But in the meantime, you're the only constant in her life and you weren't around."

"I was only downstairs," he pointed out.

"Behind closed doors."

"If I didn't have other things to deal with, Miss Castillo, I wouldn't have hired you to help take care of Riley for the summer." Now that the little girl had quieted, he set her back on her feet.

Hannah wanted to ask if his business was more important than his daughter, but she knew that it wasn't a fair question. She had to remember that the prince wasn't her own father, and she couldn't assume that his preoccupation with other matters meant he didn't care about the princess.

"You're right," she agreed, watching as Riley went over to her desk to retrieve a portfolio case. "I'm sorry. I just wish this wasn't so difficult for her."

"I get the impression she's making it difficult for you, too."

She hadn't expected he would see that, much less acknowledge it, and she conceded that she may have been a little too quick to judgment.

"I teach *Beowulf* to football players—I don't mind a challenge," she said lightly. "Although right now, the challenge seems to be finding a spare set of sheets for Riley's bed."

"I'll send Caridad up to take care of it," he told her.

"I don't mind," she said, thinking that it would at least

be something useful for her to do. "I just need you to point me in the direction of the linen closet."

Before he could respond, Riley interjected, "I need flowers for my art project."

"Why don't you go outside with Hannah to get some from the gardens?" the prince suggested. "I'm sure she would love to see the flowers."

"Can't you come with me, Daddy?" she asked imploringly.

"I'm sorry, honey, but I have a big project to finish up before dinner."

With a sigh, Riley finally glanced over at Hannah, acknowledging her for the first time since the prince had come into the room.

"I need freesias," she said. "Do you know what they are?"

Hannah smiled. "As a matter of fact, freesias happen to be some of my favorite flowers."

Michael was going to his office to pick up a file when the phone on the desk rang. He'd just tucked Riley into bed and didn't want her to wake up, so he answered quickly, without first bothering to check the display. The moment he heard his mother's voice, he realized his mistake.

"I have wonderful news for you, Michael."

"What news is that?" he asked warily, having learned long ago that her idea of wonderful didn't always jibe with his own.

"Your daughter has been accepted for admission at Charlemagne Académie."

"I didn't even know she'd applied," he said dryly.

Elena huffed out an impatient breath. "I pulled a lot of strings to make this happen, Michael. A little appreciation would not be unwarranted."

"I didn't ask you to pull any strings," he pointed out. "In fact, I'm certain I never mentioned Charlemagne at all."

"Your sister went there—it's a wonderful educational institution."

"Even so, I'm not sending Riley to boarding school."

"Of course you are," Elena insisted. "And while they don't usually accept children as young as five—"

"Riley's not yet four," he interrupted.

His mother paused, as if taken aback by this revelation, but she recovered quickly. "Well, if they could take a five-year-old, they can take a four-year-old."

"They're not taking her at all," he said firmly.

"Be reasonable, Michael. This is the perfect solution to your child-care dilemma."

"There's no dilemma, no reason for you to worry."

"I thought your nanny was leaving."

"Brigitte did leave, and I hired someone new for the summer."

"And what will you do at the end of the summer?" she challenged.

"I'm not worrying about that right now."

"The fall term starts in September."

"I'm not sending my four-year-old daughter away to boarding school in Switzerland."

"The child will benefit from the structure and discipline."

"The child has a name," he pointed out.

"A wholly inappropriate one for a princess," his mother sniffed.

"You've made your opinion on that perfectly clear," he assured her. "But it doesn't change the fact that Riley is her name."

"Getting back to my point—*Riley* will benefit from the structure and discipline at Charlemagne, and you will no longer be burdened—"

"Don't." Though softly spoken, the single word silenced her as effectively as a shout. "Don't you dare even suggest that my daughter is a burden."

"I didn't mean that the chi—that *Riley* was a burden," she hastened to explain. "But that the responsibilities of caring for a young daughter must seem overwhelming at times."

He couldn't deny that was true any more than he could expect his mother to understand that Riley was also the greatest joy in his life, so he only said, "I'll let you know if I change my mind about Charlemagne."

"I really do believe it would be best for Riley and for you," she said.

"I appreciate your concern," he lied.

Elena sighed. "I'll look forward to hearing from you."

Michael began to respond, but she'd already disconnected the call.

He dropped the receiver back in the cradle and went around his desk. Only then did he notice the figure curled up in the oversized wing chair facing the fireplace.

"I beg your pardon, Your Highness." Hannah immediately rose to her feet. "I should have made my presence known, but I didn't have a chance to say anything before the phone rang. Then I wanted to leave and to give you some privacy for your call, but you were blocking the door."

He waved off her apology. "It's okay."

"I really didn't intend to eavesdrop," she assured him. "But for what it's worth, I'm glad you're not planning to send Riley to boarding school."

He shook his head. "I can't believe she would expect me to even consider such a thing."

"She?" Hannah prompted curiously.

"My mother."

Her eyes widened. "That was your mother on the phone?"

He could only imagine how his half of the conversation had sounded to her, and shrugged. "We don't have a traditional parent-child relationship," he said.

Truthfully, there was more apathy than affection between them, especially since his wife had died. Elena had never respected boundaries and had never trusted her children to make their own decisions, and he had yet to forgive her for interfering in his marriage and convincing Sam that it was her wifely duty to provide him with an heir—a decision that had ultimately cost her life.

"Riley's grandmother wanted to send her to Switzerland?" Hannah pressed, apparently unable to get past that point.

"She even pulled strings to ensure she would be accommodated," he said.

"But she's just a child."

"My mother isn't an advocate of hands-on parenting," Michael told her.

Hannah seemed to think about this for a minute, then asked, "Did you go to boarding school?"

He nodded. "My brother and sister and I all did, but not until high school. Before that, we attended Wyldewood Collegiate."

"It would be easy to send her away," she said. "To let someone else assume the day-to-day responsibilities of her care."

"No, it wouldn't," he denied. "It would be the hardest thing in the world."

Hannah's conversation with the prince gave her some unexpected insight into his character and a lot to think about, but she was mostly preoccupied with trying to figure out his daughter. She tried to be patient and understanding, but as one day turned into two and then three, it seemed that nothing she said or did could change the princess's attitude toward her. And if there was one thing Hannah was certain of, it was that the princess's attitude very definitely needed changing.

On Saturday, after Riley had finished her lessons for the day, Hannah decided to take the little girl down to the beach. She'd made a trip into town the day before to get buckets and shovels and various other sand toys, and she was excited to watch Riley play. She should have guessed that the child would be less than enthusiastic about her plans.

"I don't like sand," the princess informed her. "And I get hot in the sun."

"That's why we wear our bathing suits—so we can cool off in the ocean after we play in the sand."

Riley folded her arms over her chest. "You can't make me go."

"Go where?" the prince asked, stepping out of his office in time to catch the tail end of their conversation.

"Hannah's trying to make me go to the beach." She made it sound as if her nanny was proposing a new kind of water torture.

"That sounds like a lot of fun."

The little girl wrinkled her nose, clearly unconvinced. "Will you come with us?"

He hesitated, and Hannah knew he was going to refuse, so she spoke quickly, responding before he did in the hope that it might lessen the sting of his refusal for Riley.

"I'm sure your daddy would love to come if he didn't have important business that needed his attention right now."

"But it's Saturday," Riley said, looking up at him pleadingly.

"Well, in that case," he said, "I could probably play hooky for a couple of hours."

His daughter's eyes lit up. "Really?"

"Sure, just give me a few minutes to change."

While the prince disappeared to don more appropriate beach attire, Hannah made sure that the princess was covered in sunscreen. Although the little girl obviously didn't like having the cream rubbed on her skin, she didn't protest. Apparently she was willing to put up with the process—and even Hannah—so long as she got to go to the beach with her daddy.

Hannah glanced up when she heard his footsteps, and exhaled a quiet sigh of purely female admiration. Over the past week, she'd come to appreciate how good the prince looked in his customary Armani trousers and Turnbull & Asser shirts, but the more formal attire had given her no indication of how muscular and toned he was beneath the clothes. Now he was wearing only board shorts slung low on his hips with a striped beach towel draped across very strong, broad shoulders, and just looking at him made Hannah's knees go weak.

She'd admired him from afar for so many years. As a teen, she'd snipped every photo of him out of newspapers and magazines and created her own personal scrapbook. Back then, she'd never expected that their paths would ever cross again. And now he was only a few feet away from her—almost close enough to touch. In fact, if she took only two steps forward, she could lay her hands on his smooth, tanned chest to feel the warmth of his skin and the beating of his heart beneath her palms. She could—

"Are we ready?" he asked.

"I'm ready, Daddy!"

It was the excitement in the little girl's response that snapped Hannah out of her fantasy and back to the present. She reached down for the bucket of toys, conscious of the warm flush in her cheeks. She should have outgrown her adolescent crush on the prince long ago, but as embarrassing as it was to accept that some of those feelings remained, it was somehow worse to realize that the man she was ogling was her boss. Obviously she had to work on maintaining appropriate boundaries.

"Let's go," she said brightly.

She'd barely taken a dozen steps out the door when she heard a familiar chime. Startled, she turned back to see the prince reaching into the pocket of his shorts.

"You weren't really planning to take your BlackBerry down to the beach, were you?" she asked incredulously.

"I've been waiting to hear back from a new client," he said without apology. And without another word, he turned away and connected the call.

Riley watched him, her big brown eyes filled with disappointment.

Hannah shook her head, acknowledging that while the prince might have a fabulous body and a face worthy of magazine covers, his priorities were completely screwed up.

Then she remembered the telephone conversation she'd overheard and the prince's adamant refusal to send his daughter away to school. Obviously he loved his little girl and wanted to keep her close—so why did he keep himself so distant from her? And why was she so determined to uncover the reason for this contradictory behavior?

Pushing the question from her mind, at least for now, she continued toward the water and the expensive private beach that had been calling to Hannah since her arrival at Cielo del Norte. "Do you want to know one of my favorite things about the beach?" she asked the princess.

The little girl shrugged but trudged along beside her.

"When the waves break against the shore, you can give them your troubles and they'll take them back out to the sea."

"No, they won't," the princess protested.

But instead of her usual confrontational tone, this time the denial was spoken softly, and the quiet resignation in her voice nearly broke Hannah's heart.

"Well, not really," she agreed. "But I'll show you what I mean."

She found a long stick and with it, she wrote in the sand, right at the water's edge: M-A-R-K-I-N-G-T-E-S-T-S.

"I'm a teacher," she explained. "And I love teaching, but I don't like marking tests."

The little girl looked neither interested nor impressed, but she did watch and within a few moments, the movement of the water over the sand had completely erased the letters.

Hannah offered the stick to Riley, to give her a turn. The princess seemed to consider for a moment, then shook her head.

So Hannah wrote again: T-O-F-U. She smiled when the letters washed away.

"What's tofu?" Riley asked.

"Bean curd," Hannah said. "It comes from China and is used in a lot of vegetarian dishes."

Thinking of China made her think of Ian, so she wrote his name in the sand.

"Who's Ian?"

"Someone I thought was a friend, but who turned out not to be. He's in China now."

"Eating tofu?"

She chuckled at Riley's question. "I don't know—maybe he is."

The little princess reached for the stick. She paused with the point of it above the sand, her teeth nibbling on her bottom lip. Finally she began to make letters, carefully focusing on the formation of each one until she spelled out: R-A-M.

"You don't like sheep?"

Riley smiled, just a little. "It's 'Riley Advertising Media.'"

"Your dad's company?"

The little girl nodded.

Hannah frowned as a strange thought suddenly occurred to her. "Did he actually name you after his business?"

Now the princess shook her head. "Riley was my mommy's middle name—because it was her mommy's name before she married my granddad."

"Oh. Well, it makes more sense that you'd be named after your mom than a corporation," Hannah said lightly.

But the little girl was writing in the sand again, this time spelling out: H-A-N-A...

She tried not to take it personally. After all, this game had been her idea, and she should feel grateful that Riley was finally communicating with her, even if she didn't like what she was communicating.

"Actually, my name is spelled like this," she said, and wrote H-A-N-N-A-H in the sand.

Riley studied the word for a moment, and when it washed away, she wrote it again, a little further from the waves this time. "Your name is the same backwards as forwards."

Hannah nodded. "It's called a palindrome."

"Are there other palindromes?"

"There are lots, not just words—" she wrote R-A-C-E-C-A-R in the sand "—but phrases and even complete sentences."

"Do you know any sentences or phrases?" Riley challenged.

N-E-V-E-R-O-D-D-O-R-E-V-E-N.

"That's pretty cool," the princess admitted. Her gaze flickered back toward the house. The prince was pacing on the terrace, his phone still attached to his ear.

She took the stick from Hannah again and wrote D-A-D.

"Good job," Hannah said, then winced when the little girl crossed the word out with so much force the stick snapped.

"Do you want to go back inside?" she asked gently.

Riley shook her head again. "I need to wash off this sand."

Michael had just ended his call when he spotted Hannah and Riley coming out of the water. Obviously he'd missed the opportunity to join them for a swim, and he was as sincerely disappointed as he knew his daughter would be. But as she made her way up the beach with Hannah toward the lounge chairs where they'd left their towels, his attention and his thoughts shifted from his little girl to the woman with her.

He hadn't expected that she would swim in the shorts and T-shirt she'd worn down to the beach. Truthfully, he hadn't even let himself think about what kind of bathing suit she had on beneath those clothes. But it wasn't the bathing suit that snared his attention so much as the delectable curves showcased by the simple one-piece suit of cerulean Lycra.

He didn't feel the phone slip from his fingers until it hit the top of his foot. With a muttered curse, he bent to retrieve the discarded instrument—and smacked his head on the rail coming up again. This time his curse wasn't at all muted.

Rather than risk further bodily injury, he remained where he was, watching through the slats of the railing as the nanny helped Riley dry off. After his daughter's cover-up had been slipped back on, Hannah picked up a second towel and began rubbing it over her own body. From the curve of her shoulders, down slender, shapely arms. From narrow hips, down endlessly long and sleekly muscled legs. Across her collarbone, dipping into the hollow between her breasts.

There was nothing improper about her actions—certainly she wasn't trying to be deliberately seductive. But like a voyeur, he couldn't tear his gaze away.

She tugged her shirt over her head, then shimmied into her shorts, and Michael blew out a long, slow breath, urging the hormones rioting in his system to settle down. But he now knew that, regardless of what she might be wearing, he would forever see the image of her rising out of the water like a goddess.

It was a good thing he would be going out of town for a few days.

Chapter Five

By the time Michael joined his daughter and her new nanny, Riley was packing sand into a long rectangular mold. She glanced up when he lowered himself onto the sand beside her, but didn't say a word. She didn't need to say anything—he could tell by the reproachful look in her big brown eyes that she was displeased with him.

He could handle her quick mood changes and even her temper tantrums, but her evident disappointment cut him to the quick. He was trying his best to be a good father, though it seemed increasingly apparent to him that he didn't know how. Every time he thought he was getting the hang of things, the rules changed.

"Sorry I missed swimming," he said, tugging gently on a lock of her wet hair. "But that was a really important client."

"They're all really important." She turned the mold over and smacked the bottom of it, perhaps a little too hard, with the back of a plastic shovel.

She was right. And she certainly wouldn't be the first person to suggest that he might be too focused on his company. But his work was at least something he understood. In his office, he was competent and capable and completely in charge. With Riley, he often felt helpless and overwhelmed and absolutely terrified that he was going to screw up—as if he hadn't done so enough already.

He glanced over at the nanny, to gauge her interpretation of the stilted exchange with his daughter, but Hannah's eyes were hidden behind dark glasses so that he couldn't tell what she was thinking. He decided he would wait to tell both of them of the meeting that would take him back to the city on Monday.

"What are you making?" he asked Riley instead.

"What does it look like?"

He wasn't pleased by her sarcastic tone, but he knew that she wasn't pleased with him at the moment, either, so he only said, "It looks like a sand castle."

She didn't respond.

"Is it Cinderella's castle or Sleeping Beauty's?" he prompted.

"Uncle Rowan's."

He should have realized that a child who had run through the halls of an authentic castle would be less fascinated by the fairy-tale versions. He should also have realized that she would be as methodical and determined in this task as with any other. Riley didn't like to do anything unless she could do it well. As a result, she quickly grew frustrated with any task she couldn't master.

Though Hannah didn't say anything, she pushed a cylindrical mold toward him with her foot. He let his gaze drift from the tips of her crimson-painted toenails to the slim ankle, along the curve of her slender calf—

She nudged the cylinder again, with a little less patience

this time. He tore his attention away from her shapely legs and picked up the vessel.

"Building a castle is a pretty big project for one person," he said to Riley. "Do you think maybe I could help?"

She just shrugged, so he picked up the small shovel and began filling the receptacle.

"You can't use that sand," she said impatiently, grabbing the mold from him and tipping it upside down to empty it out. "You need the wet stuff, so it sticks together."

She looked to Hannah for verification, confirming that this castle-building knowledge had been recently imparted by the new nanny, and was rewarded by a nod. Then she demonstrated for him—showing him how to pack the container with sand, then turn it over and tap it out again.

There were a few moments of frustration: first when one of the walls collapsed, and again when she realized the windows she'd outlined weren't even. But Michael patiently helped her rebuild the wall and assured her that sand-castle windows wouldn't fall out if they weren't perfectly level. That comment finally elicited a small smile from her, and he basked in the glow of it.

While he remained outwardly focused on the castle-building project, he was conscious of the nanny watching their interactions. He was conscious of the nicely rounded breasts beneath her T-shirt, and of the long, lean legs stretched out on the sand. He noticed that her hair had dried quickly in the sun and that the ends of her ponytail now fluttered in the breeze.

She could have passed for a teenager who'd skipped school to hang out at the beach with her friends, the way she was leaning back on her elbows, her bare feet crossed at the ankles and her face tipped up to the sun. And his immediate physical response to the sexy image was shockingly adolescent.

Dios, it was going to be a long two months. Especially if, as he suspected, he was going to spend an inordinate amount of that time fighting this unexpected attraction to her. On the other hand, the time might pass much more quickly and pleasantly if he *stopped* fighting the attraction. If he reached over right now to unfasten the band that held her hair back in order to slide his hands through the silky mass and tip her head back to taste her—

"Is it okay to dig a moat?" Riley asked, and the fantasy building in his mind dissipated.

He forced his gaze and his attention back to her construction.

"Every castle should have a moat," he assured her.

"Uncle Rowan's doesn't."

"But it should, to protect the princes and princesses inside from ogres and dragons."

She giggled. "Ogres and dragons aren't real, Daddy."

"Maybe not," he allowed. "But a moat is a good idea, just in case."

Riley tipped her head, as if considering, then nodded and began digging.

"What do you think?" he asked Hannah. "Is it worthy of the Sand Castle Hall of Fame?"

"An impressive first effort, Your Highness," she replied, and he knew she wasn't just talking about the construction.

"But I shouldn't quit my day job?" he guessed lightly.

"I don't imagine you would ever consider doing so."

He winced at the direct hit.

"But if you did, you might have a future in castle-building," she relented. "Your spire looks pretty good."

His brows rose. "My spire?"

Her cheeks colored as she gestured to the cone shape on top of the tower he'd built. She was obviously flustered by his innuendo, and he couldn't help but smile at her.

"But your flagpole is crooked," she said, and smiled back at him.

His gaze dropped automatically to her mouth, to the seductive curve of her lips. He wondered if they would feel as soft as they looked, if they would taste as sweet as he imagined. And he thought again about leaning forward to press his mouth to hers, to discover the answers to those questions.

Instead, he straightened the twig that was the castle flag and mused that it had been a long time since he'd shared this kind of light, teasing banter with a woman. A long time since he'd felt the slightest hint of attraction for a woman who wasn't his wife, and what he was feeling for Hannah was more than a hint.

He pushed himself up from the sand and picked up an empty bucket.

"Let's get some water for your moat," he said to Riley.

When the moat was filled and the finished project adequately *ooh*ed and *aah*ed over, they returned to the house. Hannah ran a bath for the princess so that Riley could wash the salt off her body and out of her hair. When she was dried and dressed, the little girl had taken a book and curled up on her bed. Hannah suspected that she would be asleep before she'd finished a single page.

After she'd showered and changed, the nanny ventured back downstairs, looking for Caridad to inquire if the housekeeper needed any help with the preparations for dinner. Hannah was embarrassingly inept in the kitchen but with so much time on her hands, she thought she might start hanging around while Caridad cooked. Even if she didn't learn anything, she enjoyed spending time with the older woman.

Unfortunately, the kitchen was empty when she entered. But more distressing to Hannah than the missing housekeeper was the absence of any suggestion that dinner might be in the oven.

She opened the door and scanned inside, just to be sure. Then she opened the fridge and surveyed the shelves.

"Looking for something?"

She started at the unexpected sound of the prince's voice behind her. When they'd returned to the house, she'd assumed that he would retreat to his office and stay there for the rest of the evening. That was, after all, his pattern.

"Caridad," Hannah said. "I haven't seen her all day."

"Well, I can assure you that you won't find her in either the oven or the refrigerator."

He smiled, to show that he was teasing, and she felt her cheeks flush. She hadn't yet figured out the prince or her feelings for him—aside from the jolt of lust she felt whenever he was in the same room. But as attracted as she was to Prince Michael, she was equally frustrated with the father in him. There were times he was so oblivious to his daughter and her needs that Hannah wanted to throttle him. And then there were other times, such as when he'd reached for his little girl's hand on the beach or when he'd slip into his daughter's room late at night just to watch over her while she slept—as she noticed he did almost every night—that his obvious love and affection for the princess made her heart melt. How could one man be both so distant and so devoted?

And how, she wondered, could one man have her so completely tied up in knots? Because there was no doubt that he did, and Hannah had absolutely no idea how to cope with her feelings.

She tried to ignore them, all too aware that Michael was completely out of her league, not just because he was her boss but because he was a prince. Her short-lived engagement to a British earl had forced her to accept that royals and commoners didn't mix, at least for the long term. Unfortunately, ignoring her feelings for the prince hadn't diminished them in the least.

"She and Estavan have weekends off," Michael continued

his response to her question about Caridad. "Unless I have formal plans for entertaining."

"Oh," Hannah replied inanely, thinking that was another check in the 'good prince' column. She also thought it was great for the housekeeper and her husband—and not so great for a woman whose kitchen expertise was limited to reheating frozen dinners.

"You don't cook, do you?" the prince guessed.

"Not very well," she admitted.

"Then it's a good thing I'm in charge of dinner tonight."

She stared at him. "*You* cook?"

"Why do you sound so surprised?"

"I just can't picture you standing over the stove with a slotted spoon in one hand and your BlackBerry in the other. Your Highness."

Rather than taking offense, he smiled. "You do that a lot, you know."

"What's that?"

"Tack my title on to the end of a reply, as if that might take the sting out of the personal commentary."

"I don't mean to sound disrespectful, Your Highness."

"I'm sure you don't," he drawled. "But getting back to dinner, maybe you could try picturing the stove as a barbecue and the slotted spoon as a set of tongs."

"I should have realized that when you said you could cook what you really meant was that you could grill meat over fire."

"You forgot the 'Your Highness.'"

She smiled sweetly. "Your Highness."

"And at the risk of spoiling your illusions, I will confess that I also make an exquisite alfredo sauce, a delicious stuffed pork loin and a mouthwatering quiche Lorraine."

"But do you actually eat the quiche?" she teased.

"You can answer that question for yourself as it's on the menu for brunch tomorrow."

"And what's on the menu for dinner tonight?" she asked, as curious as she was hungry.

"Steak, baked potato and tossed green salad," he told her.

Her mouth was already watering. "Can I help with anything?"

"You just said that you don't cook."

"Can I help with anything that doesn't involve preparing food over a heat source?" she clarified.

He chuckled. "Do you know how to make a salad?"

"I think I can figure it out."

While Michael cooked potatoes and grilled steaks on the barbecue, Hannah found the necessary ingredients in the refrigerator for a salad. When Riley came downstairs, she gave her the napkins and cutlery and asked her to set them on the table.

The princess did so, though not happily. Obviously she wasn't accustomed to performing any kind of menial chores. And when her father came in with the steaks and potatoes, she looked at the food with obvious distaste.

"Can I have nuggets?"

"Not tonight." The prince had earlier uncorked a bottle of merlot and now poured the wine into two glasses.

"But I want nuggets," Riley said.

"You had nuggets for lunch," Hannah reminded her, and gave herself credit for not adding "almost every day this week."

The little girl folded her arms across her chest. "I want nuggets again."

"If she'd rather have nuggets, I can throw some in the oven," the prince relented.

"Yes, please, Daddy." Riley beamed at him.

Hannah opened her mouth, then closed it again without saying a word.

"Excuse us," he said to his daughter, then caught Hannah's arm and steered her into the kitchen.

"What's the problem with Riley having chicken nuggets?" he demanded.

"I didn't say anything, Your Highness."

"No, you stopped yourself from saying whatever was on your mind," he noted. "And since you didn't seem to have any qualms about speaking up earlier, why are you censoring your comments now?"

"Because I don't want to get fired after less than a week on the job."

"I won't fire you," he promised.

"Then I'll admit that I'm concerned about your willingness to give in to your daughter's demands," she told him. "She's not even four years old, and if you let her dictate what she's going to eat, she might never eat anything but chicken nuggets."

"It's just nuggets."

"No, it's not just nuggets. It's that you always give in to her demands."

"I don't always," he denied.

"And if you give in on all of the little things," she continued, "she'll expect you to give in on the not-so-little things and then, suddenly, you have no authority anymore."

She picked up the salad to carry it to the table, giving the prince a moment to think about what she'd said.

"Where are my nuggets?" Riley demanded when he followed Hannah into the dining room.

"It will take too long to make nuggets now," he said gently. "Why don't you just have what we're having tonight?"

Hannah cut a few pieces of meat from one of the steaks and slid them onto a plate along with half of a baked potato and a scoopful of salad. Although the prince didn't sound as firm as she hoped he would, she gave him credit for at least taking a stand.

The princess scowled at the food when it was set in front of her, then looked straight at Hannah as she picked the plate up and dropped it on the floor.

"Riley!" The prince was obviously shocked by his daughter's behavior.

The little girl, equally shocked by her father's harsh reprimand, burst into tears.

Hannah simply retrieved the broken plate from the floor and scooped up the discarded food to dump it into the garbage. Then she got another plate and prepared it the same way again.

"I want nuggets," Riley said, but her tone was more pleading than demanding now, and tears swam in her big brown eyes.

"Your daddy cooked steak and potatoes. You should at least try that before asking for something else."

Two fat tears tracked slowly down the child's cheeks. "You're mean."

"Because I won't let you have your own way?" Hannah asked.

"Because you told Daddy not to let me have nuggets."

She caught the prince's eye across the table. He looked helpless and confused, and though her heart instinctively went out to him, she felt confident that the situation was of his own making.

"You should sit down and eat your dinner," she suggested quietly.

He sat, but he continued to cast worried glances in his daughter's direction.

"If Riley's hungry, she'll eat," Hannah reassured him.

"I'm hungry for nuggets," the princess insisted.

"You're hungry for power." The retort slipped out before she could clamp her lips together.

Riley frowned at that.

"Don't you think that's a little unfair?" Michael asked.

"No, but I do think your daughter's demands are sometimes unreasonable." Hannah finished making up Riley's second plate, but the mutinous look in the little girl's eyes as they zeroed in on the meal warned her that the food was likely destined for the floor again. So instead of setting it in front of her, she put it aside, out of Riley's reach.

Then Hannah deliberately cut into her own steak, slid a tender morsel into her mouth. Riley watched through narrowed eyes, her bottom lip quivering. Hannah ate a few more bites of her meal while the child watched, her gaze occasionally shifting to her own plate.

"I'm thirsty," Riley finally announced.

"There's milk in your cup," Hannah told her.

The princess folded her arms across her chest. "I don't want milk."

"Then you can't be very thirsty."

"I want juice," Riley said, and pushed the cup of milk away with such force that it hit Hannah's wineglass, knocking the crystal goblet against her plate so that it spilled all over her dinner and splashed down the front of Hannah's shirt.

She gasped and pushed away from the table, but the wine was already trickling down her chest, between her breasts. The prince grabbed his napkin and rounded the table, his gaze focused on the merlot spreading across her top. He squatted beside her chair and began dabbing at the stain.

Hannah went completely still. She couldn't move. She couldn't think. Heck, she couldn't even breathe, because when she tried, she inhaled his distinctly masculine scent and her hormones began to riot in her system. So she sat there, motionless and silent, as he stroked the napkin over the swell of her breasts.

Her blood was pulsing in her veins and her heart was pounding against her ribs, and he was all but oblivious to the effect he was having on her. Or so she thought, until his movements slowed, and his gaze lifted.

His eyes, dark and hot, held hers for a long minute. "I guess I should let you finish that," he said, tucking the linen into her hand.

She only nodded, unable to speak as his gaze dipped again, to where the aching peaks of her nipples pressed against the front of her shirt, as if begging for his attention.

"Or maybe you should change," he suggested, his eyes still riveted on her chest.

She nodded again.

"I want juice!"

Riley's demand broke through the tension that had woven around them. The prince moved away abruptly, and Hannah was finally able to draw a breath and rise to her feet.

"I'll be right back," she said, and retreated as quickly as her still-quivering legs would allow.

Michael sank back into his chair, then turned to face his daughter. He wasn't sure if he was angry or frustrated or grateful, and decided his feelings were probably a mixture of all those emotions—and several others he wasn't ready to acknowledge.

"Well, you've certainly made an impression today," he told Riley.

"I'm thirsty," she said again.

"Hannah gave you milk," he told her, trying to be patient. "And you spilled it all over the table and all over Hannah."

"I don't want milk, I want juice."

"You always have milk with dinner."

"I want juice," she insisted.

Though he had misgivings, he got up to get her drink. As he poured the juice into another cup, Hannah's words echoed in the back of his mind. *If you give in on all of the little things, she'll expect you to give in on the not-so-little things and then, suddenly, you have no authority anymore.*

He knew that she was right, and it irritated him that after less than a week with his daughter, Hannah had a better understanding of the child's needs than he did after almost four years. But the truth was, as much as he wanted to be a good father, he'd felt awkward and uncomfortable in the role from the very beginning. He'd constantly second-guessed everything he said and did around Riley, and whether it was a result of his ineptitude or not he knew Hannah was right: his daughter was turning into a pint-size dictator.

It was as if he was missing some kind of parenting gene— or maybe he'd deliberately suppressed it. When he and Sam got married, he knew that any pregnancy would be high-risk because of her diabetes and accepted that they might never have children. When she got pregnant, he'd been not only surprised but terrified. He knew what kind of risks she was facing, and he'd been so focused on her that he hadn't let himself think about the baby she carried.

Now that baby was almost four years old, the only care-givers she'd ever known were gone, and he'd hired a high school teacher to play nanny while he buried himself in his work, unwilling to even play at being a father. Was it any surprise that his daughter was acting out?

"Where's my juice?" she asked again when he returned to the table empty-handed.

"You can have juice with breakfast," he told her, trying to maintain a patient and reasonable tone.

"Now." She kicked her feet against the table.

"If you don't stop this right now, you'll have to go to bed without anything to eat or drink," Michael warned.

"You can't do that," Riley said, though there was a note of uncertainty in her voice now.

"I can and I will," he assured her.

His heart nearly broke when she started to cry again.

"It's Hannah's fault," she wailed. "She's making you be mean to me."

"Maybe, instead of always looking to blame someone else when you don't get your own way, you should start taking some responsibility for your own actions," he suggested.

She stared at him, completely baffled. He knew it wasn't because she didn't understand what he was saying but because the concept was completely foreign to her—because he had never before let there be consequences for her misbehavior. Instead, he'd made excuses—so many excuses, because she was a little girl without a mother.

While Riley considered what he'd said, Michael tried to tidy up the mess his daughter had made. He used another napkin to mop most of the spilled wine off of Hannah's plate, which made him recall the tantalizing image of the merlot spreading across her shirt, and the round fullness of the spectacular breasts beneath that shirt, and the blood in his head began to flow south.

He scowled as he righted her overturned goblet and refilled it. It had been a long time since he'd become aroused by nothing more than a mental image, and a lot longer since he'd been affected by a mental image of anyone other than Sam. He felt betrayed by his body's instinctive response to this woman, guilty that he could want a woman who wasn't his wife.

He knew that having sex with someone else wouldn't mean he was unfaithful. Sam was gone—he was no longer her husband but a widower. But he'd loved her for so long that even the thought of being with someone else felt like a betrayal of everything they'd shared and all the years they'd been together.

By the time Hannah returned to the table, the steaks and potatoes were cold. He offered to throw her plate in the microwave, but she insisted that it was fine. He didn't bother to heat his own dinner, either. He was too preoccupied wondering about the flavor of her lips to taste any of the food that he put in his mouth.

He'd been so tempted to kiss her. When he'd been crouched down beside her chair, his mouth only inches from hers, he'd very nearly leaned forward to breach the meager distance between them.

He didn't think she would have objected. It might have been a lot of years since he'd sent or received any kind of signals, but he was fairly certain that the attraction he felt wasn't one-sided. He was also fairly certain that he'd never experienced an attraction as sharp or intense as what he felt for Hannah Castillo.

He and Sam had been friends for a long time before they'd become lovers; their relationship had blossomed slowly and rooted deep. What he felt for Hannah was simple lust, basic yet undeniable.

It seemed disloyal to make any kind of comparison between the two women. Sam had been his partner in so many ways and the woman he loved with his whole heart; Hannah was a stranger on the periphery of his life, his daughter's temporary nanny—and the woman with whom he was going to be living in close quarters for the next two months. And he was definitely tempted to take advantage of that proximity.

"Are you hungry now?"

Though she wasn't speaking to him, Hannah's question interrupted his musings. Forcing his attention back to the table, he noticed that Riley was eyeing the plate Hannah had prepared for her, this time with more interest than irritation.

"If you dump it again, you won't have any dinner left," Hannah warned before she set the meal in front of the child.

His daughter immediately picked up a piece of potato and put it in her mouth.

"Use your fork, Riley," Michael said.

She didn't look at him, but she did pick up the fork and

speared a wedge of tomato. It was obvious that she was still angry with him, but at least she was eating. Though he'd tried to sound firm when he'd threatened to send her to bed without any dinner, he wasn't entirely sure he would have been able to follow through on his threat.

When the meal was finally over, Riley had eaten most of her potato and picked at the salad, but she'd adamantly refused to touch the steak.

"Dinner was excellent," Hannah said, pushing her chair away from the table. "Thank you."

"You're welcome," he replied, just as formally.

"I'll clean up the kitchen after I get Riley ready for bed," she told him. "And then, if you've got some time, I'd like to talk to you about a few things."

Michael nodded, though he wasn't certain he wanted to hear what Hannah was going to say. He was even less certain that he should be alone with the nanny without the buffer of his daughter between them.

Chapter Six

Riley had made it clear to her new nanny that she was neither needed nor wanted, and as Hannah finished tidying up the kitchen after the princess was tucked in bed, she began to question her true purpose for being at Cielo del Norte. Maybe she was being paranoid, but when she finally cornered the prince in his office, the first question that sprang to her mind was "Did my uncle ask you to fabricate a job for me so that I wouldn't go to China?"

The prince steepled his fingers over the papers on his desk. "I didn't know anything about your plans to go to China," he assured her. "And this job is most definitely not a fabrication."

She had no reason to distrust his response, but she still felt as if he could have hired a local high school student to do what she was doing—and for a lot less money. "But Riley's instructors spend more time with her than I do," she pointed out to him, "which makes me wonder why I'm even here."

"You're here to ensure that the status quo is maintained."

"Your daughter needs more than a supervisor, Your Highness. And if you can't see that, then I'm wasting my time."

He leaned back in his chair, his brows lifted in silent challenge. "After less than a week, you think you're an expert on what my daughter needs?"

"I don't need to be an expert to know that a child needs love more than she needs lessons," she assured him.

"Riley isn't a typical four-year-old," the prince pointed out.

"Maybe she's not typical, but she is only four."

"She is also both gifted and royal, and she has a lot to learn in order to fulfill the duties and responsibilities that will be required of her in the future."

"In the future," she acknowledged. "But right now, knowing how to make friends is more important than speaking French."

"I disagree."

"I'm not surprised," she said, and couldn't resist adding, "but then, you probably speak impeccable French."

His gaze narrowed. "Is there a point to this conversation, Miss Castillo?"

His tone—undeniably royal-to-servant—gave her pause. She hadn't been sure how far she intended to push, but in light of his apparent refusal to give any consideration to her opinions, she felt that she had no choice but to make him face some hard truths. Even if those truths cost her this job.

"I took Riley into town yesterday afternoon," she said, then hastened to reassure him—though with an undisguised note of sarcasm in her tone—"Don't worry. We weren't gone any longer than the allotted two hours of free time."

"Did Rafe go with you?" he demanded.

She nodded, confirming the presence of the security guard whose job it was to protect the princess whenever she went out in public. Although Riley was young enough to be of little interest to the paparazzi, there was always the possibility of encountering overzealous royal watchers or, worse, a kidnapper.

"Where did you go?"

"To the bookstore."

The furrow between his brows eased. "Riley enjoys visiting the bookstore."

"Right inside the door was a display case for a new book she wanted, but the case was empty. Then Riley spotted another child at the cash register with a copy in her hands. When I told Riley it was probably the last one, she tried to snatch it out of the other girl's hands."

"She is used to getting what she wants when she wants it," he admitted a little sheepishly.

"Because you give her what she wants when she wants it," she pointed out. "And it's turning her into a spoiled brat."

"Miss Castillo!"

She ignored the reprimand, because as angry as he was with her, she was still angrier about Riley's behavior the previous afternoon.

"And when the child counted out her money and realized she was two dollars short, Riley actually smirked at her—until I gave the extra two dollars to the clerk so the other girl could take it home, and then the princess threw a tantrum like I've never seen before."

Michael scrubbed his hands over his face as he considered his response. "Riley's status as a royal combined with her exceptional talents make it difficult for her to relate to children her own age," he finally said.

"Her behavior has nothing to do with her blue blood or superior IQ and everything to do with her sense of entitlement."

"If this arrangement isn't working out for you, maybe we should consider terminating our agreement," he suggested in an icy tone.

She shook her head. "I'm not quitting, and I don't think you really want to fire me."

"I wouldn't bet on that," he warned.

"If you were sincere about wanting someone to help with Riley, then you need me," she told him. "You might not want to admit it, but you do."

His brows rose imperiously. "Do you really think so?"

"I doubt you'd have much difficulty replacing me," she acknowledged. "I'm sure you could find someone who is willing to step in and manage Riley's schedule and defer to her every command, and at the end of the summer, you and your daughter would be exactly where you are now."

"I'm not seeing the downside."

Hannah had never doubted that the princess came by her attitude honestly enough. She forced herself to draw in a deep breath, then let it out slowly. She was a commoner and he was a royal and her bluntness bordered on rudeness, but someone needed to shake up his comfortable little world to make him see the bigger picture—for his sake, and certainly his daughter's.

"The downside is that, if you let this continue, the princess's behavior will be that much more difficult to correct later on," she told him.

"Don't you think you're overreacting to one little incident?"

"If it was only one little incident, I might agree, Your Highness. But you saw how she was at dinner. And I suspect that her behavior has been escalating for a long time."

"Do you really think she knocked your wineglass over on purpose?" His tone was filled with skepticism.

"I believe that she was acting out of frustration, because she's so accustomed to getting her own way that she doesn't know how to cope when she doesn't."

He was silent for a moment, as if he was actually considering her words. And when he spoke, his question gave her hope that he had finally heard what she was saying. "So what am I supposed to do?"

"You need to make some changes." She spoke gently but firmly.

"What kind of changes?" he asked warily.

Before Hannah could respond, his BlackBerry buzzed.

"That's the first one," she said, as he automatically unclipped the device from his belt to check the display.

"It's my secretary. I have to—"

"You have to stop putting your business before your daughter."

"That statement is neither fair nor accurate," he told her, as the phone buzzed again. "There is nothing more important to me than my daughter."

"And yet, when I'm trying to talk to you about her, it's killing you not to take that call, isn't it?"

Even as he shook his head in denial, his gaze dropped to the instrument again.

"Answer the phone, Your Highness." She turned toward the door. "I'll set up an appointment to continue this discussion when it's more convenient for you."

Hannah's words were still echoing in the back of his mind while Michael gathered the files and documents that he needed for his meetings in Port Augustine. He didn't expect her to understand how important his business was, why he felt the need to keep such a close eye on all of the details.

He did it for himself—the business was a way to be self-supporting rather than living off of his title and inheritance, and it was something to keep him busy while his daughter was occupied with her numerous lessons and activities. He also did it for Sam—to ensure that the business they'd built together continued not just to survive but to thrive. And while it did, his sense of satisfaction was bittersweet because his wife wasn't around to celebrate with him.

Ironically, the company's success was one of the reasons that Sam had been anxious to start a family. The business didn't need her anymore, she'd claimed, but a baby would. Michael had assured her that he still needed her, and she'd smiled and promised to always be there for him. But she'd lied. She'd given birth to their daughter, and then she'd abandoned both of them.

He knew that she would never have chosen to leave them, that she would never have wanted Riley to grow up without a mother. But that knowledge had done little to ease his grief, and so he'd buried himself in his work, as if keeping his mind and his hands occupied could make his heart ache for her less.

Except that he rarely did any hands-on work himself anymore, aside from occasional projects for a few of the firm's original clients, his pro bono work for the National Diabetes Association and a few other charitable causes. For the most part, he supervised his employees and worked his connections to bring in new clients. And although he'd claimed that he was too busy to take a two-month vacation, the truth was, he could easily do so and know that his business was in good hands. The knowledge should have filled him with pride and satisfaction, but he only felt…empty.

Truthfully, his greatest pride was his daughter. She was also his biggest concern. After almost four years, he felt as if he was still trying to find his way with her. Their relationship would be different, he was certain, if Sam had been around. Everything would be different if Sam was still around.

Your daughter needs more than a nanny—she needs a mother.

He knew it was probably true. But he had no intention

of marrying again just to give Riley a mother. He had no intention of marrying again, period.

You are still young—you have many years to live, much love to give.

While he appreciated Caridad's faith in him, he wasn't sure that was true. He'd given his whole heart to Sam—and when he'd lost her, he'd been certain that there wasn't anything left to share with anyone else.

Of course, Riley had changed that. He'd never understood the all-encompassing love of a parent for a child until he'd held his baby girl in his arms. And as Riley had grown, so had the depth and breadth of his feelings for her. But knowing what to do with a baby didn't come as instinctively as the loving, and for the first year of her life, he'd relied on Marissa and Brigitte to tend to most of Riley's needs.

And then, just when he'd thought he was getting the hang of fatherhood, he'd realized that Riley needed so much more than he could give her. So he made sure that there were people around to meet her needs—tutors and caregivers—and he turned his focus back to his business.

When he told Hannah about his intended trip back to Port Augustine after lunch on Sunday, she just nodded, as if she wasn't at all surprised that he was leaving. Of course, she probably wasn't. She'd made it more than clear the previous night that she thought he valued RAM above all else. While that wasn't anywhere close to being the truth, he wasn't prepared to walk away from the company, either.

"I'm the president and CEO," the prince reminded her. "Fulfilling those positions requires a lot of work and extended hours at the office."

"I didn't ask, Your Highness," she said evenly.

"No, you'd rather disapprove than understand."

"Maybe because I can't understand why you don't want to spend any time with your daughter," she admitted.

"It's not a question of want."

"Isn't it?" she challenged.

He frowned. "Of course not."

"Because it seems to me that a man who is the president and CEO of his own company—not to mention a member of the royal family—would be able to delegate some of his responsibilities."

"I do delegate," he insisted. "But ultimately, I'm the one who's responsible."

"But it's your wife's name on the door, isn't it?"

"What does that have to do with anything?"

She shrugged. "Maybe nothing. Maybe everything."

"Could you be a little more indecisive?" he asked dryly.

"I just can't help wondering if your obsession with the business isn't really about holding on to the last part of the woman you loved."

"That's ridiculous," he said, startled as much by the bluntness of the statement as the accusation.

"I agree," she said evenly. "Because the business isn't the only part you have left of your wife. It's not even the best part—your daughter is."

"And my daughter is the reason you're here," he reminded her. "So you should focus on taking care of her and not lecturing me."

She snapped her mouth shut. "You're right."

"Especially when you couldn't be more off base."

"I apologized for speaking candidly, but I was only speaking the truth as I see it, Your Highness."

"Then your vision is skewed," he insisted.

"Maybe it is," she allowed.

"The potential client is only going to be in town a few days," he said, wanting to make her understand. "If the meeting goes well, it could turn into a big contract for RAM."

"What would happen if you skipped the meeting?" she challenged. "Or let one of your associates handle it instead?"

"The client specifically asked to deal with me."

"And if you said you were unavailable?"

"We would lose the account," he told her.

"And then what?" she pressed.

He frowned. "What do you mean?"

"Would you miss a mortgage payment? Would the bank foreclose on your home?"

"Of course not, but—"

"But somehow this meeting is more important than the vacation you're supposed to be sharing with your daughter?"

She was wrong, of course. But he could see how it appeared that way, from her perspective.

"The timing of the meeting is unfortunate and unchangeable," he told her, "which is why you're here to take care of Riley in my absence."

"Don't you think it would be better if Riley had more than a week to get to know me before you left?"

"I agree the circumstances aren't ideal," he acknowledged. "But I trust that you can manage for a few days."

That was apparently her job—to manage. While her lack of experience had given her some concern about taking a job as a nanny, Hannah had sincerely looked forward to spending time with the young princess. But the truth was, she spent less time with Riley than did any of the little girl's instructors.

And while she rarely saw the prince outside of mealtimes, their weekend beach outing aside, just knowing he had gone back to Port Augustine somehow made the house seem emptier, lonelier. Or maybe it was the weather that was responsible for her melancholy mood. The day was gray and rainy, Riley was busy with one of her countless lessons, leaving Hannah on her own.

After wandering the halls for a while—she'd spent hours just exploring and admiring the numerous rooms of Cielo del Norte—she decided to spend some time with Caridad.

Although she'd only been at the house for a week, she'd gotten to know the housekeeper quite well and enjoyed talking with her. But Caridad was up to her elbows in dough with flour all over the counters, so she shooed Hannah out of her way.

Hannah felt as if she should be doing something, but when she finally accepted that there was nothing she *had* to do and considered what she *wanted* to do instead, she headed for the library.

It was, admittedly, her absolute favorite space in the whole house. She had always been a voracious reader, and on her first visit to the room she'd been thrilled to find that the floor-to-ceiling bookcases were stocked with an eclectic assortment of materials. There were essays and biographies; textbooks and travel guides; volumes of short stories, poetry and plays; there were leather-bound classics, hardback copies of current bestsellers and dog-eared paperbacks. She spent several minutes just perusing the offerings, until a recent title by one of her favorite thriller writers caught her eye.

She settled into the antique camelback sofa with her feet tucked up under her and cracked open the cover. As always, the author's storytelling technique drew her right in, and her heart was already pounding in anticipation as the killer approached his next victim when a knock sounded on the door.

The knock was immediately followed by the entrance of a visitor and, with a startled gasp, Hannah jumped to her feet and dropped a quick—and probably awkward—curtsy.

"I beg your pardon, Your Highness, you caught me—"

"In the middle of a good book," the princess finished with a smile, as she offered her hand. "I'm Marissa Leandres, Michael's sister."

Of course, Hannah had recognized her immediately. Although the princess kept a rather low profile and wasn't a usual target of the paparazzi, she made frequent public appearances for her favorite charities and causes.

"I recently read that one myself and couldn't put it down," Marissa admitted. "So if I'm interrupting a good part, please tell me so, and I'll take my tea in the kitchen with Caridad."

"Of course not," Hannah lied, because after being banished by the housekeeper, the prospect of actual human company was even more enticing than the book still in her hand.

"Good," the princess said, settling into a balloon-back chair near the sofa. "Because I would love for you to join me, if you have a few minutes to spare."

"I have a lot more minutes to spare than I would have anticipated when I took this job," Hannah admitted.

The other woman's smile was wry. "I guess that means that my brother, once again, chose to ignore my advice."

"What was your advice?"

"To give Riley a break from her lessons, at least for the summer."

"So I'm not the only one who thinks that her schedule is a little over the top for a not-quite-four-year-old?" Even as the words spilled out of her mouth, Hannah winced, recognizing the inappropriateness of criticizing a member of the royal family—and to his sister, no less.

"Please don't censor your thoughts on my account," Marissa said. "And I absolutely agree with you about Riley's schedule. Although, in his defence, Michael believes he is doing what's best for Riley."

"I'm sure he does," she agreed, even if she still disagreed with his decision to leave Cielo del Norte—and his daughter. Thinking of that now, she apologized to the princess. "And I'm sure the prince must not have known of your plans to visit today because he went back to Port Augustine this morning."

Marissa waved a hand. "I didn't come to see him, anyway. I came to meet you. And I would have come sooner, but I've been tied up in meetings at the hospital, trying to get final approval for the expansion of the neonatal department at PACH."

"The Juno Project."

Marissa smiled. "Of course you would know about it—your uncle has been one of my staunchest allies on the board."

"He believes very strongly in what you're doing."

"Don't encourage me," the princess warned. "Because if I start talking about what we want to do, I won't be able to stop, and that really isn't why I'm here."

Another knock on the door preceded Caridad's entrance. She pushed a fancy cart set with a silver tea service, elegant gold-rimmed cups and saucers, and a plate of freshly baked scones with little pots of jam and clotted cream.

"Thank you," Marissa said to the housekeeper. "Those scones look marvelous."

Though she didn't actually smile, Caridad looked pleased by the compliment. "Would you like me to serve, Your Highness?"

"No, I think we can handle it."

"Very well then." She bobbed a curtsy and exited the room, closing the door again behind her.

"She makes that curtsying thing look so easy," Hannah mused. "I always feel like I'm going to tip over."

Marissa smiled as she poured the tea.

"It does take some practice," she agreed. "But I wouldn't worry about it. We don't stand on ceremony too much in my family—well, none of us but my mother. And it's not likely you'll have occasion to cross paths with her while you're here."

The statement piqued Hannah's curiosity, but she didn't feel it was her place to ask and, thankfully, the princess didn't seem to expect a response.

"So how are you getting along with my brother?" Marissa asked, passing a cup of tea to her.

"I don't really see a lot of the prince," Hannah admitted.

"Is he hiding out in his office all the time?"

"He's working in his office all of the time," she clarified.

"He does have the National Diabetes Awareness Campaign coming up in the fall," the princess acknowledged. "He always gives that a lot of time and attention—and pro bono, too."

Her surprise must have shown on her face, because Marissa said, "I know Michael sometimes acts like it's all about making money, but he does a lot of work for charities—Literacy, Alzheimer's, the Cancer Society—and never bills for it."

Hannah knew that his wife had been diabetic, so she should have expected that awareness of the disease was a cause close to his heart, but she hadn't expected to learn that he had such a kind and generous heart.

"I didn't know he did any of that," she admitted.

"Michael doesn't think it's a big deal," the princess confided. "But giving back is important to him. After Sam died...I don't know how much you know about his history, but he went through a really tough time then."

"I can't even begin to imagine," Hannah murmured.

"Neither can I," Marissa confided, "and I was there. I saw how losing her completely tore him apart—nearly decimated him. I tried to be understanding, but I don't think anyone really can understand the magnitude of that kind of grief without having experienced the kind of love that he and Sam shared.

"It took him a long time to see through the fog of that grief—to see Riley. But when he finally did, he put all of his efforts into being a good father to his little girl. He prepared her bottles, he changed her diapers, he played peekaboo."

As hard as Hannah tried, she couldn't imagine the prince

she'd only started to get to know over the past week doing any of those things. While it was obvious that he loved his daughter, it seemed just as obvious to Hannah that he was more comfortable with her at a distance.

"He made mistakes, as all new parents do, but he figured things out as he went along. Then he found out that Riley was gifted, and everything changed."

"Why?"

"Because Michael was just starting to find his way as a father when one of the specialists suggested that Riley would benefit from more structured activities, as if what he was doing wasn't enough. So he asked Brigitte to set up some interviews with music teachers and language instructors and academic tutors, and suddenly Riley's day became one lesson after another. Honestly, her schedule for the past six months has been more intense than mine."

While Hannah doubted that was true, she did think the princess's insight might explain Riley's bed-wetting episode. It wasn't that the little girl was regressing to her toddler habits, just that the signal of her body's need hadn't been able to overcome the absolute exhaustion of her mind.

"I think that's when he started spending longer hours at the office, because he felt like Riley didn't need him."

"I've tried to talk to the prince about his daughter's schedule," Hannah admitted now. "But he seems…resistant."

The princess's brows lifted. "Are you always so diplomatic?"

She flushed, recalling too many times when she'd freely spoken her mind, as if forgetting not just that he was a prince but also her boss. "I'm sure His Highness would say not."

Marissa laughed. "Then I will say that I'm very glad you're here. My brother needs someone in his life who isn't afraid to speak her mind."

"I'm only here for the summer," Hannah reminded her.

"That just might be long enough," Marissa said with a secretive smile.

Hannah didn't dare speculate about what the princess's cryptic comment could mean.

Chapter Seven

It was ten o'clock by the time Michael left the restaurant Tuesday night, but he did so with the knowledge that the prospective clients were going to sign a contract at nine o'clock the following morning. He didn't need to be there for that part of things—he'd done his job, gotten the client's verbal commitment; the rest was just paperwork. The documents had already been prepared by his secretary and the signing would be witnessed by the company vice president, so there was no reason that Michael couldn't head back to Cielo del Norte right now. True, it would be after midnight before he arrived, but he wasn't tired. In fact, the drive would give him a chance to let him unwind.

But for some reason, he found himself following the familiar route toward his home in Verde Colinas.

He unlocked the door but didn't bother turning on any lights as he walked through the quiet of the now-empty house toward his bedroom. It was the bedroom he'd shared with his wife during their twelve-year marriage. Even the bed was the same, and there were still nights that he'd roll over and reach for her—and wake with an ache in the heart that was as empty as his arms.

For months after she'd gone, he could still smell her perfume every time he walked into their bedroom. It was as if her very essence had permeated every item in the room. Each time, the scent had been like a kick to the gut—a constant reminder that while her fragrance might linger, his wife was gone.

He wasn't sure when that sense of her had finally faded, but now he was desperate for it, for some tangible reminder of the woman he'd loved. He drew in a deep breath, but all he could smell was fresh linen and lemon polish.

He stripped away his clothes and draped them over the chair beside the bed, then pulled back the covers and crawled between the cool sheets.

He deliberately shifted closer to Sam's side of the bed, and he was thinking of her as he drifted to sleep.

But he dreamed of Hannah.

The prince had told Hannah that he would probably be away overnight, but he was gone for three days.

At first, despite the nightly phone calls to his daughter, it didn't seem as if Riley was even aware of her father's absence. But then Hannah noticed the subtle changes in the little girl's behavior. She went about her daily routines, but she was unusually quiet and compliant at mealtimes, and she wet her bed both nights. The first morning that Hannah saw the damp sheets in a heap on the floor, she waited for Riley's tirade. But the little girl only asked if she had time to take a bath before breakfast.

By Wednesday, Hannah was desperate for something—anything—to cheer up the little girl. It was the only day of the week that Riley's lessons were finished by lunchtime, so in the morning, she dialed the familiar number of her best friend.

"I'm calling at a bad time," she guessed, when she registered the sound of crying in the background.

"Gabriel's teething," Karen replied wearily. "It's always a bad time."

"Maybe I can help," Hannah suggested.

"Unless you want to take the kid off of my hands for a few hours so I can catch up on my sleep, I doubt it."

"I was actually hoping to take Grace off of your hands for a few hours, but I might be able to handle the baby, too."

She must have sounded as uncertain as she felt, because Karen managed a laugh. "The new nanny gig must be a piece of cake if you want to add more kids to the mix."

"I wouldn't say it's been a piece of cake," Hannah confided. "But I really would appreciate it if Grace could come over and hang out with Riley for a while."

The only response was, aside from the background crying, complete and utter silence.

"Karen?" she prompted.

"I'm sorry. I'm just a little—a lot—surprised. I mean, Grace is a great kid, but she goes to public school."

Hannah laughed. "She is a great kid, and I think it would be great for Riley to play with someone closer to her own age." Although her friend's daughter had just turned six and the princess wasn't quite four, Hannah didn't have any concerns about Riley being able to keep up with Grace. "So—will you come?"

"I'm packing Gabe's diaper bag as we speak," Karen assured her.

"Could you bring some of Grace's toys and games, too?"

"Sure. What does the princess like to play with?"

"That's what I'm trying to figure out," Hannah admitted.

For the first time since Hannah arrived at Cielo del Norte, she felt as if she and Riley had a really good day. Of course, it was really Grace's visit that made the difference for the princess. After Riley got past her initial hesitation about meeting someone new, the two girls had a wonderful time together. They played some board games, made sculptures with modeling clay, built towers of blocks—which Gabe happily knocked down for them—and sang and danced in the music room. The adults observed without interference until Grace suggested playing hide-and-seek, then Karen insisted on limiting their game to only four rooms, to ensure that her daughter didn't wander off too far and get lost.

Hannah was amazed by the transformation of the princess into a normal little girl. And while Karen still looked like she would benefit from a good night of uninterrupted sleep, she thanked Hannah for the invite, insisting that the change of venue and adult conversation were just what she needed to feel human again. For her part, Hannah was happy to have the time with her friend—and thrilled to cuddle with ten-month-old Gabe.

"Did you have fun playing with Grace today?" Hannah asked when she tucked Riley into bed later that night.

The princess nodded. "Her mommy is very pretty."

The wistful tone in her voice made Hannah's heart ache for the little girl who didn't have any memories of her own mother. "Yes, she is," she agreed. "Her mommy is also one of my best friends."

"I don't have a best friend," Riley admitted. "I don't have any friends at all."

"Only because you haven't had a chance to make friends. That will change when you go to school in September."

Riley looked away. "I don't want to go to school."

"Why not?"

The little girl shrugged. "Because I won't know anyone there."

"It can be scary," Hannah admitted. "Going new places,

meeting new people. But it's going to be new for all of the other kids, too."

"Really?"

"Really," Hannah assured her.

"When did you meet your best friend?" Riley wanted to know.

"The first year that I came to Tesoro del Mar to live with my uncle Phillip."

"He's my doctor," Riley said, then her little brow furrowed. "But why did you live with your uncle? Where was your daddy?"

Hannah thought it was telling—and more than a little sad—that Riley didn't ask about her mother. Because, in her experience, it was more usual for little girls to live with their daddies than with both of their parents.

"My daddy lived far away."

"Why didn't you live with him there?"

"I used to," Hannah told her. "Before my mother died."

The princess's eyes went wide. "Your mommy died, too?"

Hannah nodded. "When I was a few years older than you."

"Do you miss her?"

She nodded again. "Even though it was a very long time ago, I still miss her very much."

"I don't remember my mommy," Riley admitted, almost guiltily.

Hannah brushed a lock of hair off of the little girl's forehead. "You couldn't," she said gently, hoping to reassure her. "You were only a baby when she died."

"But I have a present from her."

"What's that?"

The princess pointed to the beautifully dressed silken-haired doll on the top of her tallest dresser. Hannah had noticed it the first time she'd ever ventured into the room, partly because it was so exquisite and partly because it was the only doll the little girl seemed to own.

"I call her Sara."

After the little princess in the story by Frances Hodgson Burnett, Hannah guessed, having seen a copy of the book on Riley's shelf of favorites.

"That's a very pretty name," she said. "For a very pretty doll."

The child smiled shyly. "Daddy said she looks just like my mommy, when she was a little girl. And he put her up there so that she could always watch over me." Then she sighed.

"Why does that make you sad?" Hannah asked her.

"I just think that she must be lonely, because she has no one to play with."

"Are you lonely?"

Riley shook her head, though the denial seemed more automatic than sincere, and her gaze shifted toward the doll again. "There's always a teacher or someone with me."

"You are very busy with your lessons." Hannah took Sara off of the dresser, smoothed a hand over her springy blond curls. The princess watched her every move, seemingly torn between shock and pleasure that her beloved Sara had been moved from her very special place. Hannah straightened the velvet skirt, then adjusted the bow on one of her black boots, and finally offered the doll to Riley.

The child's eyes went wide, and for a moment Hannah thought she might shake her head, refusing the offer. But then her hand reached out and she tentatively touched a finger to the lace that peeked out from beneath the doll's full skirt.

"But maybe you could spend some time with Sara when you're not too busy?"

She nodded, not just an affirmation but a promise, and hugged the doll against her chest.

"And maybe Grace could come back to play another time," Hannah continued.

The last of the shadows lifted from the little girl's eyes. "Do you think she would?"

"I think she'd be happy to." She pulled the covers up to Riley's chin. "Good night."

"'Night," Riley echoed, her eyes already drifting shut.

Hannah switched off the lamp on the bedside table and started to tiptoe out of the room.

"Hannah?"

She paused at the door. "Did you need something?"

There was a slight hesitation, and then Riley finally said, "Daddy sometimes sits with me until I fall asleep."

And as Michael hadn't been home for the past two nights, his daughter was obviously missing him. "I'm not sure when your daddy's going to be home," she admitted, because he never spoke to her when he called except to ask for his daughter and she hadn't felt entitled to inquire about his agenda.

"Could you stay for a while?" Riley asked. "Please?"

"I would be happy to stay," Hannah told her.

The princess's lips curved, just a little. "You don't have to stay long. I'm very tired."

"I'll stay as long as you want," she promised.

Hannah wasn't very tired herself, but the night was so dark and quiet that she found her eyes beginning to drift shut. She thought about going across the hall to her own bed, but she didn't want to tiptoe away until she was certain that Riley wouldn't awaken. So she listened to the soft, even sounds of the little girl's breathing...

Michael had stayed away longer than he'd intended, and he was feeling more than a little guilty about his extended absence. And angry at himself when he finally recognized the real reason behind his absence—he'd been hiding.

His sister would probably say that he'd been hiding from life the past four years, and maybe that was true to a certain extent. But for the past three days, he'd been hiding from something else—or rather some*one* else: Hannah Castillo.

Since she'd moved into Cielo del Norte, she'd turned his entire life upside down. She made him question so many things he'd been certain of, and she made him feel too many things he didn't want to feel.

After two long, sleepless nights alone in his bed in Verde Colinas, he'd accepted that he couldn't keep hiding forever.

Besides, he missed his daughter, and hearing her voice on the phone couldn't compare to feeling the warmth of her arms around his neck.

Whether Hannah believed it or not, Riley was the center of his world. Maybe he spent more hours in his office than he did with his child, but it was the time he spent with her that made every day worthwhile. It was her smile that filled the dark places in his heart with light, and her laughter that lifted his spirits when nothing else could.

Even now, as he tiptoed toward her room, his step was lighter because he was finally home with her.

Of course, being home also meant being in close proximity to Hannah again, but he was confident that he would figure out a way to deal with the unwelcome feelings she stirred inside of him. And anyway, that wasn't something he was going to worry about before morning.

Or so he thought until he stepped into Riley's room and saw her in the chair beside his daughter's bed.

He stopped abruptly, and her eyelids flickered, then slowly lifted.

"What are you doing here?" Though he'd spoken in a whisper, the words came out more harshly than he'd intended.

Hannah blinked, obviously startled by the sharp demand. "Riley asked me to sit with her until she fell asleep."

"I would hope she's been asleep for a while," he told her. "It's after midnight."

"I guess I fell asleep, too."

"You should be in your own bed," he told her.

She nodded and eased out of the chair.

He moved closer, to adjust Riley's covers. As he pulled up the duvet, he noticed that there was something tucked beneath her arm. He felt a funny tug in his belly as he recognized the doll that Sam had bought when she learned that she was having a baby girl.

It was the only thing Riley had that was chosen specifically for her by her mother. Now its dress was rumpled and its hair was in disarray and one of its boots was falling off. He tried to ease the doll from Riley's grasp, but as soon as he tried to wriggle it free, her arm tightened around it. With a sigh of both regret and resignation, he left the doll with his daughter and caught up with Hannah outside of the room.

He grabbed her arm to turn her around to face him. "What were you thinking?" he demanded, the words ground out between clenched teeth.

The nanny blinked, startled by his evident fury, and yanked her arm away from him. "I don't know what you're talking about, Your Highness, but if you're going to yell at me, you might not want to do so right outside of your daughter's bedroom."

He acknowledged her suggestion with a curt nod. "Downstairs."

Her eyes narrowed, and for just a second he thought she would balk at the command. Maybe he wanted her to balk. Her defiance would give him a reason to hold on to his fury, because touching Hannah—even just his hand on her arm— had turned his thoughts in a whole other direction. But then she moved past him and started down the stairs.

She paused at the bottom, as if uncertain of where to go from there.

"My office," he told her.

She went through the door, then turned to face him, her arms folded over her chest. "Now could you please explain what's got you all twisted up in knots?"

"The doll in Riley's bed."

He saw the change in her eyes, the shift from confusion to understanding. Then her chin lifted. "What about it?"

"It's not a toy."

"Dolls are meant to be played with," she told him firmly.

"Not that one."

She shook her head. "You don't even realize what you're doing, do you?"

"What *I'm* doing?" he demanded incredulously, wondering how she could possibly turn this around so that it was his fault.

"Yes, what *you're* doing. You told Riley this wonderful story about how her mother picked out the doll just for her, then you put it on a shelf where she couldn't reach it, so that the only tangible symbol she has of her mother stayed beautiful but untouchable."

He scowled at her. "That's not what I did at all."

"Maybe it's not what you intended, Your Highness," she said in a more gentle tone, "but it's what happened."

He'd only wanted to preserve the gift for Riley so that she would have it forever. But he realized now that Hannah was right, that in doing so he'd ensured that she didn't really have it at all.

He shook his head, the last of his anger draining away, leaving only weariness and frustration. "Am I ever going to get anything right?"

He felt her touch on his arm. "You're doing a lot of things right."

He looked down at her hand, at the long, slender fingers that were so pale against his darker skin, and marveled that she would try to comfort him after the way he'd attacked her. She truly was a remarkable woman. Strong enough to stand up to him, yet soft enough to offer comfort.

"That's not the tune you were singing the last time we discussed my daughter," he reminded her.

Her hand dropped away as one side of her mouth tipped up in a half smile. "I'm not saying that you're doing *everything* right," she teased. "But I do think you have a lot of potential."

"If I'm willing to make some changes," he said, remembering.

She nodded.

"Do you want to talk about those changes now or should we just go up to bed?"

He didn't realize how much the words sounded like an invitation until she stepped back. He didn't realize how tempted he was by the idea himself until he'd spoken the words aloud.

"I meant to say that if you're tired, you can go upstairs to your own bed," he clarified.

"Oh. Of course," she said, though he could tell by the color in her cheeks that she had been thinking of something else entirely. Unfortunately, he couldn't tell if she was intrigued or troubled by the something else.

"I apologize for my poor word choice," he said. "I didn't mean to make you uncomfortable."

"You didn't."

He took a step closer to her, knowing that he was close to stepping over a line that he shouldn't but too tempted by this woman to care. "You didn't think I was propositioning you?"

"Of course not," she denied, though her blush suggested otherwise.

"Why 'of course not'?" he asked curiously.

She dropped her gaze. "Because a man like you—a prince—would never be interested in someone like me."

There was a time when he'd thought he would never be interested in anyone who wasn't Sam, but the past ten days had proven otherwise. Even when he wasn't near Hannah, he was thinking about her, wanting her. He knew that he shouldn't, but that knowledge did nothing to diminish his desire.

"You're an attractive woman, Hannah. It would be a mistake to assume that any man would not be interested."

"You're confusing me," she admitted. "In one breath, you say that you're not propositioning me, and in the next, you say that you find me attractive."

"Actually, my comment was more objective than subjective," he told her. "But while I do think you're a very attractive woman, I didn't hire you in order to pursue a personal relationship with you."

"Okay," she said, still sounding wary.

Not that he could blame her. Because even as he was saying one thing, he was thinking something else entirely.

"In fact, I wouldn't have invited you to spend the summer here if I thought there was any danger of an attraction leading to anything else."

"Okay," she said again.

"I just want you to understand that I didn't intend for this to happen at all," he said, and slid his arms around her.

"What is happening?" she asked, a little breathlessly.

"This," he said.

And then he kissed her.

Chapter Eight

She hadn't anticipated the touch of his lips to hers.

Maybe it was because her head was already spinning, trying to follow the thread of their conversation. Or maybe it was because she would never, in a million years, have anticipated that Prince Michael might kiss her. But whatever the reason, Hannah was caught completely off guard when the prince's mouth pressed against hers.

Maybe she should have protested. Maybe she should have pushed him away. But the fact was, with the prince's deliciously firm and undeniably skillful lips moving over hers, she was incapable of coherent thought or rational response. And instead of protesting, she yielded; instead of pushing him away, she pressed closer.

It was instinct that caused her to lift her arms and link them behind his head, and desire—pure and simple—that had her lips parting beneath the coaxing pressure of his. Then his tongue brushed against hers, and everything inside of her quivered.

Had she ever been kissed like this? Wanted like this? She didn't know; she couldn't think. Nothing in her limited experience had prepared her for the masterful seduction of his lips. And when his hands skimmed over her, boldly sweeping down her back and over her buttocks, pulling her closer, she nearly melted into a puddle at his feet.

She couldn't have said how long the kiss lasted.

Minutes? Hours? Days?

It seemed like forever—and not nearly long enough.

When he finally eased his lips from hers, she nearly whimpered with regret.

Then she opened her eyes, and clearly saw the regret in his.

It was like a knife to the heart that only moments before had been bubbling over with joy. Being kissed by Prince Michael was, for Hannah, a dream come true. But for Prince Michael, kissing her had obviously been a mistake, a momentary error in judgment.

Her hand moved to her mouth, her fingertips trembling as they pressed against her still-tingling lips. Everything inside her was trembling, aching, yearning, even as he was visibly withdrawing.

"I'm sorry." He took another step back. "I shouldn't have done that."

He was right. Of course, he was right. What had happened—even if it was just a kiss—should never have happened. He was Riley's father and her employer. But, even more importantly, he was a prince and she was *not* a princess. She was nobody.

That was a lesson she should have learned years ago, when Harrison Parker had taken back his ring because she didn't have a pedigree deemed suitable by his family. But all it had taken was one touch from the prince, and she'd forgotten everything but how much she wanted him.

How had it happened? One minute they'd been arguing

and in the next he'd claimed that he was attracted to her. Then he'd kissed her as if he really wanted to. And when he'd held her close, his arms wrapped around her, his body pressed against hers, she'd had no doubt about his desire. But then he'd pulled away, making it clear that he didn't want to want her.

Proving, once again, that she simply wasn't good enough.

"Hannah?"

She had to blink away the tears that stung her eyes before she could look at him.

"Are you okay?"

The evident concern in his voice helped her to steel her spine. "I'm fine, Your Highness. It wasn't a big deal."

He frowned, and she wondered—for just a moment—if he might dispute her statement. If maybe he, too, felt that it *had* been a big deal.

But in the end, he only said, "I was way out of line. And I promise that you won't be subjected to any more unwanted advances."

"I'm not worried about that, Your Highness," she said confidently.

And she wasn't.

What worried her was that his kiss hadn't been unwanted at all.

He dreamed of her again.

Of course, this time the dream was much more vivid and real. And when Michael finally awakened in the morning with the sheets twisted around him, he knew that it was his own fault.

He never should have kissed her.

Not just because he'd stepped over the line, but because one simple kiss had left him wanting so much more.

It wasn't a big deal.

Maybe it wasn't to Hannah, but to Michael—who hadn't

kissed anyone but Sam since their first date so many years before—it was.

He didn't feel guilty, not really. His wife had been gone for almost four years, and he knew she would never have expected him to live the rest of his life as a monk. But he did feel awkward. If he was going to make a move on anyone, he should have chosen a woman he would not have to interact with on a daily basis from now until the end of the summer, and especially not an employee.

He winced as he imagined the headlines that a sexual harassment suit would generate, then realized he was probably being paranoid. After all, to Hannah the kiss "wasn't a big deal."

He would just have to make sure that he kept his promise, that absolutely nothing like that ever happened again. And count down the days until the end of the summer.

After Hannah ensured that Riley was wherever she needed to be for her first lesson of the day, she usually returned to the kitchen to enjoy another cup of Caridad's fabulous coffee and conversation with the longtime housekeeper of Cielo del Norte.

But when she approached the kitchen Thursday morning, she could hear that the other woman already had company— and from the tone of her voice, she wasn't too pleased with her visitor.

"This isn't open for discussion," Caridad said firmly.

"But it isn't fair—"

"Whoever said life was supposed to be fair?"

"You never made Jocelyn go to summer school," the male voice argued.

"Because Jocelyn didn't struggle with English Lit."

"She would have if she'd had Mr. Gaffe as her teacher."

"You complained about the teacher you had last year, now you complain about this teacher—maybe the problem isn't the teachers but the student. And maybe you should have paid a little more attention to the lessons and a little less to Serik Jouharian last term."

Based on the dialogue and the tones of their voices, Hannah guessed that Caridad was talking to her son. She knew that the housekeeper and her husband had five children—four girls and, finally, a boy. Kevin was the only one still living at home and, according to Caridad, he was responsible for every single one of her gray hairs.

"The only reason I even passed that course was because Serik was my study partner," the boy told her now.

"Then you'd better pick your study partner as carefully this time."

Hannah peeked around the corner in time to see Caridad kiss her son's cheek, then hand him his backpack. "Now go, so you're not late."

"Serik," Hannah said, as Kevin exited the room. "That's a beautiful name."

"Serik was a beautiful girl. An exchange student from Armenia, and I thanked God when school was done and she went back to her own country." Caridad sighed. "He was so smitten. And so heartbroken when she said goodbye."

"I guess he's at that age."

"The age when hormones lead to stupid?"

Hannah laughed. "He seems like a good kid."

"He is," Caridad admitted. "And smart. He's always got good marks in school, except for English. I thought if he took the next course at summer school, when he only has to focus on one subject, he might do better, but he's done nothing but complain since the course started."

"He's a teenager and it's the summer," Hannah said. "Of course he's going to complain about being stuck in school."

"He says he'd rather be working, and if I let him get a job, he could help pay for his education. But I worry that a job would take time away from his studies, jeopardizing his chances of getting a scholarship."

"I could tutor him," she offered.

"No offense, but I can't imagine that a nanny knows too much about senior English."

"You might have noticed that I don't know too much about being a nanny," she said. "That's because I'm a teacher in my real life."

"Your real life?"

"Well, nothing about this seems real to me." She looked around at the kitchen that was bigger than her whole apartment in the city. "It's as if I've fallen through the rabbit hole."

"Should we call you Alice?"

She smiled. "No. Riley's already confused enough without giving a new name to the new hire."

"So how did an English teacher end up taking a summer job as a royal nanny?"

"Desperation."

"Prince Michael's desperation or your own?"

"Both, I guess. He needed someone who could step in right away while he continues to look for a full-time caregiver, and I needed a job and a place to stay for the summer because I sublet my apartment with the intention of spending the break teaching in China." She shook her head in response to the lift of Caridad's brows. "Don't ask."

"We can't afford a tutor," Caridad admitted. "Prince Michael offered to hire one when he heard that Kevin was struggling, but I couldn't let him do that when he already does so much for us."

"I'm already getting a paycheck, and I really do love to teach."

"I wouldn't feel right—taking something for nothing."

"We could exchange services," Hannah suggested. "Maybe you could teach me to cook?"

"Not likely," the housekeeper said.

Hannah couldn't help but feel disappointed by her response. Cooking lessons would at least give her something to do while Riley was busy with her tutors, but unlike her, Caridad probably had more than enough to keep her busy.

"You don't think you'd have the time?" she guessed.

"I don't think you could learn," the older woman admitted bluntly. "You don't know the difference between browning and burning."

Hannah couldn't deny it was true—not when the housekeeper had asked her to keep an eye on the garlic bread while she put a load of laundry in the wash. All Hannah had to do was take the tray out of the oven when the cheese started to brown. But then Riley had come into the kitchen to get a drink and she'd spilled her juice, and while Hannah was busy mopping up the floor, the cheese was turning from brown to black.

"Don't you think that's a little unfair?" she asked, because she had explained the extenuating circumstances behind the mishap.

"Maybe," Caridad agreed. "But not untrue."

Hannah had to laugh. "No, not untrue," she admitted as she poured herself a fresh cup of coffee. "But is that any reason to let your son struggle?"

The housekeeper hesitated. "It's only the first week. I want to see him at least make an effort before you bail him out."

Hannah and Riley spent the following Saturday afternoon on the beach again, but the prince made no effort to join them. And although the three of them had dinner together, as usual, the prince immediately retreated to his office after the meal was done.

It was Monday before Hannah worked up the nerve to knock on his office door.

She could hear him talking, and she pictured him pacing

in front of his desk with his BlackBerry in hand. It seemed as if it was *always* in hand. His voice rose, as if to emphasize a point, and she took a step back. Maybe she should come back later. Maybe she should forget trying to talk to him at all—or at least choose a different venue for their conversation. The last time she'd been in his office with him was when the prince had kissed her.

Okay, it probably wasn't a good idea to think about that kiss right now. Except that since Wednesday night, she'd barely been able to think about anything else.

She realized that she couldn't hear him talking anymore, and knocked again, louder this time.

"Come in."

She pushed open the door and stepped inside.

He looked up, as if surprised to see her. He probably was. They'd both been tiptoeing around each other for the past several days.

"We never did finish the conversation we started to have about Riley," she reminded him.

"I assumed if there was cause for concern I would hear about it."

"Well, actually, I do have some concerns. Primarily about her eating habits."

"I have lunch and dinner with my daughter almost every day," he said. "Other than her preference for chicken nuggets, I haven't observed any problem."

"I wouldn't say it's a problem," she hedged. "At least not yet."

His brows lifted. "You came in here to talk about something that isn't yet a problem?"

She felt her cheeks flush. "Riley seems to eat a lot for such a young child, and she has dessert after lunch and dinner—every day."

"So?"

"If she continues to eat the way she does now, it won't be

long before she's battling weight and possibly even health issues."

"She's not even four."

She didn't disagree with what he was saying, and it wasn't Riley's weight that worried her. It was the pattern that she could see. She knew there was an easy fix for the problem, but only if the prince agreed to cooperate.

"She eats too much and exercises too little," she said bluntly.

"Should I hire a personal trainer for her?"

"No, Your Highness, you should stop hiring people and start spending time with her."

His brows lifted in silent challenge.

"I know I haven't been here very long," Hannah said. "But I've noticed that you don't interact with Riley very much outside of mealtimes."

"Then maybe you've also noticed that I have a lot of work to do and Riley is busy with her own lessons."

"Yes, I have noticed that, too," she admitted. "And I think that's why Riley is overeating."

"I'm not following."

She hesitated, torn between reluctance to disturb the status quo that obviously mattered to him and determination to open his eyes to some harsh truths. In the end, she decided his relationship with Riley was more important than anything else—her job included.

"The only time Riley sees you throughout the day is at lunch and dinner, so she does everything that she can to extend those mealtimes," she explained. "As soon as her plate is cleared away, you disappear, and I think that she's asking for second helpings so that you stay at the table with her. It's not because she's hungry, but because she's starving for your attention, Your Highness."

His gaze narrowed dangerously. "How dare you—"

"I dare," she interrupted, "because you entrusted Riley

into my care and I'm looking out for her best interests, Your Highness."

"Well, I don't believe it's in my daughter's best interests to put her on a diet."

She was horrified by the very thought. "That isn't what I'm suggesting at all."

"Then what are you suggesting?"

"That you rearrange your schedule to spend a few hours every day with Riley, somewhere other than the dining room."

"You can't be serious," he said, his tone dismissive. "And even if you are, she doesn't have that much time to spare any more than I do."

"Which is the other thing I wanted to talk to you about," she forged ahead before she lost her nerve.

"Go on," he urged, albeit with a decided lack of enthusiasm.

"A four-year-old needs time to play, Your Highness."

"Riley has plenty of time to play."

She shook her head. "She plays the piano, but she doesn't do anything else that a typical four-year-old does—anything just for fun. She paints with watercolors but doesn't know what to do with sidewalk chalk. She doesn't know how to jump rope or hit a shuttlecock, and she's never even kicked a soccer ball around."

"Because she isn't interested in any of those things."

"How do you know?" Hannah asked softly.

He frowned. "Because she's never asked to participate in those kinds of activities."

"Did she ask for piano lessons?"

"No," he admitted. "Not in so many words. But when she sat down and began to play, it was patently obvious that she had a talent that needed to be nurtured."

"And how do you know she's not a potential all-star soccer player if you don't give her the opportunity to try?"

"If she wants to kick a ball around, I have no objections," he said dismissively. "Now, if that's all—"

"No, it's not all," she interrupted. "There's the issue of her French lessons—"

"If there's any issue with her French lessons, you should discuss it with Monsieur Larouche."

"And I suppose I should direct all inquires about her Italian lessons to Signora Ricci and about her German lessons to Herr Weichelt?"

"You're starting to catch on."

She bristled at the sarcasm in his tone. "I thought we were past this already. Why are you acting like you don't care when I know that you do?"

"You're right," he agreed. "I do care—enough that I've hired qualified people to ensure she has everything she needs."

"When we talked the other night—" she felt her cheeks flush and prayed that he wouldn't notice "—you said that you were willing to make some changes. All I'm asking for is a couple of hours of your time every day."

He drummed his fingers on his desk, as if considering. Or maybe he was just impatient for her to finish.

"You said you wanted to get it right," she reminded him. "The only way to do that is to spend time with your daughter. To get to know her and let her get to know you, and that's not going to happen if you insist on keeping nannies and business obligations between you."

"It's the business that allows me to pay your salary," he pointed out to her.

"I'll gladly take a cut in my pay if you promise to give Riley at least two hours."

Once again, Hannah had surprised him. "I don't usually let my employees set the conditions of their employment."

"But this isn't a usual situation, is it?" she countered. "And I know you want what's best for Riley."

How could he possibly argue with that? And truthfully, he didn't want to. Although it was against his better judgment to give in to a woman whom he was beginning to suspect would try to take a mile for every inch he gave her, he wasn't opposed to her suggestion. After all, his time at Cielo del Norte was supposed to be something of a vacation from the daily demands of his company.

It's hardly a vacation if you're working all the time.

He heard Sam's words, her gently chiding tone, clearly in his mind.

It had been a familiar argument, and one that he'd always let her win—because it hadn't been a sacrifice to spend time with the wife that he'd loved more than anything in the world. But Sam was gone now, and without her a vacation held no real appeal. And yet he'd continued to spend his summers at the beach house because he knew that she would be disappointed if he abandoned the tradition. Just as he knew she'd be disappointed if he didn't accede to Hannah's request.

During Sam's pregnancy, they'd had long conversations about their respective childhoods and what they wanted for their own child. Sam had been adamant that their daughter would grow up in a home where she felt secure and loved. She didn't want Riley to be raised by a series of nannies, as he had been raised. Michael had agreed. He had few fond memories of his own childhood—and none after the death of his father—and he couldn't deny that he wanted something more, something better, for Riley. Except that without Sam to guide him, he didn't know what that something more and better could be.

Now Hannah was here, demanding that he spend time with his daughter, demanding that he be the father that Sam would want him to be. And he couldn't—didn't want to—turn away from that challenge. But he had to ask, "How do you know that spending more time with me is what Riley wants or needs?"

"Because you're her father and the only parent she has left," she said simply.

It was a fact of which he was well aware and the origin of all his doubts. He knew he was all Riley had—and he worried that he wasn't nearly enough. And he resented the nanny's determination to make him confront those fears. "Why is this so important to you?" he countered. "I mean, at the end of the summer, you'll walk away from both of us. Why do you care about my relationship with my daughter?"

He saw a flicker of something—sadness or maybe regret—in the depths of her stormy eyes before she glanced away. "Because I want something better for her than to get an email from you twenty years in the future telling her that she has a new stepmother," she finally responded.

Dios. He scrubbed his hands over his face. He'd forgotten that Hannah wasn't just Phillip Marotta's niece but that she'd lived with the doctor since coming to Tesoro del Mar as a child. Obviously there were some unresolved father-daughter issues in her background, and while those issues weren't any of his business, he knew that his relationship with his own daughter *was* his concern. And if Hannah was right about Riley's behavior, he had reason to be concerned.

"Okay," he agreed.

"Okay?" She seemed surprised by his acquiescence.

He nodded and was rewarded with a quick grin that lit up her whole face.

"I'd like to start this afternoon," she told him.

He glanced at his schedule, because it was a habit to do so before making any kind of commitment with respect to his time, and because he needed a reason to tear his gaze away from her mesmerizing smile. She truly was a beautiful woman, and he worried that spending more time with her along with his daughter would be as much torment as pleasure.

"If that works for you," Hannah said, as if she was expecting him to say that it didn't.

"That works just fine," he assured her.

She started for the door, paused with her hand on the knob. "Just one more thing."

"What's that?"

"When you're with Riley, the BlackBerry stays out of sight."

Chapter Nine

When Caridad told her that Monsieur Larouche had called to cancel his morning lesson with Riley, Hannah took it as a positive sign. Not for Monsieur Larouche, of course, and she sincerely hoped that the family emergency wasn't anything too serious, but she was grateful for the opportunity to get Riley outside and gauge her interest in something a little more physical than her usual activities.

Whether by accident or design, Karen had left a few of Grace's toys behind after their visit the previous week, including the little girl's soccer ball. And when Riley's piano lesson was finished, Hannah lured her outside with the promise of a surprise.

The princess looked from her nanny to the pink ball and back again. "What's the surprise?"

"I'm going to teach you how to play soccer."

"Soccer?" Riley wrinkled her nose.

"It's fun," she promised. "And very simple. Basically you

run around the field kicking a ball and trying to put it in the goal."

"I know what soccer is," the child informed her. "I've seen it on TV."

"It's not just on television—it's the most popular sport in the world."

"I don't play sports."

Hannah dropped the ball and when it bounced, she kicked it up to her thigh, then juggled it over to the other thigh, then back down to one foot and over to the other, before catching it again. "Why not?"

"Because I'm a princess," she said.

But Hannah noticed that she was looking at the ball with more curiosity than aversion now. "Oh—I didn't realize that you weren't allowed—"

"I'm allowed," Riley interrupted. "But I have more important things to do."

"Okay," Hannah agreed easily, slipping her foot under the ball and tossing it into the air.

"What does that mean?" the child demanded.

"I'm simply agreeing with you," she said, continuing to juggle the ball between her feet. "Playing soccer isn't important—it's just fun."

"And it's time for my French lesson anyway," the princess informed her, the slightest hint of wistfulness in her voice.

"You're not having a French lesson today."

"But it's Monday. I always have French after piano on Monday."

"Monsieur Larouche can't make it today."

Riley worried her bottom lip, uncomfortable with last-minute changes to her schedule.

"But if you'd rather study than learn to play soccer, you can go back inside and pull out your French books," Hannah assured her.

"Can you teach me how to do that?" Riley asked, mesmerized by the quick movements of the ball.

"I can try." She looked at the girl's pretty white dress and patent shoes. "But first we'd better change your clothes."

As Hannah scanned the contents of the child's closet, then rifled through the drawers of her dressers, she realized that dressing Riley appropriately for outdoor play was easier said than done.

"Who does your shopping?" she muttered.

"My aunt Marissa."

"It's as if she was expecting you to have tea with the queen every day." She looked at the shoes neatly shelved in three rows on the bottom of the closet. There were at least fifteen pairs in every shade from white to black but not a single pair without tassels or bows or flowers.

"Tesoro del Mar doesn't have a queen," the princess informed her primly. "It's a principality."

Hannah continued to survey the child's wardrobe. "Do you even own a T-shirt or shorts? Or sneakers?"

Riley shrugged.

"Well, I think before we get started, we need to find a mall."

"There's a bookstore at the mall," the little girl said, brightening.

"Shorts and shoes first," Hannah insisted. "Then we'll see."

"Maybe we could find a book about soccer," Riley suggested.

Hannah had to laugh. "You're pretty clever, aren't you?"

"That's what my teachers say."

"We'll go shopping after lunch," Hannah promised.

Though Michael didn't believe that Riley was starved for his attention as Hannah had claimed, he did make a point of paying close attention to her behavior at lunch. And he was dismayed to realize that the nanny was right. As soon as he had finished eating and she thought he might leave the table, she asked if she could have some more pasta salad. And after she finished her second helping of pasta salad, she asked for dessert.

"What did you want to do after lunch?" he asked her, while she was finishing up her pudding.

"I have quiet time until four o'clock and then…" The words faded away, and Riley frowned when she saw him shaking his head.

"I didn't ask what was on your schedule but what you wanted to do."

The furrow in her brow deepened, confirming that Hannah hadn't been so far off base after all. His daughter truly didn't know what to do if it wasn't penciled into her schedule.

"Because I was thinking maybe we could spend some time together."

Riley's eyes grew wide. "Really?"

He forced a smile, while guilt sliced like a knife through his heart. Had he really been so preoccupied and neglectful that his daughter was surprised by such a casual invitation?

"Really," he promised her.

"Well, Hannah said we could go shopping after lunch."

He looked at the nanny, his narrowed gaze clearly telegraphing his thoughts: *I agreed to your plan but I most definitely did not agree to shopping.*

"Your daughter has an impressive wardrobe that is completely devoid of shorts and T-shirts and running shoes," she explained.

"So make a list of what she needs and I'll send—"

One look at his daughter's dejected expression had him changing his mind.

With an inward sigh, he said, "Make a list so that we don't forget anything."

* * *

After two hours at the mall, with Rafe and two other guards forming a protective circle around the trio of shoppers, Michael noted that Hannah was almost as weary of shopping as he. But they had one more stop before they could head back to Cielo del Norte—the bookstore. He bought her a latte at the little café inside the store and they sat, surrounded by shopping bags, and discreetly flanked by guards, in the children's section while Riley—shadowed by Rafe—browsed through the shelves.

"We got a lot more than what was on the list."

"You said she didn't have anything," he reminded her.

"But she didn't need three pairs of running shoes."

Except that Riley had insisted that she did, showing how the different colors coordinated with the various outfits she'd chosen.

"She gets her fashion sense from my sister," he told her. "One day when we were visiting, Marissa spilled a drop of coffee on her shirt, so she went to find a clean one. But she didn't just change the shirt, she changed her shoes and her jewelry, too."

Hannah laughed. "I probably would have put on a sweater to cover up the stain."

"Sam was more like that," he admitted. "She didn't worry too much about anything. Except official royal appearances—then she would stress about every little detail like you wouldn't believe."

He frowned as he lifted his cup to his lips. He didn't often talk about Sam, not to other people. It was as if his memories were too precious too share—as if by revealing even one, he'd be giving up a little piece of her. And he wondered what it meant—if anything—that he found it so easy to talk to Hannah about Sam now. Was it just that he knew he could trust her to listen and not pass judgment, or was it a sign that he was finally starting to let go of the past and look to the future?

"Well, I should have realized that Riley's closet wouldn't be filled with all those frills and ruffles if it wasn't what she liked," Hannah commented now.

"You weren't into frills and ruffles as a child?"

"Never. And when I was Riley's age…" She paused, as if trying to remember. "My parents were missionaries, so we traveled a lot, and to a lot of places I probably don't even remember. But I think we were in Tanzania then, or maybe it was Ghana. In either case, I was more likely running naked with the native children than wearing anything with bows."

He tried to imagine her as a child, running as wild as she'd described. But his mind had stuck on the word *naked* and insisted on trying to picture her naked now. After having seen the delectable curves outlined by her bathing suit, it didn't take much prompting for his imagination to peel down the skinny straps of sleek fabric to reveal the fullness of creamy breasts tipped with rosy nipples that eagerly beaded in response to the brush of his fingertips. And when he dipped his head—

"Look, Daddy, I found a book about soccer."

Nothing like the presence of a man's almost-four-year-old daughter to effectively obliterate a sexual fantasy, Michael thought.

Then Riley climbed into his lap to show him the pictures, and he found that he didn't regret her interruption at all.

"That's an interesting book," he agreed.

"Can we buy it?"

He resisted the instinct to tell her yes, because he knew from experience that it wouldn't be the only book she wanted and he was trying to follow Hannah's advice to not give her everything she wanted.

"Let me think about it," he told her.

She considered that for a moment, and he braced himself

for the quivering lip and the shimmer of tears—or the hands on the hips and the angry scowl—but she just nodded. "Can you hold on to it while I keep looking?"

"I'll keep it right beside me," he promised.

Hannah watched the little girl skip back to the stacks. "She's so thrilled that you're here," she told him.

"I guess I didn't realize that it took so little to make her happy," he admitted.

"We've already been here longer than the two hours I asked for."

"I'm not counting the minutes," he assured her. "Besides, I'm enjoying this, too."

"Really?"

He chuckled at the obvious skepticism in her tone. "Let's just say, the shopping part wasn't as bad as I'd feared. And this part—" he lifted his cup "—is a definite pleasure."

"You better be careful," she warned. "Or you just might live up to that potential I was talking about."

He took another sip of his coffee before asking the question that had been hovering at the back of his mind. "Was your father so neglectful?"

"How did my father come into this?" she countered.

But the casual tone of her reply was too deliberate, and he knew that beneath the lightly spoken words was buried a world of hurt.

"I think he's always been there, I just didn't realize it before."

"It's true that my father and I aren't close," she admitted.

"Because he never had enough time for you," he guessed.

"He never had *any* time for me." She cupped her hands around her mug and stared into it, as if fascinated by the ring of foam inside. "I'm not even sure that he ever wanted to be a father," she finally continued, "but my mom wanted a baby and there was no doubt that he loved my mom, and I thought it was enough to know that my mom loved me."

"Until she died," he guessed.

"But then I had my uncle Phillip. He pretty much raised me after she was gone."

"I have to say, he did a pretty good job."

She smiled at that. "He was a wonderful example of what a father should be—of the kind of father I know *you* can be."

He hoped—for Riley's sake even more than his own—that he wouldn't disappoint her.

Despite the new outfit and the proper shoes, it didn't take Hannah long to realize that Riley was never going to be an all-star soccer player. It wasn't just that the child seemed to lack any kind of foot-eye coordination, but that she quickly grew discouraged by her own ineptitude. The more patient and understanding Hannah tried to be, the more discouraged Riley seemed to get.

So after a few days on the lawn with little progress and a lot of frustration, she took Riley into town again so that the little girl could decide what she wanted to try next. The sporting goods store had an extensive selection of everything, and Hannah and Riley—and Rafe—wandered up and down several aisles before they found the racquet sports section.

"I want to play tennis," Riley announced.

Since there was a court on the property, Hannah hoped it might be a better choice for the princess, who immediately gravitated toward a racquet with a pink handle and flowers painted on the frame.

Now she had a half-full bucket of tennis balls beside her with the other half scattered around the court. She'd been tossing them to Riley so that she could hit them with her racquet, with very little success. The child had connected once, and she'd been so startled when the ball made contact with the webbing that the racquet had slipped right out of her hand. But she'd scooped it up again and refocused, her big brown eyes narrowed with determination. Unfortunately, it seemed that the harder she tried, the wider she missed.

The prince would happily have paid for a professional instructor, but Hannah wanted to keep the lessons fun for Riley by teaching the little girl herself. But after only half an hour, neither of them was having very much fun. The more balls that Riley missed the more frustrated she got, and the more frustrated she got the less she was able to focus on the balls coming toward her.

"She needs to shorten her grip."

Hannah looked up to see a handsome teenager standing at the fence, watching them with an easy smile on his face.

"She needs a better teacher," she admitted.

"Kevin!" Riley beamed at him. "I'm going to learn to play tennis just like you."

The boy's brows lifted. "Just like me, huh?"

She nodded. "Hannah's teaching me."

"Trying to, anyway." She offered her hand. "Hannah Castillo."

"Kevin Fuentes," he said.

"Caridad and Estavan's son," she suddenly realized. "I've seen you helping out your dad around the yard." And she'd heard him in the kitchen, arguing with his mother, though she didn't share that information. "So you play tennis?" she queried.

"Every chance I get."

"Caridad says that Kevin's going to get a scholarship," Riley informed her. "But only if he pays attention in class and forgets the pretty girls."

Hannah couldn't help but laugh as the boy's cheeks flushed.

"You have an awfully big mouth for such a little kid," Kevin said, but the reprimand was tempered with a wry smile as he ruffled Riley's hair.

The little kid in question beamed up at him in obvious adoration.

"Do you want me to show her how to adjust her grip?" Kevin asked.

"I'd be extremely grateful," Hannah assured him.

The teenager dropped to his knees on the court beside her.

"I'm going to play just like you," the little girl said again.

"It took me a lot of years of practice." Even as he spoke, he adjusted the position of Riley's grip on the handle of her racquet.

"I'm a fast learner," she assured him.

"You need to learn to be patient," he told her, guiding her arm in a slow-motion demonstration of a ground stroke. "And to let the ball come to you."

He nodded toward Hannah, signaling her to toss a ball.

As soon as the ball left her hand, Riley was trying to reach for it, but Kevin held her back, waiting then guiding her arm to meet the ball.

The fuzzy yellow ball hit the center of the webbing with a soft *thwop,* and Hannah had to duck to avoid being hit by its return. Riley turned to Kevin, her eyes almost as wide as her smile. "I did it."

"You did," he agreed. "Now let's see if you can do it again."

After a few more easy tosses and careful returns, Riley said, "I want to hit it harder."

"You should work on accuracy before power," Kevin told her.

Riley pouted but continued to practice the slow, steady stroke he'd shown her.

"You're a lot better at this than I am," Hannah said, tossing another ball.

He gave a half shrug. "This comes easily to me. Trying

to figure out what Hamlet's actually saying in his infamous 'to be or not to be' speech doesn't."

"It's really not that complicated, although the language of the time can make it seem so," she said, not wanting to delve into the details of the tragic hero's contemplations about suicide in front of a four-year-old.

"And my teacher talks like he was born in Shakespeare's time."

"It can't be that bad," Hannah protested, tossing the last ball.

"It's worse," he insisted. "I have an essay due tomorrow in which I have to decide—in a thousand words—whether or not Hamlet really did love Ophelia."

She couldn't help but smile, thinking that—like most teenage boys—he'd much rather talk about the character's thirst for revenge than any of his more tender emotions. But all she said was, "*Hamlet* has always been one of my favorite plays."

He turned to look at her now, his expression a combination of surprise and disbelief. "Really?"

She shrugged, almost apologetically. "I like Shakespeare."

"Can we do some more?" Riley interrupted to demand.

"First lessons should be short," Kevin told her. "And the lesson's not over until you put all of the balls back in the bucket."

If Hannah had been the one to ask Riley to retrieve the scattered balls, she had no doubt the princess would have refused. But when Kevin spoke, the little girl happily trotted off to do his bidding.

"You're really good with her," Hannah noted.

"She's a good kid."

"Would you be willing to work with her on some other tennis basics some time?"

"Sure," he agreed readily. "It's not like I'm doing much of anything else these days, aside from summer school."

"Speaking of which," she said. "Why don't you bring your essay up to the main house tonight?"

His eyes lit up. "Are you going to fix it for me?"

She laughed. "You're assuming it needs fixing."

"It does," he assured her.

"Then we'll fix it together."

Friday morning after breakfast, Hannah and Riley were working on a jigsaw puzzle in the library when Caridad came in to water the plants. She looked from the little girl to the clock then back again and frowned.

"Signora Ricci is late today," she noted.

"Signora Ricci isn't coming today," Hannah told her.

The housekeeper held a towel beneath the spout of the watering can to ensure it didn't drip as she moved from one planter to the next. "Is she ill?"

"No, she's on vacation."

"She would not have gone on vacation without first arranging a replacement and certainly not without discussing the matter with the prince." The implication being that the prince would then have told her, which of course he would have—if he'd known.

"The vacation was my idea," Hannah admitted. "And more for the benefit of the princess than her teacher."

"You have talked to Prince Michael about this?" the housekeeper prompted.

"I tried, but the prince assured me that any concerns about his daughter's language instruction were best discussed with her instructor."

"I had my doubts," the housekeeper admitted, "when the prince first hired you. But now I think that maybe he knew what he was doing."

"Even if he would disagree?"

Caridad smiled. "Especially if he would disagree."

She finished watering the rest of the plants before she

spoke again. "Kevin said you're helping him with his Shakespeare essay."

"In exchange for him helping Riley learn to play tennis," Hannah explained, remembering their earlier conversation in which the housekeeper had expressed reluctance to accept help for her son without some kind of payment in return.

The housekeeper waved the towel in her hand, obviously satisfied by the exchange of services. "I have no objections," she said. "If you are half as good a teacher as you are a nanny, he will write a good paper."

Only a few weeks earlier, Hannah hadn't been certain that she even wanted to be a nanny, but in all of her years of teaching, she'd never received a compliment that meant as much to her as Caridad's.

Chapter Ten

There were still occasions when Michael had to return to Port Augustine for meetings with clients, but he rarely stayed away overnight. Unfortunately, today's meeting had stretched out longer than he'd anticipated because the client refused to be satisfied with any of the advertisement proposals presented to her.

Michael believed strongly in customer satisfaction, so he suggested that they continue their discussions over dinner. He'd learned that a less formal atmosphere often facilitated a more open exchange of information, but as they shared tapas and wine, he quickly realized that the client had chosen RAM less for the needs of her company and more for her personal interest in him.

He knew that he should be flattered, but truthfully he was growing tired of deflecting unwanted advances. Especially when he'd given her no indication that he was interested in anything more than a business relationship. But as he drove back to Cielo del Norte, he found himself wondering what was wrong with him that he wasn't attracted to an obviously attractive woman. A few weeks ago, he could have argued that he just wasn't ready, that he couldn't imagine himself with anyone who wasn't Sam.

Since Hannah had moved into Cielo del Norte, he'd realized that was no longer true. So why couldn't he be attracted to someone other than Hannah? What was it about his daughter's temporary nanny that had got under his skin?

As a result of his unproductive dinner meeting, he returned to the beach house much later than he'd intended. Not only had he missed hanging out with his daughter during the day, but he was too late to tuck her into bed, as had become their nightly ritual. When he went upstairs to check on her, he found that she was sleeping peacefully with Sara tucked under her arm. He brushed a light kiss on her forehead and her lips curved, just a little, in response to the touch.

He went back downstairs, thinking that he would pour a glass of his favorite cabernet and sit out under the stars for a while. When he approached the kitchen, he heard the sounds of conversation. The soft, smoky tone was definitely Hannah's; the deeper, masculine voice wasn't as familiar.

It occurred to him then that she'd given up her whole life to spend the summer at Cielo del Norte, and in the first month that she'd been in residence, she hadn't asked for any time off to go out. He knew that her friend Karen had visited a few times with her children, because Riley would tell him all about her "best friend" Grace and describe in great detail everything that they'd done together. But it was Hannah's visitor who was on his mind now.

Was the man in the kitchen an old friend? Maybe even a boyfriend? He frowned at the thought. His frown deepened when it occurred to him that there had been no other vehicles in the drive when he'd pulled in.

He paused in the doorway, shamelessly eavesdropping.

"Pay close attention to the characters of both Marlow and

Kurtz," Hannah was saying now. "And which one seems, to you, to be the real hero of the book."

It didn't sound like date conversation to him. On the other hand, he hadn't been on a date in more than sixteen years, so what did he know?

"But can't there be—"

Her guest looked up as he walked into the room, and the boy—Caridad's son, Michael realized with a sense of relief—pushed his chair away from the table to execute an awkward bow. "Your Highness."

He waved Kevin back to his seat. "I didn't realize you were...entertaining," he said to Hannah.

"I didn't realize you were home," she countered.

He noted the books that were open on the table, surrounded by scraps of paper with notes scribbled on them.

"We're working on the outline for Kevin's next assignment," she explained.

Michael surveyed the assortment of bottles in the wine rack, automatically reached for a familiar label. Maybe she did believe she was helping the boy study, but it was obvious to him that Hannah's student was more interested in her than in anything she was trying to explain to him.

"I thought school was out for the summer," he commented.

"For most people," Kevin said. "But my mom decided to torture me with summer school—as if spending ten months in the classroom wasn't already torture enough."

Hannah smiled as she gathered together the loose papers and inserted them into a folder. "Look on the bright side—if you get your credit this summer, you won't have to take another English course until college."

"That's still too soon for me," the boy grumbled.

"I want to see your draft outline by Wednesday," Hannah told him.

"I'll have it ready," he promised. Then he bowed again. "Good evening, Your Highness."

"Good evening, Kevin." He uncorked the bottle of wine. "So how long have you been tutoring my housekeeper's son?"

"It isn't a formal arrangement," she said. "And it doesn't interfere in any way with my taking care of Riley."

"I'm not worried—just curious as to how this arrangement came about, and whether Caridad knows that her son has a major crush on you."

"It came about because Kevin's been helping Riley with her ground stroke, and Caridad knows that his infatuation will be over before he signs his name to his final exam."

"How can she be so sure?"

"Teenage boys are notoriously fickle."

"That's probably true enough," he acknowledged, even as he mentally berated himself for being no less fascinated by the sexy curves outlined by her T-shirt than the teenage boy who had just left.

And no doubt he would have shown more interest in English Lit when he was in school if he'd had a teacher like Hannah Castillo. But all of the teachers at the exclusive prep school he'd attended had been male and seemingly as old as the institution itself.

She finished packing away her notes, then pushed away from the table. "I'm going to go check on Riley."

"I just did." He took two glasses out of the cupboard. "She's sleeping."

"Oh. Okay."

"Come on," he said, heading toward the sliding French doors that led out to the terrace. He bypassed the chairs to sit at the top of the steps, where he could see the moon reflecting on the water.

Hannah had paused just outside the doors, as if reluctant to come any closer. "It's late."

"It's not that late," he chided, pouring the wine. "And it's a beautiful night."

She ventured closer and accepted the glass he offered before lowering herself onto the step beside him. "How was your meeting?"

"I don't want to talk about the meeting." He tipped his glass to his lips, sipped. He didn't even want to think about the time he'd wasted, time he would much have preferred to spend with his daughter—and her nanny. "How did things go with Riley today?"

"I think we're making some real progress."

"I know she's enjoying the tennis lessons," he admitted.

Hannah smiled. "That's more because of Kevin than the game, I think."

He frowned. "Are you telling me that my daughter has a crush on the boy who has a crush on her nanny?"

"It's a distinct possibility," she told him. "At least the part about Riley's feelings for Kevin."

"I should have my brother talk to the Minister of the Environment about testing the water out here," he muttered.

She smiled again. "She's a little girl and he's a good-looking boy who pays her a lot of attention."

"You think he's good-looking?"

"That was hardly the most relevant part of my statement," she said dryly.

"Maybe not," he acknowledged. "But he's also seventeen years old."

"Relax, I don't think she's planning the wedding just yet," she teased.

"I was making the point of his age to you," Michael admitted.

"I know—oh!" She grabbed his arm and pointed. "Look."

Her eyes were wide with wonder as she stared up at the sky, but it was the press of her breast against his arm that snagged his attention.

"I've never seen a shooting star before," she told him.

She was still holding on to his arm, though he wasn't sure if she was conscious of that fact. And while he couldn't deny the quick jolt of lust that went through him, he realized that there was something deeper beneath the surface. A sense of happiness and contentment that came from just sitting here with Hannah. A sense of happiness and contentment that he hadn't felt in a very long time.

"It was right here on this terrace with my dad that I saw my first-ever shooting star," he told her.

She seemed surprised by the revelation, and he realized that she probably was. Over the past couple of weeks, they'd spent a lot of time together and engaged in numerous conversations, but either Riley was with them or was the center of those discussions. He certainly wasn't in the habit of sharing personal details of his own life.

"Did you spend a lot of time here as a kid?" she asked him now.

"Yeah. Although not as much after my dad passed away."

"It was probably hard for your mom, to return to a place with so many memories."

While he appreciated the sympathy in her tone, he knew that her compassion—in this instance—was misplaced. "It wasn't the memories she had trouble with, it was the lack of exclusive boutiques and five-star restaurants."

Hannah seemed puzzled by that.

"Do you know much about my family?" he asked.

"I know that your mother is the princess royal."

"And my father was a farmer."

"I didn't know that," she admitted.

"She claimed that she loved who he was, and then she spent the next fifteen years trying to change him into someone else. Someone better suited to her station."

She didn't prompt him for more information or pry for details, and maybe that was why he found it easy to talk to her. Why he found himself telling her things that he'd never told anyone else before.

"After my dad died, she changed her focus to my brother and I. She had such big plans and ambitions for us."

"I would think she'd be very proud of both of you."

His smile was wry. "She refers to RAM as my 'little company' and despairs that I will ever do anything worthwhile. And even Cameron's position in the prince regent's cabinet isn't good enough, because she wanted him sitting on the throne."

"What were her plans for Marissa?" she asked curiously.

"Lucky for her, my baby sister pretty much flies under Elena's radar."

"How does she manage that?"

"She's female."

Hannah's brows lifted.

"I'm not saying it's right—just that it is what it is. Even though the Tesorian laws were recently changed to ensure equal titles and property would be inherited regardless of gender, she's always believed that it's the men who hold the power.

"I remember how thrilled she was to find out that Sam was expecting—and how disappointed she was when she learned that we were having a daughter. She didn't even pretend otherwise."

"But Riley is such a wonderful little girl," she protested.

"And my mother barely knows her," he admitted. "She's the only grandparent my daughter has, and she doesn't even make an effort to spend time with her."

Not only did Elena not spend time with Riley, the princess royal had suggested sending his little girl away to boarding school, the mere idea of which still made Michael's blood boil.

"She's lucky, then, to have a father who's making such an effort to be part of her life," Hannah told him.

"I missed her today," he admitted, pushing all thoughts of his mother aside. "And I hated not being here to tuck her in."

"She was disappointed, but thrilled when you called from the restaurant to say good-night."

"She said you had a picnic on the beach at lunch."

"I thought it might take her mind off of the fact that you weren't here."

"She sounded as if she really enjoyed it," he said.

Hannah smiled. "She got a bit of a surprise when she threw the crusts of her sandwich away and the gulls swooped in to take them."

"Was she scared?"

"She did shriek at first, but then she was okay. She's already decided that she's keeping the crusts of her toast from breakfast tomorrow so that she can feed them again."

"Then we'll have to make sure we have toast for breakfast," he agreed.

And that was how they ended up on the dock the next morning. Except Hannah noticed that while she and Riley were tossing bread to the birds, the prince had wandered farther back on the dock. After the little girl had tossed the last few pieces to the hungry gulls, Hannah took Riley's hand and guided her back to where her father was standing, with his back to the water and his BlackBerry to his ear.

She put her hands on her hips. "What do you think you're doing?"

Michael stopped in midsentence. "I'm just—"

Before he could finish speaking, she'd grabbed the phone from his hand.

"We had a deal," she reminded him.

And he'd stuck to the deal, which had been a pleasant surprise to Hannah. At least until now. In fact, he'd been so diligent about following the rules that she was prepared to cut him some slack—after she'd made him feel just a little bit guilty.

"I know, but—"

"No phones, Daddy." It was Riley who interrupted his explanation this time, and before he could say anything further, she took the phone from Hannah and flung it over her shoulder.

Hannah gasped as Michael's head whipped around, his gaze following the instrument as it sailed through the air, seeming to tumble end over end in slow motion before it splashed into the ocean.

She knew that Riley had acted on impulse, without any thought about what she was doing or the potential consequences, and that the prince was going to be furious. The only possible way to do damage control was to get Riley to apologize immediately and sincerely. But when Hannah opened her mouth to speak to the little girl, the only sound that came out was a muffled laugh.

"I was in the middle of a conversation with the vice president of a major telecommunications company," the prince informed her.

"You'll have to tell him that your call—" she tried to muffle her chuckle with a cough "—got dropped."

He glowered at her.

"I'm sorry. I know it's not funny…" But she couldn't finish, because she was laughing.

"If you know it's not funny, why are you laughing?" he demanded.

Riley looked from one to the other, measuring her father's stern visage against her nanny's amusement, as if trying to figure out how much trouble she was in.

"I don't know," Hannah admitted. "But I can't seem to stop."

"She threw my BlackBerry into the ocean."

She was turning red from holding her breath, trying to hold in the chuckles.

His eyes narrowed. "You really *do* think it's funny, don't you?"

She shook her head, wanting to deny it. But her efforts were futile.

"Well, then," Michael said. "Let's see if you think this is funny."

She fell silent when he scooped her into his arms, suddenly unable to remember why she'd been laughing. The sensation of being held close in his arms blocked everything else out. Everything but the heat and hardness of his body—the strong arms holding on to her, one at her back and one under her knees; the firm muscles of his chest beneath her cheek. She was tempted to rub her cheek against him and purr like a kitten, inhaling the enticingly spicy scent of the furiously sexy man. Oh, if only he would hold her like this forever—

The thought had barely formed in her mind when she realized that he was no longer holding on to her at all. Instead, she was flying through the air.

The shock of that had barely registered before she hit the water.

She came up dripping and sputtering, obviously as surprised as he had been when Riley had tossed his phone in the water, then she resolutely began to swim back to the dock. Any sense of satisfaction Michael had felt when he sent her on the same journey was gone. In fact, looking at her now as she pulled herself up onto the ladder, he was feeling distinctly unsatisfied. And very aroused.

He stared. He knew it was impolite, but he couldn't help himself. She usually dressed conservatively, keeping her feminine attributes well hidden. But now, with her pale pink T-shirt and white shorts soaked through and plastered to her body, there was no disguising the delicious curves she had tried to hide—or the sexy lace bra that covered her pert, round breasts but couldn't conceal the tight buds of her nipples.

He swallowed, hard.

She was at the top of the ladder now, and he offered his hand to help her up the last step.

She eyed him warily for a moment before she accepted.

Her hand was cool, but the touch heated his blood, and he realized that he was in serious trouble with this woman. Because even now, when he should be angry and amazed, he couldn't deny the attraction between them. An attraction that continued to grow stronger with each passing day.

"All in all, I'd say you fared better than my phone," he noted, trying to maintain some equilibrium.

She shoved a handful of sopping hair over her shoulder and, with obvious skepticism, asked, "How do you figure?"

"Your circuits aren't fried." As his were—or at least in serious danger of doing so.

"Are you going to throw me in the water, too, Daddy?" Riley looked at him with an expression that was half hopeful and half fearful.

"I might," he said, scooping her off of her feet and into his arms.

Riley shrieked and wrapped her arms tight around his neck. "No, Daddy, no."

"But you did a bad thing, throwing my phone into the water," he reminded her. "So there should be some kind of punishment."

She nodded her head, still clinging to him.

"What do you think that punishment should be?"

His daughter wrinkled her nose, as if seriously contemplating an answer to his question, then offered her suggestion. "Maybe no broccoli for me for a month?"

It was all he could do not to laugh himself—because he

knew how much she hated broccoli. "Nice try, Princess, but I think the punishment needs to be a little more immediate than that and more directly linked to the crime."

"An apology?" she suggested. "Because I am very sorry, Daddy."

"That's a good start, but not very convincing."

"Very, very sorry," she said, framing his face in her hands and kissing first one cheek and then the other.

"Much more convincing," he said.

She smiled at him, and it was the kind of smile he hadn't seen on her face in a very long time—a smile full of such pure joy that it actually made his heart ache.

He glanced over her head at Hannah, hoping to telegraph his appreciation to her because he knew that she was responsible for so many changes he'd seen in his daughter in the past few weeks. She was watching them and smiling, too, and he saw that there were tears in her eyes.

Since her first day at Cielo del Norte, Hannah had witnessed more and more examples of the strengthening bond between father and daughter. They'd come a long way in a short while, she realized. From virtual strangers who shared polite conversation across the dinner table to a father and daughter who genuinely enjoyed spending time together.

Watching them together filled her heart with happiness—and more than a little envy. Because as much as she wanted to believe that she'd played a part in bringing them together, her role had been peripheral. She was the outsider, as she'd been the outsider through most of her life.

Even when her uncle Phillip had brought her back to Tesoro del Mar, she'd been conscious of the fact that she didn't really belong. All she'd ever wanted was a home and a family of her own, a place where she was truly wanted and needed. But she'd be a fool to think she could find it here—even for a short while.

But there were moments—rare and precious moments that she knew she would hold in her heart forever—when she truly felt as if she was part of their world. Like when Riley reached for her hand as they walked on the beach. Or when the little girl spontaneously reached up to hug Hannah as she tucked her into bed at night.

She'd known from the beginning that her time with Riley and the prince wouldn't ever be anything more than temporary, but that knowledge hadn't stopped her from falling for the princess. There was simply no way she could have resisted a child who needed so much and somehow gave back so much more.

No, it didn't surprise her at all that the little girl had completely taken hold of her heart. The bigger surprise—and much bigger worry—was that she was very close to falling in love with the princess's father, too.

Chapter Eleven

It was the sound of Riley's screams that had Michael bolting out of his office a few days later. The screams were coming from the tennis courts, and he raced in that direction. Caridad, also summoned by the sound of the little girl's calls, was right behind him.

"Help! Daddy! Help!"

He would have been the first to admit that his daughter had a tendency to melodrama and that she did everything at full volume. But he'd learned to tell from the tone of her cries whether she was sad or frustrated or hurt, and he'd learned to distinguish between playful and fearful shouts. But he'd never heard her scream like this, and the sound chilled him to the bone.

"Someone! Please! Quick!"

As soon as she saw him, her screams turned to sobs. "Daddy, Daddy, you have to help."

He dropped to his knees beside her. "What happened? Where are you hurt?" He ran his hands over her as he spoke, his heart in his throat as he tried to determine the nature of her injury. The way she'd been screaming, he'd sincerely feared that she'd lost a limb or at least broken a bone. But aside from the red face streaked with tears, she appeared to be unharmed, and relief flooded through him like a wave.

"It's n-not m-me," she sobbed. "It's H-han-nah."

By this time, the housekeeper had caught up to them, and he saw that she had gone directly to where Hannah was kneeling on the court. Though the nanny had a hand to her head, she didn't seem to be in any dire straits.

With Riley clinging to his side, he ventured closer.

"I'm fine," he heard her saying, trying to shake Caridad off as she helped her to her feet.

But the older woman was resolute, and as she steered Hannah toward one of the benches along the sidelines of the court, he finally noticed the blood.

He halted abruptly, his stomach clenching.

"I d-didn't m-mean to d-do it," Riley managed between sobs. "It w-was an accid-dent."

He squeezed her gently, trying to reassure her but unable to tear his own gaze away from the crimson blood dripping down the side of Hannah's face.

"You are not fine," Caridad said to Hannah. "And you need to sit down while I get a towel and the antiseptic cream."

He'd yet to meet anyone who could ignore a direct order from the housekeeper when she spoke in that tone, and Hannah was no exception. She sat where Caridad directed.

"Come on, Riley," the housekeeper said. "You can help me find what we need."

Michael knew that Caridad didn't really need Riley's assistance but was trying to distract her from the situation. And Riley was eager to help, obediently falling into step behind the housekeeper. Michael moved over to the bench to check on Hannah.

"I guess that will teach me to walk up behind a little girl with a tennis racquet," she said ruefully.

"Is that what happened?" He kept his tone light, not wanting her to know how badly his insides were shaking. He guessed that she'd been cut right above the eye, because that's where she seemed to be applying pressure, but he couldn't tell for sure.

Hannah managed a smile. "Your daughter has a good set of lungs on her."

"That she does," he agreed.

"I'm sorry about the panic. I was trying to calm her down, but she saw the blood and then just started screaming."

Riley raced over with a neatly folded towel. "This one's for your head," she said, handing one to Hannah. "You're supposed to put pressure on the cut to stop the bleeding. Caridad's bringing the rest of the stuff."

The rest of the stuff turned out to be a washcloth and a basin of warm water, which she used to clean the blood off of the area around the cut, and a first-aid kit, from which she took an antiseptic wipe to dab gently against the wound. Then she instructed Hannah to keep the pressure on and went back inside to finish getting dinner ready.

"There's a lot of blood, Daddy." Riley spoke in an awed whisper.

"Head wounds always bleed a lot," Hannah said, trying to reassure her. "I'll put a Band-Aid on in a few minutes and—"

The prince laid his hand over hers, forcing her to lift the towel so that he could take another look at the gash. The blood immediately began to flow again. "I'm pretty sure it needs more than a Band-Aid."

"I'm sure it doesn't," she insisted.

"You're not a doctor," he reminded her.

"No, but I grew up with one, and he—"

"And he would want you to have this checked out," the prince said firmly.

As it turned out, her uncle Phillip had been at a day conference in San Pedro, so he arrived at Cielo del Norte within an hour of the housekeeper's call. By that time, the bleeding had mostly stopped and Hannah was lying down on a sofa in the library, reading.

Riley was sitting with her, keeping her company while she waited for the doctor to arrive. Despite her repeated assurances that she was okay, the child insisted on staying by her side.

"You only had to call and I would have come to visit," her uncle chided from the doorway. "You didn't need to create all this drama to get me out here."

"I'm having second thoughts about it now," she told him, easing herself back up to sitting position.

"Hi, Doctor Phil," Riley said.

He smiled at the nickname and offered the little girl a lollipop that he took out of his bag. "For after dinner."

She nodded and tucked it into the pocket of her shorts.

Phillip sat down beside his niece. "So how did this happen?"

"I hit Hannah with my racquet," Riley confessed.

"Forehand or backhand?" the doctor asked.

Riley had to think for a minute before answering that one. "Backhand."

"You must have a pretty powerful swing."

"I've been practicing lots," she admitted, sounding torn between pride and regret.

"Okay, let's see what kind of damage you did," he said, moving to examine the wound.

Hannah winced when he tipped her head back.

"Headache?" he asked, all teasing forgotten.

She nodded slowly.

"I'll give you something for that after I stitch this up."

He offered to let Riley stay to watch while he fixed up the wound. The little girl had seemed enthused about the prospect, but as soon as the needle pierced through the skin the first time, she disappeared quickly enough.

"Are you enjoying your job here?" Phillip asked Hannah when Riley had gone.

"Other than today, you mean?"

"Other than today," he agreed with a smile.

"I am," she said. "There was a period of adjustment—for all of us—but I think we've come a long way in a few weeks."

"The young princess seems very taken with you."

"I think she's feeling guilty."

"That could be part of it," he admitted.

Hannah sat patiently while he tied off the sutures, thinking about the little girl.

"I still miss my mom sometimes," she finally admitted.

If her uncle thought it was a strange statement, or one that came from out of nowhere, he gave no indication of it. Instead, he said, "I do, too."

"But I have a lot of memories of the time we spent together. Good memories."

"And Riley has none of her mother," he noted, following her train of thought.

"Do you think that makes it harder for her—because she doesn't have any memories to hold on to?"

"I'm sure there are times when she's conscious of a void in her life, but she seems pretty well-adjusted to me."

"How long do you think someone usually grieves?"

He taped a square of gauze over the sutures. "I'm not sure there's an answer to that question. Each relationship is different, therefore each grieving process is different."

She thought about her father's latest email again—and her

own surprise and anger when she read his note. "I thought my dad would love my mom forever."

"I'm sure he will," her uncle said gently. "But that doesn't mean he couldn't—or shouldn't—fall in love again."

She nodded, but her thoughts were no longer on her parents' relationship or her father's remarriage. "Do you think Prince Michael could fall in love again?"

"I'm sure he could," he said with a slight furrow in his brow. "But I wouldn't want to speculate on when that might happen, and I don't want you to forget that this is only a summer job."

"Don't worry—I have no desire to give up teaching to be a full-time nanny," she assured him.

"That's not what I meant."

"What did you mean?"

"I know you had a crush on the prince when you were younger, and I'm worried that being here may have rekindled those feelings."

"I did have a crush," she admitted. "But it was a childhood infatuation. I didn't know him then, and I didn't even like him when I first came here—he was so distant and reserved."

"And now you've fallen in love with him," he guessed.

She shook her head. "No. I have feelings for him—" deeper feelings than she was ready to admit even to herself "—but I'm smart enough to know that falling in love with a prince could never lead to anything but heartache."

"You're not nearly as smart as you think if you honestly believe that you can control what is in your heart," he warned her.

As Phillip finished packing up his bag, Caridad came in to invite him to stay for dinner. He declined the offer politely, insisting that he wanted to get on his way.

Hannah was sorry to see him go—she had missed him over the past several weeks, but she was also relieved by his departure. Apparently he had shrewder observation skills than she would have guessed, and she was very much afraid he was right. And if she was falling in love with the prince, she didn't want her uncle to be a witness to her folly.

Because she knew that it would be foolish to give her heart to a man who could never love her back because he was still in love with his wife. And she feared that her uncle was right—that loving the prince might not be a matter of choice, and that she already did.

After dinner, Hannah joined the prince and his daughter in the media room to watch a movie. Riley insisted on sitting between them with the bowl of popcorn in her lap, and while the action on the screen kept her riveted for nearly ninety minutes, she did sneak periodic glances at the bandage on Hannah's head to ensure that it wasn't bleeding again.

"Bedtime," the prince told his daughter when the credits began to roll.

"I can't go to bed," she protested. "I have to stay up in case Hannah has a concuss."

"It's *concussion*," Hannah said. "And I don't."

"But what if you do?"

"Doctor Phil checked me over very thoroughly."

"But the medical book says you should be 'specially vigi—" She wrinkled her nose, trying to remember the word.

"Vigilant?" her father suggested.

She nodded. "You should be 'specially vigilant when someone gets hit in the head."

So that was what she'd been doing while Phillip stitched up Hannah's wound—reading up on head injuries.

"I appreciate your concern," she told the little girl. "But I'm really okay—I promise."

"You're not going to die?" The little girl's eyes were wide, her tone worried.

"Not today."

"Does it hurt very much?" The child didn't sound worried so much as curious now.

"Not very much," she said, and it was true now that the acetaminophen her uncle had given her was finally starting to take the edge off of the pain.

"Do you want me to kiss it better?"

Hannah was as surprised as she was touched by the offer. "I think that would make it much better."

Riley leaned forward and very carefully touched her lips to the square of white gauze that had been taped over the wound.

"Okay?"

She nodded.

"You have to kiss it, too, Daddy."

Hannah's panicked gaze met with the prince's amused one.

"It's really much better now," she said to Riley.

"But if one kiss helps, then two should help twice as much," the little girl said logically.

"You can't argue with that," Michael told her.

"I guess not," she agreed.

"Kiss her, Daddy."

So he did. He leaned down and touched his lips gently to her forehead, just above the bandage. It was nothing more than a fleeting touch, barely more than a brush against her skin, but it made everything inside of her melt. Oh yeah, she was definitely falling.

He pulled back, looking into her eyes again. All traces of amusement were gone from his expression now, replaced by an intense awareness that rocked her to her very soul.

"Is that twice as much better?" Riley wanted to know.

Hannah forced a smile. "Twice as much."

"Now that Hannah's boo-boo has been kissed all better, it's bedtime for you," Michael reminded his daughter.

"Will you take me up, Daddy?"

"You bet," he said, and swept her off of her feet and into his arms.

Hannah let out an unsteady breath as they disappeared through the doorway. She felt the tiniest twinge of guilt knowing that she'd lied to the little girl. Because the truth was that the prince's kiss hadn't made anything better, it had only made her desire for him that much harder to ignore.

When Riley was all snug under her covers, Michael kissed her good-night and went back downstairs to find Hannah. He wasn't happy when he found her in the kitchen.

"You're supposed to be resting," he admonished.

"I'm not on my hands and knees scrubbing the floor— I'm just putting a couple of glasses in the dishwasher."

"Nevertheless—" He took her arm and steered her out of the room. "I don't want your uncle mad at me because you weren't following his orders."

"I can't imagine he would hold you responsible."

"And Riley is very concerned about you, too," he reminded her.

She smiled at that. "If I'd known a little cut above my eye would change her attitude toward me, I'd have let her take a swing at me weeks ago."

"I'm not sure that's a strategy I would actually recommend to her next nanny."

He was only responding to her teasing, but his words were a reminder to both of them that the summer was almost halfway over. And when it was done, Hannah would go back to her own life, and he and his daughter would go on with theirs.

Not so very long ago he'd been thinking about the two months he'd planned to spend at Cielo del Norte as an interminable amount of time. Now that the first month had nearly passed, it didn't seem long enough.

Hannah returned to the media room and resumed her

place at one end of the oversize leather sofa. He'd been sitting at the other end earlier, with Riley as a buffer between them, but he sat in the middle now.

She looked at him warily. "Don't you have phone calls to make or projects to complete?"

"It's almost ten o'clock."

"That hasn't seemed to matter on any other night."

She was right. He was in the habit of disappearing back into his office again as soon as he'd said good-night to his daughter. But what Hannah didn't know was that he often just sat behind his desk, doing nothing much of anything except ensuring that he kept a safe and careful distance between himself and the far-too-tempting nanny. And if he was smart, he would have done the same thing tonight, except that he'd made his daughter a promise.

"Riley asked me to keep an eye on you."

"I'm fine," she insisted.

"She made me pinky-swear," he told her.

Her lips curved. "It's sweet of her to worry, but I'm not concussed and I don't need anyone watching over me."

"I know it," he acknowledged. "But Riley seems really concerned."

"A lot of kids are preoccupied by death and dying," she said. "I would guess it's even more usual for a child who's lost someone close."

Somehow he knew that she wasn't just talking about Riley anymore. "How old were you when your mom died?" he asked.

"Eight."

"What happened?"

"There was a malaria epidemic in the village where we were living at the time. I got sick first, and my mom didn't trust that the Swazi doctors knew what they were doing, so she called Phillip. By the time he arrived, I was on my way to recovery, but—" Her gaze shifted away, but not before he caught a glimpse of the moisture in her eyes. "But while she'd been taking care of me, she'd ignored her own symptoms. By the time the doctors realized that she'd been infected, too, the disease had progressed too far."

She tucked her feet up beneath her on the sofa. "I thought my dad blamed me," she confided. "And that's why he sent me away after she died."

"He sent you away?"

"No one admitted that's what happened. Uncle Phillip said that I would be better off in Tesoro del Mar, that traveling from village to village was no kind of life for a child, and my father agreed. But no one had seemed too concerned about that while my mom was alive, and no one seemed to think about the fact that they were sending me away to live with a man I barely even knew."

"I'm sorry, Hannah."

And he was. He couldn't imagine how traumatic it had been for a child who'd just lost her mother to be taken away from her only other parent.

"I'm not. At the time, I was devastated," she admitted. "But now I realize it was the best thing that could have happened. My uncle gave me not just a home, but a sense of stability and security I'd never had before. He was—and is—a constant presence in my life, the one person I know I can depend on above all others."

"Where's your father now?"

"Botswana, I think. At least, that's where his last email came from."

"The one that told you he was getting married again," he guessed.

"How did you know about that?"

"You once told me that you wanted me to work on my relationship with Riley so that she didn't get an email from me telling her that she had a new stepmother."

She winced. "I was upset. The message wasn't that he

was getting married but that he'd already gotten married. He didn't even think to tell me beforehand. And probably the only reason he thought to share the news at all is that they're coming to Tesoro del Mar in the fall and he hopes I'll get a chance to meet her."

"I can see how that would have pulled the proverbial rug out from under you," he admitted.

"But it shouldn't have," she said now. "Because the truth is, I don't know him well enough to be surprised by anything he does. In the past eighteen years, since Uncle Phillip brought me here, I've only seen my father half a dozen times.

"His work has always been more important to him than anything else. And I guess, when you trust that you've been called to a higher mission, it needs to be a priority," she acknowledged. "And I know he believes in what he's doing. He goes to the darkest corners of the world, he sees families living in poverty and he sees children struggling to learn, but he never saw me."

She sighed. "It hurt. For a long time. But I finally realized that he was doing what he needed to do, because the people he helps out need him more than I ever did."

He didn't think it was as simple as that, and he was furious with her father for turning a blind eye to the needs of his child and angry with himself because he'd been doing the same thing to Riley. And he was so very grateful to Hannah for making him see it and helping him to be a better father to his daughter.

"So will you go to meet her—your father's new wife?"

"Probably." Her lips curved just a little.

He lifted a brow, silently inquiring.

"My friend Karen suggested I show up with a husband in tow," she explained.

"Getting married just to make a point seems a little extreme, don't you think?"

"More than a little, but I don't think she was suggesting an actual legal union."

"Have you ever been married?" he asked curiously.

"No."

"Engaged?"

"Haven't we covered enough of my family history for one night?"

He figured that was a *yes,* but decided to respect her wish not to talk about it. At least for now. "So what are we going to talk about for the rest of the night?"

"If you're really determined to hang out here babysitting me, that's your choice, Your Highness. But I'm going to watch some television."

"It's my choice," he agreed. "And it's my TV." And he snapped up the remote before she could.

She narrowed her gaze. "Don't make me wrestle you for it."

"Would you really?" He was certainly willing to let her tackle him. In fact, the more he thought about it, the more intrigued he was by the possibility.

"I would, but I'm supposed to be resting."

Another fantasy ruined, he handed her the remote.

Chapter Twelve

The rain was pouring down when Michael pulled into the drive at Cielo del Norte after a quick trip into town to meet with an old friend. It had been gray and drizzling for the better part of three days, but now the skies had completely opened up.

As he ran through the deluge to the front door, a flash of lightning split the sky, almost immediately followed by a crash of thunder. He winced, knowing how much Riley hated storms. If she was awakened by one in the night, he'd sometimes find her trying to crawl under the covers of his bed, her eyes squeezed tight and her hands pressed against her ears.

Inside, he shook the rain off of his coat and hung it in the closet. From the kitchen, he could smell the mouthwatering scents of roasted pork and sweet potatoes, but it was the music he heard in the distance that drew him down the hall.

Not surprisingly, it was coming from the music room. But

it certainly wasn't Riley practicing piano. In fact, it wasn't anything he had ever heard before. And when he pushed open the door, he saw something that he was certain he'd never seen before.

Riley was dancing—spinning and twirling, with her arms flying and her legs kicking. Hannah was right into the music with her, hips wriggling and body shimmying. And both of them were singing at the tops of their lungs about…he wasn't sure if he was unable to decipher the lyrics or if they just didn't make any sense, but both his daughter and her nanny seemed to know all the words.

He winced at the volume of the music, but he knew there was no way that Riley could hear the thunder over whatever it was that they were listening to—and no way they could have heard him enter the room. So he just leaned back against the wall and enjoyed the show for a few minutes.

One song led into the next, and they continued to sing and laugh and dance, and he continued to watch, marveling at the sheer happiness that radiated from his little girl. He couldn't remember ever seeing her like this—just being silly and having fun, and he realized that Hannah had been right about this, too. His daughter, despite all of her talents and gifts, needed a chance to simply be a child.

Impossible as it seemed, Riley's smile grew even wider when she finally spotted him.

"Look, Daddy! We're dancing!"

While Riley continued to move, Hannah's steps faltered when she realized that she and the child were no longer alone, and he would have bet that the flush in her cheeks was equal parts embarrassment and exertion.

"Don't let me interrupt," he said. "Please."

But she went to the boom box and lowered the volume, at least a little.

He picked up the CD case, looked at the cover, then lifted his brows.

"Grace let Riley borrow it," she told him, then grinned. "In exchange, Riley gave her a copy of Stravinsky's *Rite of Spring*."

He was suprised to learn that his little girl, who had a profound appreciation for the classics, could find such pleasure in jumping up and down and wiggling her hips to something called *Yo Gabba Gabba,* but he wasn't at all disappointed by the recent changes in her behavior.

"So what precipitated this dance-a-thon?"

"The precipitation," Hannah said, and smiled. "The rain made us give up on the idea of going outside, but Riley had a lot of energy to burn off."

"She's changed so much in only a few weeks," he noted.

"You say that in a way that I'm not sure if you approve or disapprove of the changes," she said uncertainly.

"I approve," he assured her. "I guess I'm still just getting used to it. I would never have said that she was unhappy before—but I've also never seen her as obviously happy as she is now. And to hear her laugh—the sound is so pure and full of joy."

"She's a wonderful little girl," Hannah assured him.

He had to smile, remembering that it hadn't been so long ago that she'd warned him that his daughter was turning into a spoiled brat. But then she'd taken Riley out of the familiar, structured world that she knew and changed all of the rules.

And while there had been a few growing pains in the beginning—and he was sure there would be more to come—he couldn't deny that he was impressed by the results.

"With a real passion for dance," the nanny continued.

Watching his daughter move, he couldn't deny that it was true. She might not have a natural talent, but she certainly had enthusiasm.

"My sister has a friend who—"

"No," Hannah interrupted quickly, then softened her refusal with a smile.

He frowned. "How do you even know what I was going to say?"

"Because I know how your mind works. And Riley doesn't need any more lessons. At least, not yet. Just let her have some fun for a while. And then, if she does want more formal training, enroll her in a class where she can learn along with other kids."

When the current song came to an end, Hannah snapped the music off.

"It's not done," Riley protested. "There's still three more songs."

"How many times has she listened to this CD?" Michael wondered.

"I've lost count," Hannah admitted. Then to Riley she said, "It's almost time for dinner, so you need to go wash up."

The little girl collapsed into a heap on the floor. "I'm too tired."

Michael had to smile. "If you're not too tired to keep dancing, you can't be too tired to twist the taps on a faucet," he said, picking her up off of the floor to set her on her feet. "Go on."

With a weary sigh, the princess headed off.

Hannah took the CD out of the machine and returned it to its case.

"Did you have any formal dance training?" he asked curiously.

She nodded, a smile tugging at the corners of her mouth. "Ballet, because my uncle Phillip was a lot like you in that he wanted to give me every possible opportunity. But after two years, my teacher told him that she couldn't in good conscience continue to take his money when it was obvious that I had less than zero talent."

"She did not say that," Michael protested.

"She did," Hannah insisted. "And truthfully, I was relieved."

"You looked pretty good to me when you were spinning around with Riley."

"We were just having fun."

"Will you dance with me?" he asked her.

She looked up, surprise and wariness in her eyes. "Wh-what?"

He moved to the CD player, pressed the button for the satellite radio—and jumped back when heavy metal screamed out at him. Hannah laughed while he adjusted the volume and scrolled through the preset channels until he found a familiar song.

"This one was at the top of the charts in my first year of college," he told her, and offered his hand.

"I don't recognize it," she admitted.

"Then I won't have to worry about you trying to lead," he teased.

Though she still looked hesitant, she finally put her hand in his.

"You really don't know this song?" he asked, after they'd been dancing for about half a minute.

She shook her head.

"Okay, now I have to ask—how old are you, Hannah?"

"Twenty-six."

Which meant that she was a dozen years younger than he, and while he'd been in college, she'd still been in grade school. But that was a long time ago, and there was no doubt that she was now all grown up. And soft and feminine and undeniably sexy.

He drew in a breath and the scent of her invaded his senses and clouded his mind.

"Hannah—"

She tipped her head back to meet his gaze, and whatever

words he'd intended to say flew out of his mind when he looked into those blue-gray eyes and saw the desire he felt reflected back at him.

He'd been fighting his feelings for her from the beginning, and to what effect? He still wanted her, now more than ever. And if she wanted him, too—and the look in her eyes made him believe that she did—then what was the harm in letting the attraction between them follow through to its natural conclusion?

They were, after all, both adults…but the little girl peeking around the corner was definitely not.

"Caridad said to tell you that it's dinnertime," Riley announced.

Hannah wanted to scream with frustration.

For just a minute, she'd been sure that the prince was going to kiss her again. And his gaze, when it flickered back to her now, was filled with sincere regret.

Regret that they'd been interrupted?

Or regret that he'd almost repeated the "mistake" of a few weeks earlier?

"Thank you for the dance, Hannah," he said formally.

"It was my pleasure, Your Highness."

He lifted her hand to kiss it.

She wanted a real kiss—not some lame fairy-tale facsimile. But then his lips brushed the back of her hand, and she felt the tingles all the way down to her toes.

It wasn't the passionate lip-lock with full frontal contact that she craved, but it wasn't exactly lame, either. And that made her wonder: if a casual touch could wield such an impact, what would happen if the man ever really touched her?

She was almost afraid to find out—and more afraid that she never would.

* * *

The next day, the sun shone clear and bright in the sky. After being cooped up for the better part of three days, Riley was thrilled to get outside and run around. In the morning, Hannah took her for a long walk on the beach. Michael watched from his office as they fed the gulls and wrote messages in the sand, and he wished he was with them.

He tore his attention from the window and back to his work. He was putting the final touches on a project for the upcoming National Diabetes Awareness Campaign, and if he finished it up this morning, then he could spend the whole afternoon with Riley and Hannah.

He wasn't sure when he'd started thinking of Hannah as Hannah and not "Miss Castillo" or his daughter's nanny— or when he'd started looking forward to spending time with her, too. In the beginning, when every step in his relationship with Riley seemed both awkward and tentative, he'd been grateful for her guidance. But somewhere along the line, he'd begun to enjoy her company and thought they might actually be friends. Except that he was still fighting against his body's desire to get her naked.

He pushed that idea from his mind and forced himself to get back to work.

He did finish the project by lunch, and afterward Riley invited him down to the beach to build castles in the sand. It was an offer he couldn't refuse, and he wasn't just surprised but disappointed when Hannah begged off. She claimed to want to catch up on some emails, but he knew that she was really trying to give him some one-on-one time with his daughter.

He appreciated her efforts. After all, she was only going to be with them until the end of the summer, at which time he and Riley were going to have to muddle through on their own—or muddle through the adjustment period with another new nanny. The thought made him uneasy, but he refused to delve too deeply into the reasons why. It was easier to believe that he was concerned about his daughter than to acknowledge that he might actually miss Hannah when she was gone.

After castle-building, they went swimming to wash the sand off, then Riley talked him into whacking some balls around the court with her. Hannah had told him that Riley was learning a lot from Kevin, and he was pleased to see that it was true. By the time they were finished on the court, he noticed that Hannah had come outside and was sitting on one of the lounge chairs on the terrace.

Riley spotted her at almost the same moment, and she went racing ahead. By the time Michael had reached the bottom step, his daughter was already at the top. Then she climbed right up into her nanny's lap and rested her head against her shoulder.

"It looks like you wore her out on the tennis court," Hannah said to him.

"She's had a busy day," he noted, dropping down onto the edge of the other chair.

Riley nodded her head, her eyes already starting to drift shut. "I'm ready for quiet time now."

Hannah smiled at his daughter's code word for "nap." "Quiet time's okay," she agreed. "But you can't fall asleep because it's going to be time for dinner soon."

The little girl yawned. "I'm not hungry."

"Caridad was making lasagna," Michael reminded her. "And that's one of your favorites."

"Is Hannah going to burn the garlic bread again?"

The nanny sighed. "I'm never going to live that down, am I?"

His daughter giggled.

"Well, in answer to your question, I can promise you that I am *not* going to burn the garlic bread because Caridad won't let me in the kitchen while she's cooking anymore."

"I'm glad," Riley said. "Because if you were helping her cook, you couldn't be here with me."

Hannah's lips curved as the little girl snuggled against her, but the smile faltered as she caught Michael's gaze.

"Is something wrong?" she asked quietly.

"What?" He realized he was scowling, shook his head. "No."

But he could tell that she was unconvinced, and he couldn't blame her. Because the truth was, *everything* about this situation was wrong.

She shouldn't be there. She shouldn't be on *that* chair on *this* deck cuddling with his daughter. That was *Sam's* chair—he'd painted it that particularly garish shade of lime green because Sam had thought it was a fun color. And this was *their* special place—where they used to come to escape the craziness of the world together. And Riley was *their* little girl—the child that his wife had given her life to bring into the world.

He felt a pang in his chest. Caridad was right—Riley needed more than a nanny, she needed her mother. But that was something he couldn't give her. Sam was gone. Forever.

He thought he'd accepted that fact. After almost four years, he should have accepted it. During that entire time, while he'd gone through the motions of living, he'd been confident that Riley was in good hands with Brigitte, and he'd been comfortable with his daughter's relationship with her nanny.

So why did it seem so different when that nanny was someone else? Why did seeing his daughter with Hannah seem so wrong? Or was the problem maybe that it seemed so right?

How was it possible that after only one month, Hannah had become such an integral part of his daughter's life—and his, too? It was hard to believe that it had been four weeks already, that it was already the beginning of August, almost...

The third of August.

The pain was like a dagger through his heart. The stab of accompanying guilt equally swift and strong. He reached for the railing, his fingers gripping so tight that his knuckles were white.

Dios—he'd almost forgotten.

How had he let that happen? How had the events of the past few weeks so thoroughly occupied his mind and his heart that the date had very nearly escaped him?

He drew in a deep breath, exhaled it slowly.

"I just remembered that there are some files I need from the office," he announced abruptly. "I'll have to go back to Port Augustine."

"Tonight?" Hannah asked incredulously.

"Can we go, too, Daddy?" Riley asked.

Not *I* but *we,* he realized, and felt another pang. Already she was so attached to Hannah, maybe too attached. Because at the end of the summer, Riley would have to say goodbye to someone else she cared about.

"Not this time," he told her, stroking a finger over the soft curve of her cheek. "It would be too far past your bedtime before we got into town."

"When are you coming back?" Riley asked.

"Tomorrow," he promised.

Riley nodded, her head still pillowed on Hannah's shoulder. "Okay."

"Are you sure everything's all right?" Hannah asked.

Concern was evident in her blue-gray gaze, and as Michael looked into her eyes, he suddenly couldn't even remember what color Sam's had been.

"I'm sure," he lied.

He'd loved his wife—he *still* loved his wife—but the memories were starting to fade. She'd been the center of his world for so many years, and it had taken him a long time to put his life back together after she was gone. Losing her had absolutely devastated him, and that was something he wouldn't ever let himself forget. And that was why he wouldn't ever risk loving someone else.

Chapter Thirteen

Michael didn't remember many of the details of Sam's funeral. He didn't even remember picking out the plot where she was buried, and he wasn't entirely sure that he had. It was probably Marissa, who had stepped in to take care of all of the details—and his baby girl—who made the decision.

Thinking back to that time now, he knew that Sam would have been disappointed in him. She would have expected him to be there for their daughter, and he hadn't been. Not for a long time.

But he was trying to be there for her now, trying to be the father his little girl needed, and he thought he'd been making some progress. There was no awkwardness with Riley anymore. Not that everything was always smooth sailing, but they were learning to navigate the stormy seas together.

Hannah was a big part of that, of course. There was no denying the role she'd played in bringing him and Riley together. And sitting here now, on the little wrought-iron bench by his wife's grave as he'd done so many times before, he knew that Sam would be okay with that.

He caught a flicker of movement in the corner of his eye and, glancing up, saw his sister climbing the hill. She laid the bouquet of flowers she carried in front of Sam's stone.

"Are you doing okay?" she asked gently.

"You know, I really think I am."

She nodded at that, then took a seat beside him.

They sat in silence for a few more minutes, before he asked, "Why did you come?"

"Did you want to be alone?"

"No, I just wondered why you were here. Why you always seem to be there when I need you—and even when I don't realize that I do."

"Because you're my big brother and I love you."

He slipped his arm across her shoulders. "I'm the luckiest brother in the world."

She tipped her head back and smiled.

"It would have been our sixteenth anniversary today," he said.

"I know."

"I thought we would have sixty years together." He swallowed around the lump in his throat. "She was more than my wife, she was my best friend—and the best part of my life. And then she was gone."

"But now you have Riley," his sister reminded him.

He nodded. "The best part of both of us."

Marissa smiled again. "I heard she's learning to play tennis."

"Dr. Marotta told you, I'll bet."

She nodded. "How's Hannah?"

"The stitches should come out in a couple of days, and she's learned to keep a distance from Riley's backhand." He waited a beat, then said, "She canceled almost all of Riley's lessons for the summer."

"Good for her."

He hadn't expected such unequivocal support of the decision. "You were the one who encouraged me to find a piano instructor for Riley," he reminded her.

"Because she has an obvious talent that should be nurtured. But you went from music lessons twice a week to five days a week, then added language instruction and art classes. And I know the deportment classes were Mother's idea, but you could have said no. Instead, the poor child barely had time to catch her breath."

Which was almost exactly what Hannah had said. And while Riley never complained about her schedule, he should have seen that it was too much. He should have seen a lot of things he'd been oblivious to until recently.

"So other than tennis, what is Riley doing with her spare time?" his sister wanted to know.

"She's…having fun."

"You sound surprised."

"I'd almost forgotten what it sounded like to hear her laugh," he admitted. "It's…magic."

Marissa smiled again. "Maybe I was wrong."

"About what?"

"To worry about you. Maybe you are beginning to heal."

He knew that he was. And yet, he had to admit, "I still miss her."

"Of course," she agreed. "But you've got to move on. You're too young to be alone for the rest of your life."

"I can't imagine being with anyone other than Sam," Michael told her, but even as he spoke the words, he knew that they weren't entirely true. The truth was, he'd never loved anyone but Sam, and it seemed disloyal to even think that he ever could.

But that didn't stop him from wanting Hannah.

* * *

Hannah had sensed that something was wrong when the prince suddenly insisted that he needed to go to Port Augustine the night before. It seemed apparent to her that what he really needed was to get away from Cielo del Norte, though she couldn't figure out why.

Over the past few weeks, as Michael and Riley had spent more time together and grown closer, she'd thought that she and the prince were growing closer, too. But his abrupt withdrawal suggested otherwise.

She wasn't surprised that he was gone overnight. It didn't make sense to make the drive back when he had a house in town. She was surprised when he stayed away through all of the next day. But Caridad seemed unconcerned about his whereabouts. In fact, the housekeeper didn't comment on his absence at all, leading Hannah to suspect that she might know where the prince was.

It was only Riley, because she'd been spending more and more time with him every day, who asked for her daddy. Hannah tried to reassure the child without admitting that she had no idea where the prince had gone—or when he would be back.

It was late—hours after Riley had finally settled down to sleep—before she heard the door open. She told herself that she wasn't waiting up for him, but she'd taken the draft of Kevin's latest essay into the library to read because she knew if she was there that she would hear the prince come in.

"I didn't know if you'd still be up," he said.

"I had some things to do."

He opened a glass cabinet and pulled out a crystal decanter of brandy. She wasn't in the habit of drinking anything stronger than wine, and never more than a single glass. But when the prince poured a generous splash of the dark amber liquid into each of two snifters and offered one to her, it seemed rude to refuse.

"You haven't asked where I've been all day," he noted, swirling the brandy in his glass.

"I figured if you wanted me to know, you'd tell me."

He sat down on the opposite end of the sofa, but with his back to the arm, so that he was facing her. But he continued to stare into his glass as he said, "It was Sam's and my anniversary today."

"You went to the cemetery," she guessed.

"Just like I do every year." He swallowed a mouthful of brandy before he continued. "Except that this is the first time I almost forgot."

Hannah eyed him warily, uncertain how to respond—or even if she should. She sipped her drink cautiously while she waited for him to continue.

"We celebrated twelve anniversaries together. This is only the fourth year that she's been gone, and the date almost slipped by me."

"You're feeling guilty," she guessed.

"Maybe," he acknowledged. He tipped the glass to his lips again. "And maybe I'm feeling relieved, too. Because in the first year that she was gone, I couldn't seem to not think, every single day, about how empty my life was without her, so the important dates—like her birthday and our anniversary—were unbearable."

He looked into his glass, and frowned when he found that it was nearly empty. "And then there was Mother's Day. She wanted nothing so much as she wanted to have a baby, and she never got to celebrate a single Mother's Day."

Beneath the bitter tone, she knew that he was still hurting deeply, still grieving for the wife he'd loved.

"I wasn't happy when Sam told me she was pregnant," he admitted.

Coming from a man who obviously doted on his little

girl, the revelation startled her more than anything else he'd said.

"I knew it was a risk for her," he explained, and rose to pour another splash of brandy into his glass. "Though she'd successfully managed her diabetes for years, the doctors warned that pregnancy and childbirth would take a toll on her body.

"After a lot of discussion and numerous medical consults, we decided not to take the risk. It was enough, I thought, that we had each other."

Obviously, Hannah realized, at some point that decision had changed.

"She didn't tell me that she'd stopped taking her birth control pills," Michael confided. "We'd always been partners—not just in the business but in our marriage. Neither one of us made any major decisions without consulting the other, so I wasn't just surprised when she told me that we were going to have a baby, I was furious."

Hannah didn't say anything, because she knew the prince wasn't trying to make conversation so much as he was trying to vent the emotions that were tearing him up inside. So she just sat and listened and quietly sipped her drink.

"I was furious with Sam," he continued, "for unilaterally making the decision that would cost her life, even if neither of us knew that at the time. And I was furious with my mother, for convincing Sam that I needed an heir—because I found out later that was the motivation behind Sam's deception."

And that, she thought, explained so much of the tension in his relationship with his mother.

"But in the end, I realized that I was most furious with myself—because I should have taken steps to ensure that Sam couldn't get pregnant. If I had done that, then I wouldn't have lost my wife."

He sank into the chair beside hers, as if all of the energy

and emotion had drained out of him so that he was no longer able to stand.

She touched his hand. "You might not have lost your wife," she agreed softly. "But then you wouldn't have your little girl."

He sighed. "You're right. And now, when I think about it, I know that even if I could go back in time, I wouldn't want to. I couldn't ever give up Riley, even if it meant I could have Sam back."

"They say there's nothing as strong as a parent's love for a child," she said softly, her throat tight.

"The first time I held her in my arms, I knew there wasn't anything I wouldn't do for her," he admitted. "For a few glorious hours, I let myself imagine the future we would have together—Sam and Riley and myself. And then Sam was gone."

The grief in his voice was still raw—even after almost four years. And listening to him talk about the wife he'd obviously loved with his whole heart, Hannah experienced a pang of envy. Would she ever know how it felt to love like that—and to be loved like that in return?

She'd thought she was in love with Harrison, but when their relationship ended, she was more angry than hurt. She most definitely had *not* been heartbroken.

"I'm sorry," he said. "I didn't come in here with the intention of dumping on you."

"Please don't apologize, Your Highness. And don't worry—I can handle a little dumping."

"Strong shoulders and a soft heart?"

She managed a smile. "Something like that."

"Can you handle one more confession?"

She would sit here with him forever if it was what he wanted, but she had no intention of admitting that to him, so she only said, "Sure."

"I met Sam when I was fifteen years old and while I

didn't realize it at the time, I started to fall for her that very same day. I was lucky enough that she fell in love with me, too, because from that first moment, there was never anyone else. Even after she died...I never wanted anyone else." His dark eyes lifted to hers, held. "Until now."

She swallowed.

"I know it's wrong," he continued. "Not that it's a betrayal of my vows, because I've finally accepted that Sam is gone, but wrong because you're Riley's nanny and—"

She lifted a hand to touch her fingers to his lips, cutting off his explanation. She didn't want to hear him say why it was wrong—she refused to believe that it was. If he wanted her even half as much as she wanted him, that was all that mattered.

Somewhere in the back of her mind it occurred to her that the prince was still grieving and that if she made the next move, she might be taking advantage of him in a vulnerable moment.

Then his fingers encircled her wrist, and his thumb stroked slowly over the pulse point there as if to gauge her response. As if he couldn't hear how hard and fast her heart was pounding. Then he lowered her hand and laid it against his chest, so that she could feel that his heart was pounding just as hard and fast, and the last of her reservations dissipated.

She knew there was no future for them, but if she could have even one night, she would gladly take it and cherish the memories forever.

"I want you, Hannah," he said again. "But the first time I kissed you, I promised that I wouldn't do it again."

"You promised that you wouldn't make any unwanted advances," she corrected softly.

"Isn't that the same thing?"

"Not if I want you to kiss me," she said.

"Do you?" he asked, his mouth hovering above hers so

that she only needed to tilt her chin a fraction to make the kiss happen.

"Yes." She whispered her response against his mouth.

It was the barest brush of her lips against his, yet she felt the jolt all the way down to her toes. She caught only a hint of his flavor, but she knew that it was rich and dark and more potent than the brandy she'd sipped.

"I want you to kiss me," she repeated, in case there was any doubt.

He responded by skimming his tongue over the bow of her upper lip, making her sigh with pleasure. With need.

"I want you," she said.

His tongue delved beneath her parted lips, tasting, teasing. She met him halfway, in a slow dance of seduction.

It was only their second kiss, and yet she felt as if she'd kissed him a thousand times before. She felt as if she belonged in his arms. With him. Forever.

No—she wasn't going to let herself pretend that this was some kind of fairy tale. She knew better than to think that the prince wanted to sweep her off of her feet and take her away to live out some elusive happily-ever-after.

But he did sweep her off of her feet—to carry her up the stairs to her bedroom. And the sheer romanticism of the gesture made her heart sigh.

"Say my name, Hannah."

It seemed an odd request, until she realized that she'd never spoken his name aloud. Maybe because she hoped that using his title would help her keep him at a distance. But she didn't want any distance between them now.

"Michael," she whispered, savoring the sound of his name on her lips.

He smiled as he laid her gently on the bed, then made quick work of the buttons that ran down the front of her blouse. She shivered when he parted the material, exposing her heated flesh to the cool air. And again when he pushed the silk off of her shoulders and dipped his head to skim his lips over the ridge of her collarbone.

"Are you cold?"

She shook her head.

How could she be cold when there was so much heat pulsing through her veins? When her desire for him was a burning need deep in the pit of her belly?

His mouth moved lower. He released the clasp at the front of her bra and pushed the lacy cups aside, exposing her breasts to the ministrations of his lips and teeth and tongue.

She wasn't a virgin, but no one had ever touched her the way he was touching her. The stroke of his hands was somehow both lazy and purposeful, as if he wanted nothing more than to show her how much he wanted her. And with every brush of his lips and every touch of his fingertips, she felt both desire and desired.

Her hands raced over him, eagerly, desperately. She tore at his clothes, tossed them aside. She wanted to explore his hard muscles, to savor the warmth of his skin, to know the intimacy of his body joined with hers.

Obviously he wanted the same thing, because he pulled away from her only long enough to strip away the last of his clothes and take a small square packet from his pocket.

"I didn't plan for this to happen tonight," he told her. "But lately...well, I began to hope it would happen eventually and I wanted to be prepared."

"I'm glad one of us was," she assured him.

His fingers weren't quite steady as he attempted to open the package, and he dropped it twice. The second time, he swore so fervently she couldn't hold back a giggle. But he finally managed to sheath himself and rejoined her on the bed, nudging her thighs apart so that he could lower himself between them.

"Will you do me a favor?" he asked.

"What's that?"

"When you remember this night, will you edit out that part?"

She smiled. "Absolutely."

But it was a lie. She had no intention of editing out any of the parts. She wanted to remember every little detail of every minute that she had with Michael. Because she didn't have any illusions. She knew this couldn't last. Maybe not even beyond this one night. But she wasn't going to think about that now. She wasn't going to ask for more than he could give. She was just going to enjoy the moment and know that it was enough.

His tongue swirled around her nipple, then he drew the aching peak into his mouth and suckled, and she gasped with shock and pleasure. He shifted his attention to her other breast, making her gasp again.

Oh yes, this was enough.

Then his mouth found hers again in a kiss that tasted of hunger and passion. His tongue slid deep into her mouth, then slowly withdrew. Advance and retreat. It was a sensual tease designed to drive her wild, and it was succeeding.

She whimpered as she instinctively shifted her hips, aching for the hard length of him between her thighs. Deep inside her.

She rocked against him, wordlessly pleading.

He entered her in one hard thrust, and her release was just as hard and fast. Wave after wave of pleasure crashed over her with an unexpected intensity that left her baffled and breathless.

While her body was riding out the last aftershocks of pleasure, he began to move inside of her. Slow, steady strokes that started the anticipation building all over again.

Had she honestly thought that this might not be enough?

It was so much more than she'd expected, more than she'd even dared hope for, more than enough. And still, he somehow managed to give her more, to demand more, until it wasn't just enough—it was too much.

His thrusts were harder and faster now, and so deep she felt as if he was reaching into the very center of her soul. Harder and faster and deeper, until everything seemed to shatter in an explosion of heat and light and unfathomable pleasure.

Michael didn't know if he could move. He did know that he didn't want to. His heart was still pounding like a jackhammer and every muscle in his body ached, and yet he couldn't remember ever feeling so good. So perfectly content to be right where he was.

But his own contentment aside, he knew that Hannah probably couldn't breathe with his weight sprawled on top of her. So he summoned enough energy to roll off of her. But he kept one arm draped across her waist, holding her close to his side. After another minute, he managed to prop himself up on an elbow so that he could look at her.

Her hair was spread out over the pillow, her eyes were closed, her lips were slightly curved. She looked as if she'd been well and truly ravished, and he felt a surge of pure satisfaction that he'd had the pleasure of ravishing her. And he wanted to do so again.

He stroked a finger down her cheek. Her eyelids slowly lifted, her lips parted on a sigh.

"*Dios,* you're beautiful."

She smiled at that. "Postcoital rose-colored glasses."

He shook his head. "Maybe I've never told you that before, but it's true. Your skin is so soft and smooth, your lips are like pink rose petals and your eyes are all the shades of the stormy summer sky."

"I didn't realize you had such a romantic streak, Your Highness," she teased.

"Neither did I." His hand skimmed up her torso, from her

waist to her breast, his thumb stroking over the tight bud of her nipple. "I always thought everything was black or white—and for the past few years, there's been a lot more black than white. And then you came along and gave me a whole new perspective on a lot of things."

She arched into his palm, as if she wanted his touch as much as he wanted to touch her. She had incredible breasts. They were so full and round, and so delightfully responsive to his touch.

Sam's curves had been much more modest, and she'd often lamented her tomboy figure. Even when she'd been pregnant, her breasts had never—

He froze.

Her gaze lifted to his, confusion swirling in the depths of her blue-gray eyes.

"Michael?"

The unmistakable smoky tone of Hannah's voice snapped him back to the present and helped him push aside any lingering thoughts of Sam. As much as he'd loved his wife and still grieved for the tragedy of a life cut so short, she was his past and Hannah—

He wasn't entirely sure yet what Hannah would be to him, but he knew that even if she wasn't his future, she was at least his present.

He lowered his head to kiss her, softly, sweetly. And felt the tension slowly seep out of her body.

Yes, she was definitely his present—an incredible gift. The only woman he wanted right now. And so he used his hands and his lips and his body and all of the hours until the sun began to rise to convince her.

Chapter Fourteen

Hannah didn't expect that Michael would still be there when she woke up in the morning. She'd known he wouldn't stay through the night. There was no way he would risk his daughter finding him there. But it would have been nice to wake up in his arms. To make love with him again as the sun was streaming through the windows.

Making love with Michael had been the most incredible experience. He'd been attentive and eager and very thorough. She stretched her arms above her head, and felt her muscles protest. Very very thorough. But while her body was feeling all smug and sated, her mind was spinning.

She'd been fighting against her feelings for the prince since the beginning, and she knew that making love with him was hardly going to help her win that battle. But as she showered and got ready for the day, she knew she didn't regret it.

After breakfast, while Riley was in the music room practicing piano—simply because she wanted to—Hannah was in the kitchen sipping on her second cup of coffee while Caridad was making a grocery list.

"How many people are you planning to feed?" Hannah asked, when the housekeeper turned the page over to continue her list on the other side.

"Only the three of you," she admitted. "But I want to make several ready-to-heat meals that you can just take out of the freezer and pop in the microwave."

"Are you going somewhere?"

"Just for a few days, and I'm not sure when, but I want to be ready to go as soon as Loretta calls."

Loretta, Hannah remembered now, was Caridad and Estavan's second-oldest daughter who was expecting her first child—and their fourth grandchild. "When is she due?"

"The eighteenth of August."

"On Riley's birthday," Hannah noted.

"She mentioned that to you, did she?"

"Only about a thousand times," she admitted with a smile.

"A child's birthday is a big deal—or it should be." Caridad tapped her pen on the counter, her brow furrowed.

Hannah knew that there was more she wanted to say. She also knew that prompting and prodding wouldn't get any more information out of the housekeeper until she was ready. So she sipped her coffee while she waited.

"The princess is going to be four years old," Caridad finally said. "And she's never had a party."

Hannah was startled by this revelation, and then realized that she shouldn't be. Samantha had died within hours of giving birth, which meant that Riley's birthday was the same day that Michael had lost his wife.

"I don't mean to be critical—I know it's a difficult time for the prince. And it's not like her birthday passes without any kind of recognition.

"There's always a cake," Caridad continued. "Because I bake that myself. And presents. But she's never had a party."

"Why are you telling me?" Hannah asked warily.

"Because I think this year he might be ready, but he probably won't think of it on his own."

"You want me to drop some hints," she guessed.

The housekeeper nodded. "Yes, I think just a few hints would be enough."

"Okay, I'll try."

"But not too subtle," Caridad said. "Men sometimes don't understand subtle—they need to be hit over the head."

Hannah had to laugh. "I'll do my best."

Michael had thought that making love with Hannah once would be enough, but the first joining of their bodies had barely taken the edge off of his desire. After four years of celibacy, it probably wasn't surprising that his reawakened libido was in no hurry to hibernate again, but he knew that it wasn't as simple as that. He didn't just crave physical release, he craved Hannah.

Every time his path crossed with hers the following day, his hormones jolted to attention. Now that he knew what it was like to be with her—the sensual way she responded to the touch of his lips and his hands, the glorious sensation of sinking into her warm and welcoming body, the exquisite rhythm of their lovemaking—he wanted only to be with her again.

But what did *she* want?

He didn't have the slightest clue.

She'd been sleeping when he'd left her room, so he'd managed to avoid the awkward "What does this mean?" or "Where do we go from here?" conversations that purportedly followed first-time sex. Since Hannah was the first woman he'd been with since he'd started dating Sam almost eighteen years earlier, he had little firsthand experience with those morning-after moments. And now he didn't know what was the next step.

They had lunch and dinner together with Riley, as was customary, and the conversation flowed as easily as it usually did. There were no uncomfortable references to the previous night and no awkward silences. There was absolutely no indication at all that anything had changed between them.

Until later that night, when he left Riley's room after he was sure she was asleep, and he found Hannah in the hall.

It wasn't all that late, but she was obviously ready to turn in for the night. Her hair had been brushed so that it fell loose over her shoulders, and she was wearing a long blue silky robe that was cinched at her narrow waist. A hint of lace in the same color peeked through where the sides of the robe overlapped, piquing his curiosity about what she had on beneath the silky cover.

He'd intended to seek her out, to have the discussion they'd missed having the night before. But now that he'd found her, conversation was the last thing on his mind.

"Wow" was all he managed.

But apparently it was the right thing to say, because she smiled and reached for his hand. Silently, she drew him across the hall and into her room.

The robe was elegant but discreet, covering her from shoulders to ankles. But when he tugged on the belt and the silky garment fell open, he saw that what she wore beneath was a pure lace fantasy. A very little lace fantasy that barely covered her sexy curves, held into place by the skinniest of straps over her shoulders.

And while he took a moment to appreciate the contrast of her pale skin with the dark lace, he much preferred reality to fantasy. With one quick tug, he lifted the garment over her head and tossed it aside.

* * *

Afterward, he let her put the lace-and-silk fantasy back on, and they sat on her balcony with a bottle of wine, just watching the stars.

"Are you ever going to tell me about that engagement?" he asked her.

"It was a long time ago," she said dismissively.

Considering that she was only twenty-six, he didn't imagine that it could have been all that long ago, and he was too curious to drop the subject. "What happened?"

"It didn't work out."

He rolled his eyes.

"We met at university," she finally told him. "He was a member of the British aristocracy, I was not. As much as he claimed to love me, when his family made it clear that they disapproved of his relationship with a commoner, he ended it." There was no emotion in her voice, but he sensed that she wasn't as unaffected by the broken engagement as she tried to appear.

"How long were you together?"

"Almost four years." She lifted her glass to her lips. "They didn't seem concerned about my lack of pedigree so long as we were just dating—apparently even aristocrats are entitled to meaningless flings—but to marry me would have been a blight on the family tree."

Again, her recital was without emotion, but he saw the hurt in her eyes and silently cursed any man who could be so cruel and heartless to this incredible woman.

"I didn't imagine there was anyone living in the modern world—aside from my mother—" he acknowledged with a grimace "—who had such outdated views about maintaining the purity of bloodlines."

"And yet your mother married a farmer," Hannah mused.

"Elena is nothing if not illogical. Or maybe she believed that her royal genes would trump his." He smiled as an old memory nudged at his mind. "The first time I scraped my knee when I was a kid, I didn't know what the red stuff was, because I honestly believed that my blood was supposed to be blue."

She smiled, too, but there were clouds in her eyes, as if she was thinking of the lack of blue in her own veins.

"So did you at least get to keep the ring?" he asked, in an attempt to lighten the mood.

She shook her head. "It was a family heirloom," she explained dryly.

"He didn't actually ask for it back?"

"Before we even left the ancestral estate," she admitted.

"And you gave it to him?" He couldn't imagine that she would have just slid it off of her finger and handed it over. No, if she'd cared enough about the man to want to marry him, she wouldn't have been that cool about the end of their engagement.

"I threw it out the window."

He chuckled.

"It took him three hours on his hands and knees in the immaculately groomed gardens to find it."

"He must have been pissed."

"Harrison didn't have that depth of emotion," she informed him. "But he was 'most displeased' with my 'childish behavior.'"

"Sounds like you made a lucky escape." And he was glad, because if she'd married that pompous British twit, she wouldn't be here with him now.

"I know I did. I guess I just thought I'd be at a different place by this point in my life."

"You're only twenty-six," he reminded her. "And I don't think there are many places in the world better than this one."

"You know I didn't mean this place specifically." She

smiled as she tipped her head back to look up at the sky. "This place is…heaven."

"Cielo," he agreed. "And you are…*mi ángel.*"

After almost a week had passed and Hannah's apparently too-subtle hints about Riley's approaching birthday continued to go unnoticed, she decided that Michael needed to be hit over the head. Not as literally as she had been, she thought, rubbing the pink scar that was the only visible reminder of her clash with Riley's racquet now that her stitches had been removed. But just as effectively.

So on Thursday morning, after the little girl had gone to the tennis court with Kevin, she cornered the prince in his office.

"It's Riley's birthday next week," she said.

"I know when her birthday is," he assured her.

"Well, I was thinking that it might be fun to have a party."

"A party?" he echoed, as if unfamiliar with the concept.

"You know—with a cake, party hats, noisemakers."

He continued to scribble notes on the ad layout on his desk. "Okay."

She blinked. "Really?"

He glanced up, a smile teasing the corners of his mouth. "Did you want me to say no?"

"Of course I didn't want you to say no," she told him. "But I thought there would be some discussion first."

He finally set down his pen and leaned back in his chair. "Discussion about what?"

"I don't know. Maybe the when and where, the guest list, a budget."

"When—sometime on the weekend. Where—here. As for the guest list, I figure if it's Riley's party, she should get to decide, and I don't care what it costs so long as I don't have to do anything but show up."

Happiness bubbled up inside of her. She couldn't wait to race into the kitchen and tell Caridad the good news.

"If you let Riley decide what she wants, it could turn into a very big party," she warned.

"I think we're overdue for a big party." He slipped his arms around her waist, drew her close. "And this year, I feel like celebrating."

Her heart bumped against her ribs, but she forced herself to respond lightly. "Okay, then. I'll talk to the birthday girl when she comes in and get started making plans."

"Where is Riley?"

"On the tennis court with Kevin."

"You'll have to give me an updated schedule," he said, not entirely teasing. "I never know where to find her these days."

"We don't have a schedule—we're improvising."

"I can improvise," he said, brushing his mouth against hers.

Hannah sighed. "Mmm. You're good at that."

"How long is she going to be busy with Kevin?"

"Probably about an hour. Why?"

"Because I want to show you some of the other things I'm good at."

Her cheeks flushed. "It's nine o'clock in the morning."

"But you don't have a schedule to worry about—you're improvising," he reminded her.

"Yes, but—"

"I really want to make love with you in the daylight."

He was a very lucky man, Michael thought with a grin as Hannah took his hand led him up to her room. And about to get luckier.

When he followed her through the door, his gaze automatically shifted toward the bed upon which they'd made love every night for the past nine days—and caught on the enormous bouquet of flowers in the vase on her bedside table.

He picked up the card. "With sincere thanks for helping me survive summer school, Kevin."

She paused in the process of removing the decorative throw cushions from the bed when she saw him holding the card. "Isn't that sweet?"

"Sure," he agreed stiffly. "He's finished his course, then?"

She nodded. "He got an A-plus on his final essay to finish with first-class honors."

"Caridad must be thrilled."

"She promised to make baklava, just for me," Hannah told him.

She said it as if that was her favorite, and maybe it was. He didn't know too much about what she liked or didn't like.

"I didn't know you liked flowers," he said, as if that was an excuse for the fact that he'd never thought to give her any.

"Who doesn't like flowers?" she countered lightly.

There was no accusation in her words, no judgment in her tone. Of course not—Hannah had made it clear from the beginning that she didn't have any expectations of him. Not even something as insignificant as a bouquet of flowers. And though he couldn't have said why, the realization annoyed him.

Or maybe he was annoyed to realize that he'd never really made an effort where Hannah was concerned. He'd never even taken her out to dinner, and they only went as far as the media room to watch a movie. They came together after dark like clandestine lovers, without ever having had anything that resembled a traditional date.

He knew that was his fault. He wasn't ready to subject Hannah to the media scrutiny of being seen in public together. Going shopping with Riley didn't really count, because the press accepted that the prince would require the assistance of a nanny when he was out with his daughter.

But he knew it would be very different if he and Hannah ventured out together without Riley as a buffer between them.

It was difficult to date when you were a member of the royal family, even one not in direct line to the throne. There was no such thing as privacy, and rarely even the pretense of it. Every appearance, every touch and kiss, became a matter of public speculation.

Not that Michael thought she couldn't handle it. He had yet to see Hannah balk at any kind of challenge. No, it was simply that he wasn't ready to go public with a relationship that felt too new, or maybe it was his feelings that were too uncertain. And that he was unwilling to look too deep inside himself to figure them out.

"I don't know if I like the idea of a much younger man bringing you flowers," he said, only half joking.

"He didn't just bring flowers," she teased. "He kissed me, too."

His brows drew together; Hannah laughed.

"It was a perfectly chaste peck on the cheek," she assured him.

"Lucky for him, or I might have to call him out for making a move on my woman."

Her brows rose. "*Your* woman?"

The words had probably surprised Michael even more than they'd surprised Hannah, and were followed by a quick spurt of panic. He immediately backtracked. "Well, you're mine until the end of summer, anyway."

Hannah turned away on the pretext of rearranging the colored bottles on her dresser, but not before he saw the light in her eyes fade. When she faced him again, her smile was overly bright.

"And that's less than three weeks away, so why are we wasting time talking?" She reached for the buttons on his shirt.

"Hannah—" He caught her hands, not sure what to say, or even if there were any words to explain how he felt about her.

He cared about her—he couldn't be with her if he didn't. And he didn't want her to think it was just sex, but he didn't want to give her false hope, either. He didn't want her to think that he could ever fall in love with her. Because he couldn't—he loved Sam.

"I never asked you for any promises," she told him.

And he couldn't have given them to her if she had. But he could give her pleasure, and he knew that doing so would give him pleasure, too.

He stripped her clothes away and lowered her onto the mattress. Then he knelt between her legs, stroking his fingertips slowly over the sensitive skin of her inner thighs. He brushed the soft curls at the apex of her thighs, and she gasped. He repeated the motion, parting the curls so that his thumb stroked over the nub at her center, and she bit down on her lip to keep from crying out.

"It's okay," he told her. "I want to hear you. I want to know how it feels when I touch you."

"It feels good. So good."

As his thumb circled her nub, he teased her slick, wet opening with the tip of a finger. She whimpered.

"Michael, please."

"Tell me what you want, Hannah."

"I want you."

He wanted her, too. He wanted to spread her legs wide and bury himself in her. To thrust into the hot wetness between her thighs, again and again, harder and faster, until he felt her convulse around him, dragging him into blissful oblivion.

But first, he wanted to taste her.

He slid his hands beneath her, lifting her hips off of the mattress so that he could take her with his mouth.

She gasped again, the sound reflecting both shock and pleasure. His tongue slid deep inside, reaching for the core of her feminine essence. Her breath was coming in quick, shallow pants, and he knew that she was getting close to her edge. It wouldn't have taken much to push her over the edge, but he wanted to draw out the pleasure for her—and for himself.

With his lips and his tongue, he probed and suckled and licked. He heard her breath quicken, then catch, and finally... release.

He stroked and kissed his way up her body until she was trembling again. Her belly, her breasts, her throat. She reached for him then, her fingers wrapping around and then sliding up the hard, throbbing length of him. He sucked in a breath. She stroked downward again, slowly, teasingly, until his eyes nearly crossed.

She arched her hips as she guided him to her center, welcoming him into her slick, wet heat. The last threads of his self-control slipped out of his grasp. He yanked her hips up and buried himself deep inside her.

She gasped and arched, pulling him even deeper, her muscles clamping around him as she climaxed again. The pulsing waves threatened to drag him under their wake. He reached for her hands, linking their fingers together over her head, making her his anchor as he rode out the tide of her release.

He waited until the pulses started to slow, then he began to move. She met him, stroke for stroke. Slow and deep. Then fast and hard. Faster. Harder. This time, when her release came, he let go and went with her.

Chapter Fifteen

Once the prince had given his nod of approval to the birth-day party, Hannah was anxious to get started on the plan-ning, so she turned to her best friend for advice. Karen outlined the five essential ingredients of a successful chil-dren's party: decorations, such as colorful streamers and balloons; games or crafts to keep the kids busy; cake to give the kids an unnecessary sugar high; presents for the guest of honor and loot bags for all of her friends—all of which should somehow coordinate with the party theme. And preferably, she added as an afterthought, outdoors so that the sugar-high kids weren't tearing through the house and destroying everything.

For Riley's first-ever birthday party, Hannah took her friend's list and gave it the royal treatment. She decided to go with a princess theme, since it was too obvious to resist.

The first glitch came when she asked Riley who she wanted to invite. The little girl mentioned her new friend, Grace, then added Kevin and Caridad and Estavan before rattling off the extensive list of all her aunts, uncles and cousins. She didn't mention her grandmother, and when Hannah asked about adding her to the list, the princess wrinkled her nose.

"Do I have to?"

"She is your grandmother, and you invited everyone else in the family," Hannah felt compelled to point out, even as she wondered if she was making a mistake.

But she couldn't help remembering Michael's comment about his mother barely knowing his daughter, and though she didn't think an invitation to one birthday party was likely to change that, she couldn't help hoping that it might be a start. And maybe, if the princess royal got to know Riley, she would give up on the idea of sending her away to boarding school.

"Everyone else in my family is nice," Riley said simply.

Hannah didn't quite know how to respond to that. She'd never actually met the princess royal and she didn't want to prejudge, but the princess's response made her wary.

"Would it be nice to invite everyone except her?" she prodded gently.

"No." Riley sighed, and considered her dilemma for another minute before she finally said, "Okay, you can put her on the list. But she doesn't get a loot bag."

After the guest list was finalized, Hannah turned her attention to other details. Taking her friend's advice to heart and unwilling to trust in the capriciousness of the weather, she rented a party tent to ensure that the celebration remained outside. Of course, when she called about the tent, she realized that she needed tables and chairs for inside the tent, and cloths to cover the tables and dress up the chairs. By the time she got off the phone, she was grateful the prince wasn't worried about budget.

"I just ordered a bouncy castle," she admitted to Caridad.

The housekeeper's brows lifted. "One of those big inflatable things?"

"It fits the princess theme," she explained.

"Riley will love it."

"And a cotton-candy cart and popcorn machine."

Caridad's lips twitched. "Apparently you know how to throw a party."

"You don't think it's too much?"

"Of course it's too much, but after waiting four years for a party, it should be a party worth waiting for."

"It will be," Hannah said confidently.

And it was. The tent was decorated with thousands of tiny white fairy lights and hundreds of pink streamers and dozens of enormous bouquets of white and pink helium-filled balloons.

The younger female guests got to make their own tiaras—decorating foam crowns with glittery "jewels" and sparkling flowers. Thankfully Hannah had realized that the crowns wouldn't be a big hit with Riley's male cousins, so they got to decorate foam swords. After the craft, they played party games: pin the tail on the noble steed, musical thrones and a variation of Hot Potato with a glass slipper in place of the potato. And, of course, they spent hours just jumping around in the inflatable bouncy castle that had been set up behind the tennis court.

For a minute, Hannah had actually worried that Michael's mother was going to have a coronary when she spotted it. The princess royal had gone red in the face and demanded that the "grotesque monstrosity" be removed from the grounds immediately. But Michael had been unconcerned and simply ignored her demand, for which the kids were unbelievably grateful.

Riley loved all of it. And she was completely in her element as the center of attention. Hannah was happy to remain in the background, making sure everything was proceeding as it should, but Michael made a point of introducing "Riley's nanny and party planner" to everyone she hadn't yet met. There was nothing incorrect in that designation, and it wasn't like she expected or even wanted him to announce that they were lovers. But she wished he'd at least given a hint that she meant something more to him than the roles she filled in his daughter's life.

That tiny disappointment aside, she really enjoyed meeting his family. She already knew his sister, of course, and was pleased when Marissa jumped right in to help keep things running smoothly. She was introduced to Prince Cameron, his very pregnant wife, Gabriella, and their daughter, Sierra. The teenage princess was stunningly beautiful and surprisingly unaffected by her recently newfound status as a royal, happily jumping in to help the kids at the craft table.

She also met Rowan, the prince regent, his wife, Lara, and their sons Matthew and William; Prince Eric and Princess Molly and their kids, Maggie and Josh; Prince Christian— next in line to the throne—his sister, Alexandria, and their younger brother, Damon. Even Prince Marcus, who divided his time between Tesoro del Mar and West Virginia, happened to be in the country with his wife, Jewel, and their two daughters, Isabella and Rosalina, so they were able to attend.

They were all warm and welcoming, but it was their interactions with one another that Hannah observed just a little enviously. It had nothing to do with them being royal and everything to do with the obvious closeness they shared. As an only child, she'd never known anything to compare to that kind of absolute acceptance and unquestioning loyalty, but she was glad that Riley did.

As for Riley's "Grandmama"—well, Hannah didn't get any warm and fuzzy feelings from her, so she just kept a careful distance between them. And she succeeded, until she went into the house to tell Caridad that they were getting low on punch. On her way back out, the princess royal cornered her in the hall.

"I'll bet this party was your idea," she said.

And so was adding your name to the guest list, Hannah wanted to tell her. But she bit her tongue. Elena Leandres might be insufferably rude, but she was the princess royal and, as such, was entitled to deference if not respect.

"Riley doesn't need to play at being a princess," the birthday girl's grandmama continued. "She *is* one. And this whole display is tacky and inappropriate."

"I'm sorry you're not enjoying yourself."

The older woman's eyes narrowed on her. "But you are, aren't you?"

"I can't deny that I like a good party, Your Highness," she said unapologetically.

"Is it the party or the fairy tale?" she challenged. "Do you have some kind of fantasy in your mind that you're going to ride off into the sunset with the prince?"

"I have no illusions," she assured the prince's mother.

"I'm pleased to hear that, because although my son might lack sense and discretion in his choice of lovers, he would never tarnish his beloved wife's memory or his daughter's future by marrying someone like you."

One side of Elena's mouth curled in a nasty smile as Hannah's cheeks filled with color. "Did you really think I wouldn't guess the nature of your relationship with my son? I know what a man's thinking when he looks at a woman the way Michael looks at you—and it's not about hearts and flowers, it's about sex, pure and simple."

She forced herself to shrug, as if the princess royal's words hadn't cut to the quick. "Sure," she agreed easily. "But at least it's really great sex. And while this has been a fascinating conversation, I have to get back outside."

"You have not been dismissed," Elena snapped at her.

"I beg your pardon, Your Highness," she said through

clenched teeth. "But the children will be getting hungry and I promised Caridad that I would help serve lunch."

"Well, go on then," the princess royal smirked. "I wouldn't want to keep you from your duties."

And with those words and a dismissive wave of her hand, she quickly and efficiently put the nanny in her place.

Hannah's feelings were in turmoil as she headed up the stairs to her own room. She was angry and frustrated, embarrassed that her own thoughts and feelings had been so transparent, and her heart was aching because she knew that what the princess royal had said was true.

Not that she believed her relationship with the prince was about nothing more than sex. They had fun together and they'd become friends. But she also knew that while Michael had chosen to be with her now, he'd made no mention of a future for them together. And she had to wonder if maybe one of the reasons he'd chosen to get involved with her—aside from the obvious convenience—was because he could be confident that their relationship already had a predetermined expiration date. At the end of the summer, she would be leaving. The time they'd spent together was an interlude, that was all, and she'd been a fool to ever let herself hope it might be more.

Marissa was coming down the stairs as she was going up, and the princess's quick smile faded when she got close enough to see the distress that Hannah knew was likely etched on her face.

"Riley asked me to find you," she said. "She said she's absolutely starving and wanted to know when it would be time to eat."

"Please tell her that I'll be out in just a minute, Your Highness." She was anxious now to move things along and get this party over with, but she needed a few minutes alone to regain her composure before she could face anyone. And especially before she could face Michael.

"Hannah." The princess touched her arm, halting her progress. "I just saw my mother walk out—did she say something to upset you?"

"Of course not."

But it was obvious that Marissa didn't believe her, and that she was disappointed by the obvious lie.

"I thought we were becoming friends," she said gently.

Hannah looked away so that the princess wouldn't see the tears that stung her eyes. "You've been very kind to me, Your Highness, but—"

"Will you stop 'Your Highnessing' me," Marissa demanded, "and tell me what she said to you."

"It wasn't anything that wasn't true," Hannah finally acknowledged.

The princess sighed. "I'm not going to make excuses for her. All I can say is that she's so unhappy, her only pleasure comes from making others feel the same way."

"I'm not unhappy," Hannah assured her. She was simply resigned to the realities of her relationship with the prince, but also determined. If they only had two more weeks together, then she was going to cherish every moment.

"Actually, there is one more thing I'd like to say," Marissa told her.

"What's that?"

"That you're the best thing that has happened to my brother in a long time, so please don't let my mother—or anyone else—make you question what you have together."

Despite Marissa's reassurances, the rest of the day was bittersweet for Hannah, her happiness tempered by the realization that she wouldn't be around to witness the celebration of Riley's fifth birthday. She was only going to be at Cielo del Norte with the prince and his daughter for another two weeks. After that, they would return to their home in Verde Colinas, and she would go back to her apartment in town and her job at the high school, and she knew that she was going to miss them both unbearably.

She tried not to dwell on that fact, and when everyone joined together to sing "Happy Birthday," it was a welcome diversion. Caridad had offered to make the cake, as she had for each of the princess's previous birthdays, and Riley was stunned by the three-dimensional fairy-tale castle confection that she'd created, complete with towers and spires and even a drawbridge.

After everyone had their fill of cake and ice cream, Riley opened her gifts. She enthused over all of them, showing as much appreciation for the Little Miss Tennis visor that Kevin gave her to the elaborate back-to-school wardrobe from her aunt Marissa. Of course, her absolute favorite gift was the *Yo Gabba Gabba* CD collection from Grace, and she insisted on putting on the music for the enjoyment of all her guests.

The prince had given his gift to his daughter at breakfast: a three-story dollhouse, which she had absolutely adored. Partly because it came with dozens of pieces of furniture, but mostly because it was from her beloved daddy.

Hannah had walked the mall in San Pedro three times looking for something special for the little girl. She didn't want it to be anything showy or expensive, just something that might remind Riley of the time they'd spent together after she was gone. She finally found it in a little boutique that sold an indescribable variety of items ranging from handmade lace and estate jewelry to the latest in kitchen gadgets and children's toys. At first, it caught her eye just because it was funky and fun: a three-foot-long stuffed caterpillar with a purple body and high-top running shoes on its dozens of feet. Then when she picked it up, she noted the name on the tag: EMME.

"It's a palindrome!" Riley exclaimed happily.

"It looks like a caterpillar to me," her father said.

Riley just rolled her eyes and shared a secret smile with Hannah.

Several hours later, after the guests had all gone home and the remnants of the party had been cleared away by the rental company, Riley's eyes were closed. Even when Michael touched his lips to her cheek, she didn't stir.

"She's sleeping," he confirmed.

"She had a busy day," Hannah noted.

"A fabulous day—thanks to you."

"I tried not to go too over the top," she said.

His brows rose. "You don't think it was over the top?"

"I nixed the suggested arrival of the birthday girl in the horse-drawn glass carriage," she told him.

"I'm in awe of your restraint," he said dryly. "But truthfully, whatever it costs, it was worth every penny. I've never seen her so happy."

"Now I'm regretting that I didn't get the carriage."

"Then what would we do next year?"

She knew he'd only meant to tease her with the suggestion that this party couldn't be topped, but the words were a reminder to both of them that there was no *we* and Hannah wouldn't be around for the princess's next birthday.

"Brigitte called today," he said, in what seemed to Hannah a deliberate attempt to shift the direction of the conversation. "To wish Riley a happy birthday."

"That was thoughtful," she said. "How is she adjusting to life in Iceland?"

"Not easily."

"Does she want to come back?"

He laughed. "No. As much as she's struggling with culture shock, she is very much in love with her new husband."

"Then what is it that you're not telling me?" Because she was sure that he was holding something back.

"She did ask if I'd found a full-time nanny," he admitted. "And when I said I had not, she suggested that I interview her friend Margaux for the position."

Hannah had to remind herself that this wasn't unexpected. She'd known all along that the prince would be hiring a new nanny because she was leaving at the end of August. "Why do you sound as if that's a problem?" she asked.

"Because I was hoping that I might convince you to stay beyond the summer."

Her heart pounded hard against her ribs. This was what she hadn't even realized she wanted—what she hadn't dared let herself hope for. "You want me to stay?"

"You've been so wonderful with Riley, and she's going to be devastated if you leave."

Disappointment washed the roots of barely blossomed hope from her heart. "She'll be fine," she said, confident that it was true. The child had already proven that she was both adaptable and resilient. It was her own heart that gave Hannah concern, because she knew that when she left Cielo del Norte, she would be leaving the largest part of it behind.

"Okay, maybe the truth is that I'm not yet ready to let you go," Michael acknowledged.

Not yet ready—but he would be. Neither of them had any expectations of anything permanent or even long-term. At least none that she was willing to admit to him now. "We still have two weeks before the end of the summer," she said lightly.

"What if I'm not ready then, either?"

She didn't know what to say, how to answer his question in a way that wouldn't give away the feelings in her own heart. Because the truth was, she didn't want him to ever let her go—she wanted him to love her as much as she loved him, and she knew that wasn't going to happen.

He was still in love with Riley's mother, and even if he wasn't, she knew he wouldn't ever love her. Not enough.

Her father hadn't loved her enough to keep her with him, and Harrison hadn't loved her enough to defy his parents. And if she wasn't good enough for the heir of some obscure earldom, there was no way anyone would ever consider her good enough for a Tesorian prince. The princess royal had made that more than clear.

"Let's not think about that right now," she said, leading the way across the hall.

So long as they had tonight, she wasn't going to think about tomorrow.

Afterward, Hannah would wonder how it happened, because she knew she didn't consciously speak the words aloud. She certainly hadn't intended to tell him of the feelings that filled her heart. But when he pulled her close, tucking her against the warmth of his body so that she felt secure and cherished in his embrace, her emotions overruled reason. And as she started to drift toward slumber, the words slipped from between her lips as if of their own accord.

"I love you, Michael."

His only response was silence. She wanted to believe that he was already asleep and that he probably hadn't heard her impulsive confession, but the sudden tension that filled his body proved otherwise. The muscles in the arm that was wrapped around her grew taut, and she felt the sting of tears in her eyes.

She hadn't intended to confide her feelings. She knew she would be leaving her heart at Cielo del Norte but she'd hoped to at least take her pride. But keeping the feelings to herself certainly hadn't diminished them, and she was through pretending.

She did love him—with her whole heart. And she loved Riley as if the little girl was her own child. But accepting the truth of her feelings forced her to accept the more painful truths that were equally evident: there was no place for her here, and no future for her with the prince and his daughter.

Once again, she was trying to fit in someplace where she could never belong.

Chapter Sixteen

The night after Hannah's whispered declaration of her feelings, Michael didn't go to her room. It was the first time since their first night together that he'd gone directly to his big, empty bed. He didn't sleep well. He wasn't even sure that he'd slept at all.

But he knew he was doing the right thing. To continue to be with Hannah when he didn't—couldn't—feel the same way she did wasn't fair to either of them.

It was on Tuesday, after two restless, sleepless nights, that she knocked on his office door.

"Excuse me for interrupting, Your Highness, but I was wondering if I could have a minute of your time."

He cringed at the formal tone of her voice, hating the distance between them. He wanted to hear her speak his name, not his title. He wanted to take her in his arms and hold her so close that he could feel her heart beating against his. He wanted to touch his mouth to hers, to feel her lips yield to his kiss. But he had no right to want anything from her anymore.

"Of course, Hannah," he responded to her request.

"I got a notice from St. Eugene's that I'll be teaching a new course in the fall, and I was hoping to go back to Port Augustine at the end of this week."

This wasn't at all what he'd expected. He wasn't ready for her to leave, and he had no intention of letting her go. She had agreed to stay until the end of summer, to take care of his daughter.

"What about Riley?" he demanded now. "How can you just abandon her?"

"I'm not going anywhere until you've found someone else to take care of her."

"And what if I don't find anyone else?" he challenged.

He wasn't sure why he was fighting her on this. It was only seven days, and even if he didn't have anyone else by then, he would be happy to spend more time with his daughter during that last week. He didn't need a nanny, but he needed Hannah.

He wasn't sure where that last thought had come from— or how it could simultaneously feel so right and make him break out in a cold sweat.

"Margaux has agreed to come for an interview tomorrow."

"You're so eager to get away from here that you called her to set this up?"

"No," she denied. "Margaux called here, on Brigitte's advice, to set a date and time to meet with you. I just took the message."

"You could have said that I would get in touch with her when I returned to Port Augustine," he countered.

She looked at him oddly, as if she heard the note of desperation he tried to keep out of his voice. But all she said was, "I thought you would want this settled before then—to make sure Riley will be in good hands when you go back."

He couldn't refute the logic in that. Instead, he asked, "Is there nothing I can say to make you stay?"

She hesitated for a moment, as if considering her response, then finally said, "You really don't need me anymore. You and Riley are going to be just fine."

"Have you told her that you're leaving?"

"She won't be surprised. She knows I have to go back to my real job."

Just as he'd known it was only a temporary assignment when he'd hired her, so why was he fighting it now?

"I'll let you know after I meet with Margaux tomorrow," he told her.

"Thank you," she said.

And then she was gone.

Hannah was transferring her clothing from the dresser to her suitcase when Riley came into her room.

"Who's that lady with Daddy?" she demanded. "Is it true that she's going to be my new nanny?"

"That's for your daddy to decide," Hannah told her.

The princess crawled up onto Hannah's bed and hugged her knees to her chest. "Why don't I get to decide?"

"Because you're four."

"That's not my fault."

Hannah tousled her hair and smiled gently. "It's not a question of fault, it's just the way it is."

Riley watched as she continued to fill the suitcase. Hannah forced herself to concentrate on carefully arranging each item, because she knew that if she looked at the little girl right now, she would fall apart.

After a few minutes, Riley spoke in a quiet voice, "I don't want you to go."

Hannah's throat was tight, her eyes burning with unshed

tears. She drew in a deep breath and settled onto the edge of the bed, trying to find the words that would make goodbye easier for both of them.

But as soon as she sat down, Riley scooted over to wrap her arms around her, squeezing her so tight that the dam that was holding back Hannah's tears began to crack.

"I don't want to go, either," she admitted. "But we both knew that I was only going to be here for the summer."

"The summer's not over yet," the princess pointed out.

She rested her chin on top of the little girl's head, so Riley wouldn't see the tears that slid down her cheeks. "No, but it's getting close."

After another few minutes, Riley asked, "Can I come visit you?"

Hannah knew it would be best to make a clean break, to walk away from Cielo del Norte and never look back, but there was no way she could deny the child's request. "That's up to your dad, but if he says yes, it's absolutely okay with me."

"When?" Riley demanded.

The characteristic impatience in her voice made Hannah smile through her tears. "Anytime."

Margaux was everything Brigitte promised she would be. She was compassionate and knowledgeable and professional, and though his daughter kept insisting that she didn't want a new nanny, Michael remembered that she'd been equally resistant to Hannah at first. So he offered her the job, and she accepted. And when she agreed that she could start right away, he released Hannah from her obligation to stay until the end of the month.

It seemed pointless to have Margaux move into the beach house only to have to move back to the city a week later, so he decided that he and Riley might as well return to Verde Colinas early. Maybe his excuses were just that—certainly

Caridad thought so—and maybe it was true that he didn't want anyone else in Hannah's room. Not yet, while the memories were still fresh. By next summer, he was confident that he would be able to think of it as simply the nanny's room again and not think about all the hours that he'd spent in there with Hannah, talking and laughing with her, and making love with her.

Back in the city, Riley seemed to settle into her new routines fairly easily. Since summer was almost over, he'd started some of her lessons again, but on a much more modest scale. His daughter was polite and attentive to her teachers, and she cooperated willingly enough with Margaux, but still, something didn't seem quite right.

It took him almost a week to realize why the house seemed so somber and silent. Because not once in that entire time, not once in the six days since Hannah had been gone, did he hear his daughter laugh.

When she unpacked at home, Riley put the doll that Sam had given her back in its special place on the shelf. The silly stuffed caterpillar that Hannah had given to her as a birthday gift went on the bed, and Riley slept with it hugged close to her chest every night.

He wished that he could comfort his daughter, but he missed Hannah as much as she did. Maybe he hadn't sent her away, but he knew that he was responsible for her leaving just the same. She'd told him that she loved him, and he hadn't dared speak of the feelings that were in his own heart. Because he hadn't been willing to admit them, even to himself.

Now that she was gone, he could no longer deny the truth. Hannah hadn't just shown him how to build a better relationship with his daughter, she'd helped him heal and gave him hope for the future—a future he now knew that he wanted to share with her.

* * *

During the first week after her return from Cielo del Norte, Hannah missed Riley so much that she actually felt a pain in her chest whenever she thought of the little girl. As for the prince—well, she didn't even dare let herself think of the man who had stolen her heart.

She kept herself busy. She washed curtains and scrubbed floors; she repainted the walls and bought new throw rugs and cushions. She knew what she was doing: trying to make a fresh start. She wasn't sure that her plan would actually succeed, but she'd realized that the only way she could sleep at night was to fall into bed completely physically exhausted.

After everything was cleaned and painted and rearranged, she carted all of her boxes out of storage and back into her apartment. As she unpacked her belongings, she was amazed to think that only two months had passed since she'd packed it all away. It really wasn't a lot of time, but so much in her life had changed during that period. She had changed.

But she was doing okay—until she got a letter from Caridad. The housekeeper just wanted to let her know that Loretta had finally had her baby—almost two weeks late— and that she and Estavan were the proud grandparents of another beautiful baby girl.

Hannah was genuinely thrilled for them, and she sent a card and a gift for the baby. She'd considered hand-delivering the items, but decided against it. The memories were still too fresh, her heartache still too raw. She did hope to keep in touch with Caridad, as the housekeeper had become a wonderful friend, but there was no reason for her to ever go back to Cielo del Norte.

No reason except that she'd left her heart with Prince Michael while she'd been there. It didn't seem to matter that he didn't want it; she knew that it would always belong to him.

So many times, she thought back to that last conversation

in his office, when he'd asked, "Is there nothing I can say to make you stay?" And she'd wondered if anything might have been different if she'd had the courage to speak the words that had immediately come to mind: *Tell me you love me.*

But she knew that even if he had actually said those words to her, she wouldn't believe them. Because actions spoke louder than words, and he'd already made his feelings clear. She'd told him that she loved him—and he didn't even give her the lame I-care-about-you-but-I'm-not-ready-for-a-serious-relationship speech. He'd said nothing at all.

Still, she knew the mistake wasn't in speaking of the feelings that were in her heart; the mistake was in letting herself fall in love with a man that she'd known all along could never love her back. But even that knowledge didn't stop her from missing the prince and his little girl.

She was grateful when school started up again in September. She was anxious to get back into the familiar routines, confident that a return to her normal life would help her forget about Michael and Riley and how much she missed both of them.

Still, she thought about contacting him. Every day, she experienced moments of such intense yearning that she was tempted to pick up the phone, not just to hear his voice but to check on Riley. If she did, maybe he would give her permission to visit the little girl, but in the end she decided that wouldn't be a good idea for either of them. Margaux was the princess's nanny now, and she deserved a chance to bond with the child without Hannah in the way.

She was confident that Riley would adjust to these new changes in her life without much difficulty. She truly was an amazing child, and Hannah just hoped that the prince didn't fill her schedule with so many lessons and classes again that she forgot to be a child.

Instead of contacting the prince, Hannah busied herself working on new lesson plans for the current term. She was rereading the first play for her freshman drama class when there was a knock at the door Saturday afternoon. She was feeling desperate enough for a distraction that she responded to the summons. If it was a vacuum cleaner salesman, she might even invite him in to do a demonstration in the hope that it would possibly give her a half-hour reprieve from her thoughts of Michael and Riley.

But when she opened the door, she realized that there wasn't going to be any reprieve—because the prince and his daughter were standing in her hall.

"Hello, Hannah."

She opened her mouth, but no sound came out. She didn't know what to say—whether to invite them inside or send them away. And she was afraid that whatever choice she made would only result in fresh heartache.

"You said I could come visit, remember?" Riley's smile was uncharacteristically tentative, as if she was unsure of her welcome.

Hannah managed a smile, though she felt as if her heart was splitting wide open inside of her chest. "Of course I remember."

"Can we come in?" the prince asked.

She wished she could say no. And if his daughter wasn't standing at his side, she would have refused. But there was no way she could close the door now.

She stepped back so that they could enter, while questions swirled through her mind. Why were they here? Why now? Subconsciously, she touched a hand to her brow. The scar above her eye had started to fade, but the wounds on her heart were still raw and bleeding.

"Hannah?" the princess prompted, her little brow furrowed with concern.

She dropped her hand away, forced a smile. "Can I get you anything?"

She wasn't sure what to offer—her mind had gone blank

when she'd seen them standing outside of her door and she honestly couldn't remember what was in her refrigerator.

"Not for me, thanks," the prince said.

Riley shook her head.

Hannah led them into the living room. As a result of all of the cleaning and painting and redecorating, she knew the apartment looked good. Hardly up to royal standards, but then again, she wasn't a royal.

"So—were you just in the neighborhood?" she asked, attempting a casualness she wasn't feeling.

"No, Riley wanted to see you." Michael tucked his hands into his pockets. "Actually, we both wanted to see you."

"We miss you," the little girl said.

"How is school?" she asked Riley, forcing a note of cheerfulness into her voice even as her heart cracked wide open.

"It's okay," the princess said.

"Have you made lots of new friends?"

"A few."

Hannah swallowed. "And everything's going well...with the new nanny?"

The little girl looked at her daddy, as if deferring the question to him.

"Margaux is...almost perfect," he said.

"That's great," she said, and hoped that she sounded sincere.

"Almost," Riley repeated.

"Is there a problem?" Hannah asked, genuinely concerned.

"The only problem," Michael said, "is that she isn't you."

"We want you to come back," Riley said.

"This isn't fair," Hannah said to the prince, glaring at him through the sheen of tears that filled her eyes. "You can't bring your daughter here to—"

"It was Riley's idea," he told her. "There was no way she was letting me come here without her."

"Please, Hannah." The princess looked at her, those big brown eyes beseeching.

Hannah could barely speak around the lump in her throat. "I'm not really a nanny," she reminded the little girl gently. "I'm a high school teacher."

"We both understand that," Michael assured her. "And the thing is, Riley and I had a long talk about it and agreed that, since she's in school now during the week anyway, she probably doesn't need a nanny."

"Then why are you here?"

"Because I do need a mom," Riley piped up.

"And I need a wife," Michael said. "So—" The prince looked at his daughter, she gave him a quick nod, then they spoke in unison: "Will you marry us, Hannah?"

She could only stare at them both, her eyes filling with tears all over again.

Michael nudged his daughter.

"Oh." The little girl reached into the pocket of her skirt and pulled out a small box. She tried to flip open the lid, but it snapped shut again—catching her finger.

"Ow." Riley shook her hand free, and the box went flying across the floor, disappearing under the sofa.

Hannah had to laugh through her tears.

"This isn't quite how I imagined the scene playing out," Michael admitted.

It was a scene she hadn't dared let herself imagine and still wasn't entirely sure was real.

"Can you trust that I have a ring or do I have to dig the box out from under the furniture before you'll answer the question?" he asked.

"I don't care about the ring," she assured him.

"It's a really pretty ring," Riley said, making Hannah smile.

"But you're not saying anything," he prompted.

"I've got it, Daddy." The princess held up the box she'd

retrieved from beneath the sofa. Then she came over and opened it carefully so that Hannah could see the gorgeous princess-cut diamond solitaire set in a platinum band. "Now you're supposed to say yes."

She wanted to say yes. More than anything, she wanted to say yes, and it had nothing to do with the ring. It had to do with the fact that the prince was offering her everything she'd ever wanted and more than she'd ever dreamed of, but she felt as if they were both forgetting a couple important issues. "I'm a commoner, Michael."

"Which only means you don't carry all of the baggage that goes along with a title," he assured her.

"I realize it's not a big deal to you, but maybe it should be. And your mother—"

"Has absolutely no say in any of this," he said firmly.

"Daddy told Grandmama that if she can't accept you, then she can't be part of our family," Riley told her.

"You talked to your mother…about me?"

"I wanted her to know that I won't tolerate any more interference in my life," he said.

"I don't want to be the cause of any dissension in your relationship," she said, both surprised and humbled that he would take such a stand for her.

"You're not," Michael assured her. "If anything, confronting my mother about her attitude toward you gave me the opportunity to clear the air about a lot of things. I'm not naïve enough to believe that we came to any kind of understanding, but I am confident that she won't cause any problems for us ever again."

He spoke with such certainty, she couldn't help but believe him. But she had other—and even bigger—concerns than the princess royal.

"Needing a wife—and a mother for Riley—aren't the best reasons to get married," she said softly.

He smiled as he took both of her hands in his. "Did I

gloss over the I-love-you-more-than-I-ever-thought-it-was-possible-to-love-somebody part?"

Her heart swelled so much in response to his words that her chest actually ached with the effort to contain it. "Actually, you skipped it altogether."

"It's true," he told her. "I didn't plan to ever fall in love again. Truthfully, I didn't want to ever fall in love again."

"Because you still love Sam," she guessed.

"Sam will always have a place in my heart," he admitted, "because she was the first woman I ever loved and Riley's mother. But the rest of my heart is yours, for now and forever. So now the question I need answered is: do you love me?"

"You know I do."

"Is that a yes?" Riley wanted to know.

Hannah laughed. "That is very definitely a yes."

The princess clapped her hands together. "Now you have to put the ring on her finger, Daddy."

So he did.

"And kiss her."

And he did that, too.

He kissed her very tenderly and very thoroughly, until all of the loneliness and anguish of the past few weeks was forgotten because her heart was too full of love to feel anything else.

And still he continued to kiss her—until Riley pushed her way in between them.

"Are we married now?" she asked.

"Not quite yet," the prince said.

Riley sighed. "Can Hannah come home with us tonight anyway?"

"What do you say?" he asked, drawing her to her feet. "Will you come home with us tonight?"

Home.

She looked around at the apartment that had been her

residence for almost three years and felt absolutely no regret about leaving. It was only a collection of rooms—cold and empty without the man and the little girl she loved.

"There is nowhere else I want to be," she said truthfully.

"Just one more thing," Michael said.

"What's that?"

"If you ever retell the story of my proposal, will you edit out the awkward parts?" he asked.

She shook her head. "Absolutely not. I'm going to remember each tiny detail forever, because this moment—with you and Riley—is my every dream come true."

Epilogue

ROYAL WEDDING BELLS TOLL AGAIN
by Alex Girard

Last summer, Prince Michael Leandres was looking for a nanny for his young daughter and hired a high school teacher instead. At the time, it might have seemed that he'd made an error in judgment, but the lucky guests in attendance when the prince married Hannah Castillo at the Cathedral of Christ the King on Friday night would definitely disagree.

The ceremony began with four-and-a-half-year-old Princess Riley tossing white rose petals as she made her way down the aisle and toward the front of the church where her father, immaculately attired in a classic Armani tuxedo, was waiting. Then came the bride, in a strapless silk crepe sheath by Vera Wang, carrying a bouquet of calla lilies and freesia, proudly escorted by her uncle, Doctor Phillip Marotta.

Despite the more than two hundred people in the church,

the bride and the groom seemed to have eyes only for each other as they spoke traditional vows and exchanged rings. The couple then veered from convention by each reaching a hand to Princess Riley and drawing her into their circle, and the bride made a public promise to the groom's daughter that she would always be there for her, too, to guide her through good times and bad. The little girl chimed in to assert that they would all be good times, now that they were finally a family.

And when the bride and groom and his daughter lit the unity candle together, there wasn't anyone in the church who doubted that the young princess's words were true.

* * * * *

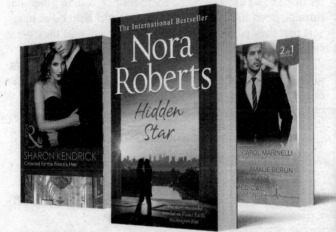

Join Britain's BIGGEST Romance Book Club

- **EXCLUSIVE offers every month**
- **FREE delivery direct to your door**
- **NEVER MISS a title**
- **EARN Bonus Book points**

Call Customer Services
0844 844 1358 *

or visit
nillsandboon.co.uk/subscriptions

* This call will cost you 7 pence per minute plus your
phone company's price per minute access charge.